Elizabeth snatched up her hairbrush and hurled it at him. He slapped it aside easily and remained where he was, glaring at her like a green-eyed predator.

'Irishman!' She said it with all the loathing she could muster. 'Barbaric Irish savage. Take your filth from my room!'

Before she could move he was on her, hands imprisoning her head. 'By Christ, I should kill you,' he grated, his face over hers. 'Anything to stop your mouth.'

And stop it he did, for she opened it to hurl another insult and he closed it with his own.

'O'Neill!' He was crushing her against him. For the first time she experienced the promise of a man's body and felt her own need rising to meet his.

'O'Neill, O'Neill,' she moaned . . .

JENNIFER O'GREEN

Royal Captive

GRAFTON BOOKS

A Division of the Collins Publishing Group

LONDON GLASGOW
TORONTO SYDNEY AUCKLAND

UN

Grafton Books
A Division of the Collins Publishing Group
8 Grafton Street, London W1X 3LA

A Grafton UK Paperback Original 1988

Copyright © Jennifer O'Green

ISBN 0-586-20030-4

Printed and bound in Great Britain by
Collins, Glasgow

Set in Times

03215081

O, sad in green Tyrone when you left us, Hugh O'Neill,
In our grief and bitter need, to the spoiler's cruel steel!
And sad in Donegal when you went, O! Rory *Ban*,
From your father's rugged towers and the wailing of your
clan!

– from Ethna Carbery's *The Princes of the North*

Prologue

The moon was full: a fat, bright disc in the night sky that painted the black water silver. The lantern lights on shore seemed to float in the darkness, unattached to the land so nearly within grasp. All was silence save for the rhythmic lapping of waves against the prow of the ship.

The *Marie* had sailed from France with empty holds. Her cargo was light indeed: two men, a woman, and two huge hounds. Ordinarily the captain would have balked at wasting so much time on so small a cargo, but the good gold in its silk purse had changed his mind quickly enough. His *Marie* had sailed from Dieppe, and now her destination was nearly at hand.

A portion of the human cargo stood on deck. Two men: the first unremarkable, of average size, clad quietly in unpretentious Italian fashion, brown-haired, blue-eyed, slender, inherently graceful even in repose. The second man was no less graceful, perhaps, but what grace he claimed came from a different source – from exceptional height, from shoulders a handspan broader than those of other men, and a complete understanding of how a human body moved. No wasted effort. None at all.

Black-haired he was, and with eyes the clear green of an uncut emerald. Eyes that fastened themselves on the black shoreline with a strange, wild hunger that was not the yearning of a man coming home but the intense need to overcome a thing that had once defeated him. The line of his mouth was pressed thin and flat, ruining its purity of form; hands gripped the taffrail so hard the sinews stood up beneath the flesh.

7

'*England*,' he said – that only, but the single word contained so much venom and bitter hatred, the first man looked at him sharply.

He thought to answer, but did not at once. He waited. And when he did speak the slender man's voice conveyed none of the alarm that had shown so briefly in his blue eyes. 'The game, then,' he said quietly, 'is over before 'tis properly begun.' He lifted his brows. 'Is it not?'

The tall man smiled briefly, but his eyes never forsook the shoreline. ''Tis a game begun eleven years ago, Bard . . . we only bring it round again.'

Bard looked out across the moon-painted water and saw what his companion saw, but could not name what emotions rose up to fill his breast. He wondered if O'Neill could name his own. And so he asked, when he dared it, 'What are you feeling, then?'

'Anger.' The answer came at once. 'Anger and hatred and bitterness and resentment and such a wild, killing rage I could wish for an English throat between my hands this very instant.' The hands released the taffrail and rose more clearly into the moonlight. Green eyes now black in the darkness stared at broad palms, long fingers, thick wrists corded with muscle. The fingers closed in a convulsive gesture that set the sinews to twisting on the bones. 'What I would give for the blood of a Sassenach! By *Christ* – what I would give!'

Bard looked at the light of battle in O'Neill's eyes and caught his breath up short. In months past he had seen the man play the part of a punctilious, silk-tongued courtier to win their release from the Pope. O'Neill had carried off the role so well that Bard had nearly forgotten what his anger could be like; the cold determination that drove him so unmercifully.

But now the moonlight, falling full on O'Neill's taut face, limned the strength in the jaw and the hardness of

8

his features; the arrogance that pride and a wild, fierce loyalty had graven into his flesh. His was a warrior's face, not a ubiquitous courtier's: nose too straight, nostrils too arched; a firm, clear-cut mouth and brilliant green eyes that saw through a man as if he were made of glass. It had been a long time since Bard had seen O'Neill outwardly exhibit his anger and impatience, for the man had become adept at hiding his true feelings. But – faced with survival or execution – a man often learns to be what he is not.

'*The O'Neill*,' Bard whispered, unconsciously speaking aloud when he meant to keep it silent.

O'Neill glanced at him sharply, black brows jerking down between his eyes. 'I have not earned the right to the title,' he said with significant distinctness, 'and until I have, you will not call me by it.'

Bard smiled benignly. 'Of course, O'Neill.'

But the man had forgotten the curtness of his command almost the moment it was given. He stared shoreward again, transfixed. And then, abruptly, he smiled. 'Apropos.'

Bard frowned. 'What is, O'Neill?'

'We will enter England at Pevensey.' O'Neill waited a moment, but Bard did not respond. 'D'ye not know your history, then?'

'*Irish* history, aye,' Bard retorted. 'What would I be wanting to know about the Sassenachs?'

O'Neill laughed aloud. His eyes, beneath slanted black brows, were bright in the light from the moon. ''Tis where the Bastard arrived on this island so long ago. Five hundred years ago it was, or so . . . I have not counted properly.' He smiled again as Bard scowled at him plainly. 'Pevensey, Bard, and on to Hastings, where Harold fell and took England with him.' One hand fisted and struck the taffrail sharply. 'By *Christ*, man – would that I could do as much myself!'

Bard leaned negligently against the rail, arms folded as he watched the shoreline draw closer. 'What would you do, then?' His tone, as he smiled, was idle. 'What would you do, O'Neill – were England truly yours?'

O'Neill smiled to himself, but it was singularly lacking in mercy or merriment. 'Sunder the realm,' he said evenly, 'and make Ireland free again.'

Bard hitched one shoulder in a brief, eloquent shrug. 'William had vast armies, O'Neill. We have only ourselves.'

O'Neill turned to face him slowly. 'We are Irishmen,' he said at last in a cold and deadly tone. 'We are Irishmen, and where a single Irishman stands, so stands a nation.'

A breeze, cloaked in the salt scent of the sea, ruffled O'Neill's black hair. It lifted tendrils from his face and the collar of his leather doublet. And Bard, looking at the blazing determination in the hard green eyes, thought the arrogant statement was perfectly true.

For wherever stood Kieran O'Neill, so stood Ireland's pride.

1

July 1617

Elizabeth Stafford was oblivious to the jolting of the poorly sprung coach that carried her towards London. It seemed a small price to pay, particularly after she had spent all of her eighteen years in the quiet Kent countryside on her father's only remaining estate. Too quiet, she felt. For all she loved the soft, sloping hills that rolled forever towards the channel, thick woods and thicker gardens, she knew there was more to the world. And now, at last, she would discover it in the halls of England's King.

She had tucked her father's letter into the bodice of her plain grey travelling gown, already creased and spotted from the rough going. That she travelled in a Stafford coach at all was something of a small miracle, since all but two had been sold. It should not matter that the leather squabs were dried and cracking, that the horses were so ill-matched, because what *did* matter was that she, a Stafford, was London-bound at last, when the name had known so little of honour in the past.

Her hand strayed to the folded parchment, fingers caressing the dog-eared paper. She did not need again to read it to know what words were there. She had committed them to memory.

To my Dere Daughter Elizabeth, by the Grace of our beloved King James:
It is my grete Pleasir to say I have procured a place for you at

Court after so much effort and money spent. You are to make your Way at once to Whitehall and take up your Place as a Quene's Lady. I am bid tell you the Quene waits upon your Attendance. Come at once.

Your loving Father,
Sir Edwin Stafford

Loving? she thought. No. Her father loved minted gold and the glory of a rank higher than the knighthood that he already held.

'Has it changed any?' asked Annie.

Elizabeth, snapping back to full awareness, smiled at her maid. Annie was a buxom, freckled young woman who had served as a housemaid at Rosewood until Sir Edwin had decided his daughter was due a proper ladies' maid. There was nothing *proper* about Annie, for she was rough-spoken and lacking refinement, but she was a good soul who was dedicated to her young mistress.

'No,' Elizabeth admitted, 'it hasn't changed at all. The words are still the same.' And then her smile burst its bounds and turned into joyous laughter. 'Oh, Annie – *London!*'

'Aye,' Annie agreed glumly. 'Lunnon. Away from the hills and meadows and into fine houses instead.'

'Rosewood is a fine house,' Elizabeth retorted, amused.

Annie's mouth twisted downward, though there was a glint of amusement in her blue eyes. 'Aye, Rosewood is a fine house. Or was, once. But don't you see what Lunnon'll do to you?' Abruptly the maid slid forward on her seat and peered at Elizabeth earnestly. 'The city 'ull swallow you up. I *been* there, once, when I was just a girl.' Her hands twitched as if she meant to reach out and capture Elizabeth's, but she refrained. 'I was a girl, just a little girl, with me mum. But I recall what all I saw – costermongers along the Thames, pickpockets in the Haymarket, women selling themselves in the stews.' She

12

did not stint in the baldness of her description. 'Not to say you'll see the same, being as you're a lady, but you must know Lunnon's different from the country.'

'And that's what I *want!*' Elizabeth reached out and caught Annie's hands. 'I understand, Annie, *I do* – but you must understand *me*. I want more than Rosewood's halls, at least for a little while. I want more than just being chatelaine of my father's estate.'

'More,' Annie agreed glumly. And she knew Elizabeth would indeed know more than quiet years spent at Rosewood – more, perhaps, than the girl herself dreamed. She could hardly avoid it. She was too beautiful, too proud, and, even in old skirts kilted up for racing her horse across the meadows, too elegant, too unconsciously alluring to be overlooked for long. Elizabeth would have men dancing permanent attendance on her and women desiring her friendship so they could share in the spoils.

The slim hand crept again to the letter tucked away. Annie, sliding back to settle her spine against the dry, cracked squabs, smiled in bittersweet acknowledgement. It was the way of the world, she knew. A court appointment was far out of her ken, but, for all she longed to keep their old life alive, such was just what Elizabeth deserved. The girl had known the freedom of the Kentish downs all her life, isolated from the rigid social hierarchy of the aristocracy, but she was one of them, and meant for something better. Something special. And Elizabeth, at court, would set the men afire. No doubt a fine marriage would follow upon the heels of her entrance into the royal circles.

Annie knew that was precisely what Sir Edwin desired. When the letter arrived and Elizabeth had run shouting the news through the halls that she was bound for London at last, gossip had run twice as fast. Sir Edwin lacked the gold to buy himself the better title he wanted. Elizabeth was flesh instead of metal, but worth perhaps even more if proper disposition of her hand bought him what he wanted.

Inwardly, Annie fretted. She was too simple for such things, but the head cook had explained it all to her. Elizabeth was now an only child, for Sir Edwin had lost his beloved son in the wars with Ireland. With his wife dead as well as his fortunes in serious decline, Stafford would be prepared to use whatever remained to him. For too long Elizabeth had been too young, for he had known instinctively it would better serve him to wait until she reached the first blossoming of her beauty.

And then, when he felt the time ripe, he discovered himself still in royal disfavour. It had taken most of his remaining gold to set it to rights, for the Old Queen's edicts held more often than not in her successor's time as well. James Stuart had come down from Scotland prepared to make England his, but on his own terms. It had taken Stafford years to catch the King's ear, but apparently he had done it at last. The Staffords of Kent were no longer expected to hide themselves in quiet country exile. Elizabeth herself would serve the Queen.

Elizabeth jumped as thunder cracked over her head. The summer storm had caught them between inns, shrouding the lush countryside in darkness and rain. The coachman's only choice had been to go on to the next inn, hoping to reach it before the fury of the storm descended upon them. But he had not, and in the darkness of early night rained turned the road into a morass of mud, sucking at the wheels and fouling the horses' hooves.

Elizabeth pulled aside the leather curtain and saw the damp darkness beyond. The full moon was hidden behind thick clouds. A flash of lightning turned the woods into a mass of clawing, twisted figures reaching skyward in supplication. A grue ran down her spine; shivering, she

14

let the curtain fall back and pulled the thin black cloak more firmly around her shoulders.

'We should ha' stopped at the last inn,' Annie said bleakly, burrowing into her coarse woollen cloak. 'Better yet, we should ha' never left Rosewood!'

'Oh, Annie, you cannot be wishing to go *back!*' Elizabeth's brown eyes, pale as sweet clover honey, stared at the maid in concern. Already a stray curl of rich tawny hair crept down her neck to dangle alluringly, escaping the elaborate arrangement Annie had pinned up that morning. Annie had hoped the pins would hold, but she should have known better. The girl had never been one for curls and fine fashions, preferring instead the freedom of loose gowns and looser hair. It seemed odd to see her wrapped in black velvet with tawny hair piled atop her head. But it suited her very well.

Annie met Elizabeth's eyes. 'I wish to go with *you*,' she said clearly, 'but I'll not say I won't miss Kent. So will you.'

Elizabeth's glowing face dimmed. She loved the beauty of Kent with all her heart. She adored Rosewood. With her mother and brother dead, and her father so often in London, she had learned to thrive upon the responsibility of running a household.

But London . . . she thought longingly. *Court. And a position with Queen Anne herself.*

Overcome with a spurt of renewed excitement, Elizabeth hugged herself within her cloak. Annie's gloomy words spilled out of her mind entirely, replaced with visions of the King's palaces and state banquets. It was the stuff of dreams, and the promise of a magical future. Great honour indeed, for even Elizabeth knew King James's Danish queen preferred to surround herself with Scottish ladies, ignoring the custom of appointing English ladies to attend the Queen of England. It had been considered a snub of the highest order for years. But apparently Queen Anne, in poor health of late, had finally relented.

And I am the one she chose.

Elizabeth sighed and shut her eyes, envisioning the riches she would see. Her father's wealth had always been spent on buying favours and position, never on his daughter's appearance, and she could but wonder what might be expected of her. Queen Anne would give her an allowance as she gave all her ladies, but it would hardly be enough to clothe Elizabeth properly. That was for a father or husband to do, and Elizabeth knew full well her father had little coin to spare.

One hand touched the fabric of her gown; the other crumpled the velvet cloak. Its nap was coarse, lacking the weight and plushness of better cloth. But it was hers. And though it undoubtedly improved her appearance, it – and she – could not compete with what would be at court.

Country girl, she thought wryly. *Is that what they will call me?*

She opened her eyes to put the question to Annie, whose opinion she always sought, but a huge cracking explosion blotted out her words. Lightning filled up the coach with daylight. Annie cried out in surprise; Elizabeth ripped aside the rain-wet leather curtain and saw the massive lightning-spawned fireball that lit up the woods.

Rain ran down Elizabeth's hand, soaking the sleeves of her gown, and beading on her velvet cloak. But she was blinded by the fireball. And then she felt the first lurching sway of the coach as the horses bolted in terror and ran.

She and Annie were thrown to the floor in a tangle of arms and legs. Elizabeth struggled up, dragging the cloak from beneath Annie's huddled figure. She was conscious of the maid's frightened prayers, but said none of her own as she sought to crawl back on to the seat. Another lurch

16

threw her down again so hard that she bruised her hip against the side, and this time she remained on the floor of the coach.

Annie wrapped trembling arms around Elizabeth's shoulders, pulling the cloak awry. 'Pray he stops the horses – *pray he stops the horses*.'

Elizabeth banged her elbow against the seat as she sought to loosen Annie's throttling arms. A handful of pins scattered across the floor and her tawny hair came down from Annie's careful coiffure, spilling over her shoulders in a mass of burnished curls. She swept it back from her face with one hand.

'He will,' she said, 'he will. John is so good with the horses.' But even as she spoke Elizabeth was thrown against the side of the coach. A hinge dug into her spine. The coach swayed, tilted precariously, then bounced so hard it left the ground entirely.

It crashed back to earth with a crack of splintering wood. Elizabeth felt fingernails bending, snapping as she scrabbled for a handhold, aware of Annie's frantic prayers and clutching fingers. Slowly, so slowly, the coach went over. For one long obscene moment she felt herself in midair, weightless, bodiless, and then she heard Annie screaming.

Elizabeth opened her mouth to add her own voice, but awareness ceased abruptly as the coach crashed down.

Darkness. Dampness. Pain. It filled up her head until she wanted to cry out with it. But she did not. She knew, somehow, that did she give tongue to her pain, the sound would intensify it.

And so she said nothing, nothing at all, floating in a cloudy awareness that told her, and insistently, that she was alive.

Alive. *Alive.*

17

And she recalled the runaway horses with a violence that made her recoil, and the recoil renewed the pain, until she thought she might vomit it out of her roiling stomach.

Darkness. Dampness. Pain. Her skirts were sodden. She lifted one hand to push her damp hair from her face, saw broken fingernails and scraped flesh in the moonlight – *moonlight; no more clouds* – and recalled it all.

Elizabeth struggled up. 'Annie? Annie?' But her head turned inside out and she felt the hinge against her spine again and knew, in the dim vagueness of pain filling up her skull, that she was injured.

Stillness. She did not move, ignoring the hinge in her spine without compunction because her head hurt worse. And the hurting was worse than mere pain, which she was beginning to understand, because what was in her head was connected to her stomach.

Elizabeth did not move. But she looked, and in looking she saw Annie sprawled in the far corner of the coach. A faint shaft of moonlight slanted through the curtainless window and Elizabeth realized the storm had passed.

Annie? Spoken silently, it did not disturb her head. *Annie?* Elizabeth saw the closed eyes and slack jaw. Annie had bled from the nose but the blood had dried in a trail across her face. She was very pale.

'Annie?' Aloud this time, in a whisper, it hissed in the dark and dampness.

Annie did not answer. She did not move. And so Elizabeth, moving so carefully, wishing not to crack the fragile eggshell that was her skull, climbed slowly on to her knees and inched across to her maid.

Rain-wet fingers touched the face and found it cold. There was no life in the flesh. Elizabeth flinched back, away from the body, and felt the bile rise up into her throat.

'Annie . . .' she gasped. 'Annie, wait – wait – I'll fetch you help at once.'

But she did not. She crouched against the floor of the coach – once it had been the side – and swallowed back the bitter bile in her throat. She wanted nothing more than to curl up in her sodden velvet and wait for someone to come, except she knew she could not. Annie needed her. Annie was badly injured and required immediate aid. And so, somehow, half blind with pain in her head, Elizabeth crawled out of the ruined coach.

Darkness filled her eyes. She thought it was the night and nothing more until she realized it was not – it was the blackness of pain and nausea and a wretched misery. She clung to the nearest coach wheel and prayed not to be ill. Not because she could not bear the disgrace – for who was present to witness it? – but because to be ill was to give in. And surrender was not within her ken.

When she could focus again she looked around. Trees. The road, stretching before her. The coach, on its side, blocked the road completely, and the horses were gone. There was nothing for it but to go herself. Alone.

A moment longer, a single moment, she clung to the wet, mud-clogged coach wheel. Though her senses seemed mostly fogged by the pain and shock of the accident, still they functioned. She heard streamlets running in the muddy ruts, rivulets pouring from the coach to splatter against the soaked ground. And silence. At night, after a storm, even when there is noise, there is silence. A heavy, oppressive silence that threatened to crush her to the ground.

'I *will* go,' she said firmly. And then, unsteadily, Elizabeth began to walk.

The leather slippers were stripped from her feet almost at once. Cold, slimy mud crept up past her ankles, sucking at her legs. The cloak and skirts, soaked through with rain and now freighted with mud, were almost too heavy to bear. Elizabeth hitched the folds up with only her right hand because her left wrist hurt, ached from some injury she had not examined, and she slowly stumbled on.

Almost, she missed it. But the moonlight suddenly bounced back at her from stone, not trees and shadows but stone. A tumbled wall edged an overgrown drive, and the brass plate was black, unreadable. But it marked the drive and she turned into it instantly, knowing a house lay at the end.

She tried to run, but skirts and cloak tangled around her muddied feet until she had to rip them away from her ankles with both hands. Breath rasped in her chest; she staggered, trying to maintain her momentum against the pounding of her skull.

And then she looked up in time to see a pair of yellow eyes and gleaming teeth lunge at her from out of the darkness.

Elizabeth cried out. Somehow, she had not thought of wolves.

Yet another came at her, growling and snapping. She closed her eyes and slipped to her knees. *Oh God – am I to be eaten?*

'Boru!' called a voice. 'Cuchullain – *to me!*'

Elizabeth's eyes snapped open. No one, that she had ever heard of, could train wolves to answer to personal names as if they were dogs. She swayed on her knees, grimy fingers gently touching one throbbing temple, and stared at the man as he strode out of the shadows and made his own.

He carried a lantern, and a sword. The light cast illumination into his face and she saw glittering green eyes under slanted black brows that lent him the look of the devil. White, even teeth showed briefly as he cursed.

'Please . . .' The voice was subdued, weak; she realized

20

the plea was her own. 'Please . . . can you help me?'

He stared down at her for a long moment and she realized how closely she resembled a supplicant before God. Well, perhaps she was.

His eyes raked her and his face tightened. 'It seems I have no choice.'

Elizabeth nearly flinched at the bitterness in his tone. But she did not. She was wet, cold, weary, and in pain, and she had no time for this man's resentment. 'My maid has been injured.' She said it as firmly, as coldly as she could, seeking to match his demeanour. 'Forgive me my intrusion – but we did not *choose* to have our horses run away.'

She saw surprise in his eyes and a quick reappraisal of her. A faint smile, albeit ironic, twisted his chiselled lips. He lifted the lantern so its light fell fully upon her. And then the smile disappeared and so did the sword. 'Come up from there.' He reached down a hand. ''Tis no place for a woman.'

But the fingers closed over her sore wrist, dragging her from the ground, and pain filled up her head. She cried out soundlessly. Then her head fell back, baring her throat to the sword he put away, and she fell downwards into darkness.

2

She dreamed. And out of the dreams came voices. Distorted voices: wavering, loud, soft, mostly unheard. But she could understand none of the words. None at all. In her dreams she knew only that some spoke *of* her – not to her – and that the topic should be of great interest to her. But she drifted, unable to summon enough awareness to make sense of the words, and dreamed.

She heard, in her dreams, a deep baritone voice saying something as if he sang, a lilting tone that expressed concern and exasperation all at once, and anger. A second voice, male as well, but lacking the same dark quality. The second remonstrated with the first, she thought. Or so it seemed. She could make no sense of his words either.

A bed. She was in a bed, a strange bed in a strange house, and it smelled. It filled up her nose with the scent of disuse and neglect, musty and close. The fabric beneath her cheek was soft enough for fine linen but it felt stiff, dry, as if it had been packed away for years. And though she lay cocooned in stiff, dry linen sheets in a strange bed, she was comfortable, for the pain in her head had faded. She drifted mutely, hearing only the cadences of the words she could not understand. She did not care to understand them any more than she cared to know where she was. For in ignorance was painlessness.

But her eyelids, no longer pinned down by senselessness, lifted. Lashes tickled her brows. She thought to see clearly, to discover where she lay, but the room was shrouded in a shadow, deep shadow, illuminated only by a single candle resting on a small table in a corner of the room. She turned her head slowly to look at the candle. She heard the sibilant scrape of her hair against the pillow, felt the renewal of pain stabbing through her eyes and into the recesses of her skull. Soundlessly, she moaned a tiny protest.

'By Christ, man, she is lovely!' The words, comprehensible now, crept into the shadowed room. She could not say from where they came, only that she heard them. 'But what am I to do with her? She cannot stay *here!*'

In the strange bed, Elizabeth stirred in mute protest. *Will they turn me out with my aching head . . . ?*

'Neither can you simply turn her out.' That from the second voice, lighter toned, but just as firm. Just as irritated. 'Not just yet. I have seen head injuries of the sort before – it will take days, perhaps a week or more, before she is fit to travel anywhere.'

The first man swore again. 'I have no intention of turning her out, man – d'ye take me for a fool? Could *you* turn a woman like that out into the darkness?' The voice paused a moment, on the brink of some high emotion, then continued. Its note was odd. 'Aye, you probably could. And without sparing it a thought.' Then, abruptly: 'I am sorry, Bard. 'Twas cruel of me. You are not a monster, and 'tis not my place to gibe at you.' Silence a moment. Then, in bridled exasperation: 'Will you stay with her?'

'I will nurse her most closely.' The other's tone was dry. 'And when she wakens I will answer all her questions.'

I am awake, she told him. But she said it silently, and the words put pain into her head, and so she went back to the soft land of sleep where there was no pain or sound.

She heard, in her dreams, her own voice calling out repeatedly. Annie's name. But there was never any proper answer, only a quiet, soft stranger's voice bidding her into silence, and before long she was accustomed to it. She quieted when the hand touched her brow and soothed its ache, instinctively turning her face against it. She felt safe with his hand upon her.

At night she was left alone. And it was at night she heard the harp music, drifting into her room like a seductive web, snaring her spirit as she slept and dreamed and healed. She heard soft, gentle ballads, sweet lullabies, and strange, wild laments that reached into her spirit and tugged, for the voice that accompanied the harp was so eloquent, so poignant. The language was unknown to her, full of strange consonants and accents, but it fit the harp to perfection. And so she lay in bed and dreamed, smiling to herself, as she conjured a man to go with the voice, and hands. Hands that made the harp song; hands that lost themselves in her hair.

When at last she came to herself fully, shedding the nausea and pain, she found sunlight in her room and a young man full in its path. He stood by the door, leaning indolently against the panelled wall, and she saw his blue eyes upon her incuriously.

As she opened her mouth in surprise he smiled, a sweet, boyish smile that put her instantly at ease. 'There is a woman in the house, mistress, and she has seen to you, so you need fear no improprieties.'

Elizabeth shut her mouth. He spoke kindly enough, and she knew from his touch that he meant her no harm. But automatically one hand covered her throat to shield herself from his gaze, and she felt the softness of a bedgown. Her hair was loose and clean, surprisingly so, and fell freely down her shoulders to tumble against the bedclothes snugged over her body. And all the while he stood there looking at her with a strange, unreadable expression in his eyes.

24

Elizabeth touched her right temple, exploring carefully. 'Is it whole?'

'Whole,' he agreed. 'Though I doubt not it aches as though it were shattered.' He pressed himself off the wall and moved closer to the bed. He wore dark, unremarkable clothing of a foreign style; his smooth, youthful face was set in a solemn expression that did not hide the mobility of his features. It was a good face, though oddly closed, accented with good bones. His dark brown hair was thick and shiny, brushed smooth against his head. 'I am Bard,' he said from the foot of her bed. 'And you, mistress?'

He spoke with an accent she could not identify. For a moment there was a hint of France about him, then Italy, but most certainly not England.

She wet her lips. 'I am Elizabeth Stafford. My father, Sir Edwin, is in London, at court.' She saw how the flesh of his eyes tightened minutely at the corners; how his brows moved up towards his hairline fractionally. 'He should be told what has happened at once, for he expects me.'

She hoped her growing apprehension did not show itself so obviously. Although he had spoken kindly enough and seemed genuinely concerned for her welfare – had he not tended her carefully? – there was something about him that set her on edge. Something indefinable. She sensed an odd restraint in him directly connected to her presence.

He made an elegant little bow but his eyes were not so subservient. His smile was a mere twisting of the lips. 'Of course, mistress, I will attend to it at once. The message will be sent. And when you are recovered enough to travel, I myself will escort you to London.'

'That will not be necessary,' she told him smoothly, summoning what calmness she could. 'There is my maid.' She took a breath and found, in relief, it did not jar her

25

head. 'Annie also was injured. How does she fare?'

'Annie,' he said bluntly, 'is dead.'

No – of course she is not – not any such thing – not Annie . . . But she knew, staring at him in shock, that he did not lie to her. 'I said I would bring her help.' Elizabeth pushed herself upright in bed, wincing as the movement sent pain lancing into her left wrist. 'I *told* her I would – do you see?' She marked the taut, speculative expression in his eyes, but could not make sense of it. 'Not Annie . . .'

'Forgive me, mistress.' But he did not sound at all repentant. 'I did not mean to speak so harshly. But there was nothing I could do for your maid.' He paused. 'Or the coachman.'

Elizabeth shut her eyes and set her forehead against her drawn-up knees. Before her rose a vision of Annie sprawled in a corner of the overturned coach, blood staining her face and the freckles so bright against the bloodless flesh. Somehow, she had known it all along. And denied it to herself.

The warmth of tears spilled out of her eyes and ran down her face. Unheeding, she let them fall. 'We grew up together.' The whisper hardly sounded her own in the silence of the room. 'Annie and I – we grew up together. She was going with me to London . . . to court . . . to the Queen.' Dazedly she looked up at the man who watched her. 'We were going there *together* – '

'And now you are not.' Still he watched her. 'Perhaps you would prefer to be left alone.'

'*No*'. She said it more sharply than she intended, not knowing, at first, that she intended it at all, why she wished for him to stay. 'Please . . . don't go just yet. Stay with me a moment. You are – you are at least *alive* . . .' She looked into his face and saw wariness in his eyes. 'It *was* you, was it not? Staying with me before?' She touched her head to evoke memories of those hours.

He smiled, but there was a strange glitter in his eyes. He was judging her.

Abruptly Elizabeth looked away from him. She wished to avoid the assessive stare. He had been very kind to her in her illness, but she was no longer disoriented, and his manner disturbed her intensely.

She looked instead at the room. The hangings were mildewed and faded and the musty smell remained. A fire burned in the fireplace but the stones were clotted and black, as if no one had seen to the tending of the flue for a long time. When she looked back at her host she saw he waited patiently for her questions, so purposely she said nothing.

'I have been – away.' He was unsmiling.

She did not miss the irony in his tone. 'Then you are not pleased to be home?'

He turned away. She saw the tension in the line of his shoulders. When he glanced back, turning, she saw a strange expression in his eyes. ''Tis time for your meal, mistress. I will see to it myself.'

'Bard.' Her voice stopped him at the door. His eyes, watching her closely, were wary and attentive as a snared animal.

He fears me . . . She realized it with a shock. *This man fears me!*

'Mistress?' he inquired.

Elizabeth inhaled a deep breath, knowing, somehow, what he answered would have great bearing on her future. 'Bard.' she said it quietly, overlooking her trepidation. 'You are not English, are you?'

He smiled and made an elegant leg. 'You are perceptive, mistress. No, I am not. I have only just arrived in England from France.'

'And before that?'

'Italy,' he said easily.

She looked directly into his smooth, implacable face. 'And before that?'

His smile was faint and slow. 'You have a good ear, mistress . . . perhaps you should tell *me*.'

She frowned, shaking her head. 'I could not say.'

'Then, mistress, it shall remain unsaid.' And he left her.

Bard brought each meal personally and stayed with her when she ate, as if he knew she needed the company. Elizabeth missed Annie badly. Bard was not a replacement, but she sensed a gentleness in him that would give her support if she needed it.

And yet, more deeply, she sensed an underlying tension in the man. Though she felt perfectly safe with him – as he had promised, there was a woman in the house; though Elizabeth had never seen her, she *had* heard her voice – he roused her suspicions as to his identity and purpose. He was ever kind, ever courteous, but he was strung so tightly she thought he might snap if she said the wrong word.

And she wondered which word it was.

'This is your house?' She asked it as he stood with his back to her, staring out of one of the mullioned windows.

He turned smiling wryly. 'Does it not suit its master well? Somewhat in disrepair and a little shabby?'

She smiled back at him. 'No more than myself.'

He laughed, surprising her, and she saw the wariness fall away for the first time. His face lost years that did not suit it and showed her the boy beneath the man. There was a vulnerability she had not seen before.

'Bard,' she said, 'who are you?'

The laughter stopped and the gaiety died out of his face. The reserve was back again, turning his face solemn and his eyes very cold. For a moment she was almost afraid of him.

'I am myself,' he answered tonelessly.

'And the other man?'

Bard moved away from the window. He came to stand by the bed, hands hanging loose at his sides and booted feet spread. His very stillness was threatening. '*Other* man?'

Elizabeth nodded. 'The one who found me.'

'*I* found you.'

She frowned, wondering if the head injury had somehow affected her memories. '*You* were the one who called off the wolves?'

He grinned again unexpectedly and the tension left his body – a tangible thing. 'They are dogs, mistress, not wolves, and aye, it was me. I went out to see what alarmed them, and they found you.'

Elizabeth, still frowning, stared at him. His arms were crossed, folded idly across his dark-clad chest, but she sensed a remaining wariness in him. 'It was not you.' She said it clearly, with all the certainty of conviction. 'It was not, Bard. He had *green* eyes – the kind of eyes I could never forget – and yours, you see, are blue.'

Elegantly, he shrugged. 'It was quite dark, mistress, in the aftermath of the storm.'

It had come down to a battle of wills. Jaw set, Elizabeth shook her head. 'I saw him quite clearly; he had a lantern. He spoke to me. And I heard him again when he spoke to *you* in some strange language that first night.'

Bard smiled again but his eyes were sharp. 'You were in much pain, mistress. You had struck your head. Such injuries often foul the senses with imaginings.' He watched her. 'There are only two of us here, mistress – myself and my serving woman. And, of course, the dogs.'

She looked into his face and knew he lied. 'Was it you who played the harp?'

'The harp,' he repeated blankly, and she knew she had won. He had given himself away. Then: 'Aye, 'twas me you heard.'

But it was not. Bard's voice was higher than the one she recalled so clearly. Lighter. It lacked the colour and timbre of that voice.

Testing him, she smiled. 'Will you play for me now?'

The line of his mouth went flat and hard. She saw a sudden flare of emotion in his eyes that he had kept carefully suppressed, and with that emotion came hostility.

Before she could speak Bard was at her bedside. He reached out and caught a handful of hair before she could jerk away, and by then she was trapped. His face, so close as he bent over her, was white and angry.

'You are all alike!' he said violently. 'With your soft lips and wide, begging eyes, and all the while you wish to trick us this way and that way so you can have fine gowns and gems and the fawning attendance of every man.' His hand tightened in her hair. 'Not from this man, mistress! I am immune to such as you!'

Elizabeth gasped as he released her. But he was gone before she could summon the voice to speak.

3

'You drink like that only when someone has got beneath your flesh,' O'Neill told him. 'What has the woman done?'

Bard, swallowing down the harsh whiskey he had poured himself, turned to find O'Neill slouching against the doorjamb. The green eyes were bright and shrewd, and Bard knew he could not keep it from him.

'Not what she has done,' he explained. 'What she has said. What she *knows*.' Bard poured himself a second glass, hesitated, then offered it to O'Neill, who shook his head. At his side, leaning against a big-thighed leg, sat one of the huge grey wolfhounds. 'She is not a fool, that Englishwoman,' Bard said flatly. 'She has already said I am neither French nor Italian, while she is quite certain I am also not English. That leaves me little ground, O'Neill.'

The big man grinned lazily, eyes aglint. 'Aye, but then you never have much to stand on, do you? 'Tis one of your more charming habits – to cut the support from beneath your own legs and then tread a virgin path.'

Bard scowled at the whiskey-filled glass. 'I cannot keep up this mummery while she knows I lie to her.'

'Women expect to be lied to.' O'Neill's tone was indifferent. ''Tis all a part of the game.'

'Those who are willing to play the game *properly*,' Bard agreed. 'This one wants the truth.'

'She'll be knowing it soon enough.' O'Neill sighed explosively and scrubbed a long-fingered hand through thick black hair. 'By Christ, what a coil! I come back to England in all secrecy and what happens? I must give succour to some Sassenach woman whose father is a king's man! What cursed luck!'

'Perhaps.' Bard's tone was idle. 'But this cursed luck will benefit us, O'Neill. Aye, offer succour – but it will be paid for with good gold. Good *Sassenach* gold – from out of her father's pocket.' He shrugged and sipped at his whiskey. 'When the ransom is paid we will be well rid of her and can tend to other business.'

'Ransom.' O'Neill put down his right hand and touched the wolfhound's grizzled head. 'Oh, aye, I know you have the right of it – 'tis a good idea to get gold for our cause from whatever source we may – but when she's sent back she'll be knowing who we are.' The Irish lilt slipped back into O'Neill's words, lending his tone the singing quality Elizabeth had heard before. 'We can't be having King Jamie learning of us so soon, man. When we are ready, aye, but not before. 'Twould spoil all.'

'As well as accounting for our executions,' Bard agreed drily.

O'Neill flashed him a sardonic glance and moved into the room. The dog followed, pacing at his heels like a huge grey shadow, sleek and deadly. O'Neill poured himself a glass of whiskey and downed it in one toss. 'I don't like this, Bard. All this creeping around like dogs on our bellies, unable to give tongue. *By Christ* – what I wouldn't give for an honest fight!'

'And we'll be having that soon enough, once we're back in Ireland.'

'Ireland . . .' O'Neill sighed and turned away, seeking a chair. He lowered himself into it, stretched out his long legs, and put a hand on the wolfhound's head as it settled next to the chair. ''Tis so long since we've set eyes on our home, Bard. D'ye think 'twill be the same?'

Bard looked down at him grimly. 'Ireland is tilled by English and Scots now, O'Neill . . . what do *you* think?'

O'Neill cursed again, softly, but no less violently for all its softness. He rubbed his fingers through the dog's coarse hair. 'And we'll be taking it back from that Scottish laddie-bastard, Bard. Leave Jamie to England and his highlands – Ireland is for the Irish.'

'You were wrong to play your harp.' Bard moved to a chair and settled himself down in it.

O'Neill looked at him as if he had lost his mind. 'My harp?'

'She heard it,' Bard said plainly. 'I had a devil of a time convincing her *I* played it, and then she asked me to do so there, in the bedroom.'

O'Neill's face reflected astonishment, then pensive consideration. 'I'd not thought of that.'

'I'm quite certain she believes I lied to her.' Bard shrugged. 'I have.'

'And does it matter to you?' O'Neill's eyes bored into Bard's. 'She is a woman . . . and you care little enough for what they think of you.'

Bard did not look away from O'Neill. 'She is a threat. That is the only concern I have for her at all.'

O'Neill settled back in his chair once more, lost in thought again. ''Tis unfair, somehow . . . you have the tending of her, when all her fairness is gone to such waste.'

Bard grinned. 'Would you be for trading places, then? You could fill up your eyes with that soft, pale English skin and golden hair, and I can be about my business.'

'That being to serve *me*.'

Bard's brows slid up as he heard the edge in O'Neill's tone. 'Do I deny it? I am your man, O'Neill . . . you'll be having me in your service forever. And I'd wish for no other master.'

O'Neill, sombre, studied Bard a long moment. Then he shrugged. 'If there is a threat arising out of this coil, I shall see to it she can no longer offer one.' He rose suddenly. ''Tis time I walked the dogs.' But as he turned to go with a word for the wolfhound, he saw the girl standing in the doorway. '*Christ and St Patrick!*' he swore, and then he swore again.

Elizabeth, clutching closed the velvet robe she had found thrown across a chair in her room, stared at him. The man was huge, towering over her even though he stood in the centre of the room. He was as she remembered him – black-haired and green-eyed and fierce as any swordsman, for she recalled also the blade he had carried in the night. Now he stood without a sword, but the light from the room fell fully on his face and limned his surprise and exasperation.

She could not take her eyes from him. Transfixed, she stared. He wore a black leather doublet, quite plain, that fit snugly against his chest, giving his wide shoulders fighting room should he require it and freeing the column of his throat. His breeches and trunk hose were also black, hugging his muscular legs, but she tore her eyes away from his big body to look into his eyes. They were hard and green and glittered with an emotion she could not name.

'*You* played the harp.' She did not know why it was important to her that she say it plainly to his face, but it was. 'I knew it. Bard does not have the voice for it.' Her eyes went to the hands hanging loosely at his sides. Big hands, strong hands, the sort a warrior would need to wield a sword. But his fingers were long and supple and she knew they would conjure magic from the harp strings. 'You said if I provided a threat, you would see to it I could no longer offer one. I heard you.' She stared at his face and saw the tautness of his sun-darkened skin stretched over bones of flawless symmetry. He was beautiful, if a man could be called that. Hard and strong and

34

fierce. She faced him squarely. She knew, instinctively, she would win respect from this man by challenging him. And, perhaps her life. 'What do you plan that I must fear my knowledge of it?'

To Bard he said something in the language she could not understand, and then he stood before her. He looked down on her silently, eyes raking her, and she would not allow her head to bow down before his gaze. Somehow she met his eyes, stare for stare, and saw him smile again, as he had the night he had found her.

'The hounds require walking,' he said in his dark-timbred tone. 'Will you lend me your company?'

Elizabeth looked again at his hands, though they were slack at his sides. She recalled the negligent tone he had used to Bard: *If there is a threat arising out of this coil, I shall see to it she can no longer offer one.* She had heard him clearly. But she thought perhaps she imagined things; what threat could she possibly offer?

'D'ye come?' he asked impatiently, and Elizabeth thought there was no question in the tone, only expectation of unquestioning compliance.

She closed one hand over the neck of the bedgown. 'I am hardly dressed for it.'

He thought it amusing. She could see it in his face, in the sardonic twisting of his mouth. 'Mistress, *that* hardly matters any longer.' And his hand was on her arm, drawing her from the doorway to another. He whistled and the second dog came running, and then he took them all outside.

Dogs, she thought. *Not wolves, perhaps . . . but they do his bidding. No doubt a death would not be so hard for them.*

Elizabeth stood there in the darkness with him, watching the dogs run out as he bid them, yet completely conscious of the man at her side. She had not feared

35

Bard, not until he had set his hand in her hair and spoken so violently, but she feared this man.

'Do you know who I am?' he asked lightly. 'How long did you lurk there listening to us?'

'I was not lurking.' But she drew back a step as she said it. He was so big, so powerful, and she could not say what he might do. 'I came down because I did not believe Bard had played the harp, and when I told him so he said something that – frightened me.' She looked at the tall man squarely, tilting her head back. 'I was frightened, and so I came down.'

'And do you know what you have done?' he asked her softly.

Her mouth was dry. 'I have overheard what I should not.'

He smiled briefly, teeth shining in the diffused light that crept from the house behind them. And yet she sensed he was not really amused but merely intent upon discovering a thing. 'Tell me, mistress. Tell me what you heard.'

Elizabeth felt the grue slide down her spine. 'I heard you discussing me.'

O'Neill laughed. He threw back his head and laughed, sending the sound up into the dark night sky. 'Did you, now?' he asked when the laughter had died away. 'All of it? Then no doubt you heard us discussing your elegant charms.'

Elizabeth felt hot colour flare up in her face. She could no longer look at him with his knowing eyes. 'I wish to go on to London. I wish to go on to my father.' She lifted her head stiffly. 'I am done listening to what I should not.'

'And therefore are deserving of my clemency.' He did not smile. 'Are you afraid of me, then?'

She inhaled a shaking breath, then let it out again. 'You have convinced me perhaps I should be.'

He smiled again. 'Aye. It might be for the best.'

Elizabeth stepped back, thinking to turn and run, but he reached out and caught her arm. She swung around, gasping a little, and saw his eyes fastened on her like twin pieces of green glass, unfaceted and unreadable.

'Sassenach,' he said softly. 'A woman – a *girl* – but still a cursed Sassenach.'

'What is that?' she demanded, stung by his tone. 'What foul name do you call me?'

''Tis an Irish word, mistress. D'ye mean to say you've never heard it before?'

Her mouth fell open as she stared. '*Irish!*'

'Aye.' It was curt. 'Have you not wondered what Bard was, and myself? *You* were the one asking him for his birthplace.'

'I was only *curious*.' Her wrist hurt in his grasp. 'I knew he was neither French nor Italian, though he spoke with both accents. And he is not English.' She caught her breath. 'But . . . *Irish* . . .'

'Does it mean something to you, then?'

'The Irish killed my brother.' She wanted to slap his face, set her nails into the flesh. She wanted to spit into his watching eyes. '*My brother* –'

'Aye.' The tone, cutting her off, was curt. 'A good many men were lost on *both* sides, mistress. But the Sassenachs won it all in the end, as they have so often before.' He moved closer, staring down upon her pale, upturned face. 'D'ye wish *me* dead, mistress? Or Bard?'

'*Irish*,' she repeated in bitterness and contempt.

'Your enemy.' His tone was implacable.

Elizabeth stared at him. 'An Irishman in England? There is no good in it, no good at all – *that* much I know from what my father has said – ' She broke off, suddenly understanding the implications of his presence. Irishmen in England, and *she* knew where they were.

'What shall I do with you, then?' he asked.

Her breath was ragged in her throat. 'Let me go,' she challenged. 'Let me go on to London.'

'Straight to Jamie's court, where you will tell everyone how it was two Irishmen gave you succour. *Irishmen*, mistress – two of them. D'ye think Jamie'll let it lie? We'll be hunted, mistress, like wolves.' Abruptly he turned from her and whistled, and a moment later the wolfhounds bounded up. He spoke to them briefly in the harsh, rough tone she had heard him use before, then gestured them towards the house. They went, skinny tails waving.

'Then you *will* kill me.' It crept out of her mouth on a whisper of discovery. She had begun to hope he would not.

His lips twisted into a parody of a smile. 'For now, mistress, I will merely take you inside.'

He took her into the room where Bard waited and poured her a glass of whiskey. She refused at once, but he put his hands over hers on the glass and guided it to her mouth. 'Drink.'

She swallowed once and choked on the harsh, fiery liquor. He tipped more down her throat until she shoved the glass away, and then he smiled.

'*Slainte*,' said Bard from his chair, ironic and solemn at once.

Elizabeth tried to catch her breath, staring at O'Neill as he filled the glass again and drank the whiskey himself. When she could speak again, she fixed him with an angry stare. 'Do you wish me made foolish from liquor? Or is it your wish to take my senses so you may kill me without a protest from me as you do it?'

O'Neill grinned. 'Most women are foolish, but I doubt liquor has much to do with it. And no, for now you are safe. I want you hearing me clearly when I tell you things.'

She looked at Bard. He sat very still in the chair but he smiled, as if amused by the predicament she had put herself in. His eyes, catching hers, were watchful, but she looked away because she found she could look at no man for very long when O'Neill was in the room.

'Tell me nothing,' she said clearly. 'I have no wish to know more of Irish connivance.'

O'Neill laughed. 'Irish connivance! By Christ, she knows us well. So quickly are we undone!'

'Sit down, mistress,' Bard suggested. 'I think you would do well to listen to the man.'

She looked at O'Neill first, then at Bard, and did as he suggested. Bard remained where he was but O'Neill, restless, paced before the fire. The dogs settled themselves on the floor near the warmth. Their yellow eyes glinted in their narrow, bristled heads, and they watched their master's every move.

As much as I do myself . . . she thought.

'What would two Irishmen be doing in England, mistress?' O'Neill asked her.

The whiskey had settled in her stomach. She felt a glow of warmth there, firing her blood until it ran through her veins like quicksilver, flushing her face with colour. She put a hand to her mouth and tasted the whiskey that had spilled over her fingers as she had pushed the glass away.

'I could not venture to say,' she told him at last, carefully. She sensed she trod a very dangerous path. 'But you are *hiding* in this house, are you not?'

'Oh, aye, hiding,' O'Neill agreed. 'D'ye have any idea what would happen to us did anyone know we were here?'

She thought of the hatred the English felt for the Irish, a race of barbarians who spoke a tongue-twisting language and demanded a freedom they could not have. She thought of the long vicious wars that had sapped the strength of England until she had nearly impoverished herself in an attempt to protect those who preferred English rule. She thought of her brother, so much older than herself, who had died fighting the Irish, butchered in the field.

Elizabeth looked up at the man as he waited before the fire. 'They would hang you,' she said evenly, 'and draw and quarter you.'

'And set our heads upon a spike on London Bridge,' finished O'Neill, so quietly she could hardly hear him.

The room was filled with silence. She did not move in her chair, not daring it. Neither did *he* move, standing so calmly before the fire, and yet she sensed in him a tautness that would strike her down did she dare utter a word against his race.

Carefully she asked, 'Why have you come to England?'

''Tis not for you to know,' he told her. 'Such knowledge could get you killed – aye, I see you understand that well enough – and for now I have no wish to spill *your* Sassenach blood.' His face was grim, though his eyes were fastened on her face. 'Enough will spill later, when we have begun.'

Elizabeth was on her feet, steadying herself against the table. '*What have you come to do?*'

'*'Tis not for you to know.*'

'She knows too much already,' Bard said idly.

O'Neill looked over at him. 'Would you have me do it now, then, in this room?'

Elizabeth felt the blood leave her face, taking her strength with it. Her head set up a clamorous protest against the exertions of the evening. She wavered, steadied herself again, then tried to turn and stumble from the room. O'Neill was there instantly, as she had expected, and his hand on her arm was not gentle.

The hand shifted, moving up to her unbound hair. For

a moment she went rigid, recalling the violence in Bard's hand, but O'Neill's touch was not the same. Not the same at all.

He pushed her hair away from her face, baring her neck, and his fingers lingered on the silk of her throat. 'Sassenach,' he said hoarsely, 'but so cursed beautiful.'

She jerked away from him, stumbling back. One hand thrust itself towards him, warding him away. 'And will it keep me alive?' she demanded. 'Will you look upon me, then, seeking pleasure? And will that pleasure win me back my life?' She yanked the folds of her bedrobe into place, hiding her body from him. Heat was in her face. She wasn't certain it if was the whisky or the expression in his eyes, those green eyes that stripped her of everything save her English blood, and that enough for him to use against her. 'I know only you and Bard are Irish. Who *are* you that such knowledge could cost me my life?'

'O'Neill,' he said softly. 'O'Neill. The Hound of Ireland.'

She looked into the face burned dark by a sun that did not shine so brightly in England, at the high cheekbones and firm jaw and the tension in his mouth. She realized he had, somehow, put a weapon into her hands, but she could not say what it was.

'A name,' she spat out between her teeth. 'Do you take such pride in a *name* that England's knowledge of it should make my death worthwhile?'

He glared at her. 'A name. Aye, mistress, it is, and a proud name, worthy of respect from every man who speaks it. *O'Neill,* mistress, got from the sons of Niall, the High Kings of Ireland. And if it means so little to you' – he did not looked pleased by her ignorance, rather somewhat affronted by it – 'then perhaps you are less dangerous than we thought.'

She had prepared herself to dash from the room. She

intended to snatch open the front door and run as far into the woods as she could, hoping to flee wolfhounds and Irishmen. But she did not. She sensed her victory in his words, and stared at him in astonishment instead of trying to escape.

'What do you want of me? To hear me say I know you and what you want here, and what you intend for England?' Elizabeth shook her head. 'I am not at court, *O'Neill*, that I know what starts a war or finishes it. That you are Irish tells me you are enemies of England, but nothing more.' She looked first at Bard, then back at O'Neill. 'What is it you wish me to say?'

The expectancy washed out of his face, leaving it softer and yet more austere. 'Perhaps you have said it, mistress.'

She drew in a trembling breath. 'Then may I go on to London?'

'No.' He smiled. 'There is a use for you yet.'

'Hostage?' She asked bitterly. 'I am not worth so much.'

At that his black brows lifted. 'Are you not, mistress? Do you say so? But then – you are not a man looking at a woman.' He gestured eloquently. 'Bard shall see you to your room.'

Elizabeth flicked a glance at the other man and saw him rise. She recalled the virulence in his voice and the threat in the hand he had set into her hair. Even now he did not put out an arm for her to take, as if he knew her thoughts, and she fixed him with a level gaze out of black-lashed, honey-pale eyes. 'If I am no threat to O'Neill, what am I to *you*?'

Bard's face was strangely still. 'A woman,' he said at last, and she knew the glove had been thrown down.

4

She dreamed of men and wolfhounds, and eyes, blue and green and yellow. She dreamed of a sword in the lantern light, and a hand upon her arm. But the hand moved from her arm to her breasts, pressing upon her with intricate demands, until even in her sleep she stretched upward to meet that demand. And then she awoke, shamed by how her *dreams* could betray her, and sat upright in her bed in the darkness of the room and tried to sort out her feelings.

Anger, yes. Resentment that he could keep her when she had no desire to be kept. Fear also; she could not say what he would do. But for all the fear filled up the marrow of her bones, she knew also another emotion. Something that had no name. Something that heated her flesh and set all her limbs to trembling with restlessness and a strange urgency.

'O'Neill.' She said it aloud, recalling how much weight the name supposedly carried. Then she drew the bed-clothes around her shoulders. '*Irishman.*' It was enough, almost, to set her teeth on edge. The Irish were the enemies of her country. They had killed her brother. And now, possibly, they might kill her.

In the darkness, Elizabeth thought of O'Neill. She thought of how he dominated a room even in perfect stillness. He was not so large as to be a giant – she had seen one, once, at a summer fair – but what flesh and bone he claimed was filled up with such fierceness of spirit and pride that it dwarfed all else. He diminished her merely by looking at her.

And yet she did not feel diminished. She felt, foremost, insulted by the expression in his eyes – who was he, an *Irishman*, to stare at an Englishwoman so? – but she could not deny that he affected her. Underlying the confusion and anger was curiosity that he could be moved to look at her so. And thinking of it sent the heat rushing through her limbs again, until she threw herself down against the bed and tried to go back to sleep.

But even in her dreams she could not escape O'Neill.

When she awoke the sun was shining and filled her room with light. She thought of her dreams and the long night, and felt the colour spill into her face at once. Mortified, she pressed two fists against her temples, and then realized her headache had gone. She felt well for the first time since the accident, free of pain and lethargy except for her sore wrist, and she wanted more than anything to get up and go from O'Neill's house.

The door opened. Elizabeth sat up at once, afraid it was O'Neill come to inflict himself upon her, but it was not. It was a woman, and in her arms was one of the gowns Annie had packed for the journey.

'I am Fiona. I've come to dress you properly,' the woman said. 'Himself thought you might be needing something more than a bedgown and a robe.'

At once Elizabeth's hand went to the place on her neck where O'Neill's hand had rested. The woman's words evoked too vividly her memory of the man, and the heat from his hand seemed to linger on her throat.

'I'll be seeing to your hair as well.' The woman set the lilac-coloured gown across the foot of the bed. 'I washed it once when you lay sleeping so hard from the pain in your poor head.'

Elizabeth looked at the woman and saw kind eyes set in a face full of wrinkles. She was not old, but her youth was far in the past. Her hair, once red, had faded to a grey tinged with just enough of its original colour to make it a rusty silver. Her blue eyes had faded, too, but her smile had not. Her hands, gnarled with rheumatism, clasped a comb and brush.

'Why have you not come up before when I was awake?' Elizabeth demanded. 'Bard said freely you were here – but you never let me see you.'

'Himself would not have it.' The woman moved forward and gestured for Elizabeth to rise and sit down on a stool before a wooden vanity with a small glass mirror.

'Himself?'

'The master.'

Elizabeth frowned. 'You mean O'Neill.'

'Aye, himself. Will you be getting up, mistress?'

Elizabeth climbed out of bed and slipped into the robe, moving to the stool as the woman waited. 'Why should he keep you from coming to me?'

'He gave me leave to come when you slept. I had the tending of you, mistress, when it wasn't right for a man.' Fiona began to brush the heavy hair, taking care to smooth the tangles painlessly. 'Until eleven years ago I lived all my life in Ireland. My tongue does not take so kindly to foreign languages himself speaks so well. He knew you would know me Irish the moment I opened my mouth.'

'And an enemy.' Elizabeth looked at the woman's reflection in the mirror. 'But his secrecy is spoiled, so it no longer matters if I know you are Irish. Is that it?'

For only the slightest moment the brush stilled. 'He thought to keep you deaf to our heritage so you would not know even a single Irishman has set foot in England – '

Elizabeth spun around on the stool, grabbing the brush from Fiona's hand. 'Because he intends to do my country harm.' She stared at the older woman and saw how unwavering were Fiona's eyes. 'Why have you come here, Fiona? What precisely does he intend to do?'

Fiona's lips were pressed flat. After a moment she shrugged. 'I'd not be knowing what O'Neill intends. He keeps it to himself.'

'*And* Bard.'

Empty, Fiona's hands clasped one another. 'Bard knows the master better than any, even O'Neill himself. But 'tis not for the likes of us to know.'

'And if they intend to kill me?' Elizabeth's fingers protested the tightness of her grip upon the brush. 'He has said it, Fiona, if perhaps a trifle indirectly. And now I ask what *you* say. Does an Irishman come into England in innocence, intending no harm to the King's realm?' Bitterly, she laughed. 'You need not answer that. I know well enough what Ireland is to England – '

' – And England to Ireland.' Fiona's tone was level, lacking all inflection. 'Mistress, I cannot say what himself intends. 'Tis O'Neill's business.'

'*And* mine!' Elizabeth returned. 'It is my life they have threatened!'

For a moment Fiona's knuckles shone white as she clasped her hands more tightly. 'Give them no reason, then.'

Elizabeth stared at her. Somehow she had expected a denial from Fiona, some measure of compassion that would soften the edge of truth. But there was nothing from Fiona save an acceptance of what could happen. 'You are as bloodthirsty as Bard and O'Neill!'

For just a moment Fiona shut her eyes. When they opened again Elizabeth saw the compassion she had anticipated before. 'No, no . . . I am not. I crave the blood of no man. But I recall what has become of Ireland,

and I find it more easy to understand what himself must be doing.'

Elizabeth heard the foreign lilt underlying Fiona's words. Less strong than she had expected, though thicker than O'Neill's. 'If you love Ireland so much, Fiona – why did you leave it?'

The woman smiled a little. ''Twas my duty to go, and my wish. I serve the O'Neills.'

Elizabeth frowned. 'Why did *they* leave, then? O'Neill has said something of the pride the name carries – why would he leave a place that so respects his family name?'

'That's for himself to be telling you,' Fiona responded. 'I may speak lightly of most things, being a bit of a gossip' – briefly, she smiled – 'but I won't be speaking of things as should not be said. Not by me – 'tis for himself to say.' The hands twisted. 'But I'll tell you this much, just so you can begin to understand what lies between us – 'twas England's Scottish King and his Sassenach court.' Fiona gently took the brush out of Elizabeth's hands. 'Shall I pin it up for you, mistress?'

Elizabeth's hand crept up to the heavy locks hanging to her waist. 'No,' she said blankly, 'braid it instead, and leave the braid unpinned. I wore it so often enough when I rode the Kentish downs.' She looked at the lilac gown spread across the bed. She had so little finery, and it was far from new. She had thought to wear the gown in London, not in some renegade Irishman's house in the Kentish woods. 'Why does he call himself the Hound of Ireland?'

Fiona smiled. ''Twas a name given to him quite young by his father. Himself has always been a fierce defender of Ireland's pride – he is the loyal Irish wolfhound.'

Elizabeth thought at once of the two O'Neill kept, both huge and fiercely loyal to their master. As he was to Ireland. 'Do you think he will kill me, Fiona?'

The woman looked at the lilac gown. "Twill be a lovely colour on you.'

Elizabeth shut her eyes.

"Tis a lovely colour on you.'

Descending the stairs, she saw O'Neill standing in the open doorway. She saw the sunlight at his back and the silhouettes of two huge dogs at his side, but she could not see his face. He was only a shape before her, but she knew his eyes were on her.

'No thanks from you?' he asked in sardonic humour, moving in to shut the door. 'But then I have only a poor Irishman's tongue, and not the smooth flattery of a Sassenach courtier.'

With the door closed she could see him clearly. She saw the ironic slant to his brows and the twist of his mouth. He had left off the leather doublet and wore a white linen shirt untied at throat and wrists, open to the waist, and she saw the mat of black hair curling on his chest. She felt the odd urgency spill into her limbs once again and the heat into her face. Quickly, she looked away.

'Fiona did well by you.'

Flattery. From *him*. Unless he only mocked her. She looked back at him and found her eyes drawn to the brown column of his throat and the V that marked where the sun had not yet touched. He seemed half undressed to her, showing so much skin, and yet had done nothing more than leave his doublet off.

'Did she?' Elizabeth asked blankly.

Gravely, he nodded. 'No more a bewildered girl but a woman.'

'Still a *bewildered* one?' She matched his irony.

She had not meant it in jest but he took it so and laughed. It put her in a foul temper – who was he to laugh at *her*? – and she glared at him. 'How much longer do you intend to keep me here?'

'Until I am decided to let you go.' He met her at the bottom of the stairs and put his hand upon her arm, drawing her into the room in which she had faced him the night before. Her eyes went to the table and she saw the whiskey decanter.

O'Neill saw it as well. 'Have you developed a taste for *uisge-beatha*, then?'

She frowned at him. '*Uis* . . .' She could not force her mouth around the syllables.

'*Uisge-beatha*,' he repeated. ''Tis Gaelic for what you English call whiskey. A heathenish twisting of its proper name, I might say. 'Tis the water of life, after all.' His green eyes glinted. 'D'ye wish some?'

'No,' she returned flatly.

He glanced behind her and saw the dogs, waiting patiently for his word. 'Boru,' he said, and the larger of the two pricked his ears. 'His name is Boru, mistress.'

'And the other?' She was startled by his softness with the huge dogs.

'Cuchullain.'

'More Gaelic,' she charged.

'Of a sort.' His face was solemn. Watchful. 'They are my bodyguards, mistress.'

Elizabeth looked at the size of him, sensing restrained power and violence. She thought it unlikely he would require anyone to guard him, human or otherwise, for she believed him fully capable of protecting himself without a second thought. But when she looked back at his face she found the shrewd eyes waiting for her, and she realized he spoke with a reason.

'Sit down, mistress, and I will speak plainly with you.'

Silently she refused, until his eyes beat her down and she did as he had ordered. But she pushed herself against the back of the chair as if to underline her calmness, which she did not feel at all, and stared back.

O'Neill, after a moment, moved to the unlighted fireplace and propped his booted foot on the fender. 'I have told you my name, mistress, and that is enough to get me killed. I can tell you little more, for it could get *you* killed, but you must understand the danger you have put yourself in.'

'I have *put* myself nowhere.'

His mouth twisted. 'Oh, aye, 'twas a storm that brought you, and runaway horses. But you are here, mistress, and that is enough for me.' His eyes were oddly emotionless. 'Were you a man, you would be dead now.'

Inwardly, she had known it. And yet she had not thought to hear it put so baldly to her face. 'Would *you* have done it?' Somehow, it mattered to her.

'Or Bard.' He shrugged. 'We cannot afford to be squeamish or negligent, mistress. This is war.'

She felt her heart move in her breast. It lurched against her ribs and then fell back again, thumping slowly and laggardly. 'England and Ireland are not presently *at* war.'

His lips compressed into a thin line. One corner hooked down, as if her statement were incidental. She understood the implication at once.

'But *why?*' she burst out. 'What would it gain you? More blood, more death, more hardship. You yourself said they would put your head up on a pike. Why would you risk yourself in something so foolhardy as this?'

He stared back. 'Foolhardy? I think not.' The words were clipped, harsh. 'Ireland is in my blood, my bones, my soul. I will not turn my back on my country.' His flaring nostrils pinched down and his eyes bored into hers. 'I have waited a long time for this, and now it has begun. I will let no one get in my way.'

'*I* am in your way.'

50

'Are you wishing to die, then?' His voice was incredibly soft.

The sudden silence of the room was oppressive. Elizabeth sensed clearly the leashed power in him, the strength so evident even in repose, and an emotion she could not name. His thick hair was so black it was nearly blue, and his eyes glittered like emeralds in his face. She wondered how easily his big hands could break her or close her throat.

When she could she answered him. 'I think, O'Neill, you will do whatever you have to do. And never look back again.'

For a moment his eyes were shuttered behind black-lashed lids, and then he smiled again. It was like the sun coming out from behind a cloud. 'Do you know anything about William, mistress?'

She gaped at him. '*William?*'

'The Conqueror,' he said impatiently, gesturing with one outflung hand. 'We are but thirty miles from Hastings, woman, the place where the Conqueror won his crown.'

She stared at him, astonished by the topic.

The black brows lanced down. 'You are as uninformed about this country's history as Bard, but he is Irish. I expected ignorance from him. *You* are English.' His tone expressed the eloquent belief that she should know precisely what he was talking about.

Elizabeth grimaced and looked briefly at the dogs, thinking perhaps *they* understood O'Neill's point. But they had settled on the floor, legs asprawl, and merely thumped their tails at her as if the introduction had made them friends.

'*What I am saying*' – O'Neill spoke with the aspect of a disgruntled tutor – 'is that I want you to think a moment. William sailed from Normandy and took England for his own. *Conquered* it, and made his ways paramount. He brought castles to England and set up the Tower to defend his right to claim this country his. Do you not see?' He stared at her. 'Think, woman, how it must have been for the English to see their King fall, and their realm with him.'

She understood his elaborate point at last. And felt moved to protest. 'But England has never *invaded* Ireland.'

'Not in so many words,' he said coldly, 'but 'twas done. Again and again, throughout the centuries. Since long before you or I were born.' One hand had closed into a fist. 'Old Elizabeth hounded us, and now Scottish James. And *I* will do what I can to stop it.'

'How?' she demanded. 'By going to war again?'

His smile was grim. 'It will take that, I think.'

'You are only *one man*.' Irritated, she glared at him. 'Bard is not enough, nor are those dogs.' She shook her head. 'You fight for a pointless cause. It will gain you nothing but your death.'

'Would that not please you?' His jawline was taut. 'When I am done, mistress, there will be more than just myself and Bard and two Irish wolfhounds. There will be an army again.'

'Then why are you *here*?' Elizabeth thrust herself out of the chair, standing rigidly before him. 'Why are you in England? Why not go home to Ireland and rouse your people *there*, instead of hiding here in Kent?'

'Because there is thing I must do first,' he told her calmly. 'A thing that could avoid this war altogether – although I doubt it – and 'tis *that* you may endanger.'

'*I*?'

'One word in the proper ear would have me taken, mistress, as I have already said. D'ye wish that on your conscience?'

'Should I not?' she threw back at him. 'What does it matter to me if one – no, two! – Irish rebels are taken into the King's custody?'

He crossed the room to her and caught her shoulders in his hands. Even as she protested the hands slipped up to circle her throat snugly. 'For the *King's justice*,' he reminded her. 'Or is it that you'd be *enjoying* the sight of my head put up on London Bridge?'

Her breath was ragged in her chest. With his hands upon her flesh she could hardly breathe, though he did not threaten her. She felt the tensile strength in his fingers and the calluses at their tips. No softness in O'Neill, none at all; she was a fool to hope for any.

'Why have you told me this?' she asked as evenly as she could. 'You have said I am in danger because I know too much – why tell me more? Why not leave me in ignorance?'

'You had that chance.' His voice, much like hers, was full of underlying harshness. There was tension in his hands, his words, his posture, even as there was tension in her own. 'You had that ignorance and I would have left you in it. But last night you came down those stairs and overheard what Bard and I discussed, and when that was done your future with me was settled.'

'There *is* no future with you.' She threw it in his face. 'You are an Irish rebel who plots against England, and England will smash you down.'

'Will she?' he asked. 'And what of the other woman?'

Elizabeth frowned. 'Other woman?'

'You.' He whispered it. 'What of the Sassenach woman I hold in my two hands?'

'What do you want from me?' she demanded. 'The truth? *You shall have it.*' Unsuccessfully she tried to peel the fingers away, locking her nails in his flesh. 'She curses you. She reviles you. She despises you.' She met his narrowed eyes squarely. 'She thinks of you what an Irish girl would think of an Englishman who treated her so harshly.'

He laughed. It was a mere breath of sound, but it was genuine laughter. 'Harsh, am I? You know nothing of harshness. You know nothing of the requirements of dedication. But most of all . . . you know nothing of O'Neill.' He thrust her away stiffly, as if he could not bear to touch her. 'Go, English. I have no desire to despoil my eyes with such as you.'

5

Banished to her room, Elizabeth took supper alone. Fiona carried the tray away after inquiring if there was anything more she could do; Elizabeth, pleading headache and fatigue, said no. When the woman left Elizabeth sat on top of the bedclothes, propped up by pillows, and stared at the walls.

She waited. She heard O'Neill take the dogs out, as apparently he did each night, and heard him return. His voice echoed oddly up the stairway to her room; he spoke what she had learned was Gaelic. It reminded her of her first few nights under O'Neill's roof – how she had heard him speaking of her, and how he had played the harp. His skill with the instrument seemed at odds with his harshness, but she had heard the eloquent ballads and laments from his own mouth.

Bard, downstairs, answered something, and then she heard nothing more. They had shut themselves off from her. She did not desire their company, but she desired less their disdainful dismissal of her. As if she were chattel, sent here and there. But perhaps it was their heritage. She knew little enough of the Irish, save the stories she had heard. It would not surprise her to discover any amount of crudity in O'Neill, or even brutality.

She waited. And when at last it was quite dark outside, Elizabeth got up. She went to the clothing chest salvaged from the coach and opened it, digging down until she found the dress she sought. It was black, suitable for mourning, and she had taken it with her only because she had not so many dresses she could leave any behind.

Then, because she could not manage the laces down her back without help and did not dare call Fiona, Elizabeth ripped the bodice of her lilac gown to her waist and slithered out of it.

When she had put on the black dress she laughed softly into the shadows. She had remembered that she could not unlace the lilac gown, but she had forgotten the other would require lacing up. Elizabeth smoothed the plain black skirts over her hips, then craned her head around so she could peer down her back. The gown gaped open, baring her undershift and the flesh beneath it.

Foolishness? she railed silently. *How better to illustrate rank and honour than by requiring at least one servant to do up a gown? And how stupid is such rank when I am trapped in this renegade's house!*

Grimly she looked at the chest, which held most of her life. She could take nothing with her, for she had no means to carry it. She would simply have to content herself with merely herself, and hope her father would give her money enough to replenish her missing wardrobe. Once he understood her predicament, he could hardly refuse.

Elizabeth moved to the window and peered out, satisfied no one was about. She thought O'Neill and Bard most likely plotted Irish atrocities as they drank their heathenish whiskey; they would prove no obstacle to her escape. She had only to get out of the house, go to the stables, and take a horse. Then she would be off for Rosewood – much closer than London – and safety.

She gathered up the velvet cloak O'Neill – or perhaps Fiona – had taken from her that first night. It was water-stained and torn, but she flung it around her shoulders. It covered her completely, including the bare expanse of her back, and she wrapped herself in it as she quietly opened the door. An ear to the crack gave her nothing but silence; she crept out and started down the stairs.

In the corridor leading to the front door, Elizabeth paused a moment. She heard the muffled voices of Bard and O'Neill. As she had guessed, they were in their cups, discussing things in the Gaelic she could not understand. O'Neill's voice was arrogant and impassioned, rising as if he spoke of something that meant more than life to him; Bard's tones were quieter, more contemplative, a counterpoint to O'Neill's intensity. She thought the voices indicative of the men.

Her slippers were silent as she moved towards the door. Praying the hinges were oiled, Elizabeth closed her eyes and pulled.

It opened without a sound. She smiled, thinking it likely O'Neill himself had seen to the oiling. A man in hiding would be certain to cover his tracks. She slipped through the opening and pulled shut the door behind her, waiting for her eyes to adjust to the darkness.

The July evening was only a little cool, but still she shivered. Elizabeth clutched the cloak around her body and went out into the darkness, moving away from the house and around the corner. Looming before her were the stables; their similarity to Rosewood's architecture was unmistakable.

She found, as she walked, that she was frightened. At home she went where she liked in total safety and freedom, secure in her position as Sir Edwin's daughter and chatelaine of Rosewood. Occasionally she ventured out of a summer's evening for a moonlight ride, but never alone, and never in such straits. Her chest felt tight with apprehension and the anticipation of what might lie ahead, for she would have to make her way – alone and without money – back to Rosewood. Only her name might see her through safely, for in this part of Kent the Stafford name would promise gold to any who aided her.

Inwardly, she grimaced. Little gold, at that; noneless, someone would surely aid her.

And yet fear was not all she felt. There was also an odd exhilaration, as if a part of her wished to enjoy the evening's activities. She thought perhaps it came from a desire to spit in O'Neill's face, and her escape would do precisely that. Did he intend to belittle an Englishwoman, she would show him of what metal she was made.

'Sassenach, am I?' she muttered. 'Hound of Ireland, are you? Well, let this Sassenach pull the teeth of the hunting dog.'

When she reached the stables she found only two horses. A coach was tucked into the shadows. One mount for each man, and likely neither of them tame beasts. But the potentiality for a hot-blooded mount did not disturb Elizabeth in the least; she had ridden since childhood and was not at all put off by the thought of a spirited horse. Even better, a fleet horse would aid her escape. She had no intention of allowing O'Neill to catch up to her.

She had to work in darkness, for she dared not light a lantern. The nearest horse was a dark bay, the other a black; she chose the black because the stallion would blend into the darkness better. Softly she spoke to him, wondering if he understood English in place of Irish, then reflected both must be English-bred horses. It was unlikely O'Neill would have brought them from the Continent.

At Rosewood a stable boy had the chore of tacking out her horse. Here there was no one. She had learned as a child the intricacies involved in bridling and saddling a horse, but it had been years, and at that time her mount had been a gentle pony. Now she faced a horse significantly larger.

She lifted the bridle down from its peg on the wall, then sorted out the leather until she had headstall and reins untangled. The metal snaffle was cold to her touch as she tucked it into her left hand, spreading the rings apart. Speaking softly to the big horse, she moved close to his head and slipped the headstall over erect ears. She pressed the bit against his lips, inserting thumb and fingers gently, urging him to accept the snaffle. He did so. She settled it properly and made certain the buckles of the headstall were fastened correctly and comfortably.

She considered, for a moment, going bareback. It would be quicker; all she had to do was get herself mounted and they were gone. But though she occasionally indulged in wild bareback gallops across the downs, she thought it dangerous in view of her situation. Better to use a saddle, even if she *did* ride astride.

The stallion, an appealingly gentle sort for all his size, turned his head and watched with great interest as she settled the fleecy pad on his back. Elizabeth felt his muzzle in the folds of her cloak; the material slid aside and the stallion's velvet nose moved across her bare flesh. It was an oddly intimate gesture, almost a caress, and she felt her flesh contract. Quickly she pulled the cloak over her shoulders again, then swung up the saddle with a clank of iron stirrups.

She bent to catch the girth and buckle it. Her head set up a sudden unexpected throbbing, nearly driving her to the ground. Dizzily she leaned against the stallion, setting her face against his heavy shoulder. She took strength from the clean horse smell of him and waited, feeling dampness along her brow. When she could she did up the buckles properly.

'Now,' she said quietly, and led the horse from his stall to the door of the stables.

'I thought it might be done more quickly,' O'Neill said, 'but I was forgetting your head.'

Elizabeth stepped back so abruptly, her back slammed

into the stallion's questing nose. He took offence and lurched away, scraping his muzzle up into her hair and knocking her forwards again.

O'Neill caught her as she stumbled. 'Even my horse wants you to stay here.' He took the reins from her numb hand.

'How long have you been watching me?' she demanded.

'Long enough to see how an English gentlewoman deals with a great brute of a horse.' He grinned. Even in the grey shadows she could see the glint in his eyes and the gleam of white teeth.

'You've done well, mistress. Better than I expected.'

'I am no soft, helpless woman!' she lashed. 'Do you think I will sit still and do nothing while you plot your plots?'

'Ah, no, not a soft helpless woman,' he said intently. 'That I see clearly . . . now.' He stepped closer. 'Did you think it so easy to slip my bonds, mistress? Were you forgetting the hounds?'

She looked past him and saw the two dogs, ephemeral shapes in the moonlight. Their coarse hair was silvered and their yellow eyes glinted. 'I did not hear them bark,' she challenged, thinking he lied, that his distrust of her had led to his discovery of her escape.

'You won't, often. 'Tis only when they must, for they know what it means to take down a man unaware.' For a moment his face was solemn, his mouth grimly set. 'So I came out to see what you would do.'

'And have you seen?'

'I see, mistress, that I have misjudged you.' He put out his hand and took her sore wrist into it, drawing her out into the moonlight. She heard the stallion behind them, free, snuffling in the dirt and straw for fallen grain.

'O'Neill – ' But he put a hand across her mouth. She tasted the whiskey on it, and the salt of his flesh.

'Let me speak.' The lightness was gone from his tone. 'I am many things, mistress – rogue, scoundrel, whoreson – so many other things you might be wishing to name me. But what then are you? Not the meek, soft little thing I first believed. You are here because of a capricious fate and I'm not a man to be turning my back on a woman requiring aid, but you also are – inconvenient. You might have proved no trouble initially, but now you know enough to do me harm. And *now*, mistress . . . now that I have seen your willingness to undertake a dangerous journey, I must believe you might offer even more of a threat to me than before.'

'I only wanted to go home!' she cried. 'I only wanted to go away from *you!*'

His eyes narrowed. 'Not to London?'

Elizabeth laughed wildly. 'To London? Like *this?*' She slipped the cloak from her shoulders and turned, showing him the unlaced gown and bare flesh. She meant only to support her claim of innocence; she realized, with sudden insight, he might be a man stirred by such a sight.

Instantly she tried to spin around, aghast at what she had done, but O'Neill's hand was on her arm. It stopped her, holding her still before him, and she stared up into his face.

For a moment she saw surprise flicker deep in his eyes. She had won, or nearly so; then the victory crumbled into ashes. A mask dropped over his face. He clasped her arm in his hand. 'Has someone sent you?' he demanded.

Elizabeth's mouth fell open. She could only stare at him dumbly, astonished by the question. The thought of a woman putting herself in such danger purposely was something she could not comprehend, and even O'Neill had to admit her shock was too absolute to be unfeigned.

Grimly he smiled. 'I was mistaken, mistress. Forgive me.'

61

She wanted to bend down and retrieve her fallen cloak, but the hand on her arm prevented her. And then the other hand slid up to her shoulder. She felt him move the collar of the gown away from her neck. '*No!*'

'You have saved me some trouble already, mistress, by leaving the laces undone.' His voice was rough, husky as smoke. 'Does a woman have any idea how clumsy a man feels with all these laces beneath his hands?'

'O'Neill!' She tried to move. She felt the gown gape open across her back. His hand slid down, widened the gap, slipped beneath the soft undershift to caress bare flesh.

Elizabeth stiffened in outrage. But for just that moment the memory of the stallion's soft muzzle sliding across her spine rose in her mind; she could not help but liken O'Neill – so powerful and equally arrogant – to the animal. 'Let me g – ' But his mouth closed on hers and she never finished her command.

He tasted of whiskey, too much whiskey, and she nearly gagged on the assault. He had moved, moving her, setting her against the wall of the stable so she had nowhere to go. The hand on her back slipped lower still, moving across the upswell of buttocks; the other arm was set firmly around her neck. Her head was bent back against it until she could not move.

He was hurting her. He took her breath away, stole it out of her chest, and used it for his own. She could feel the hard, warm length of him against her, one knee set between her legs. He caught her lips in his teeth a moment, tugging gently, nipping, then released the quivering flesh and soothed it with his tongue. Elizabeth whimpered deep in her throat and tried to pull away, but he had caged her very well.

When he took his mouth away she could not repress a sob, then looked away in anguish. But when he spoke she could not help but snap her head up to stare at him in shock.

'No one sent you,' he said. 'Otherwise they'd have never sent me a virgin.'

The way he said it made an insult out of the word. There was no kindness in it, just a wry cynicism and vague amusement. At her expense. Elizabeth stiffened in the hard circle of his arms and glared at him, ignoring the clamour in her own body.

O'Neill laughed. 'Have I made you angry? 'Tis the truth, is it not? Or are you simply a good actress?' He paused reflectively a moment. 'A *very* good actress.'

Frustration and rage welled up inside. 'Are *so* many women willing to accept the mouthings of an Irish renegade?'

One corner of his lips twitched. 'Most of them do more than accept them,' he said gravely. 'They participate as well.'

Heat surged into her face. She knew now what it was to be a woman kissed by O'Neill – except she felt the experience had, somehow, been lacking. Still, it was not something she was likely to forget, regardless of the circumstances. 'I have no intention of such lewdness, Irishman. You forced yourself upon me.'

'And about to do so again.' He grinned at her inarticulate protest. ''Twould be cruel of me to leave you wondering how easy it was to discern your girl's virginity. So I'll be showing you how 'tis properly done, mistress, simply to make matters easier in the future.'

'You great Irish oaf!'' she shouted. 'Take your hands from me!'

'Ah, but I cannot, Mistress Stafford. You are too warm and soft and the moonlight is so gentle with your face . . .' His lips came down against her throat, sucking at the tender flesh so that she shivered in outrage and something she could not quite name even to herself. His tongue was hot against her, tracing down across her shoulder as his mouth moved. She felt the faint roughness of his beard, for he was a man who no doubt shaved twice a day to keep the colour from his jaw. He would have to, with such thick black hair.

Irrationally, Elizabeth wondered what he would look like with a beard . . . and then she was so angry with herself she wanted to scream. 'I thought you did not wish to despoil your eyes with me,' she challenged breathlessly.

''Tis not my eyes I'm despoiling,' he said against her flesh.

'O'Neill – you *Irish filth* – let me go!'

He felt the tension in her. He knew well enough what he did to her; he had seduced so many women he had lost count. He had surrendered his own virginity years before, before he had even left Ireland at fifteen; in France and Italy he had known great opportunity to sample that foreign field. It was the English ones that had always been denied him.

Until now.

His hand cupped down to capture the cool silken skin of her buttocks, pressing her hips firmly against his groin. He felt the line of her pelvis and the straining in her body as she tried to deny him. So badly she wanted free of him, but he could hardly let her go so soon, when she had no idea what was between a woman and a man.

His mouth closed again on hers before she could protest, for he could see the cry rising to her lips. Her honey-pale eyes were wide and frightened, dilated black in the darkness; he did not want to frighten her – *Christ, no!* – but neither did he wish to let her go. He knew of only one way to still her fear, and that was to show her there was no need for it.

Still pressing her against him, O'Neill used his free

hand to pull the loosened material away from her shoulder. He knew why she had not laced the gown. He blessed her rank for once, and her pride, and her willingness to attempt escape. He hated laces and other feminine adornment that merely got in his way; when he wanted a woman he wanted one whose clothing came off easily, without interruption, without reluctance. And without intending to, the girl had aided him.

Elizabeth felt the hand strip the gown from her shoulder. So easily was she made half naked, bared to the world, and felt bitter regret mixed with frustration, rage, and apprehension wash through her in a drowning wave as his hand moved down to explore her cringing breast. The undershift was no impediment and did little to aid her modesty. In a moment, if he continued, he would have the gown from her entirely.

Elizabeth made a small sound. She sagged in his arms. She did not feel faint, but thought it might provide a moment's distraction for him. She felt him shift his stance as she went slack, supporting her automatically, and through half-shut lashes she saw his eyes open to look at her. Abruptly she brought up her cupped right hand and smashed the heel into the underside of his chin, driving it closed. His head snapped back; she heard a muffled sound of surprise and protest and, she thought with pleasure, pain.

O'Neill fell back with an oath, the back of one hand pressed to his mouth. Elizabeth moved quickly, lunging aside and out of his reach. Hastily she pulled up the disarranged gown and turned to look for the stallion, meaning to mount and flee. But O'Neill caught her sore wrist, spinning her around. There was blood on his mouth and smeared on the back of his hand. Had she cut his tongue, then, or his lip? The thought made her smile.

O'Neill eyed her. The smile he understood, being a

man who understood revenge; he could not deny her her victory. At least she had knocked a little sense into his addled head, for he realized he had drunk too deeply of the *uisge-beatha*. It made him reckless sometimes, although ordinarily he was not a poor drinker.

'Well,' he said. Then he grinned. 'Well met, mistress. 'Tis no wonder England has reigned supreme so long if her women are such staunch fighters.' He fingered his bottom lip carefully. ''Tis not a blow *I* might choose, ordinarily, but I'll not be denying it had the desired effect.' He bent and swept the cloak off the stable floor. 'Come, Eilis . . . I'll be taking you back to the house now.'

'*Eilis?*' she demanded.

He draped the cloak around her and purposely kept his hands from straying to the silk of her throat. ''Tis Gaelic,' he answered evenly. 'For Elizabeth.'

6

'Where is O'Neill?' Elizabeth asked grimly as Fiona did up the laces of her gown.

'Himself?' Fiona sounded startled.

'O'Neill. I have something to say to him.' Elizabeth pulled her hair out of Fiona's hands and began to braid it severely, forgoing the elaborate coiffure she would have to wear at court. Doing her hair reminded her of Annie – poor dead Annie, buried in the Irishman's wood – and she felt her resolution harden. 'Well?'

'Mistress, 'twould not be wise – '

'*Where is he?*' Only rarely had she ever employed rank to manipulate a person. Now, facing a servant reluctant to betray her master in any way, Elizabeth used the tone of command she had heard in her father's mouth.

Fiona's lips pressed themselves flat. 'In the chapel.'

Elizabeth swung around to face her. 'And where is *that?*'

''Tis at the back of the house. But – mistress – '

Elizabeth ignored the protest and swept out of the room, quite certain of her course. She understood O'Neill now; she would get nowhere with him unless she faced him like a man and demanded her freedom. Asking would do no good; pleading was not in her repertoire.

Fiona's vague directions didn't help her much, but Elizabeth discovered the dogs sprawled outside a closed door and assumed she had found the proper place. She put out her hand and swung open the door, prepared to do battle, verbally or physically.

But as she stalked into the room she finally realized

exactly what Fiona had said. *The chapel*. O'Neill?

She saw him then, kneeling before a small prie-dieu with his black head bent. He wore black clothing, as usual, and blended into the grey shadows of the small, ill-lit chapel. It surprised her that the chapel was in use; Henry VIII's break with Rome and the Papacy had ended Catholicism's rule in England, and the chapels had mostly been shut up. But this one, quite obviously, had escaped the fate.

O'Neill seemed not to have heard her brazen entrance, but Bard, also on his knees in an attitude of reverence, turned sharply towards the door. His eyes were fastened on her in a combination of surprise and irritation.

The tableau took Elizabeth utterly by surprise. Never would she have dreamed of seeing O'Neill on his knees in prayer. A man humbling himself before God?

More likely telling God what O'Neill wants! – and yet there he was before her, either lost in communion with God or purposely ignoring her.

Elizabeth thought the latter more likely. But in all decency she could not interrupt him in this place, no matter what he was doing, so she backed out. But before she could shut the door Bard was up, coming towards her purposefully, and he caught the door to keep it from closing in his face. He slipped out into the corridor and shut it softly.

His face, when he turned to Elizabeth, was masklike. 'Well, mistress?'

She smoothed the skirts of her indigo gown. Then she put up her chin. 'Praying?' she asked. *'O'Neill?'*

''Tis Sunday,' Bard said briefly. 'We have no priest to say mass, and so we do what we can by ourselves.'

Elizabeth recalled the kindness he had used with her initially, only a few days before, and the comfort of his companionship. He was not the same man, not since she had seen O'Neill face-to-face. 'I should not believe it of either of you,' she told him flatly. 'You do not appear the religious sort.'

Bard's smile was humourless. 'You know nothing of either of us, mistress . . . and I suggest you do not judge what you cannot possibly understand. As for religion – aye, we are both devout in our own way.' His mouth twisted. 'We are Catholic, you see, in addition to being Irish. A double burden, here in England.'

'And were you petitioning God for divine aid in this treasonous war you plan?' she demanded, stung by his condescension.

'Quite possibly.' He took her arm and turned her away from the door, leading her down the corridor to the front of the house. 'What is it you want?'

'To speak to O'Neill.'

'Speak to me instead.'

Elizabeth tried to pull out of his grasp, but Bard was as strong as O'Neill, if in a less obvious way. He had the same sort of dedicated determination in his eyes.

He escorted her firmly into a room and bade her be seated. Unwillingly, she sat. Then, looking at his cold, unfriendly face, she could not help herself. 'What has changed you, Bard? You are become different. Harsh. You are not as you were at first.'

'Did you think me a *kind* man, mistress?' The irony was quite plain – that, and mockery.

Elizabeth disliked the cynicism in his tone. 'Aye,' she said flatly. 'I did.'

Something flickered briefly in the blue eyes. He turned away abruptly, moving purposefully towards the table with the whiskey decanter, but he stopped. She wondered if he would not drink liquor on a Sunday.

When he turned back his face was a mask again. 'I am not a kind man. I am an Irishman come to England to intrigue against the Crown. I will do whatever I must in order to succeed, even to playing the mummer with a foolish Sassenach woman.'

Elizabeth gasped at the cruel matter-of-factness in his tone, even as he admitted to treason. 'That is honest, at least. And the first time either of you has been so with me.' Her own measure of irony showed itself in her tone. 'I thank you for that much, Bard.'

He stared at her silently a long moment, as if he weighed her against some secret criteria of his own. And then his mouth twisted in the faintest shadow of a feral grimace. She saw an odd obsessive light in his eyes and knew him deadly serious. 'Keep your covetous eyes from O'Neill, mistress. He needs no woman just now, when there are more important things to concern ourselves with.'

'Covetous eyes!' she was outraged. 'How *dare* you?'

'I dare what I please,' he answered. 'I have seen you look at him.'

'He is a cruel, unfeeling beast, and he keeps me here against my will,' she told him angrily, recalling clearly the impatience and overwhelming power in O'Neill's body as he pressed her against the stable wall. Colour flared in her face. 'I want *nothing more* than to be free of you both!'

Bard's smile was faint, but she saw it. And was frightened. 'You play an old game, mistress,' he said gently, too gently. 'There is not a woman alive who has seen him and does not want him.'

'*I* am!' she declared. '*I* am alive, and *I* have seen him, and I *do not want him!*'

There was tension in him as he spoke, a taut vibrancy that lent significance to the studied lightness of his tone. 'You are not the first to protest precisely that, while all the while your nights are filled with dreams of him – dreams of O'Neill in your arms, between your legs,

70

whispering love words to you. *You beg him to lie with you, woman . . .* though you do it silently.'

Elizabeth was on her feet, wishing he were close enough for her hand to slap across his mocking Irish face. '*Bastard!*' she cried, using with all the force of her anger a word she had never thought to utter.

Bard smiled. 'No weapon, mistress – not when it is the truth.' Idly he turned to the decanter and lifted it, pouring a glass of the smoky, amber liquor.

Elizabeth recalled the taste of it in O'Neill's mouth, the way his tongue had caressed her throat and shoulder. She felt the hot flush of shame and unexpected response flood her body; she recalled also the conviction in Bard's tone when he had accused her of dreaming of O'Neill, and how possessive he had sounded.

'What are you?' she asked abruptly. 'His slave?'

Bard turned back, glass in hand. 'I am the Hound's hound,' he said obscurely, and smiled. 'Make you what you will of that, mistress . . . I doubt you would understand.'

Affronted – and offended by the truthfulness of the final statement – Elizabeth opened her mouth to challenge him again but was interrupted by the dogs. The wolfhounds bounded through the door, toenails scraping the wooden floor, and came to an expectant halt before her. Their heads were level with her waist; they were great, huge beasts, yet they regarded her with bright anticipation in their yellow eyes. Narrow tails waved.

'What do they want?' she asked apprehensively.

'Likely they'll be wanting their freedom.' O'Neill stood in the doorway. 'Come, Eilis – we'll take them out.'

Elizabeth looked at him. She looked at him and thought of the things Bard had said, and felt an odd tingling begin deep in her abdomen. 'No,' she said, but the sound was lost in the whine of one of the hounds.

71

'Come,' O'Neill said again, and she went.

The morning was clear and crisp and yet Elizabeth knew the sun would warm them too well before much longer. She needed no cloak or mantle.

The dogs raced ahead of them both, streaking through the trees as great silver blurs. She fully expected them to bark but they made no sound, as she recalled O'Neill's explanation for their silence. Somehow it made them more frightening – a man could die of fright alone if leapt upon by two silent, bestial dogs nearly as large as ponies.

'How much longer?' she asked abruptly.

'Is that the question you wished to ask me when you came bursting into the chapel?'

So he *had* known she was there. 'Were you really praying?'

The black brows lanced down. 'Of course I was praying. What else would I be doing on my knees in a holy place?'

'It hardly suits you,' she retorted.

'You have no idea what suits me.' O'Neill matched his stride to hers, which was significantly shorter than his own. 'For the moment what suits me is to keep you here.'

'And when shall I be allowed to leave?' She turned to face him squarely. 'What purpose does it serve to keep me here? If you mean to kill me, do it. If not, let me go.'

'No,' he answered. 'Until the ransom is paid, you go nowhere.'

The breath rushed out of her throat. '*Ransom!*'

'You are not a hostage, mistress . . . you have no political value. You are, however, worth a sum of money to the man who sired you.'

Elizabeth stared at him. 'But – my father – ' she broke off, seeing clearly the danger implicit in telling O'Neill her father had no gold to spare. She wondered how much he had demanded.

'Your father?' O'Neill prodded. 'Aye?'

72

'You are waiting for his answer, then,' she said. 'And when it comes I am to be freed?'

'Dependent upon his acquiescence.' O'Neill watched her. 'And, of course, your willingness to keep silent.'

Her chin rose. 'You are asking a great deal of me, after what you have done.'

'I am asking very little in return for your life,' he told her calmly. 'Silence, and you survive.'

'*You* seem dedicated enough to your Irish cause to risk your life in it,' she threw back. 'What if I am willing to risk my life for *my* country? What if I speak and am therefore killed? Will you not be taken regardless, and your rebellion thrown into disarray?' Purposely she kept her tone conversational. 'What is accomplished if the thing is ended before it is begun?'

'And you are thinking I am the only Irishman in the world?' he asked softly. 'D'ye think I am the only O'Neill? Oh, Eilis, do not be such a fool. Aye, you could see me thrown into chains, and doubtless it would please you to ride in a fine coach across London Bridge to see my head upon a pike – but you act too hastily. You dismiss the responsibilities of the Irish to one of their own.'

'Revenge.' She spat it out. 'You threaten me, then?'

'I do.' He faced her in perfect stillness. 'Speak of me, Eilis, and you and your father are dead. If not by mine, then by the hand of another O'Neill.'

She was trembling. She could not help herself. She faced him with what determination and defiance she could muster, and yet his pride and intensity smashed it down again. He had only to put his hands around her neck and squeeze, and her life was done. But she thought he might not do it – that if he intended it, surely he would have done it already. Instead, he chose to silence her with threats. She did not doubt he meant them, but she knew also it ensured her safety.

73

O'Neill does not really wish to kill me.

It was a power, of a sort. Elizabeth knew it in that moment. Looking at him, looking at his strength and pride and fierce intensity, she knew also how it was that Bard could say no woman could look on O'Neill without wanting him. Her senses clamoured for him, even as her morality withdrew from the realization in stunned shock.

Irishman. Enemy. And so vibrantly male as to overwhelm her completely, even in her innocence.

'Does your hand hurt?' he inquired, and she stared at him in confusion. ''Twas a great hard blow you fetched my poor chin last night.'

She glared. 'You deserved it, and worse. It would be worth *breaking* my hand to do it all over again.'

He caught her wrist and lifted her hand, setting the heel against the firm bone of his jaw. 'Then try,' he said softly. 'I am moved to force myself on you again.'

Elizabeth jerked back, trying to withdraw from his grasp. 'You are a lewd, licentious beast!'

'And worse,' he agreed cheerfully. 'But there you were, Eilis, attempting to escape – and only half dressed. No man would have denied himself the pleasure of stealing a kiss or two.'

'*I* denied you,' she retorted. 'Do you think I want an Irishman's kiss?'

His hand tightened its grasp on her wrist. 'Then 'tis well for an *Englishman* to kiss you?' he asked in a deceptively gentle tone. 'Is your welcome determined by nationality?'

'My welcome is determined by such things as betrothals and marriages,' Elizabeth said angrily. 'I am not a loose woman.'

'Yet you go to London.'

'I go to serve the Queen!' she exclaimed. 'An honourable service, O'Neill, such as you will never know.'

His nostrils were pinched and white. His mouth was a grim line. 'And you mean to accept it.'

'Why should I refuse it? How could I?'

'By saying no. And you should. Do not prate to me of your morality when you will sell yourself to a man in Jamie's court. Some whey-faced Sassenach nobleman, I do not doubt.'

Furious, she managed to twist her arm from his grasp. 'What does it matter to *you* what man I wed, O'Neill?'

'Cold,' he said grimly. 'Bloodless. Grasping, as Bard says.' Contempt was in his hard green eyes. 'So, mistress, you will trade your body for a grand title, sharing your bed with whatever man has gold enough to afford you.'

'I will *not!*'

'Then why do you go?' he demanded. 'What are you thinking a king's court *is*, mistress, if not one huge bedchamber for the lords and ladies to make use of? You will be besieged, I do not doubt, and will have difficulty choosing one man out of so many.' His jaw clenched. 'Or will you choose them all?'

Elizabeth felt herself shaking. She was so angry she wanted to scream at him, but instead she steadied herself and matched him stare for stare, putting all her rage into her voice without raising it. 'You mistake me, O'Neill. I am English . . . not Irish. Our sensibilities are somewhat different.'

He said something in Gaelic. Though she could not understand the meaning, she understood the tone clearly enough. She had managed to make him angry. She had touched his prickly Irish pride. And it pleased her.

'You are innocent, mistress,' he said flatly, 'and that innocence must be quickly discarded or Jamie's court will swallow you whole.' He laughed briefly, bitterly – a short bark of derisive sound. 'Do you think I have no knowledge of courts, mistress? Where d'ye think I have been these last years?'

'I could not say.' Her tone implied that neither did she care.

'I am O'Neill,' he told her distinctly. 'Kieran O'Neill. Are you *quite* certain you know nothing of me – or my family?'

Elizabeth laughed. '*There* speaks humility,' she said scathingly. 'Do you believe the whole of England knows you?'

Narrowed, his eyes studied every inch of her face, brows drawn down. She felt the intensity of his stare and knew he judged her somehow. It angered her, and yet she knew of no effective way to protest it.

'I think,' he said finally, 'you do not lie. Bard may suspect you, but I think you are telling the truth.' He shook his head and turned her, escorting her through the trees once again. 'Let it suffice you to know I have spent some time in the presence of royalty, mistress, in France and Italy. I understand courts quite well, and I think you shall learn for yourself how deep the waters can be when you have gone wading in Jamie's pond.'

'He is my King,' she responded stiffly.

'He is a man.' One of the wolfhounds came bounding up, throwing himself against his master's legs. O'Neill, chiding him fondly in Gaelic, recovered his balance and scrubbed the dog's ears affectionately.

'Boru?' Elizabeth asked.

'Cuchullain.'

'What names,' she said in disgust. 'One can hardly get a tongue around the sounds.'

'They are both heroes of Irish history,' he said – defensively, she thought.

'The dogs?'

'The men.' He scowled. 'I named them after men.'

'Ah.'

'Brian Boru was a king. A great king. And Cuchullain was a hero such as the English never had.'

'And *you*, O'Neill?' she inquired in an elaborately patronizing tone. 'What, precisely, are you?'

He smiled, unoffended. 'I am an Irishman. 'Tis more than enough for me.'

'The Hound of Ireland?'

'Aye' – he swung her roughly against his chest, locking one hand in her hair as he cradled the back of her head – 'and desiring to mount the English bitch – '

Even as she struggled he crushed her mouth with his own. He kissed her thoroughly, violently, with such a powerfully restrained passion that it left her breathless, gasping against his chest when at last he loosed her mouth. In his arms she felt fragile, brittle, as if she might break at his merest whim. And yet such a great rage built up inside that she thought she might burst.

'Take your hands from me! Take them from me! I will not suffer you to touch me – '

'And if I were English?' His splayed fingers nearly crushed her skull. 'If I were an Englishman with staid English appetites, would you welcome me then?'

'No *Englishman* would do as you do!' she retorted. 'O'Neill – let me go – '

'D'ye not want it?' His voice was husky again, almost breathless. 'D'ye not want *me*?'

'*No!*' She dug her nails deeply into the flesh of his shoulders as she sought to push away. 'I do not traffic with scum!'

'Oh, Eilis,' he breathed, 'you will. I promise it. One day you will writhe in carnal consummation with this Irishman' – she tore herself from his arms even as he loosened them – 'and you will *beg* me for it!'

77

7

Elizabeth took dinner alone in her room once again, though she had not been banished to it. She had no wish to face O'Neill or Bard while she ate; their presence would ruin her appetite. And so Fiona brought her a tray and removed it when she was done picking at the food, and then the Irishwoman returned to help her disrobe and prepare for bed.

Fiona had just begun to unlace Elizabeth's gown when O'Neill came into the bedroom. He did so without ceremony, thrusting open the door so hard it slammed against the wall. 'Fiona,' he said, 'you may go.'

'No,' Elizabeth said sharply at once, knowing the woman was her protection. 'I desire her company.'

O'Neill's eyes narrowed. 'And whom do you think she serves, woman? A *Sassenach*, or The O'Neill?'

The O'Neill. Not merely O'Neill. Elizabeth thought it a strange way of putting it, but then she understood nothing of the Irish, nothing of O'Neill, save he was a brutal, angry man.

Quietly Elizabeth matched him, stare for stare. 'You set her to serve me,' she answered. 'When I was ill, and now. Do you take from me what little propriety there is in this house?'

'I take from you what I will,' he said harshly. 'Fiona – I have said you may go.'

'Fiona!' Elizabeth appealed to the woman. 'You know what he means to do!'

There was conflict in Fiona's ageing face. Gnarled hands twisted together in the folds of her apron; her lips were pressed flat. And in that instant of conflict – and its resolution – Elizabeth saw which had more claim on Fiona's loyalty. There was no question of woman supporting woman against the impatient demands of this man. Himself had spoken, and Fiona was Irish before all else, a servant of The O'Neill.

Silently the woman took her leave. O'Neill did not bother to shut the door. He faced Elizabeth, blocking the exit and watched her expressionlessly. 'I have come, mistress, to say it would be wise not to attempt escape again.'

'And if I do?' she demanded. 'Will you beat me? Throw me in chains? Stretch me on the rack?'

'No,' he said. 'I will kill you.'

She meant to answer him. She meant to throw a retort in his teeth. But in the face of his calmness, his absolute conviction, she knew he did not lie.

'Would you?' It was mostly a whisper. 'Could you truly take my life?'

It was an honest question born out of fear and realization, not a ploy to challenge him. But she saw a grim light in his green, green eyes and realized she had been misunderstood. And now he meant to show her.

He caught her before she could retreat. His hands encircled her throat. Fingers pressed against the junction of spine and skull; thumbs pushed in to crush the fragile windpipe. 'Could I?' he said. 'Oh, aye.'

'O'Neill!' Her own fingers clawed at his hands, seeking to peel away the choking fingers. '*O'Neill* – '

'There are times,' he said quietly, 'when a man is more than willing to be turned from his goal by a woman . . . when he is willing to set aside an intention and bed with her instead. But I am an Irishman, mistress, with a free Ireland as my goal, and no woman – *Sassenach or otherwise* – can turn me from that with her wiles.'

Elizabeth's head was filling up with pain and darkness. Frenziedly she dragged at his hands, but he did not release her. She sagged, thinking to pull him off balance and free herself, but he stood firm and tightened his hands. And then, at the moment she thought she might fall into senselessness, he let her go, and she fell down from his hands to kneel gasping on the floor.

When she could speak she turned her face up towards his, so far above her, and asked him a simple question. 'Is killing me so easy for you, then?'

For an instant she thought she saw something in his face, in his eyes. A fleeting emotion that fell away almost at once. And then his mouth was a grim, flat line and his hands were clenched into fists, and she thought to herself, *No, it is* not *so easy after all*.

'Get up from there.' He said it harshly and reached down to catch her wrist, tugging her upward, and she recalled how they had met. How she had knelt in the mud with her head and heart pounding and pain all through her body; how he had pulled her from the ground even as he did now. But this time she did not faint. This time she faced him, saying nothing, hating him with her eyes.

He muttered something in Gaelic – a fierce, harsh curse. And then he took her into his arms and nearly crushed her against his chest and she knew, somehow, she had won.

This time there was no whiskey. What she tasted was O'Neill himself, and the sweet harshness of a man's mouth. She was stiff, resisting as he locked his arms around her, meaning to deny him utterly, but then something rose up to claim her, something that overwhelmed her, and she felt herself responding even against her will.

It was not surrender, not the sort O'Neill might have wished for, being a man who dominated, but it was more

80

than she had ever thought to give, she found her mouth moving of its own to fit his, tasting his tongue as it crept between her teeth, learning that a man could duel with something other than a sword. She moaned, thinking to pull away, but he did not let her. And neither, she knew, did she want it.

'Eilis.' He said it against her mouth on a breath ragged and quickening. 'Eilis – say me yea or nay.'

She wondered, fleetingly, why he asked at all. Did O'Neill not simply *take?*

'Nay . . .' she whispered, and yet her arms of their own accord crept up to lock around his neck.

He lifted her. He carried her the briefest distance to the bed and lay her down upon it. He moved on to it himself, one leg thrown on top of her thighs as he braced himself over her. She felt his knee insinuate itself between her legs.

She was made prisoner so easily, and so willingly. Deep in the recesses of her mind she was horrified at her response, but the forefront would not deny him. She felt his leg shift, and then his hand slipped down to move beneath her skirts, caressing first her ankle, then calf and knee, then thigh. And upward, softly, until his fingers whispered against her hip. Elizabeth quivered in one convulsive shudder that ran the length of her body, and moaned against his mouth.

'O'Neill.' It was Bard, standing in the open doorway. 'You said I should tell you at once.'

O'Neill, cursing, pulled away from her. He swung around until he sat on the edge of the bed, staring at Bard, and Elizabeth found Bard's cold blue eyes fastened on her in a perfect contempt.

She sat up at once, knowing what manner of appearance she presented. Her hair was tumbled, unbound; her face was flushed from O'Neill's attentions. Her breathing

81

had quickened to match his, so that her breasts strained against the bodice of her gown. The nipples were hard, outlined against the fabric. She set her lips, self-consciously, knowing they were roughened from O'Neill's kisses, and made herself look Bard in the eye.

'Your pardon, mistress,' he said drily.

O'Neill's voice was sharp. 'What is it?'

'The ransom has arrived,' Bard said simply. 'We are done with our need of her.'

O'Neill rose at once, straightening his twisted doublet, and left the room without a backward glance at Elizabeth. Bard followed him smoothly, and she sat stunned and humiliated in the centre of the rumpled bed.

Elizabeth did not see O'Neill again. Fiona saw to preparing her for bed after all, and then was gone, and Elizabeth, in her night-shift, discovered the room was horribly empty without O'Neill to fill it up.

She considered the man who had nearly seduced her. She thought of the face that had been so close to her own. It was pure as any sculpture – straight, narrow nose with arched, flared nostrils and a smooth, broad brow that betokened an intelligence she had not considered before. Black hair that needed cutting, yet she thought it suited him – a wild Irish savage, utterly unpredictable. And his wide, reckless mouth, capable of cruelty and also gentleness. The former she had seen too often; the latter, more rarely, had been intended for Fiona and the dogs.

For a long time Elizabeth sat on the edge of the bed. And then, with the window black from the darkness outside, she lifted her candle and set it close to the glass. The light set up a reflection nearly as good as any mirror. Elizabeth rose and slipped out of her nightshift.

She saw her naked body reflected in the glass – a pale, ghostly luminance. She stared at the tawny braid that hung over one breast, obscuring it from view. Slowly she pushed the braid over her shoulder so that nothing blocked her gaze.

She was slender, yet not delicate to the point of fragility. She was the colour of new ivory all over, flushed with the merest pink, save for the rosy nipples and the tawny, burnished curls between her legs. She traced the line of one full breast, felt the softness of the nipple that had been hard against her gown, against O'Neill's hand, then down between her breasts and across her flat stomach. She wondered what it was O'Neill saw when he looked at her.

Elizabeth recalled her body's response to him, felt an answering tingle deep in her abdomen, and quivered. Her eyes were black in the window reflection. 'God in heaven,' she whispered numbly, 'what was it I wanted from him?' Her breath caught in her throat. 'What was it I *needed* from him?'

Bard came when she had finished breakfast and was fully dressed. 'The coach is waiting, mistress.'

She stared at him. She had known it would come. She had known, by the look in O'Neill's eyes, that he would keep her no longer than he must. And now the money had come and she was free.

Elizabeth thought O'Neill must be outside waiting for her. She rose and twitched her skirts into place. She watched Bard lift and shoulder her chest and preceded him into the corridor, then down the stairs and outside. She saw the coach and two horses waiting there, and no sign of O'Neill.

Bard tied the chest on top of the coach and then dropped down again easily. She noted how lithe he was, how smooth his movements. He had none of the size and

83

power of O'Neill, but there was a hidden strength in him she had not marked before.

''Twill take us all day,' Bard said. 'D'ye not think we should be going?'

Fiona, already inside the coach, put her head out the open door. 'Best go, mistress.'

Elizabeth hesitated an instant. But it was long enough for Bard's laughter to cut into her unmercifully. 'Did you think he would say good-bye?' he asked scathingly. 'No. You had all you'll be getting from him last night.'

Her face flamed with colour. She spoke through her teeth. 'How is it he keeps such a spoiled, petulant lapdog by him? How is it he tolerates a yapping puppy like you?'

Bard smiled, unoffended. 'I am of the O'Neill kennels, mistress. The Hound has little choice.'

She recalled he had said it once before. '*You* are an O'Neill – '

'Aye,' he interrupted. 'A large family, mistress.' He gestured towards the coach. 'Now . . . if you will . . . ?'

Elizabeth gathered her skirts and climbed into the coach, disdaining Bard's outstretched hand. She settled herself on the wide leather seat and stared blindly at Fiona, who was wise enough to hold her silence.

Bard shut the door and fastened it, then climbed up into the coachman's seat. He called out something in Gaelic to the horses, repeated it impatiently in English, and the coach started with a jerk. Slowly it rolled from the house.

Elizabeth faced Fiona, who sat across from her. 'How will he do without you or Bard? With no one to serve him?'

Fiona laughed. 'Oh, mistress, 'tis nothing to himself to be alone. He's been alone much of his life, even when surrounded with the spies.'

'Spies!'

'Aye, mistress. A man like himself will know them always. 'Tis why he was so wary of you.'

Elizabeth frowned. 'But . . . why? Who is he that *spies* must surround him?'

Fiona said nothing at once. Elizabeth heard the rattling of the coach wheels and the creak of leather harness. And then, in the distance, the deep, imperative barks of two dogs. Elizabeth closed her eyes.

'Will you listen to me, then?' Fiona asked. 'Will you listen with your English ears, and hear me, and then understand the man better?'

'I would like to know why he hates my country so,' Elizabeth said flatly.

'There is reason,' the woman returned. 'To you, being English, perhaps not enough, but to any born of Ireland – ' She broke off, sighing. 'Mistress, you won't be liking what you hear. You'll be naming me a liar. But I'll tell you, and tell you true, and we can argue about it later.'

Elizabeth nodded. 'You said there were spies.'

'Oh, aye, of course.' Fiona's tone was matter-of-fact. 'With himself, there would be always. He is an O'Neill.' She smiled a little. 'And the only surviving son of The O'Neill.'

Elizabeth shook her head. '*The* O'Neill – what is that? What does this Irish title mean?'

'Then I'll give you an English title.' Fiona's eyes were speculative. 'Have you ever heard of the Earl of Tyrone?'

'Of course,' Elizabeth returned. 'He was the Irish rebel who cast off his English title and roused Ireland into rebellion against England.'

'He was Hugh O'Neill,' Fiona said quietly. 'Nephew to Shane O'Neill, called The Proud, father to that man back there.'

I have told you my name, and that is enough to get me

85

killed, he had said. They would put my head upon a pike on London Bridge.

Kieran O'Neill. Eldest son to Hugh O'Neill, the former Earl of Tyrone, kin to Shane the Proud, who had once – in all his Irish audacity – sought the Old Queen's hand in marriage when he had only wanted her dead and Ireland free forever.

Kieran O'Neill, who had suckled on rebellion.

'I'll be telling you the truth,' Fiona's voice was harsh. 'Not lies, not tales, not legends, but the absolute truth of it all. And I do know it, mistress, because *I was there*.'

Elizabeth looked at the lined face and the rusty-silver hair, at the gnarled hands that clasped one another so rigidly.

Slowly Elizabeth nodded. 'Tell me the truth, Fiona.'

8

''Twas eleven years ago,' Fiona said slowly. Then she fell silent, twisting her hands in her skirts; Elizabeth saw she had gone back those eleven years, lost to the present. For a moment she feared she would get no more from the woman, but Fiona nodded to herself and went on. 'I had served in the household all my life; they could not leave me behind now. I asked to go, though The O'Neill said he would not require it of me.' She smiled. ''Twas for all the lads I went – Kieran and Brian, Hugh and Shane.' Her blue eyes darkened. 'Himself was fifteen, and old enough to beg for further fighting. But The O'Neill himself said no, the fighting was done; he was old and tired and saw no more good in it. He had no wish to feed the ravens in the Tower, nor stare sightlessly at passersby on London Bridge.'

Elizabeth, transfixed by the weary resignation in Fiona's tone, could hear the man himself. She could see the ravens, the head upon London Bridge . . . She shuddered. 'So they left Ireland . . .'

'They left Ireland. *We* left Ireland.' Tears welled into Fiona's eyes. 'The Flight of the Earls.'

Elizabeth frowned. 'The Flight . . . ? What was that?'

Fiona rubbed absently at one silver eyebrow. 'We met at Lough Swilly,' she said. 'The O'Neill, his wife, his four sons – at least fifty of us, mistress, including household servants and kinfolk. And there was Rory O'Donnell – *The* O'Donnell – and him with all his folk. The Earl of Tyrconnell, once, when he held an English title.' Her mouth moved into a faint smile and her eyes took on the glow of memory. 'Such proud men they were, so tall and strong and fierce. And how they had united so many of Ireland in rebellion against the Crown. But – they knew there was no more to be done against Scottish James and his Sassenachs, and so we took a ship to France, and then went on to Italy, where we were welcomed by the Pope himself.' Tears ran down Fiona's face. 'In a year The O'Donnell was dead. Then Shane and Hugh O'Neill, both dead of a fever. Brian was killed by English spies. And they tried for Kieran too . . . only they failed. But – last year The O'Neill himself died.' She shook her head and dabbed at her eyes with a corner of her apron. 'So many of them dead.'

'Save – Kieran.' It seemed odd to say his first name. To her he was simply *O'Neill*.

'Aye.' Fiona sighed. 'Save him.'

Elizabeth's mouth twisted. '*So* – now he wants his father's title.'

Fiona frowned. ''Tis not a *title*, The O'Neill. 'Tis a proper chieftainship. Only the people can give it to him; 'tisn't something a king or queen can do, like giving over earldoms such as Tyrone and Tyrconnell.' Fiona's face was austerely proud. ''Tis something *earned*, mistress.'

'But he wants it.' Elizabeth was certain of that. Hadn't he once called himself The O'Neill?

'He wants *Ireland*,' Fiona said fiercely. 'He wants *freedom*.'

'Then why,' Elizabeth inquired deliberately, 'has he troubled himself to come to England?'

Fiona looked straight back at her. 'That, mistress, I cannot be telling you.'

'Because I'm a *Sassenach*.' The derisive Gaelic word seemed to curdle on her tongue.

'Because I don't know.' Fiona smiled. 'D'ye think I care who you are? You can't be hurting the cause. If you could, himself would stop you. And as for me – oh, aye, I have no cause to love the English . . . but I can't be laying the blame for what has happened at *your* door, mistress, just because you were born in England and I was not. 'Tis too easily done.' She sighed and smoothed the wrinkles out of her apron. 'No doubt himself would be chastising me for saying so, but 'tis the truth. I'd not be foolish enough to say every Englishman – or woman – in the world is wanting us dead. And I don't doubt there are Irish who'd rather have Ireland made over into England.' She shook her head. 'Poor souls, having lost so much of their independence.'

'These spies,' Elizabeth said, frowning, 'they think O'Neill will rouse Ireland to war again?'

'They are certain of it,' the woman said flatly. 'They fear The O'Neill and his power. 'Tis why they killed Brian, once the others had died, and why they tried for himself.' Fiona shrugged. 'They are not wrong, mistress . . . he *will* rouse Ireland to war.'

'And do they know where he is?'

Fiona shook her head decisively. 'He'd have been taken, did they know that. We were very careful leaving Italy for France, and slipping out of France. I doubt they know he's in England yet – they would expect him to go straight to Ireland – but they will discover it. All too soon, I fear.'

Elizabeth saw, in her mind's eye, the grisly execution. Her father had told her, once, of an execution he had witnessed. O'Neill would be hanged until he was nearly dead, yet still alive, then strung up by his arms and legs, spread-eagled, his belly laid open so his intestines could be pulled out and thrown into the fire. And then they would cut him into pieces and put his head on a pike upon London Bridge.

She shuddered convulsively. 'If they catch him . . .'

'They won't,' Fiona said. 'Not himself.'

And what lay between them, unspoken, was the knowledge that Elizabeth herself could be his downfall.

It was dark when the coach at last rattled into London. Elizabeth, pulling aside the leather curtain, saw the Thames glinting in the moonlight, narrow cobbled streets lighted by lanterns set on posts, boys with lamps escorting gentlemen about the city. There was nothing of the magnificence she longed to see.

Fiona dozed against the squabs and Elizabeth impatiently settled back again. She felt a strange sense of buoyancy at knowing she would see her father again, and yet it was underscored with a residue of regret. When she explored it she found herself thinking of O'Neill and savagely she thrust him from her mind. She had no time for him.

At last the coach was halted. She heard Bard jump down. Then he pulled open the narrow door. He spoke in a full spate of Gaelic to Fiona, who answered in the same language. The woman seemed to be protesting something, but at last she gave in.

Bard looked at Elizabeth. 'Fiona must stay here. I will escort you the rest of the way.'

'Can we go no farther in the coach?' She did not care to walk a single step with him.

His smile was very faint in the shadows. 'I have no doubt you would prefer it that way, for the end result would most likely be my death, but no – we can go no farther in the coach. Come with me, mistress, and say nothing. I will see you to safety.'

After a searching glance at Fiona, which told her nothing, Elizabeth climbed out of the coach. She wished she could ignore Bard's helping hand, but she needed it after so many hours spent in the coach. Her legs were stiff and her head ached a little.

Bard shouldered her trunk and nodded in the direction of a large building of Tudor style, half timbered and painted white between the dark timber stripping. ''Tis there we're bound for.'

'What is it?' She was not at all certain he would not kill her. She was not at all certain O'Neill had not ordered him to.

Bard laughed once. 'Your home, mistress. 'Tis a part of the King's Whitehall residence. *Court*, Mistress Stafford.'

Elizabeth gazed at the buildings in surprise, for she had envisioned an imposing pile of stones, crowned with turrets and battlements. But it was quite dark, too dark to see very much, and she doubted her father could command the authority to install himself near the King. No doubt his quarters were both small and unpretentious, though her father was neither.

Bard took her to the nearest doorway and set down her trunk. A single flame in an iron sconce lighted the area, but the shadows were deep. Looking back, she could only barely see the coach.

His hand was on her arm. It was a proprietary grasp and she started back. 'Do you mean to kill me *here?*'

'I would not mind.' His tone was cool, yet she heard the echoes of an underlying violence. 'But no, mistress, I do not kill you here. What I do here is exact a promise from you.'

'I will give you nothing!'

'Not for me,' he said intently, 'for O'Neill.'

She searched his tone for smugness, for coyness, for utter contempt. But there was none. No taunt she could uncover. His face was solemn and smooth, as first she had known it. And the tension in his body was such that it radiated until it encompassed her own.

'What is it you want?' she managed.

'When you see him again, say nothing.'

'*See* him again?' Elizabeth stared at him in shock. 'How could that come to pass?'

'*Promise me.*'

She looked into his shadowed face and sensed the urgency that lay so unquietly beneath his mask of calmness. She realized Bard was afraid. Not for himself, who had come so precipitantly into the very city that would demand his head, but for O'Neill.

I am an O'Neill, Bard had said. And he served the man Fiona said should be The O'Neill in his father's place.

Coolly, she answered him. 'He has warned me – *threatened me* – already. Surely you need not add your voice to his.'

Bard nodded. 'You'll be going to hell if you lie.' And then he was gone into the shadows.

God help me. She recalled how she had felt in O'Neill's embrace. *God help me, but I think I am already there.*

Elizabeth turned to pull the bell.

Sir Edwin Stafford was in his small private study when his daughter at last arrived in London, and he wished to be interrupted for no reason. He stood contemplatively by a large oaken desk, carefully sorting through a stack of papers. Most of them he tossed aside with a negligent hand so that there was a cascade of parchment atop the desk; his gesture was both eloquent and graceful, yet displayed a symbolic rejection of their importance. *Those* papers no longer held any meaning – letters from Queen Elizabeth's Privy Council suggesting politely he voluntarily surrender his position within the Queen's army. And then, later and less polite, the suggestions that became demands, until he could no longer ignore them. They threatened attainder. Like a steel sword scabbarded in velvet, Elizabeth of England had destroyed his position in the land with one stroke of her pen. The elegant sprawling signature attached to a bill of attainder that expressed a desire – *an order!* – for him to surrender most of his lands in addition to the position as adviser to the Lord Marshal of Ireland.

She said nothing of Essex himself. Was Devereux's memory conveniently forgotten the moment his head rolled off the scaffolding on Tower Green? The axe had not fallen on Sir Edwin Stafford, nor had imprisonment swallowed him up, but the Queen's will was just as sharp as the axe and just as hard as the stones of the Bloody Tower. Essex, Marshal of Ireland – and desirous of making himself King in place of the Queen – was dead. He no longer had to concern himself with such things as wealth and position within the peerage of the realm. But Stafford was not, and he did, and he had lost what was most valuable to him. The old woman – *the whore Nan Bullen's bastard daughter!* – had reduced him to a mere knight with a small holding in Kent, caring little that he had served her most faithfully for so many years – forgetting also he had lost a son to that same royal service.

But Stafford did not entirely blame the motives behind the Old Queen's actions. He understood the convenience of a faulty memory. Many times it served when something else would not.

With a faint frown of displeasure at a recalcitrant subconscious, Stafford swept away the memories of his service to Robert Devereux, Earl of Essex. The Queen's favourite was now dead of his ambition and subsequent treason; Stafford was not. And now was the time to recover from King James that which he had lost to Queen Elizabeth.

He found the paper he wanted. The order reclaiming his lands in the name of the Crown. Smiling, Sir Edwin set the edge of the parchment to the candle flame and watched it burn. When the flame threatened his fingers he let it fall, smiling as the royal seal melted and ran on to the desk in a sticky gobbet of wax and the rest turned to ash that blew away on a single aristocratic breath. The wax, cooling on the wood, he ignored entirely. Then he took up another piece of paper and read it, though he had read it a thousand times before.

We hereby confer this Royal Appointment on your Daughtere, Elizabeth Stafforde, that she may serve Her Majesty Quene Anne, Commencing as soon as maye Be.

He smiled. The Old Queen's skinny arse had fouled England's throne long enough. Now another royal rump sat in her place, and Stafford had every intention of cushioning that rump with the finest pillow in the land. That James Stuart was Scottish was cause for minor irritation – Old Bess had been enough like her father to give no sons to the throne – but the irritation faded as he considered the possibilities of the thing.

James had come down from Scotland to take up his English throne. He distrusted the fine houses of England for the simple reason that they had fought against his own for so long, the Scots, like the Irish, being somewhat displeased by England's consumption of their independence. But now the House of Stuart was in ascendency, even in England, rising through the bloodied heavens like the brightest star of all. It was bound to wink out, Stafford knew – they all did, from Plantagenets to Tudors – but for now it burned quite brilliantly.

James needed an Englishman he could trust, for the English themselves distrusted the Scottish noblemen. It was a paradox, Stafford believed, that might stand in his favour. James required English advisers the English could identify with, but James did not wish to employ those who had served Elizabeth. And so he turned to the noble houses that had been in eclipse, driven into obscurity by Elizabeth herself. Stafford, whose name had once been coupled with Essex's great, glittering venture, would fill the gap. He would make himself invaluable to James, and the king would reciprocate. Wealth, honours, lands restored . . . perhaps even a title of some preeminence. Perhaps Sir Edwin Stafford would become more than a dishonoured knight, reaching the heights from which he could look down and laugh at all the others, crawling on their knees for a hint of the Scotsman's favour.

His daughter's appointment as lady-in-waiting to Anne of Denmark was part of Stafford's plan. He was shrewd enough to understand the waiting game; he could not march into Jamie's royal presence and demand his favour. He must work quietly, carefully, until James believed himself responsible for discovering one loyal Englishman among so many false faces. And Elizabeth – beautiful, gullible, naïve – would be the perfect tool to use. The court, already jaded by the King's peculiar sexual tastes, would welcome new game. And Stafford could watch, and wait, and choose the best stud for his unbroken filly.

The servant knocked at the door just as Stafford was seating himself in the chair. He bade the man enter and waited impatiently as the servant passed on his news. Stafford stood up immediately, frowning. 'Bring her to me at once.'

As the servant bowed out Stafford stared down at the hardened red wax scarring the desktop. With one thumbnail he picked at it until it had buckled and broken, pinkish in the candlelight. Irritably he brushed the remnants away. But as the door opened again and the servant announced his daughter, Stafford rearranged his face into an expression of suitable concern. He strode across the room with hands extended, murmuring kind words that held no meaning for him. When he closed his hands on her shoulders he felt again the elegant slenderness that so amazed him, for she was finely bred as an Arab filly and yet bold as an uncut stud.

'Elizabeth.' He searched her face, seeking blemishes, scars, anything that would affect her value. 'I have worried so. Are you well?'

'I am fully recovered,' she said – that only.

His hands closed more firmly on her arms. She felt the tensile strength in his grasp, so at odds with his elegant demeanour. Her father had always been two men to her – quiet, subtle, unruffled by ordinary irritations, yet underneath his coolness she sensed banked fires burning. He was a tall man, spare of frame, with thin features both austere and intelligent. His eyes, a darker brown than her own were sharp as he looked at her. His grey hair was brushed smooth, back from a high forehead, and he wore dark grey clothing pointed up with black and cream.

How did he get me? she wondered. *I am nothing like him.*

'Be seated,' he said gently, and turned to pour her wine from a sideboard. She could not help but recall the whisky she had drunk at O'Neill's hands and the warmth that had flushed her body.

Elizabeth sipped slowly when he gave her the wine. As she drank he watched her, and she knew what he was thinking. 'There was a woman,' she said calmly. 'She came with me to London.'

He stood before the fireplace, backlighted, his face masked in the ochre shadows of the panelled room. He reminded her suddenly, oddly, of a lean alley cat, hungry yet fastidiously careful of what he ate, so as not to place himself at risk. She could not help but compare him to O'Neil, a green-eyed panther, and therefore more dangerous than her father.

96

'Did they harm you?' he asked.

'No harm was done.'

His eyes moved from her face to her breasts, then downward. Appraising her. When they returned to her face she saw a strange blankness in them, an implacability that made her inhale a trembling breath. Having had O'Neill look at her, Elizabeth understood what her father did – he judged her as a man judges a woman, not a father seeking to learn of a daughter's welfare.

'Did they touch you?'

She thought again of O'Neill's mouth on hers, his hands on her breasts and buttocks, and the warmth of his body pressed so intimately against her own. Something deep inside shivered, but it was not from fear. It was not from anger at the question or humiliation at what had been done. It was from something she could not name. Something she dared not name.

'No harm was done,' she repeated.

Stafford moved then, turning to glide to the desk. She saw the papers stacked upon it, some spilled aside negligently. After a moment his hand dipped and came up with a creased, brownstained paper, and he held it out to her. His eyes waited, and so she took it.

Your daughter is well and shall remain so, providing the sum of one thousand pounds in gold is paid accordingly. The bearer is entrusted to carry the sum. If he does not, your daughter dies.

The note was unsigned. The spelling, unlike her father's, was excellent, and the hand was obviously schooled. She thought of Bard's Italianate manners, O'Neill's faultless French, and wondered which had written it.

She looked at the note again. *Your daughter dies*. She recalled the passion in O'Neill's voice as he spoke of his longing for Irish independence. She recalled his hands upon her throat. She recalled – No, she did not. She cut the thought off at once.

Elizabeth looked at her father's face, at the ascetic lines and thin skin stretched over patrician bones. Knowing how he hated to part with money, she wondered that he had done it so quickly. She had not been with O'Neill a full fortnight.

'You have my thanks,' she said quietly.

Stafford smiled. 'You are my daughter. What else could I do? I would pay three times the amount for you, and more.'

But Elizabeth hardly heard him. She was thinking of O'Neill again, knowing how easily he had used her. And yet she had been ready to swear he was as lost as she was when faced with the thing called desire.

'Elizabeth,' her father was saying, 'you must let no word of this go from this room. I have told no one the truth, merely that you were delayed because of a coach accident. The truth must not be known. It would ruin your reputation at once. We cannot afford that, not if you are to retain your post at court. Queen Anne can have no one with any scandal attached to her name in the retinue. You must keep this to yourself.'

'I have no intention of discussing it,' she returned grimly.

He frowned faintly, hearing a trace of bitterness in her voice. Something in her had changed; something in her was different. There was a knowledge in her eyes that had not existed before.

For a moment he wondered if her captor had bedded her; he dismissed it instantly. For all there was the faintest trace of hardness in her eyes, there was also innocence. Elizabeth had not known a man yet, and he intended to keep it that way. For now. He was willing enough for her to surrender her virginity before marriage, but only to the proper man. The man with the coin to buy it.

'Well,' he said kindly, 'doubtless you are wearied from the journey. I have ordered one of the serving girls to become your maid, replacing Annie; she has some experience with court life. Your bedchamber should be prepared. Come' – he took the wine and note from her icy hands – 'I will see you to your rooms.'

Elizabeth went with him, hardly aware that he had tucked her arm into his as if he thought she needed support. Perhaps she did. And when he left her at the door of her chamber she turned her face so he could kiss her cheek, and as his mouth brushed her flesh she thought again of the power in O'Neill's body and the glow of passion in his eyes.

She turned her face away and went at once into her room, shutting the door behind her.

9

Bard made his way past the wolfhounds and went directly to the whiskey, pouring himself a generous measure. He downed the first two warming swallows, felt better almost at once, and permitted himself a sigh that issued from the soles of his boots. Then he looked at O'Neill, who stood at the leaded, mullioned window with his back to the room.

'She is in London,' Bard said. 'And safe. And I got a promise from her.'

O'Neill turned slowly. He had got little sleep the night before, and Bard saw the weariness and restlessness in his face. 'What promise?'

Bard swallowed more of the whiskey. Then he shrugged. 'That she would say nothing.' He studied O'Neill's face a little more closely. 'You will see her again, of course, at court. How can you avoid it? She is to be one of the Queen's ladies, while you – '

O'Neill lifted a hand and dropped it to his side, as if he sought to silence Bard and then regretted the gesture. He rubbed at his red-rimmed eyes. The irises were brilliant green, even in the shadows of the room. 'I doubt our fine Sassenach lady will keep to her promise.' He crossed to a chair and dropped into it, flanked at once on either side by the hounds. He put a big hand on each of the narrow, wiry heads and sat very still.

'She will,' Bard said lightly. 'I asked her to do it for you.'

O'Neill snorted inelegantly. '*That* will not keep her silent. We asked ransom for her, Bard – it will somewhat prick her pride. And I threatened her life.' His wide mouth twisted. 'I threatened her life, and that of her father, with the hand of O'Neill, be it mine or another.'

Bard nodded, brows raised. 'Aye. True enough. If she gave you away . . .' He did not finish, as if he knew there was no need. 'What is it, O'Neill? Are you wanting her to think so highly of you, then?'

O'Neill shrugged and set his head against the high back of the chair. 'I care little enough what she thinks of me.'

Bard strolled idly towards the chair. 'I have seen you with women before, O'Neill. I have seen you pursue them with only a moment's pleasure in mind, I have seen them pursue *you* with far more than that in mind, and I have seen you pay court to the elegant French ladies who are no ladies at all. I know you, O'Neill, and I know what is in your mind.'

'*Do* you?' O'Neill's tone was distant, detached.

'She is a Sassenach bitch,' Bard said deliberately. 'But young and innocent, for all you have sought to change the latter, and I think you have her precisely where you want her.' He smiled. 'Half in love with you – or thinking she is – and willing to say nothing at all.'

O'Neill shut his gritty, burning eyes. 'I did not seek to do that.'

'No? Then you gave a good imitation of it.' Bard stood just behind the chair, looking down on O'Neill's head. ''Twas no different than what you have done before when you needed a woman's tongue stilled.'

'Kissing them into silence is better than killing them, Bard. Though the latter, I warrant, is more permanent . . . and I will do it if I have to.'

'I have yet to see a woman betray *you*.'

O'Neill's sigh was faint, but Bard heard it. ''Tis only that I am concerned for our plan,' O'Neill said. 'Nothing more.'

'Because *she* could ruin it.' Bard's mouth twisted wryly. 'Why could she not have been plain as a post, and poxy to boot? Always it is the beautiful ones who fall swooning into your arms, or drop so conveniently at your feet, waiting for you to pick them up. Had I not seen the storm and shattered coach for myself – and the bodies of maid and coachman – I'd have said it was *too* convenient.'

'I believed it possible at first,' O'Neill agreed. He stretched out an empty hand and Bard put the glass into it. O'Neill downed what whiskey remained and then slouched deeper into the chair, long legs stretched out before him. The dogs had settled on to the floor, heads on massive paws and yellow eyes closed, but they did not sleep. Like O'Neill, they never lost their wariness.

'But no longer?' Bard asked curiously.

'She is not the sort for the game,' O'Neill answered. 'I'd wager my life she has never been with a man, and that would be no way to catch my interest.' His smile was grim. 'With all their spies, they must know that.'

'Perhaps 'twould be *just* the way to catch your interest.' Bard moved a step closer. 'And you.'

'I'll not be caught by the machinations of a woman,' O'Neill said flatly. 'I'll meet my death in battle, God and St Patrick willing, but not by so underhanded a trap. I am not a fool, Bard.'

'No,' Bard said quietly. 'Not a fool . . . but a man. And she is a lovely thing, for all her innocence.'

O'Neill startled him by laughing. 'Even you admit it, then?'

'You said you are not a fool.' Bard's tone was a trifle sharp. 'Nor am I, but neither am I blind. I am an admirer of art, O'Neill – I have that much of our years in Rome. And I can look at her and see the perfection any artist might strive for.' His tone hardened. 'But also I see that it is the hand of the artist who made her and not any soul from within. I know what tools have shaped her.'

O'Neill thought of the delicate bones of her face arranged in such perfection. Flawless sculpture, were she made of marble. But she was not; she was flesh, blood, bone, and his own demanded to quench itself in her body.

He shifted restlessly. 'English tools,' he said, and thought of his hands on her ivory skin and lost in her tawny hair.

Bard's voice was very quiet. 'Better you think of *Irish* girls, O'Neill . . . and home.'

'Nothing will make me forget either one, Bard.' O'Neill's tone was harsh. 'Not a king, not a pope, not an army . . . and certainly not an Englishwoman.'

Bard, standing behind the chair, looked down on O'Neill's head. The hair sprang thickly from the scalp, so black it was blue in the candlelight, capping his head like the inky pelt of a panther Bard had once seen at the French court. It was not like a woman's hair, for there was no silken fineness or scent of perfumed soap. It was simply part of O'Neill – masculine, arrogant, bold, undefeated by anything so tame as comb or brush.

Bard's hand went down to it before he could help himself, but he stopped his fingers from touching it. He closed his eyes and fastened both hands on the back of the chair, gripping it as if it provided rescue to a drowning man.

But then he had always thought himself a drowning man, and so willingly walked the plank that stretched over an ocean of black, consuming passion.

Sir Edwin Stafford spared no expense at making his daughter presentable. Expecting to be introduced at court immediately so she could take up her duties, Elizabeth found her father had no intention of allowing her to begin her career unfashionably. He ordered dressmakers to her to see that she was properly attired, selecting the lace and fur trimmings himself, in addition to the pearl necklet and amber earrings. There was no sign of his traditional closefistedness. Suddenly he lavished upon her all the gowns she had longed for since childhood, praising her face and form and admiring her self-possession, which derived from shock more than a natural inclination. He was not the father she had known, but then she had never known him.

Elizabeth wanted his attention, which she had lacked most of her life. She wanted to see the flash of pleasure and pride in his eyes as he looked at her in a new gown, to see the satisfaction moving his thin lips into a faint smile. Edwin Stafford had always seemed immensely cold to her, unmoved by normal emotions. Now she wondered how she could have thought it, for he was attentive and complimentary, as if he courted her for himself.

'You must please the eye of the court,' he told her one day as she turned in a circle to show him the fit of her newest gown. 'You must never think to please only yourself.'

'I should think the *Queen's* opinion most important.'

'Of course.' His smile was indulgent. 'It is the Queen you must always think of first, never yourself. But the eye of the court is a discerning one, and not to be discounted.' He chose his words carefully, as he chose the gowns he bought for her. 'As one of the Queen's ladies, you will hold a high place at court. Not to be confused with one of significance, of course' – he knew better than to fill her head with dreams – 'but there will be people who seek you out, believing you can aid their cause.'

Elizabeth stopped turning and looked at him directly. 'How could *I* possibly help anyone's cause?' And then she remembered O'Neill's, and recalled how it was she could *hurt* it.

Stafford, leaning indolently against the mantel of the fireplace, permitted himself an easy smile as he spread his hands in eloquent resignation. 'How can I say? But I have spent many years learning the ways of the court, and I know even the Queen's ladies may sometimes effect the course of politics.' A nice touch, he thought, damascening the ambiguity of her position with a hint of power. He could not move quickly with her or she would bolt. He could see it in her eyes.

'My duty is to the Queen,' Elizabeth told him. 'Not to carrying messages for others like a maid.'

Stafford inclined his head. 'Nicely put, my dear, but that is an excellent summation of what you *shall* be.' He saw her frown and moved quickly to turn the bluntness aside. 'Of course the Queen's ladies are not like others. You will do whatever *she* asks of you, for she is the one you serve and no other, but you will quickly learn that because you have the Queen's ear, others will seek yours.' He straightened and paced around her, quickly appraising the gown even as he continued speaking. 'There will be those who seek you out to curry favour with the Queen, who has the King's ear. And *that*, of course, is the ultimate desire of most people at court – to get the King's attention.'

Inwardly, he thought it unlikely Danish Anne could do much good with her husband; of late James had been more preoccupied with a pretty boy than with his sickly, long-nosed wife. But Stafford would not tell Elizabeth that. Part of her charm and appeal lay in her innocence of court ways. She would have the two-legged hounds and the bitches in skirts snapping at her heels soon enough, but if he told her the truth of matters she would go to court suspicious and wary, lacking the patina of freshness that would draw them to her like moth to flame.

Stafford was very pleased. She was unpretentious and

therefore lacking the tediousness of most court ladies. The artful artlessness of them could not touch his daughter, whose natural refinement and bearing would threaten even the most well-established of ladies. He would enjoy watching his daughter move through the intricacies of the dance even as he himself bid the musicians play on.

Elizabeth, standing quite still in the centre of the room, touched a hand to the necklet ringing her throat. The pearls were very fine, perfectly matched, and glowing with an ivory sheen that matched her skin. Her fingers slipped over each one, counting them.

She looked at her father. 'Is that *your* ultimate desire?'

His attention snapped back. 'What, Elizabeth?'

'I said, is that *your* ultimate desire? To catch the ear of the King?' Elizabeth's mouth twisted. 'Is all of this a careful plot for personal gain?' A wave of her hand included pearls and gown. 'Where did you find the money to finance this court appointment?'

Stafford's eyebrows – black though his hair was grey – rose in faint surprise. For a moment he was irritated by the questions, but he hid it with a smile. 'Come now, my dear, surely you must concern yourself with other matters.'

'No,' she said firmly. 'Surely I must concern myself with *these* matters. Have you forgotten? I have undertaken to administer Rosewood for some time, in your absence. I understand such things as bills and payment.' She did not smile. 'How far have you put us in debt?'

'You must dismiss from your head the requirements for running a household while at court,' he returned smoothly, with only a trace of parental disapproval in his tone. 'There are other matters of more pressing concern.'

Her hand twitched at the velvet of her skirts. 'I am not forgetting the sum paid for my release, in addition to what you have spent to clothe me. How much have you spent?'

'Impudence,' Stafford said.

'Curiosity,' his daughter retorted. 'Am I not to have any at court?'

One corner of his mouth jerked flat, though it was not an indication of amusement. 'You may have everything at court, Elizabeth. That is your answer. I have spent *enough*. *Enough* to make you worthy of this court.' He moved to her until she had to tilt her head back to look into his stern face. 'You know how we have lived these past years . . . out of favour and relegated to the emptiness of country life. It is not what I want for you. You are worthy of far better, and I intend to get it for you. This appointment is a godsend – though I admit I did what I could do to procure it – and I will not allow anything so trivial as money to upset it.'

'But so *much* –'

'I got it from the Jews,' he said roughly. 'They will wait.'

'With what security?' Elizabeth demanded in alarm. 'Not *Rosewood!*'

Stafford saw the fear in her face and heard it in her tone. She loved the country manor, he realized, even as he himself hated it. It represented his fall from favour, for the Old Queen had stripped him of all other holdings in the name of the Crown, leaving him only the acreage in Kent. It meant nothing to him that Rosewood was a lovely, warm manor, only that it had been the den to which the fox had retreated while the hunt passed by.

But now the fox was free again, leading the hounds a merry chase, and he had no intention of using the den again.

'Not Rosewood,' Stafford answered, knowing it would please her. And it was the truth. The manor was free, but his daughter's future was not. He had been extended credit on the understanding that once a wealthy marriage

107

was made, the money – with interest – would be repaid. He had needed only to show the letter of appointment with its royal seal and the gold was in his hands.

But he would not tell her that. As in a game of chess, the Queen was the last to know of her precarious position when her knights and pawns fell and all the castles captured.

'Elizabeth,' he said, 'you are lovely. And on the morrow all the court will know it.

10

The colours seemed brighter, the sounds louder as Elizabeth walked the length of the Queen's Presence Chamber with her father. Her hand rested on Stafford's left arm but she did not feel the figured fabric beneath her fingers. Most of her was numb. Most of her was too caught up in the magnitude of the moment, stunned by the realization of it all, to be particularly aware of herself, only of her surroundings.

She was aware of the ladies in their fine gowns and exotic scents, high-piled hair and painted faces, gems glowing and sparkling as they moved. Pearls, so many pearls; Elizabeth knew the Old Queen had been partial to them, and her influence lingered on even after her death.

Some of the ladies wore quiet, muted colours and unpretentious styles, counting on sheer beauty to win attention away from the fabric and jewels. Others vied with the peacocks in the gardens, pitting silks and velvets and brocades against bright feathers and iridescence. But all was a blur to Elizabeth as she moved with her father.

Stafford himself was quite pleased. He had always had great faith in his taste, but no man could be fully satisfied with his decision until the end product was seen on the woman it was intended for, and in the proper surroundings.

Elizabeth more than lived up to his expectations – she surpassed them. Her tawny-gold hair was burnished in the candle-light, pinned up in a simple, elegant style that became her, lacking the ornate twists and coils and hairpieces other women demanded for extra weight and colour. Elizabeth's hair was quite obviously her own, clean and shining and smelling of the perfumed soaps he had purchased for her. Her eyes, set so widely in a face of magnificent bones, were dilated dark, but the pupils were rimmed with the odd honey colour he could not quite put a name to. Because she was lady-in-waiting to the Queen she could not purposely compete with the high-ranking ladies of the realm, but it had not prevented him from choosing colours and fabrics carefully. She wore bronze-brown silk stiffened with gold thread, and although the colour might have been drab on another woman, it was not on Elizabeth. She was suitably attired for service to the Queen, and yet no man's eye would be able to leave her.

Stafford was quite certain of that. Tall and straight, he led her down the length of the Presence Chamber, carefully noting the eyes that followed them and the accompanying whispers. Already the women were marking her out, claws showing and teeth bared as if to bite, but he did not concern himself with the women. Elizabeth would have to deal with them on her own. It was the men Stafford took note of – the wealthy, titled noblemen who had been slow to acknowledge his place among them and yet now elbowed one another aside in order to see more clearly the woman on his arm.

Sir Edwin Stafford, smiling pleasantly at them all, felt jubilation well up within his soul. He heard the whispers asking who she was and others answering with a simple 'Stafford's daughter' and knew he had them all. It would be such a simple task to win them to his side, and then he would select the richest hound to whom he could throw the elegant bone.

Elizabeth was only vaguely aware of the people lining the sides of the chamber. Her eyes and attention were

110

fixed on the woman in the ornate chair at the end of the chamber, under a canopy of crimson silk embroidered with the thistle of Scotland and the leopards of England. Another crest she took to be representative of the House of Stuart – or did they call them clans? But Elizabeth forgot the intricacies of Scottish royal customs and concentrated on the nearness of English royalty, for this woman was her Queen.

Anne of Denmark, had she ever been beautiful, had clearly lost whatever favour she might once have known. Her thinning hair was fair and combed in such a way that it resembled a stiff cloud around her head. Her complexion was sallow from the illness that plagued her, except for spots of hectic colour in her cheeks. Her nose was quite long, drawing her face down into an expression of perpetual discontent, and the eyes that watched Elizabeth approach were a milky, watery blue. At forty-four the Queen of Great Britain, Scotland and Ireland had absolutely nothing to recommend her, except that she was wed to James Stuart and was, therefore, the second most important key to the intrigues and politics that snarled every court in contention and discord. James himself was the paramount key and he, more often than not, was the *cause* of contention and discord.

Elizabeth halted as her father halted, waiting with eyes downcast. Her heart hammered in her chest until she feared it would burst, but she wasn't certain if it was from fear or excitement – perhaps both. She heard her father's quiet, unctuous voice presenting her, and then she dipped into a curtsy that spread her bronze skirts around her like a glowing cloud.

'Your Majesty.' She could think of nothing else to say.

'Rise,' the Queen told her, and Elizabeth managed to do it without losing her balance. She looked into the plain face and wondered if the rumours she had heard were true, that the Queen was sick of the same lung fever that had taken her son, Henry, Prince of Wales, five years before.

'Mistress Stafford,' the Queen said distinctly, as if tasting the name. Her lips were thin, compressed, and her accent foreign. Even in all the years of marriage to her Scottish lord she had not lost the Danish flavour of her speech. 'As a rule I do not keep English ladies about me. I prefer women from my husband's, the king's, country.' For a moment Elizabeth feared she was being summarily dismissed, but the Queen went on. 'Your father, Sir Edwin, has convinced me there is a time for all things, and I think it is right I should honour some of the English ladies with my favour, lest your people think me unjust. Are you willing to serve me in all things?'

'Of course, Your Majesty.' Elizabeth wondered what her father could have said that would convince this woman of anything.

'*All* things?' the Queen repeated sharply.

Elizabeth looked at the blue eyes and found them shrewd, not nearly as weak as she had at first believed. The Queen was thin, her body burned up by illness, but she had not given up. She ruled still.

Elizabeth lifted her head. 'I will do whatever is required of me, Your Majesty.'

'And if I said you should go home to Kent and bide your time there?'

Elizabeth felt the silence behind her as the chamber waited for her answer. She wondered what it would mean to her father if the entire thing had been little more than a charade; if it would destroy all his plans to have her sent back to Rosewood like a child too young to understand the world. She cared little enough now what it meant for her; if this was what court was all about, she was not certain she wanted it.

Calmly she smiled at the Queen. 'Then I should go, of course. Is that what you wish?'

The Queen glanced at a group of ladies standing off to one side. Elizabeth realized they were the Scotswomen the Queen had referred to and wondered how much of her future depended on them. Their faces were perfectly blank. They waited, like everyone else.

Anne of Denmark smiled, and suddenly Elizabeth no longer saw the long nose or the sallowness of the complexion. 'I am Queen of England in addition to Scotland, and perhaps it *is* time I admitted some Englishwomen to my circle. Be welcome at court, Miss Stafford, and be happy.'

Elizabeth drew in a careful breath, knowing she risked all with what she would say, yet determined to be completely honest. 'Your Majesty, the honour is too great for me. Surely you realize I have no experience serving royalty.'

Anne laughed. 'And I have none at commanding a woman who has more right to this country than I. Perhaps we shall muddle through together, mistress.' She turned her attention to the man at Elizabeth's side. 'You have a lovely daughter, Sir Edwin. But it remains to be seen if she has your facility with words.'

'Your Majesty.' He executed a smooth bow. 'I am certain Elizabeth would do or say nothing that would displease you.'

Elizabeth recognized the subtle warning. It amused her, for no doubt her father thought her too dense to understand it, but she understood it all too well. She might be admitted to the Queen's circle, but it did not mean it was a permanent appointment. Other women would be seeking her place.

The Queen gestured with one hand. 'You have my leave to present her as one of my ladies. As for now, I will adjourn with my women.' She fixed Elizabeth with a

113

stern eye that twinkled a moment later. 'This time, you are excused. After this you shall have to leave as I leave, which may at times prove – inconvenient. But necessary.'

Elizabeth curtsied again, marking that as Anne rose everyone in the Presence Chamber either bowed or curtsied. She held her own deep curtsy until the Queen was gone, and then rose as her father's hand brought her up.

'Do not swim so deep,' he advised obliquely. 'You will drown.'

She understood him at once. Smiling at him, she said coolly, 'I am honest in all things, father, as a dutiful daughter should be.'

Stafford glanced at her sharply, wondering if he had heard her aright. Her expression was meek enough, yet he was certain he saw a glimmer of amusement deep in her eyes. If she had understood him, as he doubted, it meant she was deserving of closer attention.

He did not really know his daughter, not as he had known his son. Edward had been a well-intentioned fool, but he had been malleable enough. Stafford had thought the girl much like him. But now, as he looked at her guileless eyes and gentle smile, he wondered if he had misjudged her.

Then again, if she thought as he did and decided she wanted what he wanted, she would be an ally worth having. Stafford smiled at Elizabeth and pressed her arm again. 'If you please the Queen half as well as you please me, your place is secured.'

With what? she wondered grimly.

Bard very carefully stripped away the last of the lather on O'Neill's face. He was concentrating hard, he scowled blackly, and as he straightened he set a hand to his spine and groaned. ''Twill be the death of me just shaving you,'

114

he said aggrievedly. 'What will become of me once we are in the English court?'

O'Neill waved him aside and rose, wiping his face with a rough towel. He went immediately to the mirror set against the wall and stared at his reflection, tracing the careful line of the beard.

Bard had taken great pains to keep the thick growth even, trimming it with scissors and then putting a precise, straight-edged line from sideburns to the points of his jaw to his chin, where it reached a finger towards his bottom lip. The beard's clean line gave him the look of the devil, O'Neill thought, but he hoped it made him look less Irish and more Italian. Or at least French.

He fingered the moustache absently. It also was narrow, blending in with the beard, but he was not certain the disguise was necessary. He had a face not easily forgotten, bearded or no.

Bard, however, had left his own face uncluttered by hair, although he admitted freely the beard only enhanced O'Neill's striking dark good looks. He himself was not the sort to place much stock in his appearance, save to dress quietly in dark colours cut from good cloth. He had learned, early in life, he was not the sort others took much note of, which was just as well. It was O'Neill they recalled, which left *him* free to serve his master in other less obvious ways.

'Well?' O'Neill asked. 'Will I do?'

Bard thought the question moot. O'Neill would always *do*, even when he did not intend it; he claimed the sort of unconscious magnetism that would always draw men to his service, no matter what that service was. It was unlikely their cause would find much aid in England, but once they went home to Ireland the true test would begin. And they would badly need O'Neill's gift for acquiring loyal men.

Bard, grinning, bowed with an exaggerated flourish. '*Signore*, I am honoured by your presence. You have only to ask and it shall be yours.'

'By Christ, I wish it were that easy!' O'Neill swore several vile oaths in Gaelic and then switched back to English in mid-spate. His hands clenched. 'Would that James Stuart would listen to me as an O'Neill and not some foppish Italian fool!'

Bard thought privately that O'Neill could never conduct himself as either a fop or a fool, but he would not say it. And O'Neill *was* a good dissembler when pressed to it. The mummery might work.

'You have the letters?' Bard asked.

O'Neill strode across the room to a table. He slid one hand into a flat leather pouch and withdrew several parchments that crackled. He flashed them at Bard, showing him the heavy wax pendant seals closing the letters. His mouth, shadowed by black beard, moved into a smile, but his green eyes did not. 'Jamie'll not be knowing the difference, by God. I swear it!'

'He had better not.' Bard said it lightly, but his tone still underscored the message he intended for O'Neill. 'Or the game is up before 'tis properly started. And the ring?'

O'Neill pulled it from the pouch. It was a huge, massive ring, far too large for a man to wear on his bare hand, but made instead to go over the gloved finger of a man on horseback, riding cross-country with a message from His Holiness the Pope.

Bard nodded, satisfied. He had spent long hours in Italy training himself to forge the handwriting of the Pope's personal secretary. After that had come days of scrawling the Pope's signature over and over again until it matched the genuine letters got from the Pope's messenger, along with the ring.

Bard almost regretted it. He had slain the messenger

116

with very little compunction, because it had been the only course. O'Neill himself had given tacit approval for the murder, although his eyes had had a strange, blank look about them. When Bard returned he had found O'Neill missing. And when at last O'Neill returned he said only he had been to church. Praying for their souls, Bard did not doubt, for to kill the Pope's own messenger was a sin redoubled. They had killed men before, both of them, and would again, but this was almost as if they killed a part of the Holy Catholic Church herself. Bard was quite certain O'Neill would never fully forgive him, no more than he would himself, but they had needed the ring and letters too badly to let the opportunity escape.

'When do we leave for London?' Bard asked.

O'Neill tumbled the heavy ring across the palm of his hand. 'In the morning. I have waited too long already to begin this war. I wish to get it done.' He stared harshly at Bard. 'Jamie Stuart will be ruing the day he kept Ireland for himself!'

Bard merely smiled.

11

'Please . . . I must go to the Queen.' Elizabeth tried, without success, to draw away from Sir Henry Tavistock.

His face was very near hers as he bent over her from his impressive height. Had he the weight to go with it, he might have resembled a stork a little less. His smile left no doubts as to what he wanted of her.

'Say it again, mistress,' he implored. '*Exactly* as you said it the first time.'

Elizabeth, still trying to edge away, scowled at him in irritation. He was an odd sort, full of excess verbiage and flattering platitudes, but she had yet to see the slightest hint of sincerity about him. He had attached himself to her a fortnight before, not long after her arrival at court, and she had not yet quite learned how to deal with the men who made a career of acquiring and discarding ladies. Tavistock seemed to ignore her polite entreaties to be left alone so she could attend the Queen, and even now was professing to be enchanted by her voice.

'Please – ' she began it again, deciding to accede to his strange wish that she speak. The moment the word left her mouth his hand was on her lips, preventing her from finishing the sentence.

'*Ah!*' His blue eyes glinted. '*That* is what I have longed to hear from you. I shall oblige!' And fastened his mouth on hers the moment he removed his hand.

Astonished, Elizabeth stood there as he kissed her. She felt nothing except a wild surprise that he would trick her so and that she could be foolish enough to be so easily taken in. Then, as the astonishment faded into anger, she lunged away from his encircling arms.

'Sir Henry!' she cried, outraged.

But his hand was over her mouth yet again as he cautioned her to silence. 'Hush, my sweet . . . no noise, I implore you.'

Elizabeth ripped his hand away. 'Let go of me *at once!*' She felt great relief as he did so. Quickly she twitched her skirts into place and made certain his sudden ardour had displaced none of her bodice. She still felt the pressure of his lips on hers and made a moue of distaste. 'Sir Henry, I beg you – you *must* stop seeking me out!'

'But why?' His large blue eyes were half shuttered by droopy lids. His face was quite fair, almost childlike, but Elizabeth felt the film of powder he wore dusting her own face. His mouth was droopy, too, like a petulant child's, and she felt a moment of revulsion so acute she almost gagged.

'I serve Her Majesty the Queen.' She felt a little foolish repeating what everyone knew. But it was her only armour, for Anne had made it quite plain to everyone that her ladies were not to be dallied with. Elizabeth was not certain if the Queen knew how often that royal command was ignored; she had been pursued diligently by Tavistock and several others since her arrival. 'You must not continue this mummery, Sir Henry.'

'*Mummery!*' He gazed at her as if she had dealt him his death wound. 'Mistress, surely you know how much I care for you. It is a genuine emotion, I assure you. I have every intention of showing you how *very* much you mean to me.'

Elizabeth glared at him a moment, then hid her irritation behind a shy, ingenuous smile. 'Then you wish to wed me?'

For a moment she thought Tavistock was undergoing

119

some sort of fit. His fair face, even powdered, flushed an alarming shade of red, then the colour drained away to leave him white as death. His pale hair glistened in the candlelight, for he oiled it with a scented unguent from the East.

'Mistress,' he said through lips pressed closed together, 'I beg you to recall I already *have* a wife.'

Elizabeth bit back her smile. 'Then where is she?'

'Not at court,' he said in a clipped manner. 'She is at my country estate, awaiting the birth of our first child.' His blue eyes fastened themselves on her mouth. 'But surely you can understand how lonely I am for a good woman's – *company*.'

'Surely,' she agreed smoothly, 'just as you understand how I could not possibly wish to dally with a man who cannot offer marriage.' Elizabeth disliked the mercenary tone of her words, but it was the only escape she could find. Carefully she bestowed upon Tavistock a sweet, lovely smile. 'You *do* understand?'

'Only too well, mistress.' Bowing almost rudely, Tavistock took his leave. Elizabeth watched him move off in his stiff-kneed, disjointed manner and turned away so she would not laugh.

But the amusement quickly faded, for her predicament was genuine. Tavistock was only the first to declare his intentions openly; the others would surely follow. So far she had fended them off easily enough, for none of them seemed to be in any hurry, but Elizabeth knew the game would end soon. They would demand their payment. She was a green country girl trying to deal with the demands of a court full of men quite accustomed to tumbling ladies as they chose. She held no illusions about herself. That she had escaped so far had to do with luck. She was fast learning to choose her words carefully, lest she mistakenly lead one of them on even as she sought to put him off.

Tavistock was gone. Elizabeth released a sigh of relief and put a hand to her hair distractedly, wondering how she could protect herself against the advances of an entire court – wishing also she had a measure of her innocence back. She could no longer fool herself into believing it was only conversation they sought. It was because she was the newest of the new, therefore providing a jaded court some entertainment. Having heard of the wagering that went on – a month's worth of women's gossip had enlarged her education immeasurably – Elizabeth wondered if there were odds being laid as to which gentleman would bed her first, and when.

She shuddered convulsively in visceral reaction to the gamesmanship of the court. At least with O'Neill there had been no dissembling. She knew now he had wanted her without pretence, without the silk-and-lace language of the court; had Bard not interrupted them, it was likely O'Neill would have succeeded in overcoming her hesitation. *Then* she had not fully understood what he wanted, knowing only she wanted something also; now she did. Now she knew too well. She was surrounded by it. And she found, much to her surprise, she preferred O'Neill's brutal honesty over the elaborate courtesies of a court that employed words as a snare to trap the fleetest doe unless she was smarter than the rest.

And am I? she wondered. Her mouth tautened. *I will be. I swear it!*

Elizabeth knew she could not go at once to the Queen, not while she recalled so clearly Tavistock's assault upon her mouth. She had never been good at hiding what she felt and knew all of the Scottish ladies would guess at once what she had been doing. It wouldn't matter to them that she had been forced to it, merely that she had been foolish enough to entangle herself in such disgraceful circumstances, and they would lose no time informing their mistress.

Elizabeth did not hate the Scotswomen and knew they did not hate her, but neither were they willing to include her in their circle. She was English – *O'Neill's voice: Sassenach!* – and they were Scottish. It would be a long time, if ever, before Elizabeth was admitted to their circle. She had to content herself with serving the Queen as necessary and keeping herself busy when she didn't. The hours she spent with the women in private, sewing fine linens or embroidering altar cloths, were lonely ones, for she was rarely included in their conversation. She listened and learned, and began to know the nature of the court before she had been properly introduced to it.

The gallery in which Elizabeth stood was deserted. Tavistock had deliberately stalked her there, following quietly as she tried to escape, and now she was alone in a part of the palace she had never seen.

The wooden floors were polished until they gleamed. Paintings hung on one long wall, lighted by the windows in the other wall. Elizabeth stared up at the faces of royalty she had only heard stories about, looking into solemn eyes and unsmiling mouths. The colours seemed murky, without life and spirit, merely a way of making certain that reigning sovereigns did not forget who had gone before them.,

She stopped in front of a painting of a red-haired man in silver armour. His eyes were dark and probing, staring out of the canvas as if he wished to speak directly to her, and she very nearly answered. His was an imposing face, bold, excessively determined. The armour was an affectation for the painting, but Elizabeth had no doubts he had worn something very like it into battle. Like O'Neill, there was the hard shine of determination in his eyes and an aggressiveness that would carry others along in his wake – unquestioning, unspeaking, merely doing whatever was required.

'Ye admire the man in yon painting, mistress?'

Elizabeth spun, startled. One hand flew to her breast, then downward to gather her skirts as she swept into a deep curtsy. She had no doubt this was the King himself, for there was no mistaking the Scots burr in his voice or the richness of his apparel.

'Your Majesty!' She spoke breathlessly, wondering how she could have been so foolish as to linger in a private part of the huge palace.

James himself, smiling, raised her. He was a short man, not much taller than Elizabeth herself; his bearded face was pudgy. The royal eyes were brown, bright and sharp as a bird's, drifting quickly from her face to her breasts to the hem of her skirts, then back again.

Elizabeth's breath quickened. She had seen that reaction in men before, no matter how proper her attire, but to see it in a king? She felt unsteady, staring at him solemnly like any fool – like any or all of the unsmiling faces in the paintings.

'Aweel, mistress?' He stretched out his vowels until they more closely resembled another language. The faint, attractive catch she had heard before in the queen's Scottish women, but it sounded more intriguing in a man.

Abruptly she recalled this man was a king. She wanted to curtsy again at once, but he held her hand and shook his head. Elizabeth glanced around quickly, searching for his ever-present servitors, councillors, and courtiers, but for once he was alone. Elizabeth had never met him before – she had not even *seen* him – but she had heard all about him from the queen's ladies and others at court. James Stuart was ever a topic of conversation.

'I am sorry,' she said unsteadily, 'I should not be here.' Abruptly she recalled *why* she was there, and knew she could not tell him. What would he think of one of his wife's ladies fleeing the advances of a peer of the realm? Elizabeth drew careful breath and gestured towards the wall. 'I came to see the paintings.'

His eyes searched her face, and then he smiled again. He turned towards the wall, tucking her hand into his arm. The sunlight from the windows turned his brown hair reddish. 'D'ye know who yon man is?'

Now she was trapped. 'No, Your Majesty. But his face arrests me.'

''Tis my grandfather,' he said solemnly. 'James V, who wed a Frenchwoman and gave Scotland her sad Queen.' His eyes moved from the painting to her face. 'Ye *hae* heard of my mother, hae ye not?'

Elizabeth untangled the cadence of his speech. 'Yes, Your Majesty. Of course.'

'Of course,' he agreed, a trifle sadly. 'Ye're English, and ye'll know all about my mother.' His eyes turned from Elizabeth again, studying the portrait of his grandfather, who had sired Mary, Queen of Scots, the woman who had so foolishly laid claim to her cousin of England's throne when she already had her own.

'Your Majesty,' Elizabeth said quietly, 'forgive me, but I must return to the Queen.'

His attention was firmly back on her again. 'Return to the Queen?'

'I serve her, Your Majesty. I am one of her ladies.'

James frowned. 'My wife keeps the guid Scotswomen by her, mistress.'

'And one English one,' she told him. 'Elizabeth Stafford, Your Majesty – daughter of Sir Edwin.'

James's face brightened. 'Ach, of course! I recall Annie saying to me she wanted Sir Edwin's daughter by her. Forgie' me, mistress, I should hae known ye.'

Elizabeth wondered how he could possibly have known

124

her. It was flattering speech from a king, who doubtless had more important matters on his mind, but it made her uncomfortable. She wanted to get away, back to her safe harbour with people she knew.

James grinned at her. She was a bonny thing, he thought, much more beautiful than the 'guid Scotswomen' his wife kept by her. There was a delicacy mixed with strength in this young woman, lending her the aspect of a rose – lovely and rich in colour, yet protected by sharp thorns. But she was no rose, he decided, with her old gold and ivory colouring. More like a sprig of heather on the hills of his beloved Scotland.

He kept her hand trapped in his arm and turned away, leading her down the gallery. He noted how she kept her silence and wondered if she was afraid. She didn't *seem* afraid. Merely astonished, though her astonishment was tempered with quiet self-possession. She kept her head bowed slightly, so as not to step out of her place by looking directly at him. It was something he had accustomed himself to early in life, such subtle deference, and generally it pleased him. But he wanted this woman to look him in the eye. He wanted her to smile at him.

James halted abruptly another painting, turning her towards it. 'Who is yon man, mistress?'

Elizabeth wet her lips. 'I could not say, Your Majesty. My knowledge of Scottish royalty is little, I fear.'

He admired the honesty of her answer; she might have prevaricated with an elaborate excuse. But he had trapped her unfairly, and it was time to tell her so. 'What were ye doing here, mistress? Not admiring the portraits. Not when ye dinna even know who this man is.'

Elizabeth stared blindly at the painting. The man was big, heavy-shouldered, powerful. He wore rich, stiff clothing of another time, and the hose exposed the swelling muscles of powerful calves and thighs. *Like O'Neill's*, she thought fleetingly. But this man was bearded, his hair ruddy-gold, and his shrewd blue eyes stared out of the painting with arrogance and pride. Still, she wondered how not knowing the portrait would brand her a liar before the king.

'Your Majesty – ' she began.

James held up a silencing finger. 'Tell me why you were here, mistress.'

She stared at the polished floor. 'I sought to get free of an entanglement I did not desire.'

James smothered a laugh. 'D'ye mean to say 'twas a man pursing ye for yer favour?'

This time he did laugh. It was a startling sound coming from a king; she had not expected amusement from him, but anger. Dismissal. Banishment to Kent, and all her father's plans ruined.

'And who was the bold cockerel, mistress?'

'Sir Henry Tavistock,' she said very quietly.

'Tavistock!' James stared at her in astonishment. 'That skinny-arsed Sassenach? And I'd hae thought 'twould be Monkton or Sommerset, or even Onslow. But *Tavistock?*' He shook his head. 'Coom, mistress, can ye nae find better men than him to pursue ye?'

Incredibly, it seemed the king was not angry. Elizabeth tried to recover her course. 'Your Majesty . . . I had little choice in the matter. Sir Henry *forced* me – '

'Forced a kiss on ye?'

'Yes.'

'But nothing more?'

Elizabeth's flace flamed. '*No*, Your Majesty! I swear – '

His hand was up again. 'Enough, mistress, I believe ye. 'Tis guid to know there's yet a virtuous woman still to be found in my court.' His smile was small, secretive, but his eyes seemed merely amused. 'Does my Annie treat you well?'

Elizabeth tried to visualize the woman he called 'my Annie,' but all she could see was the regal woman who was Queen. 'Of course, Your Majesty. The Queen is the best of all mistresses.'

She used the word within its proper context, but James suddenly preferred the other, that which meant a woman in his bed for as long as he desired her. Elizabeth's body was lush even in its slenderness. So different from the boy he had lately been so taken up with. And quite suddenly James knew he was tired of the boy. He would give him a jewel or two – for the boy was as bad as a woman when it came to demanding fine clothes and gems – and would send him from court. He would go home properly grateful, richer than he could have imagined, while *this* one took his place.

James smiled. 'Tell me, mistress, why hae we not seen ye before now?'

'I serve the Queen, Your Majesty.' Elizabeth did not say what everyone knew, that Anne and James kept separate courts as well as bedchambers because James enjoyed the fawning attentions of male and female alike, while Anne did not. But admission to the King's presence was difficult, and the Queen's was better than nothing.

Elizabeth had learned early that those who frequented the Queen's company almost invariably gained permission to enter James's sphere, and once that was done they almost never returned to the Queen's – unless, of course, they had to start over again. She had met very few of the established nobles of England – the King had named three of them already – but she knew *of* everyone. She knew also she had little chance of joining the glittering crowd that thronged James's Presence Chamber because she served the Queen and would remain in obscurity.

Or so she had always believed.

'And did we bid ye coom to court so ye could escape the pursuit of Tavistock and his ilk, looking instead to proper lords?' the King asked.

Elizabeth stared at him in astonishment. 'Your Majesty – I did not come to court hoping to gain a husband. I came to serve the Queen.'

''Tis one and the same,' James answered flatly. But he smiled to take the sting from his words. 'Nae, mistress, dinna take fright from what I say. 'Tis the simple truth, and has been so for years upon years. Ye knew all of Annie's women are wed?'

'Of course.'

'They were not when they came here. And now they've all wed with Englishmen.' His beard was red in the sunlight. 'Tell me again ye hae no wish to wed a titled man, mistress.'

Elizabeth squared her jaw. 'It is not my *intention* to do so.'

'Nae doot 'twas Sir Edwin's, then.' James grinned at her obvious discomfiture. 'Nae, nae, dinna harden yer face to me. 'Tis what any father would do with a prize like ye at hand. Nothing to be ashamed of, mistress, 'tis the normal way of things. Ye'll be wed, and well . . . hae no doot of't. But I think ye'll nae catch the sort of fish Sir Edwin wants by staying with Annie. I think 'tis time ye met the rest of this court, mistress.'

'But . . . Your Majesty . . . I cannot desert the Queen!'

'Nae, nae, mistress, ye'll nae be desertin' yer Queen.' James patted her hand and allowed his to linger just a moment. ''Tis time we paid more attention to Annie anyway, so we'll simply hae her join our court. And all her ladies, of course.' He smiled benignly at her, and she saw he had small, uneven teeth. 'We hae missed our guid Queen's company of late.'

But Anne's company was easily dispensed with. He had only to get 'bonny Lizzie' into his court and the thing was done, for even the Queen would not interfere with the King's pleasure. Elizabeth would keep her position as lady-in-waiting – for it would not do to dishonour her name entirely – but she would be serving another master.

James wondered, as he drank in the purity of her features, if she were truly the virtuous woman she claimed. He had not believed a single maidenhead could survive a week at court.

The king smiled at her. 'Coom, mistress, we'll take ye back to the Queen.'

He led her from the gallery. As they left Elizabeth twisted her head to glance back at the huge man in the painting. 'Who is he, Your Majesty?'

'Henry,' James answered. 'The eighth king of that name.'

Elizabeth shut her eyes.

12

Elizabeth's world exploded into a shower of rich, glittering fragments. What she had known was gone. No more the boring days of sewing and embroidering, serving a Queen cranky from ill health and unhappiness. The 'guid Scotswomen' faded into obscurity even as Elizabeth shot out of it, elevated by the hand of the King himself.

James's court was entirely different from his wife's. Elizabeth compared the personages of the two courts to bread: The men in Anne's were like so much dough, unformed, unbaked, without substance or shape. Those in the King's were loaves, hot, fresh, steaming, food in a starving man's hands. She was now among the greatest names in England, overwhelmed by the wealth and titles and fine manners. Tavistock paled to utter imbecility by comparison, and Elizabeth began to understand why James had so arrantly dismissed him.

Tavistock's pursuit of Elizabeth also paled to utter insignificance. Though she did not doubt he had meant it, for whatever reasons, she now realized there were better ways of going about it. Ways that nearly guaranteed the outcome, for suddenly she was stalked by the most proficient of huntsmen. The fleet doe was quickly ringed by the archers, and she was not certain she could escape. The hounds might bring her down.

The King seemed to have forgotten all about her. She did not really expect his personal attention – who, after all, was *she?* – but she was vaguely aware of apprehension. He had brought her into this world for reasons she could not name, and now she was forgotten like a cuddly kitten growing into a plain cat. Elizabeth conducted herself with decorum and armed herself with a natural reserve that put off a few of the men initially, but they soon resumed the game. She was not certain she would live to see it completed.

Her days spilled into the nights, robbing her of sleep and leisure. Suddenly she was coming and going with the rest of them, serving the Queen when she could and yet quite aware that her place was not so much dependent on Anne's goodwill as it was on James's. Elizabeth believed he was only being kind to her that day in the gallery and now had forgotten her utterly. But she heard a few whispers behind hands haphazardly placed over mouths and wondered how it was possible for the court to believe her fair game.

She was tired, so tired, yet afraid to stop running. They might catch her. And then she would be no better than most of the 'ladies' at court, who played at virtue as if it were some game in which the jewel would be bestowed on the handsomest, wealthiest player. Her illusions were tumbling around her, and she began to wonder if she would wake up one morning no different than anyone else. Accessible, won with the proper combination of fine words, arousing hands and mouth, wealth and title. She did not want that for herself.

Elizabeth stared at her reflection in the mirror. Her face seemed devoid of character, a blank palette on which she would have to paint an expression. There was a downward curve to her mouth similar to that on the Queen's face, and she hated it. With effort she smiled, but it never reached her eyes.

Listlessly she pushed her freshly washed hair behind her shoulders, letting it dry in the morning sunlight. There were faint shadows beneath her eyes and little colour in her cheeks; slowly she took up a pot of pink cream and rubbed some into her face. Her cheekbones took on some colour, but she was careful to make it subtle, not overpowering. She disliked the subterfuge, but she had learned that a woman who looked weary in the King's court was believed tired from bedsport rather than late hours and troubled sleep. Elizabeth would pay almost any price to escape that stigma. So she painted her face, tipped her lashes in soot mixed with scented oil, and rubbed her lips with crushed rose petals.

Alice brushed dry her tawny hair and pinned it up, chattering about some tall, handsome man who had lately come to court. Elizabeth paid little attention, lost in some corner of her mind that recalled the sweet freshness in Kent and lush woodlands. Alice talked on about the man's impressive height, powerful hands, and imposing looks, all of which was complemented by his wealth and standing.

Not O'Neill, Elizabeth thought. *No wealth and standing* – She broke off the thought at once. He had gone from her life as much as she from his, although occasionally he intruded into her dreams and spoiled what sleep she found in the crowded hours.

'. . . but he has little to do with women,' Alice was saying. 'He is serious and solemn, they say, with little regard for the flattery of the court – '

O'Neill. Elizabeth smiled crookedly. *Except for the first part.*

'No doubt he is used to such flattery, with his face and wealth, so 'tis nothing to him,' Alice continued. 'But they say 'tis no wonder he received all the attention.' Her voice lowered to a hushed whisper of excitement. 'What will you do if you meet him, mistress?'

Elizabeth looked at Alice's face in the mirror. The girl was so giddy and free, untouched by all the intrigue and subterfuge of the court. Alice took what lovers she wished, expecting nothing but a few coins, a little kindness, and perhaps a small jewel in return. At court even the lowliest kitchen maid could become rich.

'I will doubtless say I am impressed by his reputation.' Elizabeth laughed as Alice's face fell. 'You silly goose, what do you expect me to say? That I wish to bed with him? Doubtless he hears that often enough, if he is as well-favoured as you say.'

'He *must* be, mistress,' Alice declared. 'The Queen sets fine store by him, and she's not one to play *that* sort of game.'

Elizabeth's brows rose. This was something new. Anne of Denmark only rarely indulged in the sort of diversions her husband sought regularly, for she had little stamina for the courtship rites the men enjoyed so well. Elizabeth had heard it said the Queen had taken a lover once or twice, but she wondered if it were merely rumour magnified. Anne enjoyed having handsome young men by her, but the disquiet in her eyes did not augur well for a lasting relationship.

'Who is he?' Elizabeth asked.

'Sir Simon Bagenal,' Alice answered. 'He has been in Scotland seeing to things for the King himself, and now he is back.'

'But if it is the *Queen* who values him . . .' Her voice trailed off as she considered it.

Alice, still pinning Elizabeth's hair into place, laughed giddily. 'Oh, the King values him too. 'Tis said he is a crafty, careful man, dangerous because he says so little and yet knows so much. 'Tis likely the King sees him as a threat, for he prefers knowing the Queen keeps no man by her side – so he takes Sir Simon away by sending him to Scotland.' She pinned the last curl into place and patted it, shrugging. 'Now he is back.'

Elizabeth laughed. 'If he is so careful, so solemn, it is

unlikely he will ever be brought to *my* attention.'

'But what if you were brought to *his?*'

Elizabeth smiled and gestured for assistance in getting into her pale green brocade gown edged with white coney fur. 'I think it unlikely,' she said absently. 'I think it *very* unlikely.'

Sir Edwin Stafford, standing in the King's Presence Chamber with a small knot of men, saw Simon Bagenal enter. Almost as one each head swivelled around, assessing the man who had James's ear. Everyone knew it was because the Queen doted on him and the King merely desired to sever the bond, but there was more to Bagenal than simply a pleasing turn of phrase calculated to win the queen's favour. The man was cold as ice. His tongue, when he used it, was razor-sharp. He did not appear to care whom he offended, and yet he had never offended his King and Queen.

Stafford knew James Stuart was a shrewd judge of men, even if he did too often prefer them in his bed. And James understood Bagenal better than most. He wanted to use him, and yet he distrusted him. He needed some outward sign from Bagenal that the man would serve the King as devotedly as the Queen, and James had yet to see any. Bagenal kept to himself. His guard was always in place, although there were quiet rumours he had an eye for women. That eye was cold, ruthless, and discerning, and few of the court ladies kept his attention for long. Was it the Queen he sought? Stafford wondered. Or her power? If it were the latter, Bagenal must surely know he stood a better chance with James, who could unmake him in a moment if he chose. Or *make* him.

Bagenal wore a dark blue velvet doublet and short padded breeches over black trunk hose. His boots were soft Spanish leather dyed blue, but he had left off the spurs of knighthood. The doublet was fastened with diamond studs and he wore a heavy signet ring on his right hand, but that was the extent of his bow to conventional finery. He was not the sort of man who required ornamentation to make himself stand out in the crowd. In shoddy wool Simon Bagenal would outshine them all.

Like Elizabeth, Stafford thought. Very like Elizabeth.

Bagenal was tall and quite blond, reflecting the old Saxon blood got long before from Norse ancestors. He wore his hair brushed back from a face that seemed devoid of life . . . until one looked at his eyes, so cold and blue. It was no wonder the ladies considered him a challenge and an even finer catch; he was handsome with the hard edge of a blade, scintillating and unpredictable. There was nothing remarkable about his looks – Stafford had seen handsomer men – but he exuded power and confidence and an arrogance that made him stand out in a court full of preening peacocks.

The chamberlain announced Bagenal to the King and the court fell silent, expectant. Stafford, watching, smiled. How like Simon Bagenal to ignore the grandiose tones of the chamberlain and stare at James instead, as if he had no patience for such petty customs.

The King waved the chamberlain away before he was properly done and acknowledged Bagenal with a faint smile. 'We are somewhat surprised to hae ye back wi' us so soon.'

Bagenal bowed with cool grace. 'Your Majesty, I believe my task is completed.'

'And what did my proud Scots hae to say to a *Sassenach* cooming among them like a king?'

Bagenal did not smile, but there was a faint glint in his glacial blue eyes. 'I have known men more accommodating, Your Majesty, but when I showed them your letter and seal they were all attentiveness.'

'I imagine so.' James fingered his beard, aware – as always – how the Englishman's height and self-possession put even his own kingly bearing to shame. 'Hae ye seen the Queen?'

Bagenal's expression did not change. 'I came straight to you, Your Majesty. Of course.'

'Of course,' James mocked. 'But do ye nae wonder what she will say when she knows ye're back?'

'I prefer to be – surprised.' Bagenal's tone held a hint of dryness in an otherwise expressionless voice. 'And, as ever – I serve my *King*.'

The emphasis was subtle, but quite clear to James. He wondered if Bagenal's attendance on the Queen was nothing more than a ploy to win the King's jealousy and therefore his attention, but he thought it unlikely. Any love he might once have felt for his Danish Queen had long since vanished, replaced with a grudging respect and faint affection. She had borne him six children, though only three survived, and she had conducted herself with great endurance when Prince Henry had sickened and died. She herself had the same illness, he knew, though the doctors insisted it was only a slight fever in the lungs. She brought up blood when she coughed and her body was wasting away on the sturdy Danish frame James had never truly felt comfortable with. Annie would die, leaving him alone, and he would miss her.

Nevertheless, Bagenal had always been *her* creature, and James refused her that victory.

He wanted badly to be certain of Bagenal. He wanted to give him something that would make him indebted to his King. James was not foolish enough to think any man served him out of love or blind loyalty. His power attracted them all, and their own personal greed bound them to him. He did not doubt Simon Bagenal was precisely the same, though he took care to present himself differently.

James had no doubt he could buy the man. He bought them all, like Edwin Stafford. He had only to discover Bagenal's price.

Lands would not do; Bagenal had inherited too many from his father, Sir Henry, the Old Queen's handpicked Marshal of Ireland. A title might do, more than a mere knighthood, but not yet. That was too promising a trinket to bestow so quickly. What, then? Not gold, for the man had more than most.

Instantly James's mind flashed to flesh and bone. Bagenal had no liking for boys, the King knew, preferring women. Could he give him a woman? But surely Bagenal had his choice of those at court, and they were not such a fine gift after a year or two of court life. He knew his court had become a fine forest in which the wolves could hunt the does, but he thought there must be at least a *few* does yet remaining who had not gone down beneath the grasping jaws of his velvet-clad wolves.

And then he recalled Elizabeth Stafford. He had meant to keep her for himself, but now he wondered if she might be the key to Bagenal. Certainly the Queen would never consider bestowing a *woman* on Bagenal, no matter how well he served her. And the entire court was full of discussion over Mistress Stafford. She was a quiet, considerate, unpretentious woman who did not use her great charm and beauty to bind men to her. And if she would not, *he* would.

James smiled. 'We are pleased, Sir Simon. Later ye may speak to us in confidence regarding yer time in Scotland. As for now we wish ye to be at ease, perhaps feasting yer eyes on a court ye hae been away from so long.' His fingers stroked his beard. 'Mistress Stafford, will ye coom forward?'

Elizabeth, lost in the crowd, felt it part and move away from her. The King's eyes searched for her, found her; a hand beckoned her forward. Slowly she went, eyes averted from the throne and the man in it. She halted before him, curtsying gracefully.

'Yon man has been long from court,' James told her conversationally. 'Dootless he wishes to know what has gone on in his absence. Will ye do us the sarvice of informing him, mistress?'

Alarm stiffened Elizabeth. She stared blankly at James a moment, then glanced at the man near her. He stood very still, seemingly at ease with himself, but she sensed a readines coiled in him like a wire bound too tightly.

Her first instinct told her to refuse. But no one refused the King. And so she did not. 'As you wish, Your Majesty.'

James smiled at her, then turned his attention to Bagenal. 'She is Mistress Elizabeth Stafford, lady-in-waiting to the Queen. I hae nae doot she can answer all your questions. And I hae nae doot at all her answers will please you well.'

Bagenal bowed again. 'As you wish, Your Majesty.' His words echoed Elizabeth's, but she heard in his tone the faintest hint of irony.

James, seated on his dais, looked over their heads to Edwin Stafford, who was now free to make any protest he might wish. The King could overrule him, of course, but James thought it a nice touch to act the part of a man sensitive to the nuances of the moment.

He waited, but Stafford said nothing. His eyes were on his daughter; his mouth, so thin and controlled, moved into a faint, satisfied smile.

Contempt twisted James's mouth. So the father would sacrifice the daughter? So be it. There would be some manner of reward for him . . . one day.

He waved his royal hand. 'You may go, Sir Simon. Dootless ye're weary from yer journey. Perhaps Mistress Stafford can tell ye what ye should know as ye go from here.'

Elizabeth felt a chill seep into her bones. Her flesh rose up as if an icy blast of arctic air had swept through the chamber to make a home in her chest. But a glance of appeal at the King showed her his smile, and she realized she had to go with Bagenal or face royal censure.

But why? she wondered. *Is this what he intended from the beginning?* No longer was she naïve enough to believe she had no part to play in the politics of the court. Queen's woman or no, she was as much a pawn as any of them.

And now the King had put her firmly into the game.

Bagenal turned to her. His face was expressionless. There was no warmth in his blue eyes, none at all – no pleasure, no admiration, no lust. He gazed at her silently, seemingly unmoved by her person or her face, and suddenly she felt no better than a whore parading her wares before a man who wanted nothing to do with any of them.

He put out an arm at the instant before his hesitation became blatant rudeness. 'Mistress Stafford?'

Slowly Elizabeth accepted it, conscious of his height and the breadth of his shoulders. And suddenly, looking at him, she realized how like O'Neill he was. They shared the same powerful body, the same force of will and lithe movements. Bagenal was blond and blue-eyed in place of O'Neill's black hair and green eyes, but Elizabeth sensed the same sort of ambition in the Englishman.

O'Neill.

Abruptly, too abruptly, Elizabeth realized why she had been so unmoved by all the skilful flattery of the courtiers.

None of them was O'Neill.

'My lord.' Her lips felt stiff as she mouthed the words, and he took her from the chamber.

Bagenal said nothing as she dealt with her realization and subsequent acknowledgement of its accuracy. He merely took her out of the Presence Chamber and into a private solar, away from prying eyes, and settled himself against the mantel of the fireplace. He lounged indolently, boneless as any cat, and she sensed he merely waited.

He is so like O'Neill . . . She could say nothing immediately, searching for sense in the confusion, seeking words for an explanation she could not find.

'Well?' he inquired.

Elizabeth turned sharply to face him. Stamped over his features were those of another man, and she had no words for him.

Bagenal's smile was not quite a smile. 'Are you struck dumb?'

'No,' she said flatly. 'Neither am I deaf. What I heard the King say just now is something I cannot decipher.' She shrugged. 'There is nothing I can tell you about this court that you do not already know.'

'*Honesty,* from you?' The question was strictly rhetorical. 'No sweet evasions?'

So, he was not the sort to devise poetry or summon pledges of devotion. Nor, did she think, was he the sort who would admit to any sort of affection for any, save perhaps himself. 'No evasions,' she returned. 'I have no more wish to be here – *in this position* – than have you.'

Bagenal smiled. It softened his face, though the hardness remained in his eyes. 'Is this Jamie's way of casting you off, *mistress?* Or has he discovered he cannot bribe me with boys?'

Elizabeth felt the colour run out of her face. Honesty she admired; honesty she *desired*, after so much time at court, but such bluntness she had never faced, particularly

140

when she was the target of it. 'I am not the King's mistress,' was all she could manage, thinking it enough.

Elaborate condescension. 'Then what, pray, *are* you?'

Her teeth clicked together. 'Lady-in-waiting to the Queen.'

He made a sound of derision. 'That good lady would never approve of bribery entailing *flesh*. She is above such things. A courtesy title, perhaps, designed to protect your – *good name?* – but little more.'

Elizabeth's head snapped up. 'Then ask her yourself! I was brought to court on her order, because she appointed me to the position. You have only to ask my *father* if you do not believe me.'

'Edwin Stafford?' The tone was bored. 'That man would sell his soul for a restored title and the wealth and lands to go with it. Surely one less daughter will trouble his conscience not in the least.'

'I am his *only* daughter!' she snapped.

'Then it does make the sacrifice somewhat more dramatic, but no different.' He came off the mantel and Elizabeth was again reminded of O'Neill. 'Do you think I believe you have not shared the King's bed?'

'I have not.' It was all but toneless; anger robbed her of everything save distinctness.

'Not *yet*.' Elaborate distinction.

'Not ever.' She nearly bared her teeth. 'Plainly there is no point to my remaining in your company. And so I will take myself from it. If you will excuse me – ' She turned sharply to go.

'No,' he said. 'I will not excuse you. I wish you to stay with me and explain quite plainly what your purpose is.'

'I *don't know!*' Elizabeth cried angrily. '*You* heard the King call me forward. How could I know what he intended to do?'

'You *would*, had you been privy to his plans. A reward,

141

I trust, for my good service in the King's name.' His voice was full of eloquent irony. 'Jamie pays his debts, and while doing it plans for the next service that will incur yet another. Well, *mistress* . . . shall we to bed?'

Elizabeth gaped at him, forgoing any elegance she might once have claimed. '*Bed* . . .'

Bagenal gestured with a negligent hand. 'This chamber, perhaps, is not what you are accustomed to, but it is more private than my bedchamber. At present my servants are unpacking my trunks. But I trust this floor will do . . . or perhaps this chair?' He moved forward and place two big hands on the padded back of a tall chair.

'What manner of beast *are* you?' Elizabeth stared at him. 'Do you believe *I* asked for this? No! And I will not share this room with you a moment longer than I must!'

He was across the room before she could tug open the heavy door. His hand was on her arm, turning her though she tried to keep him from it. She was stiff with anger and humiliation, longing to scream at him and yet knowing it would only brand her a mannerless whore in his eyes.

'How long have you been at court?' he demanded.

'Two months.' And two words, holding all the venom she could summon.

Bagenal frowned faintly, blond brows drawing down over intent blue eyes. 'Do you lie to me?'

'Ask anyone you wish.'

His scowl deepened. 'Two months is hardly enough time for you to wheedle your way into the King's favour . . . not when he generally keeps himself to boys.' He ignored her moue of distaste at his bluntness. 'Am I to believe you are what you appear to be – a young woman with no knowledge of how she can be used?'

'Not entirely.' She met his gaze squarely. 'I *do* know how I can be used, a little, judging by how others here are used. But that career is not what I choose for myself.'

142

'What *do* you choose?' he demanded.

'To go from you, at once.'

He smiled. 'I begin to believe you, mistress.'

'And is it not what *you* prefer?'

Bagenal released her arm. 'I have yet to find a woman who can even *begin* to know what I prefer.'

Elizabeth tugged open the door and went through it. And shut it in his face.

13

In the days following the King's public disposition of her attentions, Elizabeth found it more and more difficult to face the knowing eyes and whispering mouths in the Presence Chamber. Although nothing had transpired between herself and Simon Bagenal, the entire court believed it had. That she and Bagenal now took no notice of one another seemed only to make them appear unduly circumspect. At the very worst, everyone believed they had merely quarrelled; Elizabeth was quite certain every man and woman in Whitehall was convinced they had shared a bed at the King's instigation.

James himself appeared unaware of the distasteful position in which he had placed her. He kept Bagenal by him most of the time, as if he thought he had bound the man; Elizabeth began to wonder if perhaps that was precisely what James had intended for her. It hadn't worked, and yet to all intents and purposed it *appeared* to have succeeded, for Bagenal took his place at court. He enjoyed all the privileges of a high-ranking peer of the realm and the power that came with playing the King's game. Elizabeth saw him often, but they never spoke.

She tried once to explain to her father what had happened and how she felt about it, but Stafford seemed harried by other concerns. He expressed his confidence in her ability to handle such matters without bothering to look closely at her face, which expressed her misery more eloquently than her careful words. Elizabeth considered asking him if she could go home to Kent, but Bagenal's words had aroused her suspicions. Was it true her father wished merely to use her? He was land-hungry and quite obviously striving to recover the former glory of the Stafford name – that much she knew quite well – but would he sacrifice her as easily as a pawn in a chess game?

The thought made her uneasy. She had learned, even in her brief stay at court, there was little room for innocence and naïveté. What at first had seemed unbelievable she now knew to be quite real; power politics and sexual intrigue were the rule, not the exception, and for her to continue turning a blind eye to it all was ludicrous. Elizabeth was no longer innocent in mind, although her body remained her own.

She could not simply go home on her own; she needed her father's permission. She also needed the Queen's, and – although Anne might be glad to see her go – James could easily overrule his wife. Elizabeth thought he might. He wanted Bagenal content, and although there had been nothing between them, she thought the King would not hesitate to dangle the bait again.

And when Simon Bagenal approached her one day, in the eyes of all the court, Elizabeth knew it. The game was on again.

She turned a shoulder to him, hoping he would go, but he merely stepped around it until he faced her. Conversations continued throughout the chamber, but every eye was on them, and Elizabeth wanted little more than to rail at them all to keep their thoughts to themselves. But she didn't. She stood silently, refusing to meet Bagenal's eyes.

'Mistress,' he said, 'I would wish to speak with you.'

His excessive politeness cut no ice with her. 'There is nothing you could have to say that would possibly interest me.'

'Perhaps not,' he agreed. 'But even if we stand here and argue – politely, of course – they will think we are

145

planning a tryst. So why not forget them and think about what I might have to say to you instead?'

Unwillingly she looked at him. He was so tall, so hard, so much like O'Neill and yet so unlike him. She had, of late, discovered a tendency within herself to measure *every* man against O'Neill . . . and none of them had been able to stand in his shadow.

Bagenal might . . . But she answered him coolly. 'I would prefer we were not seen together.'

He shrugged slightly, unmoved by her preferences. 'It would make no difference. Surely you must understand a little of this court, mistress, when it comes to such things. Even with only two months under your belt.' His eyes, on her waist, forced her to acknowledge his imagery even though she wished not to.

'*What* would you wish to say to me?' she demanded impatiently.

He seemed oblivious to the eyes, the ears, as he spoke in a negligent tone. 'That, perhaps, I misjudged you.'

'You did.'

'And will you accept my apology?'

Elizabeth glared into implacable eyes. 'Are you offering one, Sir Knight? Or is this merely another move of the innocent little pawn?'

Bagenal smiled. She saw the glint of appreciation in his eyes, so cold and hard. 'So you name yourself by the truth at last.'

Elizabeth was hideously aware of the stares and whispers. 'I acknowledge I am innocent,' she told him between her teeth. 'I acknowledge I am a pawn. I acknowledge there is, indeed, a game. But I *deny* any wish to be a part of it, willingly or unwillingly.'

'I misjudged you,' he repeated. 'I think you understand what the king intended, *now,* and I wish to apologize for treating you so harshly upon our – *introduction.*'

His final words, though lacking the intent to incriminate her, made their former meeting sound like a passionate union of two bodies. Elizabeth knew what the eyes and ears believed. Nothing she could say would change that now, no matter how strongly she denied any liaison between herself and Bagenal.

'I believe, Sir Knight,' she began through gritted teeth, 'you have made yourself *quite clear*.'

Bagenal frowned slightly, as if thrown off by her words. Then she saw him think back on what he had said, and how he had said it, and saw realization move into his eyes. His head came up and he glanced around. Without haste, without seeming to take much note of those who listened, yet she knew he comprehended what he had done to her. Whatever reputation Elizabeth Stafford had managed to keep intact was now completely destroyed.

His smile was faint but also rueful, an expression she had never thought to see from him. 'Mistress, I apologize yet again. What more can I do?'

'You might leave,' she pointed out distinctly, 'before they think to see us couple on the floor like two rutting hounds.'

Bagenal laughed. Elizabeth had not intended the remark for his amusement, and certainly not to provoke a verbal response. It made her angry, turning her flesh hot and then cold with humiliation until she wished to sink into the ground, but then she saw the astonishment on the watching faces. And she realized he was not laughing *at her,* but at what she had said, and where.

'Mistress,' he said finally, when his outburst had subsided, 'I have *certainly* misjudged you. And I apologize yet again.' Blond brows arched upward. 'Three times, is it?'

'How many more times?' Elizabeth was past control. 'Or is this all part of the game?'

'No game,' he told her, and his smile was genuine. 'Or rather – part of another game. One which is not so displeasing.' His face was no longer so rigidly austere; his eyes lacked the iciness all had seen. He looked at her intently, as if he had never seen her before, and Elizabeth found herself wondering uneasily what she had done to alter his opinion of her. She was quite certain there had been some sort of change, for his manner had undergone a subtle and yet almost startling transformation.

'Mistress.' His tone was quite deliberate. 'Do you *care* what these yapping little dogs and bitches really think of us?'

Elizabeth looked at the yapping dogs and bitches. They were clustered in little groups around the huge chamber, talking over strategies for liaisons and bids for royal favour and the latest conquest by a popular nobleman of an even more popular lady. She was no longer so impressed by the great names and fabulous wealth and eloquent words. The court was, she realized clearly, precisely the bedroom O'Neill had said it was.

She smiled, thinking what O'Neill would say to all of Jamie's posturing and the mettle of the court. She knew what *she* would say . . . only it would be to Bagenal since she lacked O'Neill, but she thought he would understand.

Elizabeth laughed. 'No,' she said, 'I do not care. *Let the puppies bark.*'

Bagenal's answering smile lacked all traces of irony and icy disdain. He bowed and extended his arm. 'Then, mistress, shall we leave them to their royal kennel? We have things to discuss – and better apologies to be made.'

Elizabeth accepted his arm. Silently she walked the length of the chamber with Simon Bagenal, leaving the room to the sighs of the men and the jealousies of the women.

He led her to the gallery where she had first met the

King. It seemed so long ago. For a moment she thought to say it was not their place to make themselves at home in the private rooms of the palace, but she did not. Bagenal moved with the ease of a man accustomed to going wherever he would. Had he in truth been the Queen's lover, it would provide a lot of answers.

'James will no doubt be pleased.' He matched his stride to her shorter one as O'Neill had done so long before. 'It will seem as if I have fallen into his trap.'

'Then he *did* intend me as a bribe.' Disgust rose up in her breast that a man could use a woman so, and that another man would accept it.

'Not a bribe,' Bagenal said. 'A reward. A bribe is made before the thing is done, a reward after.' He smiled. 'Perhaps James does not know quite what he wants of me – yet.'

'And what do you want of *me?*'

He paused. The September sunlight was dull, hardly illuminating the gallery, but the weak light still set Bagenal's fair hair to shining and the diamonds in his green doublet flashing. Elizabeth had learned those jewels were his only vanity, for he openly disdained much of the self-absorption of the court.

'What do I want of you?' he echoed. 'Your company, mistress. And your forgiveness.'

'You may have the latter,' she told him, 'but I think the former must not be so. We can do one another no good.'

Coolly, he smiled. 'You said you do not care for what the dogs and bitches think.'

'I do not,' she agreed, 'but it is foolish to willingly *contribute* to the awkwardness of the situation.'

'No,' he said contemplatively, 'you are not the woman I believed you. You are neither a conniving bitch willing to give anything for what she wants, nor are you the empty-headed little country girl I heard you were.' He smiled at her wince. 'That was what the ladies called you. The men had another description.'

Discomfited, she turned away from him to stare at one of the portraits. 'Why have you brought me here?'

'To judge you for myself.' He did not move to stand beside her, but remained a few steps behind. 'I did you a disservice, and myself as well. I am not a man who puts much stock in what other people say, preferring to judge for myself, but in this instance past experience overcame better sense. At court women are traded as easily as coin in a dice game, and I believed you a willing participant. When I realized you were not I thought it a new sort of game . . . one in which the child sheds her innocence in front of the man so she can win the prize she wants.' He moved closed to her. 'Do you understand? The King wanted to give you to me so I would be properly grateful. I did not accept. And when you were so angry I thought it was because I had repudiated you.' Irony underscored his tone. 'A woman whose favours are rebuffed is generally disinclined to think *kindly* of the man. I believed you angry because your gambit had failed.'

'There is no game,' she said unevenly. 'I refuse to play.'

'Oh, there is,' he returned, 'and you will not refuse.' He paused. 'When you know what there is to win.'

Elizabeth turned to face him squarely. 'Well?' she demanded. 'What is there to win?'

'Land,' he told her, 'and wealth. A title. *Security*. Whatever a woman wants.' His mouth hooked down at one end. 'A husband to give you all those things.'

Elizabeth laughed. 'And are you *offering?*'

Bagenal's big hands moved up and caught her face, imprisoning her jaw. His mouth was close to hers, and his eyes – so blue, so cold – pinned her in place until she could hardly breathe. 'No,' he said simply. 'I do not offer. *I take.*'

150

She was trembling. His hands were so hard on her and yet they held without pain, as if promising the pain to come. She thought she wanted it. She thought she wanted *him*, as he stood so close with his hands on her and his eyes holding her so still and her heart hammering so hard against her chest.

Elizabeth felt a strange shuddering weakness run through her breasts to her stomach, then lower, until her thighs ached with it. And she was somehow quite certain that if she fell, he would catch her.

She tried to say his name, to protest, but then his mouth was on hers and she thought she was drowning. She thought only his hands kept her above water, and the air she gulped was his own.

His fingers were in her hair at the back of her neck, his thumbs spread to cup her jaw. He imprisoned her there, moving his mouth on hers until she was breathless and shaking harder than before. And yet something within her drew back. Something told her it was *O'Neill* who had had the beginning of this, not Bagenal at all. *O'Neill* who had first violated her mouth and taught her what a man's could do to her soul.

And it was the Irishman she wanted.

Elizabeth shuddered once, convulsively. And then Bagenal's mouth was gone. His eyes held the hard, cruel glint she had seen before, but he was smiling very faintly.

'I do not offer,' he said again. 'What I will have, I take. And you will have to come to me.'

The odd languor Elizabeth had begun to experience slid away abruptly. She felt stiff and awkward, staring at him in confusion that became a slow, rising anger. 'What did you say?'

'You will have to come to me.'

She stared up into the face of male self-assurance in utter disbelief. 'Do you think I *would?*'

151

'No. I know it. And you will.' He reached up to push a fallen tawny curl into place. 'I am a very patient man. I can wait.'

Elizabeth drew back stiffly. 'Then you will wait forever! Are you as patient as *that*?'

Bagenal laughed. 'Oh, yes, mistress. I am.'

14

She left him. She went from the gallery at once, wanting only to get as far from Simon Bagenal as she could. What had possessed her to go with him in the first place?

Elizabeth knew the answer. Because for a moment she had thought he might be different. And for a moment she had *wanted* his mouth on hers, his hands touching her, and now she was sickened by her wantonness. Had the King's court done it to her? Had she become like everyone else, seeking a man out for physical pleasure that had nothing at all to do with the bonds of marriage? Was she becoming as hard and cold as so many of the other women, playing for a man's protection even as Bagenal himself had said she would?

Elizabeth was disgusted with herself. But she was also frightened suddenly. Never before had she experienced such tension within her body. Never before had she looked at a man's mouth and wanted it to fasten itself to her own. When Bagenal had captured her head in his strong hands she had wanted them to do more, sliding lower to caress the silken flesh of her shoulders, moving lower still. As O'Neill's hands had.

Dear God – what has that savage Irishman done to me?

Outside a private entrance to the Presence Chamber, she stopped. Hands flew to make certain her skirts were in order, that her bodice showed no effects of Bagenal's kiss. Her hair – was it loosened? Was her face flushed? Dear God, what had she allowed herself to become?

Elizabeth shut her eyes and tried to regain her composure. She could not stand outside the chamber much longer; someone would surely arrive, desiring to go in or come out, and though they would not question her, they would wonder. She could not afford it.

She cleared her throat and drew a deep breath, then fabricated a smile. And she pushed open the door and went in.

The room was much as she had left it. James was not present, but the King's absence did not necessarily hamper the ordinary goings-on of his court. If anything, it allowed everyone more freedom in what they said, what they planned, what they hoped for.

Elizabeth drew in a deep breath of relief, hoping no one would note her rather abrupt return after a somewhat less abrupt departure. And then the doors to the main entrance flew open as bowing footmen pushed them, and the chamberlain was announcing His Majesty James I of England, VI of Scotland. Dropping into a curtsy even as the other women did, Elizabeth wondered if James himself ever got confused by the ordering of his realms. First of this, sixth of that.

The chamberlain continued, and she realized James was accompanied by two men. She heard the chamberlain announce one as Messere Andrea Lucca, personal emissary from His Holiness Pope Paul, and Matteo Pelli, his personal secretary. She glanced up in absent curiosity – and froze.

His face was smooth, bland, a stranger's beneath an unfamiliar beard. He wore his customary black, but gone were the leathers and rough woollens he had worn before. He was attired in rich velvet trimmed with gold, and worked into the left breast was the papal crest.

Papal crest? O'Neill? What is O'Neill doing in Vatican livery?

James waved his hand, giving permission for all to rise from bows and curtsies. Elizabeth automatically settled

154

her green skirts into place and tried not to stare at O'Neill. She was not altogether successful, though she managed to keep herself from gaping like a fool. But then it wouldn't have mattered. Every other woman in the chamber gaped.

Next to O'Neill, the King faded into nonexistence. All of James's satins, silks and velvets, pleats and lacy collars made him resemble a capon prepared for dinner. O'Neill – hard-faced, green eyes slitted – was a cat in the aviary; a panther, stalking through the forest with all his prey before him.

And Elizabeth, looking at him, felt a surge of sheer physical response that nearly overwhelmed her senses.

Dear God – what has he done to me?

'Are you quite well?'

She started as the hand was placed upon the junction of neck and shoulder. Bagenal. She should have known. 'Well enough,' she said brusquely.

'You are pale, Elizabeth. Have you taken ill?'

She looked into his smooth, bland face. 'No,' she said distinctly, 'I have not. Though if you press your attentions on me again, I might.'

Bagenal's laughter was soft, intimate. 'But you desired it as much as I, mistress. Do not seek to tell me otherwise. I am somewhat more experienced at judging a woman's readiness than you are.'

Elizabeth opened her mouth to retort, then shut it again. Like all the others, Bagenal was looking at O'Neill as he and Bard and the King made a slow circuit of the chamber. 'Who is this?' he asked in an idle tone. 'Who does Jamie present?'

'The chamberlain said his name was – Lucca.' For a moment she had forgotten the assumed name. 'Andrea Lucca, from the Pope. And – Matteo Pelli. Secretary to Lucca.'

'The Pope?' Bagenal frowned. 'What could the Pope be wanting with James?'

Elizabeth shrugged. 'Surely it is the King's business.'

He glanced down at her. 'The King's business is quite often my own. But you will learn that.'

She could not answer him because the King stood before them. And with him, all blandness and polite attention, was O'Neill.

'Lucca,' James was saying, 'let me present to you one of my especial favourites. Mistress Elizabeth Stafford, my bonny Lizzie.' James smiled. 'Is she not a bonny lass?'

O'Neill's answering smile was merely polite. 'Of course, Your Majesty. A very bonny lass.' There was only the slightest hint of recognition in his eyes. She looked past him and saw Bard, whose eyes held all the wary possessiveness she had seen before. And abruptly she recalled the promise she had made to him.

'And one of my most trusted aides,' James was saying. 'Sir Simon Bagenal.'

Elizabeth saw the merest flash in the green glass of O'Neill's eyes, and then it was gone. 'A distinct honour, *signore,* to meet an Englishman of such high repute.'

The accent was different. No more Irish lilt. It sounded foreign somehow . . . and then she placed it. Italian. But of course. An Italian named Andrea Lucca from the Pope. Gone was the Irish rebel she had known, and yet even as he stood before her he filled the chamber with rebellion.

Irishman, she thought, *I have only to say a word or two to the King* . . . But she did not. she recalled how he had threatened her life. She recalled how he had included her father in that threat as well.

Bagenal's hand remained on the soft flesh of shoulder and neck. His touch was eminently possessive, particularly as one finger gently caressed her neck. James was

156

pleased; she could see it in his eyes. But in O'Neill's eyes she saw nothing. No hint of jealousy, dislike. Not even amusement. Merely a calm acknowledgement of the Englishman's possession of her.

She wanted to scream at him. She wanted to shout at him that she was not Bagenal's, that she was the same woman he had kissed in the stable. The same woman he had so nearly seduced in her own borrowed bed, when she had been so close to giving in. But she did not scream at him. She couldn't. She did not dare reveal she knew him.

And so she stood there staring at him, wishing he would say something to her, while Bagenal kept his hand on her shoulder.

The King indicated it was time to go on. O'Neill swept into a elegant bow. *'Madonna,'* he said graciously, and moved on, with Bard accompanying them.

Elizabeth waited until they were out of earshot. Then she turned out from under Bagenal's grasping hand and faced him, so furious she was white-faced. 'What in the name of God was *that* mummery about?' She dared not shout it, as she longed to – the court would hear. But her furious whisper transmitted her rage quite clearly.

Bagenal was unmoved. 'That mummery, my dear, was all part of the game.'

'I am not playing,' she said grimly, through gritted teeth. 'Find another partner. Better yet – choose another opponent.'

He smiled. 'No, mistress . . . I find I like the one I have.'

'You embarrassed me before them,' she accused. 'You made them think – '

He interrupted smoothly. 'I know what I made them think. I do very little without good reason.' Before she could respond he reached out and caught a tendril of her hair that coiled on her neck. He stretched the strand out, as if he intended to banish the curl, and touched the tips to his mouth. His eyes were fastened on her own in silent challenge as he kissed the hair provocatively.

Elizabeth reached up and jerked the hair away. 'I would *suggest*,' she said in bitter frustration, 'you turn your attentions elsewhere.'

His shrug was faint, indolent. 'I am bored by court conduct. I am bored by the usual game. I make my own, and the rules – or absence thereof – to accompany it.' His blue eyes glinted oddly a moment. 'Mistress, I think we are much alike. And when you have realized it you will understand me.'

'I understand only that I wish you to leave me alone,' she said clearly. 'Please go.'

His face was quite bland as he smiled, blue eyes implacable once more. He bowed. 'As you wish, mistress. You will find, upon occasion, there are times I *will* do your bidding.'

Elizabeth watched him move away into the other groups. She was alone again – if it was possible to *be* alone in a room holding more than two hundred people. She felt locked in stone, as if the sculptor's chisel and mallet had brought most of her to life while leaving her feet unmade, still bound to the raw stone. She was utterly alive, breathing and trembling and trying very hard to understand what was happening to her. But she could not. She could think only of Bagenal's cool possessiveness and O'Neill's apparent indifference.

Does he think me a whore, then? Does he think me the cold, scheming woman who went to court to catch a wealthy, titled husband, as he once suggested? Does he believe I have lain with Bagenal when I would not with him?

She shut her eyes, shoulders drooping. For a moment

158

she felt helpless, filled with emptiness and futility and the hollow pain of repudiation.

And then she recalled how she had run from O'Neill in the darkness, and how she had run from Bagenal in the sunlight, and wondered if she would run from every man.

Elizabeth yanked her skirts into place with a silent, unladylike curse and went out of the Presence Chamber.

Alice stared at her mistress in astonishment. She had served her devotedly for more than two months, and while Elizabeth had always seemed happy enough to be at court wearing all the finery her father had purchased, never had she seemed fully caught up in the proceedings. Now she bathed with a vengeance, scrubbing at her legs with a soft cloth and scented soap until her ivory skin shone pale pink. Her shining hair was piled on top of her head, but a few heavy strands fell down to curl in the dampness. Alice thought her mistress the most beautiful woman she had ever seen; she knew for a fact most of the men at court thought so as well.

'Mistress?' she ventured. 'May I help you?'

'Make ready the burnt-rose gown,' Elizabeth told her absently. 'And the pearls.'

Thoughtfully Alice took the gown from the clothespress and began to shake out the heavy watered-silk skirts. The bodice was heavy brocade, cut lower than Elizabeth usually wore. At the narrow waist it was stiffened with whalebone. The puffed sleeves, matching the skirts, were also of watered silk, slashed to show an undersleeve of sheer Brussels lace. Overall the colour was a rich burnt rose, subdued enough not to overwhelm Elizabeth's old-gold and ivory colouring, but exquisite enough to point out her fairness with palest dusty pink. It would lend colour to her mouth and cheeks.

Elizabeth climbed out of the bath, drying herself with a

thick towel draped conveniently near the tub. Then, with Alice's help, she slipped into the cool, soft undershift, liking the way its silken folds slid down over her breasts and hips. She was more aware of her body than she had ever been before, and for the first time in her life she intended to see just how much attention it won her.

She sat down before the mirror and let Alice dress her hair. Once again the heavy tawny hair was brushed until it shone, dried where she had dampened it in the tub, then pinned up on her head. Alice coaxed a few strands back down to curl against Elizabeth's slender neck, enhancing its elegant length.

Around her neck Elizabeth placed the pearl necklet her father had purchased. In her brief time at court she had had jewels of all sizes and cuts thrust upon her, and she had refused them all. Accepting them would make her no better than a whore in her own eyes, and she refused to give in.

'Mistress,' Alice breathed, 'you are so beautiful.'

Elizabeth stared at her reflection. For only a moment she saw a stranger, and for that moment she saw the delicacy of the features – the straight nose and curving lips, wide-spaced honey-pale eyes, flawless skin stretched so smoothly over magnificent bones. But the strangeness faded and she knew the face for her own, and she could no longer see it as others did.

Beautiful enough? she wondered.

With Alice's assistance she put on her gown and stood silently as all the laces were done. Elizabeth was suddenly reminded of O'Neill's hands spreading the unlaced back of another gown, sliding a big, callused hand across the soft expanse of flesh no man's hand had touched before.

She recalled quite clearly the possessive strength in his hands as he cupped her buttocks and cradled one breast, his mouth burning down across her shoulder. Then, she

160

had hardly been aware of what he did, too angry to receive the signals her body sent her. Now, though knowing little more than she had then, she was beginning to understand. She had somehow sensitized herself to his touch, and her body merely waited for fulfilment.

Elizabeth felt a knot of tension form deep in her belly. For a moment she thought she might be ill, and then she realized it was not the discomfort of nausea. It was something quite different. She stood there with her arms hanging loosely at her sides while Alice did up the laces and wondered how long it would take O'Neill to *undo* them.

Elizabeth felt the fiery blush surge into her face, so hot and sudden it scalded down across her throat and touched her breasts. *What in God's name has become of me? What am I doing garbing myself for a man and then wondering how he might undress me?*

And was it possible O'Neill's assessment of her character had been correct – that she would sell herself to the man with the oldest, proudest title?

'There.' Alice settled the folds of the skirts into place. 'You are ready, mistress.'

Am I? she wondered grimly. But she gathered up her silken skirts, with a word of thanks to Alice, and left the room.

Elizabeth was admitted to the Presence Chamber without fanfare, which is precisely what she wanted. And yet as she entered, making her way slowly through the ever-present throng, she was intensely aware of the male eyes moving to her, following her progress. She knew most of the men by now. Some of them had pursued her diligently while others had given up the chase for easier game. But all were fascinated by her, and for once she was intensely aware of it.

She saw the King rising from his throne. It was time for

the throng to exit the chamber and move instead to the banqueting hall, where tumblers and musicians would entertain throughout the meal. And with the King, towering over the smaller man, stood O'Neill, black on black with a hint of gold and green.

'My dear.' It was Edwin Stafford, moving to her side. 'You are *magnificent*. But a trifle pale. Are you quite well?'

She looked up into his face for one blind instant, still seeing O'Neill's brilliant eyes. Then the image dissolved itself into her father's austere face, and Elizabeth saw the frown marring his brow. 'I am well enough,' she answered.

'Are you?' His hand was on her arm. 'You look as if you had seen a ghost.'

How apropos. But Elizabeth smiled and shook her head. 'I think I am merely a trifle weary. The meal will improve my spirits.'

His hand moved to her elbow, steering her towards the series of corridors that would empty the Presence Chamber and then fill up the banqueting hall. 'You are really quite remarkably lovely,' he said calmly. 'Should I ask which man it is you honour with this gown?'

She glanced at him sharply. How could he know? How could he so easily unmask her, when she hardly knew what she sought herself?

Stafford smiled blandly. 'I saw you and Sir Simon in conversation earlier. And I saw you leave with him. For a woman who has so valiantly guarded her virtue in such a licentious court, it was a departure that everyone marked with some astonishment.'

Her tone was curt. 'And no doubt there was some discussion of it.'

'But of course,' he answered. 'The women are quite disturbed that you have cut them out yet again, for Sir

162

Simon Bagenal is one of the most highly desired suitors in the realm. You have stolen their thunder yet again.'

'I have stolen nothing,' she retorted. 'He is not my suitor.'

Stafford smiled indulgently. 'Not yet, perhaps, but things seem to be progressing well. Bagenal does not care for the games other women so often play.'

No, she agreed wryly. *He plays his own.*

'It *is* unusual for Bagenal to single out a woman before the eyes of the court,' Stafford went on as they made their way down a second corridor. 'He has paid you particular honour.'

'And isn't that precisely what you desire?' Elizabeth ignored the flash of irritation in his brown eyes. 'Haven't you brought me here in order to bargain me away for a bit of gold or – better yet – a title?'

'Elizabeth – ' His hand tightened on her arm. 'I beg you, keep your voice down. And I begin to think perhaps you *are* ill. A tray in your chambers might serve better.'

'No,' she said calmly. 'That would not serve at all. Then Sir Simon could not see me – nor could any of the others.' She looked him squarely in the eye. 'I begin to understand you, my lord father . . . there is no further need for dissembling.'

Stafford looked at his daughter. The gown did exquisite things for her colouring, but the rest was a natural grace he was not responsible for. Elizabeth's time at court had dispelled some of the innocence and put just a hint of worldliness in her eyes, a new sophistication, but she retained the elegance and freshness that so captured the eyes and hearts – and the desires – of the men. But the sweet, lush mouth had lost much of its sweetness, set in a rather hard line as she stared at him. It made her chin rather pronounced in a delicate, defiant way.

'I do not dissemble before you,' he answered smoothly,

leading her onwards. 'Like any father, I desire a happy union for my daughter. Naturally I also desire the man most able to provide for her to become her husband. Would you expect less?'

'How could I?' She put no inflection in her tone.

Satisfied, he smiled. 'Then you understand that *everything* I do is done for you.'

Her mouth flattened further. 'Of *course*.'

'Then I may expect you to do as I, your father, say you must?'

Elizabeth looked into his cold face and saw the faintest trace of Bagenal there. Perhaps the man was more like her father and less like O'Neill, who was brutally forthright if nothing else.

And then she recalled the Irishman had come to court as an emissary for the Pope, a cock-and-bull story she could not possibly believe. Perhaps she knew none of them after all, or what they wanted.

'I will do as you say,' she agreed coolly, 'provided it agrees with what *I* want.'

Stafford looked at her sharply. 'What *do* you want, Elizabeth? I assure you, if it is within my power to get it for you, I shall.'

Her eyes sought and found O'Neill as he strolled the corridor with his royal host. *No,* she thought, *O'Neill is not the sort to do any man's bidding . . . save his own.*

15

The high table rested on a dais that stretched the width of the hall. It was here the King and Queen sat, plus any particularly favoured or honoured guests. The rest of the court had to accept placement at the lower tables set in regimental lines the length of the hall, so that the arrangement was in the shape of a large, rectangular U. The centre was kept clear for serving, and for the entertainments that attended every meal.

Most of the time James ignored the entertainments, preferring to make his own with his current favourite. Elizabeth felt rather sorry for the tumblers and dancers and musicians who came to court hoping to receive royal notice and equally royal gold; most of the time they performed in obscurity and vanished into the same. Meals were noisy affairs, with men calling across the opening to others while servants arrived with platters overflowing with meats and breads and delicacies enough to make the heartiest trencherman groan. Wine flowed freely. So did conversation.

The salt, as always, marked the border between the favoured and the unpopular, or those of lower rank. The huge silver cellars stood sentinel in the exact centre of each table; lest a body forget precisely where he or she should sit, a chamberlain made certain of the placement by directing each individual to the proper seat on the long benches.

Elizabeth allowed the liveried man to escort her to her place at the table and then stopped short as she saw the man who was placed at her right.

Simon Bagenal rose at once, bowing elegantly. One hand reached out and took her elbow, gently urging her to take her place. Elizabeth flashed him an angry glance but allowed him to seat her. If she made too much of a protest, she might well be banished to the lower end of the table, and too many people would be happy to take her place permanently. She could not risk it.

'Was it *your* idea to have me placed here?' She caught up a silver wine goblet from a passing servant.

'*I* assumed it was yours.' His voice was quite bland as he smoothed a smudge from his own goblet.

'No,' she said briefly. 'I would prefer we did not meet again, as we sup or otherwise.'

Bagenal's smile was very faint, and it did not melt the pale iciness of his eyes. 'As you wish, mistress.'

Elizabeth glanced at him sharply. She realized, somewhat abruptly, that she knew nothing about the man. He irritated her and yet she could not say why, except to believe it had something to do with his arrogant manner. She had heard nothing but how much the ladies of court wanted him; as far as Elizabeth was concerned, they could have him. She wanted nothing to do with him.

And yet she could not suppress the flicker of curiosity within herself. Simon Bagenal was an intriguing man, and she wondered precisely what he wanted out of life.

Idly Elizabeth glanced to her left and discovered an old man nearly asleep in his food. His was an ancient name and an even older title; she wondered that it did not pass quickly to a younger heir. And so she was faced with a choice between a senile bag of brittle bones or a coolly composed man who frightened her in some strange, curious way.

But she could not ignore Bagenal. He served her from passing platters until her plate was piled with eels and salmon and sweet roast beef; her cup was filled with good wine the moment she emptied it. Elizabeth wondered if she would lose herself in liquor the way men did. It made them feel reckless and insensible, and she had the feeling she might need the latter if she succumbed to the former.

But he did not talk to her. He merely watched her, as if he waited, and though Elizabeth was quite determined to keep her silence, his was more powerful than hers. She felt herself become clumsy under his watching eyes and knew once again the hot blush climbed into her face. She stared angrily across to the other table in an effort to ignore Bagenal and found herself suddenly looking directly at O'Neill.

For a moment Elizabeth could not breathe. She stared at him in frozen silence, seeing the rich black velvets and the papal crest on his left breast. He lifted a shining goblet and drank, but all the while his brilliant eyes were fixed on her so compellingly she could not look away.

Her heart thumped heavily once, so hard she thought it would tear the flesh from her bones, and then it settled down into an uneven rhythm that did nothing to help her peace of mind. What was he thinking as he saw her with Bagenal? Did their apparent closeness merely confirm what he had seen in the Presence Chamber?

More than ever Elizabeth wanted to leave Bagenal, and yet she could not. She wanted to go at once to O'Neill and demand an explanation for his presence, hoping he would ask one from her so she could tell him she cared nothing at all for Bagenal. It was important he know that, and yet she was quite certain he did not care. He looked at her as any man would – as all of them *had* – a gentleman momentarily impressed by a woman's beauty, and yet he gave her no more than a moment's fleeting consideration.

With deliberation O'Neill looked away from her, and she felt her hands turn icy on the wine goblet she held.

'Do you know him?' Bagenal asked.

She wrenched her eyes from O'Neill, realizing how intently she stared. 'No. No – of course not. I merely consider him an arresting man.'

Bagenal's smile was patronizing. 'Women are so often attracted to the unusual – or the foreign. Are you like all the others?'

Elizabeth smiled back, though it lacked all humour. 'How could that be? I am not attracted to *you*.'

'Are you not?' The tone was idle.

'Surely you have heard about me.' She spoke with studied lightness. 'Surely you know that no man at court has been able to win anything more than a kiss from me, and that unwilling.'

Bagenal looked at her directly. He did not smile. 'Mistress, I intend to *win* nothing from you . . . as you should well recall from the intimacy we shared earlier in the gallery. What I want, I take.'

The fish Elizabeth had eaten suddenly swam in her stomach. She choked down the bile that threatened to disgrace her and covered her mouth with a linen napkin. It was Bagenal who held the cup to her lips and made her drink, and when she had swallowed she felt better almost at once. But she could not thank him.

The tumblers began their entertainment. The troupe built human pyramids and ladders and intricate knots of contorted flesh, but no one paid them much mind. Elizabeth, staring blindly at the moving bodies, suddenly realized O'Neill had looked in her direction again. Their gazes locked across the blur of movement and she saw how brilliant were his eyes and how solemn his bearded, unsmiling face.

And then he smiled. It lacked the recognition she longed to see – merely a tribute to a lovely woman any foreigner might bestow – but it was more than she expected. Something deep inside twisted as she saw the mocking glint in his eyes and the familiar curl of his lips. The expression was gone in an instant, but she understood it.

He has satisfied his curiosity about me. No more does he care with whom I am seen.

And so she knew the truth. The rejection hurt so badly, she wanted to cry, knowing she dared not. There was nothing between them. She was nothing to him, and he was somehow becoming *everything* to her.

'He had better look elsewhere,' Bagenal said lightly. 'He is a stranger at court, and I think it more likely he will find easier conquests in the serving maids, who will so eagerly spread their skirts for coin, foreign or no.'

What has O'Neill done to me? He is an Irish rebel – *enemy to my country and my king* . . . Elizabeth looked at Bagenal swiftly, but his glacial eyes were fixed on O'Neill. She felt the hollowness of fear enter into her chest. *O'Neill is a traitor. He means harm to England* . . . But she knew she would not give away his identity, and not only because he had threatened her.

'Do you know why he has come?' Bagenal lifted the silver goblet to his mouth.

Elizabeth's heart leapt up, then settled down. 'No. Of course not.'

Bagenal frowned. 'He is from Pope Paul.' The faintest trace of emotion underscored his tone – disdain. 'He thinks to win the King's sanction for withdrawing our settlers from Ireland. He bears a message from the Pope, he claims, asking that the King of Great Britain, Scotland, and Ireland give Ireland back to the Irish.' And suddenly there was colour in his face and the hard glitter of hatred in his eyes. 'As if we would *ever* allow those savages to take back what they could not hold before!'

Elizabeth sat very still upon the bench. She was aware of Bagenal's closeness and the sudden tension in his body, tight as wire. 'Will the King do it, do you think?' She spoke only because she had to lance a boil that was so close to exploding.

'*Ha!*' Bagenal's disgust was unfeigned. 'James keeps what is his – what others before him have fought to hold. Andrea Lucca is a fool if he believes the Pope can sway the King.'

'He spoke to you?' she asked in surprise. 'The . . . Italian?'

Bagenal's nostrils were pinched. 'He spoke to several of us, though only after the King gave him leave. I doubt not they will have private meetings, but James is shrewd enough to let the business be known by all. It is an underhanded trick of a Papist Italian to come begging on Ireland's behalf when he has no interest in it except personal gain.' His lips twisted in contempt. 'I wonder what the Irish promised him? I wonder what the *Pope* promised him!'

Ireland, Elizabeth thought, *and he has promised it to himself.*

'The King is leaving.' Bagenal rose, for when royalty departed it was acknowledged the meal was finished. Those who had not eaten would go hungry, unless they bribed the kitchen maids to bring them a tray.

Elizabeth got to her feet. Before Bagenal could say any more she slipped away from him, joining the knots of people drifting from the banqueting hall back into the corridors. She did not consciously look for O'Neill among them, but she knew he would be there.

And yet he wasn't. When she reached the entrance to the Presence Chamber she found many there before her, but none of them was O'Neill. She turned to go in, suddenly so disappointed that she wanted only to leave, and came face-to-face with Bard.

'*Madonna,*' he said smoothly. 'Forgive me – I have no acquaintance with your name.'

Elizabeth glared at him briefly, then altered her expression into one of polite indifference as others glanced at them. 'Mistress Stafford,' she told him, 'in service to Queen Anne.'

He escorted her into the chamber. 'And how does such fortuitous service serve *you?*'

She wanted to glare again; could not. 'At the moment, poorly.' She maintained an even tone. 'There are times when the company leaves much to be desired.'

Bard's blue eyes flickered. 'Does *madonna* refer to the gentleman with her now? The gentleman who wears His Holiness's livery? Or could it be the gentleman who accompanied her at table?'

Then he senses the tension between Bagenal and myself. . . . It was something. If Bard felt it, perhaps O'Neill would.

Elizabeth favoured him with a genuine smile. 'The company at table was unexpected – and quite displeasing.'

'But not this afternoon?' he inquired; delicate contempt.

She knew he referred to Bagenal's possessiveness. Elizabeth smiled again, showing bared teeth a moment, and then hid her mouth with a coquettish hand for the benefit of others. 'This afternoon *in particular* was distressing.' She affected a shrug. 'But what can one do?'

'Surely you expected it.' Bard watched the others moving around the chamber in their eternal dance. 'Why else come?'

'To serve the Queen.' Her words were elaborately distinct. 'Nothing more.'

His eyes looked past her. 'The King.' His voice registered a peculiar note, and he ran a hand down one black-hosed thigh. 'It is time I served my own master.'

171

Elizabeth arched her brows. 'The *Pope?*' she inquired.

Bard bowed. 'But of course, *madonna*.' And then she was alone again, but only until she sensed O'Neill behind her.

'The colour becomes you.' His voice was very quiet. 'But then I have yet to see you in one that does not.'

He spoke with the Italian accent, but the tonal quality was the same. Elizabeth heard the rich, dark timbre and longed for the lilting cadences she had come to know in Kent. But that O'Neill was gone, banished beneath a smooth, courtly outer shell that hid the man entirely.

'Do you truly serve the Pope, *signore?*' She turned to face him. 'Or have you somehow elevated yourself to the right hand of God without benefit of sacraments and ordinations?'

'His Holiness desires peace in all lands,' he replied unctuously. 'He is genuinely concerned that, as a Catholic country, Ireland is being suppressed.'

'And so you have come to plead *his* cause before the King.'

'I plead Ireland's cause,' O'Neill said evenly, 'at the Pope's behest.'

She did not believe him. She knew him. 'Who are you, *signore?* Tell me your history.'

He smiled. 'I am the son of an Italian nobleman and an English mother. My English blood is what accounts for the colour of my eyes of course.'

Elizabeth nearly laughed at him. 'Your *English* mother? You?'

'But of course.' His face and voice were quite bland.

'*You* would claim Sassenach blood, even for this?'

'*English* blood,' he stressed calmly. 'When I must.'

'And now you must.'

'I think it most politic.' He was standing next to her now, and, like Bard, he kept his eyes moving idly over

172

the others in the chamber. It would not do for them to be seen in deep conversation. 'I do not look particularly Italian.'

Elizabeth agreed with him emphatically. But she said nothing. And when O'Neill turned to her again, letting his eyes drift down across her shoulders to her breasts, and lower still to the slender waist and belling skirts, she felt the knot of tension form and break, spreading heat throughout her body. She was suddenly intensely restless and quite short of breath.

'Where can we be alone?' His eyes did not move from her face.

Elizabeth thought she misunderstood him. O'Neill would not *ask* – he would tell.

But this was not O'Neill. This was Andrea Lucca, and if he wished to play *that* game, she would as well.

Her throat was tight. 'There is a gallery. There are paintings in it. Go from this room through the corridor and turn to your right. There you will find two doors. Open them, and you will find yourself surrounded by royalty.' She drew in a trembling breath and tried to smile. 'The kings are quite fierce, but I think they will do nothing.'

He was unsmiling. He himself looked terribly fierce, with his black brows drawn down and his eyes fastened on her so intently, but then the intensity vanished. He was smiling again, as if they shared a meaningless conversation in a room full of such.

But when he spoke his words turned her bones to ice. 'I thought you had no intention of wading in Jamie's pond.'

She stared at him. 'Wh-what?'

'Had I asked you where we could be alone two months ago, you would have cried insult. And *now* you give me careful, precise directions on how to reach my destination.' His mouth, shadowed by the beard, was taut. 'Mistress – you have given me the answers to questions I asked myself some time ago.'

She felt numb. 'Questions?'

He swung around to face her squarely. 'I asked myself if you would remain innocent for long. I asked myself was I a fool to let you go with your virtue intact. I think it is no to the first and aye to the latter.'

She stopped herself from crying out his name. She saw a flicker in his eyes and wondered if he was at all concerned that his future was held so firmly in her hands, but the answer was obvious. He held hers already, and he would not say such cruel things otherwise.

She wavered, trapped between a desperate longing to flee the chamber, and escape the humiliation of what he thought of her, and the knowledge that to do so would betray him and place herself in danger.

'*Go,*' he said roughly. 'Did you think I would not come?'

Elizabeth went. And when she reached the gallery she realized what she had done, and what it meant, and what he would expect of her.

She stood before the portrait of James V. His piercing eyes were still as bold and compelling and his face bore no trace of kindness. And yet he had sired a daughter who had been too kind, giving her favours to any man she thought handsome enough, and kind enough, and it had resulted in the murder of her second husband and the imprisonment of her third, who had conspired to murder the second, and who went mad in a Danish prison. For Mary herself there had been the long journey to the scaffold.

Is there any kindness in O'Neill? she wondered. She thought not. She thought him a hard, ruthless, cold man, intent on war no matter what the cost. And she was an

Englishwoman – a *Sassenach* – who even now considered what it would be to let a savage Irishman take her to bed.

Elizabeth shut her eyes, shivering as she hugged herself. She knew she should turn and walk away from the painting; away from the gallery; away from O'Neill, seeking safety in her own rooms until her father found the man he wished her to wed, and the longing for a man's mouth and arms would become right in the sight of God.

She heard him come. He moved silently as any cat, and yet she knew he was there. She felt it the moment his presence entered the gallery.

The doors he closed soundlessly, and then he was behind her. She felt his hands come down on her shoulders; he pulled her back against his chest as she faced James V. He said nothing. His arms slid down over her breasts to rest around her rib cage, imprisoning her, and Elizabeth knew she was lost.

'*Eilis*,' he said, and all the singing lilt of Ireland was in his voice.

A tremor ran through her body. Suddenly her skin flushed with a warmth that brought a fine sheen of perspiration to every inch of her body, and she knew only the dress was too heavy, too hot, and she wanted it off. Her lips, breasts, and thighs tingled with a dull ache that was exquisitely painful, yet it was the pain of need, of longing, and not of injury or illness. Something contracted deep within her stomach, flushing her inner thighs, and she smelled the faint musky scent that had nothing at all to do with the perfumed soap she had used.

'*O'Neill*,' she groaned, and his arms tightened until she could hardly breathe.

Elizabeth twisted, moving out of his arms so she could face him. From a great distance she saw her hands go out to the collar of his velvet doublet, tugging at the frogged fastenings.

His mouth moved into a familiar mocking smile. 'So impatient, mistress? Have you drunk the heady wine of love and found you crave its taste?'

The first fastening was undone, baring his browned throat. Her hands moved against his skin, creeping up to clasp his neck, revelling in the warmth of his flesh that must be equal to her own. Elizabeth stood on tiptoe against his great height and lifted her face, her mouth begging for his.

'Have you?' he asked. 'Do you seek to compare an Irishman against a Sassenach?'

'O'Neill!'

He smiled. 'Better. It sounds more like you, mistress. I thought the faeries had put a changeling in your place, for how else do I explain your sudden desire for my – company?'

She drew back from him. 'Then this was a *test*? Your way of discovering how easily you can make an English-woman answer an Irishman's bidding?'

'Has Bagenal bedded you?'

'No!'

'The King?'

'*No!*'

'Then who has?'

'*No one!*'

'Are you sure?' he asked intently. 'Are you *quite sure?*'

'Yes!' she shouted, and then he had her in his arms and was crushing the life from her.

Elizabeth felt the cry rising from the depths of her soul. But it wasn't a cry of outrage or fear. It was a sound she could not hold back, bursting forth as she welcomed his assault on her mouth. But it was lost in a muted whimper as she pressed herself against him.

'By Christ!' he said finally, raggedly. 'What is this armour you have on?'

'Armour?'

'*Laces!*'

She laughed. The sound came from deep in her chest and sounded as if it issued from a throat other than her own. 'I wore it for you.'

'Were you so certain of me, mistress?'

'No. No more certain of you than of myself.'

His hands were at the back of her gown, fumbling with the tiny knots. She felt his frustration as keenly as her own, and she laughed again.

'By Christ, woman – 'tis better than a chastity belt!' His breathing was quite unsteady. 'D'ye wish me to lift your skirts like any serving wench and forget a sweeter part of lovemaking then?'

'You have lost your accent, O'Neill.' She giggled. 'The *Italian* one.'

His hands crushed her shoulders. 'D'ye wish me taken, mistress? Say again my name!'

'Do you think I would?' she demanded. 'Do you think I would betray you to the King when you have threatened my life?'

He snorted inelegantly. 'Your life, indeed . . . this moment, I threaten something else entirely.' His fingertips moved softly across her lips, stilling them with a gentle caress. But his voice was harsh. 'Where are your chambers, Eilis?'

Her heart quickened. For the moment he had stopped fumbling at her laces. 'I share a room with my maid.'

'By Christ, first 'tis laces and now a maid! D'ye *want* me, mistress, or is this your way of driving me mad?'

'*O'Neill.*' She whispered it against his mouth, savouring the name, and then thrust her tongue into the warmth beyond his teeth.

He growled in sheer, unbridled frustration and picked

her up, swinging her into his arms. 'Then I'll be having you in *my own* chambers!'

'No!' She twisted in his arms. 'What of Bard?'

'To hell with Bard!' O'Neill strode towards the end of the shadowed gallery. 'Likely he is too busy with the King's pleasures to pay any mind to mine.'

Elizabeth gripped his arms as he set her down by the doors. 'What is *Bard* doing with the King?'

'Seducing him, I assume. 'Tis what he planned to do.' O'Neill's hand was on the doorknob.

Elizabeth frowned at him, confused by the reference. 'But – what does *Bard* have that would interest the King?'

O'Neill stood very still. His eyes, in the faint starlight coming through the windows, were strange. 'Himself,' he said quietly. 'Are you so blind, Eilis, that you cannot see a man may love a man instead of a woman?'

She collided with the door as she took a giant step backward. Her head bounced against the wood. 'Bard?' she whispered. '*With the King?*'

O'Neill shrugged. 'Jamie has a liking for boys. Surely you must know that, being part of his court.'

She *had* known that, but: '*Bard . . . ?*'

O'Neill's voice was very quiet. 'Bard does not care for women. I though you knew that.'

'N-no . . .' She shook her head. 'No.'

He shrugged again. 'I had forgotten how cloistered you were in your father's house. 'Tis common enough, especially in courts. Jamie's is no different from the French one – unless one counts the Sassenach prudery, which has some effect on outward displays of such feelings.'

Elizabeth put her hands to her face, aware of an odd numbness. 'You said . . . you said he *planned* this . . .'

'Oh, aye. Women know how to buy favours with their bodies. Why should a man not play at the same game?'

'You *approve?*' It tainted him somehow.

His voice was cold. 'I will do whatever I must for my country, mistress. So will Bard.'

'My God . . .' Elizabeth closed her eyes. *You are harder than I thought.*

'D'ye think it might be *catching?*' he asked scornfully. 'D'ye think he and I have shared a bed, then, and that I might *infect* you?' He shook his head. 'No, mistress, 'tis not true. 'Tis women for me, as you should know.'

Her trembling hand was on the knob. 'I know nothing,' she said unsteadily. 'I know nothing about you, except that you will use anything – *anyone!* – to further your own goal. Are we *all* tools, then? Do you look at *each* of us as if measuring us against the task ahead? My God, O'Neill, he is a *person!* He serves *you!* I care little enough for his bed partners, but to be so callous about it all! What manner of man *are* you?'

'An Irishman.' His face was white. 'A savage, barbaric Irishman, with no manners to speak of and very little sense. Else I would never have deluded myself into believing a Sassenach woman might be as warm and giving as some others I have known, no matter how brief the loving.' His hand closed on her throat. 'Perhaps I should have killed you when I found you . . . as I killed your coachman.'

'My *coachman!*'

'He was not dead,' O'Neill said curtly. 'He might have survived his injuries, though 'twas unlikely. But I could not have him saying where we were, and so I killed him.' His fingers dug into her flesh. 'I snapped his neck, mistress – *like so much brittle wood.*'

Elizabeth was shaking. She pressed herself flat against the door and tried to look away from his face, but she could not. She could only stare at the cold, glittering emerald eyes and cry inwardly for the woman who had so nearly loved him.

O'Neill leaned closer yet. His breath warmed her neck. 'Many of us believe *all* Sassenachs – regardless of sex – should be put to the sword. And if you mean to betray me, I will do it. I promise you.'

'You have already done it,' she said thickly. 'It is only that the corpse is still walking.'

He took his hand from her throat. He waited, and when she could move again she turned from him and went out of the gallery, shutting the door behind her.

16

When Elizabeth had gone O'Neill stood staring at the closed door. He had heard the knell of finality in its closing click, and suddenly he wanted to snatch it open again and shout after her, telling her she had no reason to fear him, that he would never harm her.

And yet he couldn't. He knew there might come a time when he *would* harm her, because she was an enemy and might mean danger to him and all of Ireland. She was a woman, only a woman, but she had learned the truth of him and his plans, and was therefore highly dangerous.

O'Neill swore. He recalled all too clearly the look of incomprehension and dawning shock in her eyes, turning her face deathly pale as she listened to him. He had not meant it to come out so cruelly. He had not meant to speak so plainly of Bard's sexual tastes, but she had given him no time to soften the truth. He had been too fired with the wanting of her, the *needing* of her, and even now his loins ached and his breathing echoed raggedly in the gallery. But he had told her, disliking himself for his bluntness, and now she understood more fully why it was Bard was so set against her.

'My Christ!' he rasped into the silence. 'Was he right after all? Do I endanger our plans because I chase a Sassenach woman like any dog smelling a bitch in heat?'

He had known he would see her at court. He had expected it. He had assumed himself capable of dissembling before them all, including the woman, because he had done it for years. But he had *not* expected the sudden stoppage of his heart as she had come into the Presence

Chamber in her rich rose gown with matching high colour in her face and her clover-honey eyes wide and bright. He had thought himself invulnerable to women whenever he chose to be, being accustomed to doing the choosing himself, but the moment he had seen her again he knew he wanted her as badly as before.

No. *Worse.*

O'Neill swore. The sight of her with Simon Bagenal had infuriated him. He had seen the man's hand upon her, heard him mouthing her name as if she were his, had known the man intended possession of her immediately, if he had not already had her. Seeing her flushed face, dilated eyes, and reddened lips told him plainly enough Bagenal had been kissing her; it had enraged him utterly before he had the chance to consider the reasons *why*. He only knew that in Kent, in his stable, she had been innocent and afraid. And now, quite obviously, she had been more than prepared to show him she was neither any longer. Why else had she met him so willingly in the gallery?

He did not fool himself into thinking his mere presence had accounted for her sudden surrender. He knew women – knew them well – and had seduced many of them precisely as he had intended to seduce Elizabeth. Only suddenly the seduction had been taken out of his hands and placed in hers, for she had shown him she wanted him as badly as he needed her. He had felt the tremors of rising passion in her body and the sudden warmth of her skin. He had seen her eyes, gone black with the wanting, and the soft alteration of her mouth, from merely lovely into lush and inviting. By Christ, it was *she* who had wanted him out of his clothes! *Her* hands had been on him first.

She said she had lain with no man, and he had believed her. He had felt such a surge of triumph in his body he thought he might die with it, so exultant was he to know she was still his. *He* would be the first to plumb the depths of her passion, the first to taste her honey and take her soaring to the heights he knew so well, wanting her to know them with him. In one brief moment he had not cared that his Italian accent was lost, intending to take her at once to his rooms, dismissing the thought of propriety. In James's court there was no such thing, and he had been quite certain Elizabeth wanted it as well, no matter what the cost.

And yet now she was gone, and permanently, because he knew she had seen a part of him she could not bear. The Kieran O'Neill who had been forged in the fires of hatred and war and the consequences of exile.

He set his spine against the door through which she had exited. His head smacked back against the wood as he clenched his teeth and shut his eyes in response to the futility of it all. A brief spasm passed over his face, a contortion of such anguish he could hardly bear it. By all the gods of ancient Erin, what had the woman done to him?

O'Neill swore violently. And then he spun and jerked open the door. He went out into the corridor, smiling a predator's smile, and walked. He walked away from the gallery. There was still his task to be done before his plans continued.

Elizabeth trembled convulsively as she walked away from the gallery and O'Neill. The sudden dispelling of tension and need by the shock of O'Neill's words had drained her of emotion. She knew only that there was a residual ache of unfulfilment in her body, telling her clearly how much she had wanted him. Her thoughts spun wildly in concert with the beating of her sore heart. She could make sense of nothing at all.

Bard. O'Neill's man. And a man who hated women.

She did not for a moment believe the master and the servant had shared the same bed, but the mere thought of Bard with any man was enough to send a trickle of utter incomprehension and distaste throughout her body. What O'Neill had charged was quite true – she *had* been cloistered in her father's house – but James's court had taught her there was all manner of licentiousness and depravity. She had known about the King's tastes. But the King was *the King;* the knowledge no longer shocked her because James himself had spoken of the *divine right of kings*. Kings were different. Kings were entitled to things other men did not desire or could not have.

But the truth of Bard's preferences disturbed her mostly because she knew him. He was more than just a nameless bed partner, more than the latest unknown conquest for James. More than the King's favourite, whose fame was fleeting at best and often ridiculed, while his power was courted for the moment. Bard was someone she *knew*.

Someone who cared for me as I lay ill. Someone I had considered perfectly normal, as normal as O'Neill . . . until O'Neill's revelation stripped it all away from me.

And in that moment she understood her shock, understood the slow beat of anger that was only just beginning to rise. Bard had betrayed her. She had always been on edge with him, sensing and yet not comprehending the complexities that drove him, but she had never hated him. She had seen him only as O'Neill's man, sworn by the bond of the Irish blood and the kinship they apparently shared. And he had used it, as he used everyone else.

Bard was O'Neill's hound as much as Boru and Cuchullain; he had said it once, and she was enraged that the master would so callously set his hound against the wolf.

'*Dear God* . . .' Elizabeth whispered. 'If the King finds

out . . .' She did not *like* Bard. He was too cold, too controlled, too dedicated to whatever demons wound themselves around his soul. And he did not like her. His dislike had reached out subtle tentacles until it affected her own feelings, shaping her regard of him into one of apprehension and resentment. *Anyone,* knowing a person dislikes them, wonders at the reason. And now she knew.

Elizabeth sensed the small tide of hurt rising in her chest. She knew he had harmed her in a way he could not imagine. He had shattered another piece of her innocence, and for that she would never forgive him.

'Mistress Stafford,' intruded the cool voice, 'you seem somewhat discomposed. It there a thing I might do for you to put it right again?'

Elizabeth looked into Simon Bagenal's blandly smiling face and stopped dead in the centre of the corridor. He seemed to be waiting for something, and she had not the strength to send him away.

'No,' she said. 'There is nothing you can do.' For he could not turn back the earth and make new again the days that had gone before, when she had not known a renegade Irishman who had put his mark upon her soul.

Bagenal's hand was on her elbow. 'Then perhaps I can escort you somewhere. Are you feeling quite well?'

She thought to put him off. 'No. I am not. And I think I would like to go to bed.'

He led her down the corridor regardless. '*Alone,* Mistress Stafford?'

In her benumbed state, it aroused only a flicker of irritation. '*Quite* alone, Sir Knight. I find I have a sudden distaste for men of any ilk.'

He laughed softly. 'And would this sudden dislike have anything to do with a green-eyed Italian I saw leaving the King's Presence Chamber – discreetly, of course – quite obviously in pursuit of the woman who has taken all of Jamie's court by storm?'

'It has nothing to do with an *Italian*.' The truth was doubly bitter.

'Ah, then perhaps I was mistaken.' But his icy eyes assured her he was not.

They had reached her rooms. Elizabeth curtsied briefly as he removed his hand from her arm. 'I thank you, sir.'

'It is a pity you choose to retire so soon,' he said smoothly, 'the revels are only just beginning.' His eyes were cold, so cold. 'His Majesty had discovered a new favourite, so I think we shall be an Italian court for a while . . . until Pelli's appeal fades, as it always must for James.'

Distaste and emptiness curled deeply in her stomach. 'Good evening, Sir Knight.'

He made an elegant leg. 'Good night . . . *Eilis*.'

Eilis – She felt a crushing weight descend upon her chest. She fought to regain her composure before she gave herself – and O'Neill – away, but she knew he must surely see the sudden pallor of her face and the widening of her eyes. 'What name did you call me?'

'Eilis?' He shrugged. 'It is Gaelic for your name, mistress. I had an Irish nursemaid, you see, when I was but a boy in Ireland.'

'*You* were in Ireland!'

He inclined his blond head. 'Briefly, during the wars. My father, you see, was Marshal of Ireland under our late Queen – before Essex. *He* kept his head, unlike poor old Devereux, but he lost his life to the Irish.' His eyes moved idly over her body. 'I think you are a likely successor to Gloriana's fame and pride, mistress . . . you bear her name better than she.'

Elizabeth could not discern his intent. She could not read any meaning into his words, though she was quite

186

certain he intended her to. She wondered if he thought she would blurt out that the papal emissary was as Irish as his old nursemaid, so Bagenal could betray him to the King.

Elizabeth smiled blandly. 'Do you remember much of Ireland? Surely it is a savage place. My brother died there . . . in the wars.'

His expression did not alter. 'I remember the pain of great loss, mistress, and the revelation of hatred's intensity.' A muscle ticked in his jaw. 'My father died in the Battle of Yellow Ford, fighting Hugh O'Neill.'

Hugh O'Neill, she echoed silently. *My dear God – O'Neill's father killed* Bagenal's.

With effort, she spoke evenly. 'I am sorry.'

'I am quite certain you are.' He bowed again. 'Good evening, mistress. I wish you an untroubled sleep.'

Elizabeth watched him walk away, and then she went slowly into her room. And she knew, quite plainly, she would get little sleep that night.

In the days that followed Elizabeth heard rumours of O'Neill's – *Lucca's* – mission from the Pope. Nearly every one was different: the Pope wanted Ireland made completely Catholic, with the Protestants banished to England; the Pope wanted Ireland declared a part of Rome herself; the Pope wanted all of the Scottish settlers converted to Catholicism.

But the truth also surfaced, and Elizabeth realized what O'Neill had come to do. He wanted James to loosen the reins upon Ireland so the Irish would know some peace. He wanted – in the Pope's name, of course – the English and Scottish settlers ousted, so the Irish could take back their homes. He wanted Ireland made *Irish* again, without the foreign influences of England and Scotland.

And she knew he would never see it. James would

never let a part of his kingdom go, not for any pope's pleading. No matter how eloquent the emissary, how passionate the emissary's secretary.

From Andrea Lucca Elizabeth learned how James, taking up the policies begun by Gloriana, had disrupted the clans by taking the lands and turning them over to the English and Scottish aristocracy. She learned how he had parcelled out the divided estates into settlements for English and Scottish farmers, so that the backbone of Ireland was broken. She learned how the clans had been driven into the hills to live like animals, without a proper home to call their own. But she learned it all through the eloquent words of Andrea Lucca, who spoke for the Pope and not for O'Neill himself. Elizabeth thought the fine, flowing words would be replaced with anger and scorn and a challenge, could the Hound of Ireland speak his mind.

But the hound was too careful. Never once did Elizabeth see a hint of his rebellious spirit or his hatred for the English. Never once did he exhibit the slightest trace of scorn for the Sassenachs and their Scottish King. Never once did he look at her with anything more than bland disinterest, and she felt the knife twisting deeply in her heart. She knew him better than anyone, save Bard himself, and she could not bear to see the hardness in his eyes.

O'Neill did not speak to her, except to say a word or two for appearances if they came face-to-face in the constant movement of the court. He did not touch her, even when required to escort her in to dinner. *Then* they walked side by side and very close, but a thousand miles apart.

Only once had she been placed next to him at table and it had been a dreadful affair. O'Neill said nothing more than custom required, and Elizabeth had been painfully aware of Bagenal's icy eyes watching them both from across the open space separating the tables. She had dared not speak to O'Neill, even had he been willing to listen.

Mostly Elizabeth was aware of what was said of O'Neill in his guise as Lucca. How the women longed for his embraces, how generous he was with such. Never was his name linked with a particular woman's more than once, as if he set himself the task of conquering them all, when there was no conquering to be done. They fell into his hands like ripe fruit from the vine, and before long she saw angry looks cast his way from the English and Scottish noblemen, *and* the inviting smiles of the women who waited for his notice. The Papal Bull, they called him, in a clever play on words. Elizabeth found herself longing for the blade that would put the bull out of his misery, though she could not say he looked particularly miserable. *He* seemed content enough with his lot; she was not, with hers.

But to Bard she spoke only once, when she was seated next to him at dinner. She was stiff and clumsy, unable to meet his eyes, and the glint in his own told her he understood. His politeness cut at her until she wanted to scream at it, and finally she turned on him.

'Do you find it amusing that you have so discomfited me? Do you enjoy baiting women into a place they do not know? Does it please your vanity to destroy any good feeling towards yourself if it issues from a woman?'

Bard did not pretend to misunderstand. '*Madonna*,' he said coolly, 'I thought you would not care.'

Elizabeth cast a glance at the man seated at her left, found him deep in conversation with his partner, and turned back to Bard. She was careful to keep her voice low. 'You tended me when I was injured and ill. You were kind. I was properly grateful – until you threw such

189

feeling back in my face as if it soiled you. Do you hate *every* woman?'

'I do not hate women at all.' He still used the Italian inflections. 'But neither do I love them.' He shrugged crookedly. 'You could not possibly understand it, so I will not trouble myself to explain.'

'It might make a difference if you did.'

His look on her was wryly curious. 'Do you think I *want* your regard?'

Elizabeth felt the hot blush steal up into her face, staining her throat as well. 'No. I imagine you do not.' And then, past caution, she asked the question she had been longing to ask since O'Neill had so blatantly informed her of Bard's preferences. 'Have you ever had a woman in your bed?'

He looked directly at her with a new intensity, shedding his affected indolence, and pinned her with his eyes. 'Yes, *madonna*. I have.'

She frowned. 'Then *why* . . . ?'

His smile lacked all humour. It was a mere twisting of his lips. 'I found I liked men better. I will not tell you why, *madonna*, or surely you would swoon. It would be too much for your delicate sensibilities.'

'But if you found the *right* woman – '

He laughed, cutting her off. It had a bitter, scornful undertone, and Elizabeth found herself flinching away from it. '*Madonna*, if only you knew. That is what everyone believes. But it has nothing to do with it.' His voice mocked her. 'Is it so very hard to understand that what it is a woman wants in a man is what *I* want in a man? His touch, his strength, his force of will, his tenderness and violence. I want it *all*.' His eyes did not move from her face. 'I like the feel of a man in me,' he said crudely, 'and I have no intention of putting my pleasure aside. Certainly not for a woman.'

Elizabeth recoiled from him. At the core of her being she understood he sought to shock her, to sicken her into retreating so he would not have to deal with her. But she could not comprehend what it was that drove him to seek men instead of women.

She disliked the contempt in his eyes. And so she sought to drive it away by echoing his own bluntness. 'And is the King a good lover?'

Bard's brows lifted. '*Madonna* . . . what would you say if I asked you the same of Simon Bagenal?'

She flinched. 'I do not share his bed!'

'The court says you do.'

'*The court!*' Elizabeth controlled herself with effort. When she could look at him without venting her anger once more, she saw the expectancy in his eyes, as if he anticipated her answer. And so she gave him one. 'Surely *you* have learned – in your years spent at foreign courts – that there is very little veracity in such idle gossip.'

Bard smiled. 'That gossip also linked you with Andrea Lucca – however briefly.'

The bolt struck home. Elizabeth stared blindly at her plate. 'The gossip, again, is wrong.'

'I warned you.' The tone was elaborately idle as he lifted his wine goblet to his mouth. 'I did warn you, *madonna*, not to cast covetous eyes upon him. He is not the man for you.'

'And do you want him for *yourself*?'

Her bitter question had been instinctive. But she saw the abrupt recoiling in his eyes and was stunned by the intensity of it. Quickly, so quickly, he hid it, masking his face and eyes in his customary manner, but she had seen it.

And she knew. She knew what he did and why he did it; how he could so easily stalk a king while he himself

191

was the prey, sacrificing himself without the slightest hesitation.

She *knew*.

His face was still and white as death. Elizabeth saw the hard line of his mouth as he fought to show her sublime indifference, but all the world was in his eyes. He looked away almost instantly, but she saw where his gaze had instinctively gone.

To O'Neill, who sat near the King.

Elizabeth *knew*, in that single timeless instant as she looked at the man, that she was in love with O'Neill. And that Bard was too.

She made a movement of withdrawal, but Bard's hand came down on her arm roughly. She flinched, for he held her as firmly as he could without breaking the bone. 'Do not meddle in what you cannot understand,' he hissed between his teeth. 'Christ, woman, I swear I will kill you myself!'

'And is killing so easy, then?' she whispered back. 'You and your *master* accept it so carelessly, as if that is your only answer. Do you kill everyone who stumbles across what they should not know? Do they conveniently disappear?' He teeth clicked together. 'Do you *enjoy* killing, Messere Matteo Pelli?'

'Oh yes,' he agreed sardonically. 'It is another facet of my depravity.'

She tested his grip. He released her arm. She did not flinch away from his eyes. 'And will you kill *me?*'

Distinctly, he said, 'I would not hesitate.'

Looking at him, she knew he would not.

But then she would give him no opportunity.

17

'The King does not place so much trust in a pope's power,' O'Neill said grimly. 'I think my eloquence has met an impenetrable wall of Protestantism.'

'He's Scottish,' Bard said. 'You must thank John Knox for that.'

'His mother was Catholic.'

'And a fool.' Bard shifted on his stool. 'James Stuart is King of England now in addition to Scotland; he dares not allow the Catholics to gain a foothold here again. We knew it was probably a losing cause to appeal to him in the name of the Pope.'

'Damn Henry VIII,' O'Neill muttered. 'Had he not decided he must have a divorce in order to wed that whore, Nan Bullen, there never would have been a Reformation. And England would still be Catholic.'

'In which case, we could not even *hope* to fool James with this papal appeal,' Bard retorted. 'We would be found out in an instant.'

They were in O'Neill's bedchamber. It was full night and moonless; only a few candles shed light in the room and illuminated their faces. O'Neill was sprawled on his narrow bed, unbooted, propped up against thick bolsters. He had left off his crested doublet and wore only breeches and a crumpled linen shirt, untied and open to the waist. The candlelight turned his bared chest into a gleaming pelt of black hair, so thick it nearly rivalled that on his face and head. For a moment white teeth were bared in a feral grimace.

'Would that I could tell him in my *own* words, instead

of these milk-and-honey phrases I must use to all but you!'

Bard smiled. Milk-and-honey phrases indeed, and from O'Neill it was doubly incongruous. 'I have no doubts he knows what he has done to the Irish. And I have no doubts he intends to change nothing.'

O'Neill slanted him a sharp glance from beneath half-shut lids. 'Have you had no luck at all?'

Bard sighed. 'Jamie swears he loves me, but he is a fickle man. And he likes women occasionally as well, which means I have no singular influence with him. I please him for now, but who is to say who will please him tomorrow? He grows jaded quickly – in this court, how could he not? – and I doubt there is much I can do. He professes sympathy for the Pope's concerns for the Catholic Irish, but he says there are Protestant Irish he must concern himself with as well.' Bard grimaced and shook his head. 'He is slippery as an eel, this King – and unlikely to be swayed by you or I or even the Pope.' For a moment Bard grinned. 'I wonder what the Pope would say if he knew what we did in his name?'

'He would say the words of excommunication,' O'Neill answered flatly. ''Tis bad enough we must tread the road to hell, but I would prefer to do it *with* his blessing rather than without.'

Bard rubbed at his eyes. 'We cannot stay here in England much longer.'

'I know.' O'Neill stared balefully, up at the roof timbers. 'I think we must go home very soon.'

Bard sat very still upon his stool. 'Home,' he said reflectively, so soft it was nearly a whisper. 'Ireland. Land of the faerie folk and heroes . . . and war.'

'D'ye hate me for it?' O'Neill asked abruptly.

Bard looked at him blankly. 'Hate *you*, O'Neill? For what?'

'For using you. For setting you at kings and princes as if you were a woman flaunting her wares before an attentive eye.' O'Neill's jaw tightened. 'For making you my whore.'

The strength trickled out of Bard's limbs as he sat on his stool and with it went his breath. He could only stare at O'Neill, his eyes fixed on the person who had walked through his dreams since childhood. The boy first and then the man, ever compelling, ever demanding, ever worthy of the love and respect of all who knew him. He was the sort men would die for, women turn whore for. Ruthless. Ambitious. Impatient and angry. And so filled with hostility for England you could smell it on him.

And yet none of O'Neill's ambitions were for himself. It was all spent on Ireland. He beggared his soul as well as his purse, and would do so forever.

And for him, Bard would do anything.

He drew in an unsteady breath. 'You have held no knife to me, telling me what I must do.'

'Words are sometimes more compelling than a knife,' O'Neill said curtly. 'Have I stripped you of your dignity?'

Bard's smile was very faint. 'Most men would say I have none. But that has nothing to do with you.' He drew in a ragged breath. 'What I am was begun when I was very young, and I was never *forced* to it.' He shrugged. ''Twas what I wanted, once I had known it.'

O'Neill's green eyes were fixed on Bard's face. 'You have never told what began it.'

'No,' Bard agreed. ''Tis not the sort of thing one man tells another.' He looked away from O'Neill, staring at the floor. 'I was afraid to tell you. I feared you would despise me.'

'How could I despise someone who has been with me since boyhood? Who has served me for so long?'

Bard set his teeth. 'Easily enough. Most men, when

they learn of it, turn against me as if I mean to threaten *them*. I am dust beneath their feet.'

'Useful dust.' O'Neill's eyes did not move from Bard's averted face. 'They are blind to see only that, and not the man you are.'

'They would not say I am a man.' Bard's voice was expressionless.

'Who knows what comprises a man?' O'Neill asked harshly. 'What hangs between our legs does not – I have known women with more courage than some men. Strength? I have known priests with more determination than some men, and they place no stock in hardening the body . . . unless it be calluses on their knees.' For a moment his eyes glinted. 'As for a *mind*, I think Elizabeth of England proved a man is not the only one on this earth capable of conducting attrition against another land. So what does it leave?'

Bard shook his head. 'You cannot know what it is like.'

'No,' O'Neill agreed, 'unless you tell me.'

After a moment Bard met his eyes. 'You never asked before.'

'Because no one threw it in my face.' His voice was harsh. 'No one ever accused me of measuring everyone against the task I have to do.'

'Someone has?' Bard asked in astonishment. '*Here?*'

'The woman.' And O'Neill swore.

'The *Sassenach?*'

O'Neill sat up abruptly. 'My Christ, she is driving me mad! I swear she is in my blood, and I cannot get her out of it. She is a witch!'

'Holy Mother of God, d'ye know what you're saying?' Bard demanded. 'She's *dangerous!*'

'I know it. I know it. But 'tis the truth.' O'Neill was up, striding across the room like an angry panther. His hands were fisted and the breath hissed between his teeth. 'By

Christ, I *burn* with it! I look at her and she sets me on fire, and there is no one to put it out but her.' The look he flung at Bard was angry and defiant. 'Call me a fool if you will, but 'tis a thing men must suffer when they want a woman so badly.'

'I know what it is to want someone,' Bard said drily. 'But . . . I think you are a fool to think of *her*.'

'Would you have me chasing some other?' O'Neill asked. 'Would you have me taking up with some diseased whore of the streets?'

'It might prove less dangerous,' Bard retorted.

O'Neill swore, pacing back towards the bed. 'Every time I see her she is with that cold fish.'

'Bagenal?'

'Aye. He turns my stomach.'

'That is simple jealousy. He has what you cannot.'

'More,' O'Neill said. '*More*. You know who he is.'

'I know.'

'I cannot stand to see his hands on her.'

'And will you stop him?' Bard demanded harshly. 'Will you risk our lives for one night spent between her thighs?'

O'Neill swung around. 'I'll have none of that from you. Not contempt. *That* I expect you to understand.'

Bard, abashed, nodded. 'Aye.'

O'Neill frowned faintly. 'You've never said a word before about the women I choose for bed partners,' he said curiously. 'Never. Why d'ye hate this one so?'

Bard would not tell him the truth, that he saw in Elizabeth Stafford a genuine threat. Always he had known O'Neill would one day meet the woman he wanted for life. O'Neill would marry, and the old companionship between them would be banished because a woman always came between men. It had less to do with Bard's love for O'Neill than the knowledge that the companionship would change – once the service ended, a completely new life would begin. In the past he had not cared how many women O'Neill took to bed because Bard knew they meant nothing to him. But Elizabeth Stafford was different. Even he knew that.

And he was afraid.

'She is a Sassenach,' he said finally, hoping it was enough.

O'Neill swore again. 'Why couldn't the Lord see fit to make her Irish?'

Alarm spread through Bard. He stood up, overturning the stool. 'Are you serious, O'Neill? Do you mean to have her, then?'

'I would have her,' O'Neill said grimly, 'but she will not have *me*.'

'Would you *wed* her?'

O'Neill stopped pacing. He turned slowly, staring at Bard in amazement. 'Wed a Sassenach? Have you gone mad? The Hound of Ireland wed to an English bitch?' He laughed incredulously. 'All this English ale has addled your wits. 'Tis time we went home to Ireland and set them straight again.'

Bard, relief rushing through him, grinned. He bent and righted the stool, sitting down on it again. ''Tis all right,' he said, hiding his elation. ''Tis all right, then.'

O'Neill resumed his pacing.

Elizabeth stood in the exact centre of the gallery. She refused to look at the portraits, knowing they would stare back at her with accusing eyes. She could hardly bear to be in the place, for it brought back memories of her confrontation with O'Neill.

Suddenly she was sickened by the knowledge of what she had almost done, clinging to him like some whore begging for his kisses. Such action showed she was not the innocent young woman she believed. In those moments she had wanted him badly, without really knowing what she wanted. The need for him had not diminished. Seeing him with all the fawning women reawakened the frustration and desire, and the pain of knowing there was nothing between them now. O'Neill had seen to that.

And so had she.

Elizabeth waited in the gallery because she had been told to. One of the King's personal servants had told her James wished to meet with her where they had first met, and so she had gone directly to the gallery to wait. She had not the slightest idea what he might want from her, but she had no choice but to do as he wished. And so she stood waiting, hands clasped tightly and her heart grown too large for her chest.

It was evening. The gallery was lighted only by a few candles, which lent it a sinister ambience. The faces stared down at her spine as she stared blindly at the curtained windows, and she waited.

The door at the end of the gallery opened and closed. For the barest moment Elizabeth hoped it was O'Neill; instantly she dismissed it and waited silently, hearing the quiet footsteps. At last she turned and dropped into a graceful curtsy. 'Your Majesty.'

James raised her, his fingers lingering on her hand. His eyes watched her closely, and a little smile was half hidden in his beard. He was nothing, she thought irrationally, like his grandfather on the wall behind them.

'Ye please me, mistress,' he said. 'Ye please me well. I would reward ye for it.'

Elizabeth drew in a careful breath. 'Your Majesty, I serve the Queen. That requires no reward, for it is honour enough in itself.'

He smiled more widely. 'And a pretty tongue too. Well, mistress, will ye serve yer King as well as yer Queen?'

There was no other answer possible. 'Of course,' she answered instantly.

James's eyes gleamed. 'But ye dinna know what I'm asking, mistress.'

Her hand was still in his. Elizabeth felt the cool dryness of his palm and the faint pressure of his fingers stroking her skin. A twinge of apprehension shot through her body. 'Your Majesty – '

'Ye bring beauty to my court,' he said, 'and a grace I admire. Ye dinna flaunt yersel' like so many of the women, hoping they'll catch their King's eye.' His gleamed as he said it. 'Ye dinna use yer body to gain wealth and lands and a title, like so many, and ye never pit one man against another.'

'Your Majesty – '

'I like a virtuous woman, mistress, and ye are that.'

For a moment she felt relief rushing through her body. If the King was so well pleased by her conduct, he could not be intending what she had initially feared. Perhaps James had some propriety after all.

Elizabeth smiled at him, relieved past measure, and saw the flare of desire in his eyes. Before she could react he guided her hand to his mouth. 'Better yet, I like a woman who will be pleased with what a man intends her.'

His beard tickled her wrist, but it was not a pleasant sensation. This was James of Scotland who held her hand and kissed her arm, not some eloquent nobleman who hardly heard what he said, having said it so often before. This was the King himself, and she recognized the demand in his eyes. She, who had seen it in O'Neill's, and even Bagenal's, cold as he was.

She did not dare twist her arm out of his grasp. 'Your Majesty, I beg you – '

'Ye beg me,' he said huskily. 'What d'ye beg? My favour? Ye hae it. What more would you want?'

200

Elizabeth took a very deep breath. 'A continuation of the virtue you admire so very much.'

James laughed. He released her hand. 'Mistress, every woman gives in at last. She canna go a whole life withoot a man. Ye've been circumspect and above reproach, for all there're those who'd reproach ye anyway, and I admire ye for it. But more than that . . . I want ye.' He spread his hands. 'I'm a plain and simple man, mistress . . . I'd hae ye know straight.'

She struggled to keep the desperation from her voice. 'You are wed, my lord king. It would be adultery.'

'Och, God willna punish *me* for taking a woman where I will. And Annie doesna please me that way. I leave that to others. As for *you*, mistress . . . 'twill not be adultery. God willna punish ye. Ye are an unmarried woman.'

'What of – what of the Italian?' Her voice was little more than a whisper. Did people say such things to the King? 'What of Matteo Pelli?'

'I'm done with him,' James said flatly. ''Twas nae more than a brief thing. And I grew weary of his prating about Ireland and the Pope. I'll rid myself of him tonight, or perhaps tomorrow.' He looked thoughtful a moment, as if recalling what he and Bard had shared. Then James moved closer to her. ''Tis time I took a woman again.'

She moved back, stiff with alarm. 'Your Majesty, I beg you – do not ask this of me.'

'I am not, mistress. I am *telling* ye.'

Elizabeth retreated. Most of her longed to shout at him that he could not *order* her into his bed, but she did not dare. James Stuart was the King. With one word he could banish her father and take Rosewood for his own. His power was absolute, as he himself had made it. *The divine right of kings*. If she made him angry, he could do whatever he wished in reparation.

'I am not worthy,' she said unevenly.

James smiled. 'Ye're worthy, mistress. Worthy of any of us. And I want ye.'

'Please,' she begged.

'Dinna cross me, Lizzie,' he warned. 'There is nothing to stop me. Ye hae no husband. And I am yer King.'

She bowed her head with a respect she did not feel. 'Your Majesty, I know this is great honour. But I do not wish for it.'

James frowned a bit as he stared at her. And then he smiled. 'Yer king has decided to be magnanimous – ye'll hae it anyway.' He waved a hand. ''Tis an end to it, mistress.' He circled her slowly. 'Ye sleep alone?'

'I have a maid.'

Again he waved his hand. 'Easily dismissed. Well then, mistress – there is nothing to stand in my way. I canna say what night I will coom, but I will. Ye'd best be ready for me.'

He waited, and she dropped into a curtsy that did not show him how badly her legs shook. James Stuart gave her a little bow and then took his leave, and she watched him go.

Then she went directly to her father.

Edwin Stafford was not pleased to see her. Of late he had been quite involved with planning his next assault upon the King's generosity, hoping to win a partial restoration of his lands. Elizabeth's arrival interrupted. But he took note of her ashen face and motioned her to a chair. He poured a goblet of wine and handed it to her.

She did not drink. She stared at him. 'The King,' she began without preamble, 'has said I am to be his mistress.'

He made no movement. He stood silently before her, looking at the slow flush rising in her cheeks and the anger filling her eyes. How many women would be *angry* to have the King's favour? He thought only his daughter was capable of it. 'What has he said?'

'That I am to be ready for him, though he cannot say when he will come. Only that he will.'

'Well?'

Elizabeth stared at him. 'He means to make your daughter a *whore*. Does it mean nothing to you?'

He turned from her, thinking rapidly. He had carefully watched the relationship with Bagenal develop, hoping he could wed her to the man. Bagenal had no great title yet, but surely the King would confer one on him soon. And then his wife would be a duchess or a countess and Edwin Stafford would be elevated along with her . . . providing, of course, that wife was Elizabeth.

But the King . . . the King *himself?*

Stafford swung back to face her. 'You cannot refuse the King.'

'I can. I will.' Her fingers tightened on the silver goblet. 'The thought of it makes me ill. I will not play the whore for James.'

'He is the King.'

'I can go home,' she said flatly. 'To Rosewood. Bury myself in the country, and he will forget about me.' She shrugged. 'He will have forgotten me in a day, replacing me with another woman or some pretty boy.'

'He might. But he might seek retribution.' Stafford guided the goblet to her mouth and made her drink. 'It is a great honour, my dear. There is no disgrace in being the King's mistress. Nearly every woman at court longs for the opportunity.'

Elizabeth pushed the goblet away after a few swallows. 'I want none of it, or of him.' She looked up into her father's shrewd, implacable face. 'Can you not understand?'

He thought of the years he had invested trying to buy

his way back into favour, spending his gold like water in hopes of smoothing the road back to position and pride. He thought of the snubs he had received, how he had been the butt of jests, when every man thanked God it was Stafford in disgrace and not himself. He thought of the times he had abased himself trying to win the Old Queen's welcome again, and how she had ignored him. He thought of how he had hoped to win back respectability and position through the disposition of his daughter's hand.

'I think,' he said smoothly, 'you are upset. We can speak of this another time. But you should recall he is your King and should be obeyed in all things.'

'You will not send me back to Rosewood, then, though I would prefer it?'

'No,' he said. 'Your place is at court.'

Elizabeth rose. She put the goblet into his hands and met his eyes directly. 'You should be in my place,' she said clearly. 'You play the whore better than I.'

Elizabeth sat before the mirror as Alice brushed her hair until it shone in the candlelight. It was like spun silk, rich in texture and colour and, until the King had said she must be his mistress, Elizabeth had always been proud of it. Now she wished it was dull and coarse and greying, so that James would look on her and see a plain woman who would not tempt him at all.

'Shall I braid it for bed, mistress?' Alice asked softly.

'No. Leave it loose.' And as she spoke she saw James's small, dry hands moving through her hair in perfect satisfaction, knowing he had bought it as easily as he bought her.

'Mistress,' Alice said tentatively, 'your robe?'

Elizabeth rose, sinuous in her silken night rail, and allowed Alice to wrap her in the rich tawny velvet. On

204

her feet were matching slippers, but she kicked them off and climbed into the huge bed. She sat in the middle, enveloped in the velvet robe, and tucked her legs beneath her. She stared fixedly at the door, hoping James would not choose tonight to visit her.

She smiled without the slightest trace of humour. *I am not my father's daughter for nothing, James Stuart. You have given me the weapon I need to fight you, and fight you I will. The sacrifice will be worth it, if only to show you I do not capitulate. You will not get the woman you are expecting – if you get her at all.*

And that was what she gambled on.

Elizabeth looked at Alice. 'I want you to find Sir Simon Bagenal for me and bring him here.'

Alice gaped at her. '*Here,* mistress?'

'Here. And then you may sleep with Morag's maid.'

Alice's eyes were enormous in her little face. '*Mistress –* '

'Do as I say, Alice.'

'Yes, mistress. But – what if he shouldn't wish to come?'

Elizabeth laughed, but it had a brittle sound. 'He will come, if only to gloat.' *Because he said I would come to him, and so I do.*

Alice bobbed a curtsy. 'Yes, mistress.'

Elizabeth watched the door close behind the maid. She shut her eyes as her teeth ground together and her hands curled into fists. 'I have no choice,' she said aloud into the shadows of her chamber. 'None at all.'

But she would have even less if Bagenal chose to repudiate her entirely.

18

He came. He shut the door behind him with a thud of finality, and she heard it with a calm she did not feel. She faced him, still in the big bed, and waited for his comment.

He said nothing at first. He simply stood with his back against the door, leaning on it, completely at ease. She saw the icy glitter in his eyes and the faint, mocking smile, but he said nothing.

'Did I interrupt?' she asked at last.

He shrugged carelessly. 'It was nothing that could not be done another time. You did not expect me to ignore such a summons, did you?'

'I could not say what I expect of you,' she told him flatly. 'Ever.'

'Good.' His eyes appraised her coolly. 'But I must say the same, for you have taken me quite unaware.'

'Have I?' She wondered if they would spar all night. 'But you said I would come to you. You *said* it.'

His eyes were on her face intently. 'I am a very good judge of people, women especially. But let us say I did not expect to be summoned to your bedchamber quite so precipitately.' The smile was very faint, the merest movement of the corners of his mouth. 'Generally there are some formalities that precede such invitations.'

Elizabeth felt herself at a disadvantage. She knew what she did, and yet she could not possibly know what *he* did. No one could. Simon Bagenal was too unpredictable.

She drew in a careful breath. 'But you came.'

One blond eyebrow slid up. 'Of course I came. What man would not?'

O'Neill. But she said nothing of that. She merely looked steadily back at Bagenal and wished she knew how to begin.

'I think,' he said calmly, 'you had better tell me why it is you have summoned me here.'

Her chin lifted a little. 'It should be obvious.'

'No. From another woman, perhaps, but not from you.' His eyes did not move from her face. 'You show no signs of wanting me in your bed, no matter how alluring you seek to be.'

Elizabeth felt the slow flush rising from her throat. Suddenly she wanted to shout at him to leave, to go, to find his pleasure on another woman. But it would be the destruction of her final, desperate chance, and so she said nothing at all.

'Elizabeth,' he said quietly. 'Speak.'

Slowly she wet her lips. 'Do you want me, Sir Simon? Do you desire me?'

He was very still against the door. 'And if I said . . . no?'

Her blood ran cold. She felt as if a crushing weight had landed on her chest, squeezing until she had no breath left. For a moment she nearly cried out with the humiliation, and then she consciously reached out and tapped her pride, her self-control, her determination.

Elizabeth looked straight into his eyes and smiled slowly. 'But you will not,' she said. 'Will you?'

'No,' he said. 'Oh no.'

'Then you may have me.' She lifted her head, knowing the candlelight spilled over her tawny burnished hair and the rich sheen of good velvet. She had planned well. She was all gold and bronze in the bronze-coloured counterpane, and she could tell by the darkening of his eyes that she had won. Colour moved through his face in waves, flushing it, and his icy eyes glittered. She could feel the tension and need radiating from him.

Elizabeth smiled. 'There is, of course, a price.'

'Of course.' He mocked her, but it did not lessen his need. 'Say it.'

'Your name,' she said clearly. 'And your protection – against *any* man.'

He did not smile. 'Any man would give you both. Why do you ask it of me?'

'I do not want "any man",' she told him, feeling more certain of herself. He was not so different from any of the others. They could all be bought, providing the price was right.

His face was smoothly expressionless. 'Do you truly expect me to believe you want *me?*'

Elizabeth laughed a little. 'Every woman at court wants you. Why should I be different?'

'Because you are,' he told her flatly. 'Oh, mistress, you are.'

She put an arrogant note in her voice. 'Then am I to assume you are refusing me?'

It was his turn to laugh. 'Refuse you my name and my – protection?' The laughter stopped, but the ironic smile remained. 'Since I will not get you otherwise, I would be a fool to refuse.'

Elizabeth felt a flicker of relief that her plan had worked. But even deeper she felt the nagging fear that she had put herself in an even more dangerous position, for Simon Bagenal was not a malleable man. If she married him to escape the King, she would *be* his, for him to do with as he pleased. It was simply another sort of prison.

But one she preferred to the King's.

'Will you wed me, then?' she asked.

Bagenal laughed. 'My God, woman, do you hear yourself? It is for the man to do the asking.'

'But you will not,' she said steadily. 'You told me that once. You offer nothing, you said . . . *you take.*'

'I take,' he agreed. 'And believe me, mistress, I will take you.'

She thought he might insist on sleeping with her now, since she had all but promised him she would. She had known it might be the price of her desperate plan, but if he intended to wed her there seemed little sense in putting off the inevitable. He would be the same man after the wedding as he was now, so what difference did it make?

But Bagenal surprised her. 'There is another thing.'

'My father will agree,' she said grimly.

'I know your father will agree. I think he will be well pleased.' Irony underscored his tone and sent colour into her face. 'I speak of the King, not your father.'

'*The King!*'

'I am a nobleman, mistress, and your own name is old. We must have the King's permission.'

Elizabeth had not thought of that. She had thought of everything *but* that. And now all her planning had risen up to strike her in the face. 'The King . . .' she whispered. 'Will he refuse?'

Bagenal's smile was slow. 'I think not. I think he will give his permission.'

She was not so certain. But she could not withdraw now. 'When will you ask him?'

'On the morrow,' Bagenal answered. 'This thing is better done quickly.' His hand went to the door as if he meant to leave.

Elizabeth stared at him. 'I thought – ' She broke off, wishing to show none of her confusion to *him.*

'I told you,' he said coolly. 'I am a very patient man.'

And he went out, leaving her to wonder if she had offered him anything he could not have taken anyway.

Elizabeth dressed carefully the next day because she could not say whom she would have to face. Her father, surely, because it was for Bagenal to ask Stafford permission to wed his daughter. But possibly also the King, and that was what she feared. Would James Stuart see the sudden betrothal for the escape it was and vent his royal wrath upon them both? Or would he think it merely the fruition of the plan he had made when he first set Bagenal on her heels? She could argue it was the anticipated outcome, for tongues had wagged about their nonexistent intimacy for weeks. But she did not dare tell him she sought Bagenal only because she could not see herself in the King's bed, and his arms.

A shudder ran down her spine as Alice dressed her hair. The thought of James's mouth and hands on her disgusted her. She felt her gorge rise as she thought about, and knew her decision to take Bagenal as a husband best. She did not desire Bagenal to any great degree *either*, but he was a fascinating, enigmatic man who drew her attention more and more of late. And she knew people rarely married for love. She was a fool if she thought she could have the man she wanted, as she had dreamed as a young girl. Her father had worked quite hard to put her in precisely this positon. As it was, she faced a lifetime with a man she did not fully understand.

But then she had desired O'Neill without understanding him in the least.

And she thought Bagenal enough like O'Neill that she might find the bedding satisfying enough.

Elizabeth shivered again, disliking the realization she *herself* had set out to snare Bagenal, like any of the other ladies at court. She had known exactly what she did when

210

she did it, and what it meant, and she thought it showed she was no better that her father. No better than O'Neill, whose single-mindedness would rouse Ireland into war again.

She thought of the responsibilities she would know as Bagenal's wife. Her time as mistress of Rosewood had been like the headiest wine, for those responsibilities had filled some need in her to contribute, a desire to make a difference. At court she had been swept up into circumstances she could not control, swayed this way and that by the whims and plottings of men, and when she had seen a way out she had taken it. She would be wife to Bagenal, perhaps, but she would not be mistress to the King. It was a minor sort of victory, for all its limitations.

There was a knock at the door. Alice answered, then stepped aside as a liveried page boy stepped into the room. He bowed briefly. 'Mistress Stafford, you are to come at once to the King.'

Her lips were numb. 'The . . . King?'

'Yes, mistress. Will you come?'

Slowly she rose, steadying herself against the table. She gathered wits and dignity as best she could and went with the boy. Alice's eyes were huge and questioning as she passed, but she could spare no word for an explanation. Not yet.

The page took her into one of the King's private chambers, and she expected James had every intention of reviling her for her poor attempt at escape. But instead she found Bagenal there, and her father. No King.

Bagenal lounged bonelessly against the wall; her father stood stiffly near the fire, dark eyes cold. The boy bowed himself out and shut the door. Elizabeth faced the two men.

'Your father' – Bagenal began it in a negligent tone –

'tells me the King has said he wishes you to be his mistress.'

She looked at his face and saw the cold, implacable eyes, the calm set of his mouth, but she was not fooled. Under the ice was fire, but she could not tell yet how hotly it burned.

'It is true,' she admitted clearly. 'I will not dissemble with you.'

His pale brows rose minutely. 'Why not? You did last night.'

Heat flushed her face. 'Do you think I meant nothing of what I said last night? Do you think I would have offered my person otherwise?'

He smiled very slightly. 'I think you gambled last night. I think you knew there was a chance I would claim nothing of you last night. And I imagine you were quite relieved when I left you alone in your bed.'

Eliabeth knew the truth was in her face for him to see. She was not like her father, who could dissemble so well. Bagenal had only to look at her, and it was there for him to see.

'I admire your plan.' Edwin Stafford spoke for the first time. His tone was quite dry. 'It is worthy even of myself. But is it truly worth the sacrifice?'

She heard the irony in his tone and realized he had dropped all pretence with her. No longer would he portray himself as the kind father concerned only for the welfare of his daughter. The truth, at last, she had from him, but it was a bitter revelation.

Elizabeth ignored her father and looked directly at Bagenal. 'You are the sort of man who sees what he wants and takes it. Your – methods – may be different than those of others, but the end result is the same. I think you want me, Sir Simon, and I think you will take me. That I seem less than enamoured of the idea should

212

not matter a whit – I *will* wed you. As for using you to escape the King, I admit it. I have no wish to be his mistress, but I *will* be your wife.'

'And therefore turn Jamie away, as he likes to consider himself a man with some honour. Oh, yes, *he* may bed whom he pleases, even married – it is his right. But he is unlikely to trouble *you* once you are wed.' His tone was quite lazy. 'You said you wanted my protection.'

'Yes. As any husband would give.' She faced him squarely. 'What man would *want* to see his wife so dishonoured?'

'It would depend,' he said, 'on who did the dishonouring.'

She glared at him. 'I thought better of you.'

He laughed. 'Well spoken. Touch the man's pride, and surely he is won. Well . . . you have won me. I understand your motives – I even applaud them! – and I admire the mind that saw a way out of a situation you despised.' The ironic smile returned.

'You have got yourself a husband, Mistress Stafford, and all with the father's permission.'

She looked at the tall, thin man who had sired her. 'You *will* permit it?'

'Oh yes,' Stafford said. 'I would be a fool not to, as Sir Simon has assured me he cannot possibly administer all of the vast estates he holds.' The mouth was set in a grim, narrow line. 'He even went so far as to offer me an estate near Rosewood.'

'You *sold* me.' Her voice was unsteady. 'Bartered me for more land.'

His shoulders lifted in a slight, dismissive shrug. 'Most fathers contribute a dowry when their daughters wed. What is so wrong with the father gaining instead of losing?'

'And what does the King say?' she asked.

213

'James speaks for himself,' Bagenal remarked. 'We have only to wait.' A faint glint was in his eyes. 'For all we know, this is quite futile. He may refuse us all.'

But the King, when he came, did not refuse. He listened to Bagenal's explanation of his wish to wed Elizabeth Stafford, and then looked very thoughtful. There was no mention of Elizabeth's discussion the night before with Bagenal; it was made to sound as if it were Bagenal's idea entirely. And when James at last looked at her, she contrived to look suitably demure.

'D'ye wish this marriage, mistress?' he asked. 'There is an alternative for ye.'

She lifted her head. 'Yes, Your Majesty. I wish this marriage – regardless of alternatives.'

'An I to think this is why ye put me off yesterday?' His eyes bored into her own.

She maintained a steady voice. 'Yes, Your Majesty. Why else? I knew Sir Simon intended to ask for me, and I would not spoil his pleasure by telling you myself.'

'And ye want him more than yer own King?' But it was said meditatively, and she thought she could refrain from answering.

James's eyes travelled over her face and figure, as if stripping her of her gown in his mind. It made her face burn, but she stood silently, knowing anything she said might be turned against her. If he refused permission, they could not be wed, and she would be no better off than she had been the day before.

'Aweel,' the King said on a sigh, 'methinks we'll allow it. 'Tis not so displeasing as all that.' His eyes were on Bagenal. ''Tis no secret the man thinks much of ye, mistress, and 'twill be no surprise to the court. Ye may wed.'

Elizabeth did not move.

The King did. He rose. ''Tis for ye to do the plannin'.

I've other things to see to.' But his eyes dwelled on her a moment longer, as if he knew what she had done.

She dropped into a curtsy, aware that Bagenal bowed with lithe grace beside her. And then James was gone and she was bound to the man who looked at her so calmly.

'Elizabeth.' Now he had every right to use her Christian name. 'Shall we have the wedding soon?'

She smiled coolly. 'You told me once you were a patient man, Sir Simon.'

'*Simon,*' he said. 'And I am. But why be patient when the game is won?' He smiled, bowed again, and took his leave.

When he was gone Stafford turned on her. 'You *fool!* You could have had the King himself, and you choose *Simon Bagenal?* The man can give you *nothing* compared to the King! Did you not think?'

'I thought,' she told him clearly. 'I thought well and hard. And it was my choice.'

'You are like your mother,' he said with icy venom. 'Useless and weak. I should have left you in Kent.'

'But *then* you would still have only Rosewood.' She smiled sweetly. 'This way you gain a few more acres. And no doubt you will parlay them into even greater glory.'

His face was white. 'Had the King refused Bagenal, you would have been left with nothing. No man would accept a mistress who prefers other company to his own. You would have been sent from court to moulder in the country.'

'Mouldering has *some* dignity,' she said calmly. 'More than whoredom such as yours.'

He was across the room. His hand went out and struck her across the face so hard that Elizabeth staggered. She felt the heat of the mark rising on her face and could not banish the tears that so quickly filled her eyes. She hated herself for seeming weak before him, but she had not expected her cold, collected father to react so violently.

'By God,' he said hoarsely, 'you have learned an ugly tongue. I wish Bagenal luck in taming it!'

'My tongue is my own,' she retorted. 'Even if my person is not.'

'Your *person*' – he said it between his teeth – 'was brought and paid for. You are more the whore than I.' And he spun on his heel and went out of the room, so quickly she could not summon a retort.

When she could speak again she was alone, and so she said nothing at all.

19

Elizabeth looked up in shock as the door to her bedchamber was pushed open. For one wild moment she thought it might be Bagenal come to claim her at last, but it was not. It was O'Neill.

'Get out,' he told Alice curtly.

The maid turned at once to Elizabeth. *'Mistress!'*

Elizabeth was on her feet. 'Go, Alice. Wait until I call for you again.' She knew what the little maid must be thinking – first Bagenal, now the foreigner. 'I will be all right.'

Alice scurried out with a single terrified glance at the angry man and was gone. O'Neill slammed the door closed and turned to face Elizabeth. 'My Christ, woman, you waste no time.'

She stared at him. 'You know?'

''Tis all over the court. Your father has taken pains to make certain *everyone* knows.'

'We agreed only this morning,' she said blankly.

He strode across the room and caught her shoulders. 'What are you doing, woman? D'ye know?'

She tried to pull away and could not. His hands hurt, and yet she felt a perverse stab of pleasure shoot through her body simply because he touched her. She stared up into his dark face, made darker by the devilish beard, and saw the glittering of his emerald eyes. He was very, very angry, and suddenly she was afraid. 'O'Neill – '

'You fool!' he said. 'Can you get yourself free of this coil?'

'We were formally betrothed this afternoon.' Then she

glared at him. 'Why should I *wish* to get myself free?'

'The man is a beast,' he said curtly. 'I'm not wanting to see you hurt by him.'

The Italian accent was gone from his words. She heard again the lilt of Ireland and thought how much she longed for gentle, tender tones from him, caressing her name like a lover, not this angry, defiant voice that sounded like he wanted to harm her. She wrenched herself out of his hands with an effort, straightening the fit of her gown. 'Simon Bagenal means me no harm.'

'D'ye want him, mistress? D'ye want that cold fish in your bed when you could have a man?'

'*You?*' she retorted.

His breath rasped harshly in his throat. 'You know nothing of the man, mistress. You've betrothed yourself to a beast.'

'What do *you* know of him?' Elizabeth was stung by his tone. 'He is an Englishman, of course . . . is that your reason? Or is is simply jealousy, because I will lie with him and not with you?'

Colour stood high in his face. His hands were clenched fists. She thought she had never seen him so angry, and she began to sense the glimmerings of another man. A muscle ticked in his cheek, though it was half hidden by the beard, and his eyes were narrowed, as if he judged her as he judged the enemy.

'D'ye want a name so badly, then, mistress? A fine title? You said you did not – that you came only to serve the Queen. I do not see you serving her, mistress . . . I see you serving yourself.'

'I want his protection,' she said sharply. 'His name is part of that protection, because that is the way this world works. Do you think I care for wealth and titles? *No!* But how else am I to get the protection I require?'

'Protection!' His tone was disgusted. 'A woman's way

of saying she longs for the security of such things as a nobleman can give her. D'ye expect me to believe you wed him out of love?'

'Who marries for *love*?' she flung back. 'You? You will not even look to a woman as anything other than a bed partner. What do you know of women?'

A growl of purest rage issued from his throat. 'I may know little enough of *most* women, mistress, but I know enough of you. Are you your father, then, selling your best acreage for a single royal favour?' His eyes raked her. 'But your fields are unploughed, and who knows if they will be barren or fertile?'

Elizabeth snatched up her hairbrush and hurled it at him. He slapped it aside easily and remained where he was, glaring at her like a green-eyed predator. She was shaking with rage and humiliation, longing to gouge out his eyes and claw his face to shreds, but inside there was another instinctive response rising. She could not keep herself from wondering what it would be like to go to bed with him, feeling his flesh against hers and the touch of his mouth on her breasts. She felt hot to the roots of her hair, and then cold, and she face him like a fury.

'*Irishman!*' She said it with all the loathing she could muster. 'Barbaric, Irish *savage*. Take your filth from my room!'

Before she could move he was on her, hands imprisoning her head. She felt the strength in his fingers as they spread to cage her skull, and suddenly she was deathly afraid. He was so tall, so strong, so powerful, and whenever he put his hands on her she wanted more. Inwardly she groaned, and knew it came from the roots of her soul.

'By Christ, I should kill you!' he grated, his face over hers. 'I should crush your skull or snap your neck – anything to stop your mouth!'

And stop it he did, for she opened it to hurl another insult and he closed it with his own.

It was a violent assault. There was no tenderness in him as he raped her mouth with his own, plunging his tongue past her teeth until she whimpered with the discomfort. His hands still entrapped her head, forcing her face against his, crushing her lips until they were bruised. As she struggled she felt the magnitude of his strength. Elizabeth pushed against his chest with both hands, felt muscle unyielding as stone, and knew she could not win.

His mouth moved. It left her lips and moved downwards, to her throat, and she felt his teeth against her flesh. Her breath caught in her throat as she felt the warmth of him there. He nipped, then began to suck, as if wanted the blood from her. But she knew he wanted something else.

'O'Neill!'

'Christ . . .' he groaned. 'You set me on fire, Eilis – '

'O'Neill!'

He was crushing her against him. One arm encircled her waist, holding her firmly, and she felt the hardness of his hips and the demand of his loins. For the first time she experienced the promise of a man's body and felt her own need rising to match his. Something quivered deep inside her body, demanding *his* attention, not hers, and she moaned with the realization that he had his mastery of her.

'Say again you will wed that fool!' he rasped against her ear.

'O'Neill, O'Neill – I *must!*'

'*Why?*'

'There is – a man.' She pulled her face away from his. 'He wants me to be his mistress.'

'Tell him no!'

'I *have*. He will not listen. He is powerful, and my

father approves of the liaison. O'Neill – I have no choice!'

'You have. There are ways of saying no that are – permanent.'

'Would you have me kill him? Is that the Irishman's answer to unpleasantness?' She nearly laughed at the ludicrousness of the idea. Kill the King because he desired another mistress? And yet she could not tell O'Neill that James was the one who wanted her. He was simply too unpredictable.

Like Bagenal, she thought hollowly. *Like the man who will be my husband.*

'*I* will kill him, Eilis.'

'For me?' This time she did laugh. 'Oh, my savage Irish warrior, do you think that would win me?'

'Christ, woman – d'ye mean to *wed* the man?'

His hands were hurting her again. 'Yes!' she cried. 'I will!'

He released her so abruptly she nearly fell. His eyes were blackened with rage and desire, and she knew her own must match his. But they stood glaring at one another like wary beasts, both wanting and needing the other and too proud to give in.

'Is it because I'm Irish and he English?' he asked levelly. ''Tis *that,* then, my haughty Sassenach bitch?'

She glared. 'No.'

'Then what? You want me. I can see it easily enough. You rut after me like a queen cat howling out her need. But you naysay me again.'

'I must. He offers marriage.'

'Will you trade your body for a ring, then?' His disgust was obvious. 'Like all the others?'

'Get out.' She shook. 'Get out of my room. Go back to your beloved Ireland and raise your army, so you can lead your foolish people into defeat yet *again*.'

He was white with anger. His teeth showed in a sudden

221

feral baring, and then his hand was on her wrist. Squeezing, hurting, so tight she wanted to cry out. 'And would it make a difference if I told you half of *me* is English?'

'*English!* You? Do you expect me to believe that?'

''Tis true,' he said grimly. 'My mother was a Sassenach.'

Elizabeth stared at him. At O'Neill the Irishman, whose very Irishness sentenced him to death. Half English?

'No,' she said.

'Aye,' he retorted. 'God knows I've cursed it often enough, but 'tis true. My father, The O'Neill, took an English wife.' He shrugged. 'The union did not last long. She died five years after they were wed, but she had already given him a son.'

'A rebel,' she whispered.

'That woman's name,' he said clearly, 'was Mabel Bagenal.'

Elizabeth's wrist was numb in his hand, but she thought her senses more so. Slowly she lifted her head to look directly into his eyes, seeking the truth, and there she found it. Her breath was unsteady. 'Mabel *Bagenal?*'

'Her brother was Sir Henry, Marshal of Ireland,' he said. 'Simon's father.'

'My God – you are *kin!*'

'Cousins.' His voice grated. ''Tis not a kinship I claim with any pride.'

Fear and horror rose up to engulf her soul. 'Does he know?' she asked. 'Does he know who you are? That you are here?'

'He knows I live,' he told her, 'but he has never seen me. Nor I him, until we met here, and I with another name.'

'He would want you dead.' That she knew.

'As I do him.'

'He is your cousin!'

'He is my enemy.' O'Neill released her aching wrist and

paced across the room. 'His father, Sir Henry, was Marshal of Ireland under Elizabeth. Henry Bagenal fought Hugh O'Neill at the Battle of Yellow Ford and died. Much of that battle rose out of Henry Bagenal's hatred of my father, because he eloped with his sister.' O'Neill shook his head. 'So much hatred has grown out of one man's desire for a woman, and hers for him. But what could they expect? He was Irish, she English . . . it was cursed from the start.'

'Half English.' Elizabeth stared at him. 'Then why do you hate us so much?'

O'Neill turned to look at her. 'Ireland has been all but razed by the English. Any man – or woman – with a shred of compassion would hate the land that brought so much destruction upon us. And yet the fight continues, because England wishes to exterminate the Irish.'

'No.' It was snapped out of her mouth. 'Ireland rebels, and England answers.'

His smile was devoid of humour. 'You spit that out so easily, Eilis. Am I to think you were weaned on hatred, as I was. If 'tis true, we are much alike . . . and forever doomed to be enemies.'

'O'Neill,' she said helplessly, 'I have to marry him.'

'Because of the *other* man who wishes you to be his mistress?'

She looked away from him. 'Yes.'

'You fool,' he said. 'There is another way.'

'Killing him?'

'No. That might prove too dangerous, for all I would like to do it. No. You could away . . . to Ireland.'

'*Ireland!*' Her head snapped around. 'When do you mean to go?'

'Soon.' He stopped pacing and faced her. 'Bard and I must go before we are discovered. 'Tis a dangerous game we play, and time is running out.' His voice was very

223

steady. 'You could come with us, Eilis, and escape all this clamour for your bed.'

For a moment she could say nothing. And then she could. 'What of yours? Would you want me in it?'

He was unsmiling. 'That would be the price.'

Bereft, betrayed, she felt tears welling into her eyes. 'Then you are no different from any other.'

'D'ye expect me to *wed* you?' he demanded. 'No, mistress, 'tis foolish to consider it. I will not do what my father did.'

'He must have loved her,' she challenged.

'Oh, aye,' he agreed. His eyes did not move from her face. 'But I do not love you.'

Oddly, it shook her. It hurt her. More deeply than she could have imagined. She had not expected him to say he did, and yet having the beginnings of a hope crushed hurt worse.

'You want me,' she told him curtly. 'I see it. I have seen it from the beginning, and felt your hands upon me.'

'Oh, aye,' he said gently. 'But wanting and loving are two different things, and you are a fool to think otherwise.'

She flinched. He had not struck her, had not touched her, but his words fell heavily as any blow. And suddenly she knew the futility of her position, and that she would know nothing else with him.

'Go,' she said. 'Leave me.'

'Eilis – '

'Irishman,' she said in icy contempt, 'get yourself from this place before I call a guard.'

'Then you will have him.' He did not move.

'Oh, aye.' She mocked his accent. 'I'll be having him, O'Neill.'

White-faced, he went from her room. And then she sat down and cried.

* * *

224

O'Neill got himself thoroughly drunk and then sat in the chair and stared. The flames of the fireplace played across his face, turning his eyes into glittering jewels and limning the harshness of his features. There was none of the slackness of the drunken man about him, and Bard knew it might be dangerous to cross him. O'Neill angry was one thing, O'Neill drunk another, but O'Neill angry *and* drunk meant Bard had to be very, very careful of what he said to him or risk the sort of wrath that would bring the roof down around their ears and get their heads put up on London Bridge.

O'Neill sat and stared. He was unmoving as stone, hunched forward in the chair with his elbows resting on his knees. His hands were loose, fingers hanging half curled, and the black brows were drawn down into a scowl. He did not even blink. Any other man might wonder if he still lived; Bard knew.

He got up from his own chair and poured himself some of the wine O'Neill had sucked down like a drowning man – or a man desirous of washing away a foul taste that will not leave his mouth. Bard said nothing to O'Neill immediately because he doubted the man would hear him; O'Neill could be deaf when he chose. But he was never, never blind.

Bard took his cup and himself and went to stand in front of the fire, his movement interrupting the fixedness of O'Neill's gaze. He waited.

Finally O'Neill stirred. His hands twitched, then fisted, then went slack again. 'Christ,' he said, and thrust himself back into the depths of the chair. His legs stretched out in front of him. 'Holy Christ, Bard . . . what am I to do?'

'You could kill him,' Bard said lightly. 'Or kill *her*. That would deprive Bagenal of a wife and you of this – and other – problems.'

O'Neill appeared to consider it. His voice was

detached. 'I cannot kill him. Bagenal keeps himself surrounded. 'Twould be difficult.'

'Then what of her?'

''Twould be a terrible waste,' O'Neill said seriously. 'God would surely punish me for that.'

Bard smothered a laugh. The green eyes flicked up to fix on his face a moment and Bard sobered instantly. 'O'Neill. She is nothing to you. A Sassenach. So is he. What does it matter?'

'It matters.'

'Christ, man, there are enough women for the taking!' Bard exclaimed. 'Are you needing this one in your bed to prove your manhood? You've sired enough bastards on the French court's whores – how many, four? – and at least one in Italy. No doubt you've got a few started here. What does it matter if you cannot have this woman?'

'It matters.'

Bard himself was angry now. 'And you think *I* am the fool, for avoiding such entanglements! You think *I* am the fool for looking to men – when most men do not seek to wed for title or wealth. Say to me who is the fool, O'Neill – a man who ruts after a woman who holds his life in her Sassenach hands or a man who avoids such relationships altogether?'

'Close your mouth,' O'Neill said grimly. 'You know nothing about what I feel.'

'Do I not?' Bard disregarded his normal caution. 'D'ye think I don't know what it is to want what I cannot have? Christ, man, because I prefer men to women does not make me invulnerable to pain. 'Tis the *same!*'

''Tis *not!*' O'Neill shouted. 'How can it be the same when what you do is a sin, a perversion in the sight of God?'

Bard blanched. He threw down the cup and stared at O'Neill, shaking. 'D'ye believe it that, then? Do I have

226

the truth from you in your drunkenness? D'ye tell me now that you feel the same as all the others? A *sin!* For wanting someone, loving someone, and laying with him? Is it any different from what you want? Holy Christ, O'Neill – *what is the difference?*'

'Woman was made for man,' O'Neill said slowly, enunciating carefully. 'Not man for man. 'Tis said in the Bible.'

'D'ye turn priest on me?' Bard asked angrily. 'Kieran O'Neill, who would sooner see all of Ireland razed than give up one inch to England! You kill in the name of Ireland and God, O'Neill, and you ask for absolution afterward. You confess your sins to a priest like an innocent boy, as if a few words can purify your soul and buy you a place in heaven. And you preach to *me* what I do is a sin, a *perversion,* when what you intend for Ireland is the same!'

'I am not speaking of Ireland!' O'Neill cried. 'Christ, man, they are two different things.' He rose from the chair and stood very still, but his breath rasped harsh in his throat. 'And do you think what I do for Ireland is *wrong?* You?'

'No.' Bard said between his teeth. 'Else I would not aid you. But you are wrong to say such things to me when your soul is no cleaner than mine.'

'I am not speaking of souls.'

'But you are! Lying with men is a sin, you say, while you parade your virility through all the beds of Paris and Rome and now London. What is the difference? At least *I* cannot get my partner with child!'

'You have not the right to rail at *me* about how I conduct my affairs,' O'Neill said dangerously.

'Why not?' Bard retorted. 'You have just now done it to me.' His face contorted and he turned away. 'Christ, O'Neill – have you hated me all these years?'

O'Neill looked at Bard's rigid back and realized what

he had done. He would not have hurt him for the world, for Bard was a part of him, and his words rang in his ears until he could hear nothing else. 'Bard,' he said helplessly. Then he dropped back into his chair and put his face into his hands, rubbing at tired eyes. 'Christ, man, what has happened to us? What has come between us?'

'The truth.' Bard's tone was empty. He swung around and faced O'Neill, trying to suppress the note of anguish in his voice. 'I would die for you, O'Neill! I would walk out of this room and straight to Jamie's dungeons if you asked me. I would kill anyone you wanted, expecting no thanks, no blessing, but knowing I had pleased you. For me, that is enough. But if you speak again of sin and perversion, I swear I will leave you and serve another master.'

'Bard,' O'Neill said hoarsely. 'Oh, Bard, I am drunk on too much wine and made stupid by the infernal longing of my loins. I would not hurt you. Never. Yet I have done it, and cannot undo it.' He scrubbed a hand through his hair. 'Oh Christ, I am so weary. So confused. I live on hatred instead of meat, and spice my wine with intolerance. How is it you have stayed with me this long?'

'I am an O'Neill,' Bard said tonelessly. 'I serve The O'Neill.'

'I am not he. That man was my father. And I am an unworthy son.'

'Hugh O'Neill did not sire unworthy sons.'

O'Neill stared at the fire again, propping an elbow on the chair and leaning his head into it. He looked half asleep, but he was not. 'Bard,' he said in despair, 'what shall I do with the woman?'

'Let her go,' Bard said softly. '*Let her go.*'

20

Elizabeth dropped into a curtsy before the Queen. Anne had summoned her unexpectedly and she had dressed hastily, wondering what the woman could have to say to her. It had been weeks since she had served the Queen properly; James's invitation had put her in his presence instead of Anne's. No doubt the Queen meant to censure her.

Elizabeth rose as Anne signalled her to. Two spots of colour burned high in the Queen's cheeks, otherwise her face was very pale. Her hair was dull and thin, though it had been dressed to lend her the appearance of a well woman. Her eyes watched Elizabeth with a strange desolation.

'You are to wed Sir Simon Bagenal,' Anne said listlessly.

'Yes, Your Majesty.'

'When?'

'The banns have been read. Very soon.'

Anne sighed. Her hand picked absently at the rich gown she wore, but its richness was not enough to hide the wasting of her bony·frame. Even in the few months Elizabeth had been at court the Queen's health had worsened, and rumours said she would not live out the year.

They were not alone in the room, for the Queen had her Scottish ladies, but the women had retired to a corner to lend them some semblance of privacy. Elizabeth, very alone, faced Anne silently.

The Queen sighed again. 'I cannot blame you for this,

mistress. You know what manner of man I am wed to.' For the briefest instant her lips tightened. 'He has appropriated my ladies before and left me very little to say about it. I know no woman would dare refuse the King.' Her eyes dwelled on Elizabeth solemnly. 'Do you love my Simon?'

Elizabeth felt colour stain her cheeks as she heard the Queen's possessive tone. But she kept her eyes lowered. 'Few people wed for love, Your Majesty.'

Anne laughed harshly. 'Yes, that is true. But you have more choice than most, mistress. If you do not love him, you do not have to wed him.' Her eyes suddenly sharp. 'Unless, of course, there is cause.'

Elizabeth saw the Queen's eyes drop to her slender waist. She automatically put one hand across her stomach. 'Your Majesty – no. There is no cause. That I swear.'

'You are lovely,' Anne said meditatively. 'Simon truly appreciates loveliness. But I think you will find he is not the man you believe.'

Elizabeth wondered if it was the Queen's way of saying she and Bagenal had been lovers. The whole court whispered it, but if any knew the truth, it was kept very quiet. The King could conduct lengthy and varied affairs if he wished to, but the Queen's reputation had to remain untarnished.

'Sir Simon seems a good man,' Elizabeth said quietly.

'A good man?' Anne's brows rose. 'No. A man, yes, but not a good man. You are young – too young, perhaps – but you will come to understand what I mean.' She shifted in her chair. 'I give you my permission, mistress. And perhaps it will be good for him.'

And for me? Elizabeth wondered. She swept into another curtsy. 'Your Majesty, I thank you.'

'I give you one piece of advice,' Anne said intently. 'My wedding present to you. *A man is never predictable, in bed or out of it.*' And she smiled a strange little smile.

Elizabeth stared at her. The Queen looked so odd. And then Anne waved a hand and Elizabeth knew she was dismissed, so she quietly took her leave.

The wedding gown was of rich blue brocade trimmed in fox and sable. The puffed sleeves, stiff with seed pearls, were slashed to show silver tissue undersleeves; the skirts stood out from her body like a bell, hardly moving as she walked. From her waist hung a girdle and pomander of pearls and gold, a gift from Bagenal, and she wore the pearl necklet at her throat. Her father had given her a pair of pearl earrings to replace the amber ones that would not match, and she felt as if she were a doll dressed for an occasion she could not possibly comprehend. Alice had washed her hair and brushed it dry, leaving it loose as became a bride, and it hung to her hips like golden mantle. Her hands were cold, but no amount of rubbing would warm them, for the chill came from within her soul.

The ceremony took place in the smaller chapel at Whitehall. At the altar stood Bagenal with the Anglican minister who would join them. Bagenal's blond hair was brushed smooth, capping his head in fair, shining waves that would do justice to a woman. He wore blue as well, a deep midnight colour that set his pale eyes to glittering. The sleeves of his doublet were full and slashed to show the silver tissue lining. His breeches were the same; his trunk hose were black. He wore shoes instead of boots, and on his left hand glittered a huge blue-white diamond.

Elizabeth closed her eyes a moment, took a deep breath, and went down the aisle with her father.

She hardly heard what the minister said. Words, just words, but they could not be undone. All her life she had wondered what she would feel on her wedding day; now she knew, and wished she did not. She felt empty. Swept clean of all emotion save for a faint sense of regret. This was not how it was supposed to be. She was to feel happy and joyous and thankful instead of old and alone and afraid.

Bagenal's face was solemn, cold, and unmoved as he listened to the words. His hand held hers lightly until he was required to say the vows, and then his fingers tightened. It was not a gesture of support, she realized, but of possession.

Elizabeth closed her eyes. She head Bagenal stop speaking and realized it was her turn. When she looked at the minister's face she saw kindness and infinite patience, and as he led her through the vows she felt as if he were binding her soul with iron.

Was I wrong? she wondered. *Should I have gone willingly to the King's bed? Would that somehow erase this horrible guilt I feel?*

The words were said. She felt a cold, heavy circlet of metal slipped on to her left hand and stared at it blankly, seeing the intricate crest of the Bagenal family that was now hers as well. With it he put his mark on her and made her his possession, as much as a horse or whore.

'God . . .' she whispered.

'No,' her husband said. 'Simon.' And then he bent to kiss her and she knew the thing was done.

He took her from the chapel to one of the smaller halls. There they would be feasted to honour their marriage, but the faces Elizabeth saw were all a blur. Men and women came up to give her best wishes, but so many of them were the mouths that had spoken dishonour and a grasp that exceeded her reach. They smiled and nodded and spoke courteously, but none of them meant a word. They said it because they must, because her husband stood high in the King' favour, and now she did as well.

It was a bitter wine she tasted, with very little warmth.

'Come,' Bagenal said. He led her to the dais. For the first time she was seated at the high table, looking down at all the others, but she did not feel particularly victorious. She felt ill. But she did not dare show it to him.

She ate what he put on her plate and drank what he poured into her goblet, but she tasted nothing. She felt detached from all the chatter and confusion and ribald jesting that sped around the tables. It was her wedding feast and she felt cheated, as if the Fates had somehow conspired to spoil the entire day. And she was tinglingly aware of Bagenal at her right, watching her with his cold, pale eyes.

'Are you ill?' he asked at last.

'No. Weary.' She could summon no more than that.

'More wine, perhaps? I would not want you too weary for the evening's sport.'

His allusion was crude and it sent colour leaping into her cheeks. She slanted him a disdainful glance and saw his smile. And she realized he had got from her what he wanted.

Bagenal's hand came down on hers. She felt the pressure, the promise, as he rubbed her flesh with his thumb. It was an intimate gesture from a man who made very few, and it was oddly unsettling.

She began to see faces. There were the Queen's Scottish ladies, without the Queen herself, and some of the most prominent of the King's advisers. Her father, deep in conversation with a knot of men. And the King himself, laughing over a jest with some of his Scottish friends.

Elizabeth knew she should feel honoured. Only the highest in the land hosted the King at a wedding; suddenly she had left behind the sterility of her childhood. Her life was London now, and court, and she would never know the peace of Kent again.

The hall swung around her in a slow, dizzying circle. She closed her eyes and put a hand against her brow, praying she would not disgrace herself by falling ill.

She heard Bagenal's curt question and felt his hand on her arm, and at last she was able to answer. 'I am . . . well enough. Only dizzy for a moment. It will pass.'

'By God, woman, if you are breeding – '

Her head jerked up and she stared at him. 'No! Oh God, how can you say it? Do you think I would have gone through this mummery if I were?'

'Yes,' he said flatly. 'To get a father for the child. But I swear, madam, I will raise no bastards as my own.'

'You will not have to!' she flared. 'What you get on me will *be* your own!'

'Then we had best be about it.' He rose and dragged her to her feet. The hum of laughter and conversation died. Bagenal smiled. 'If you will permit it, my lady wife and I should like to retire. Surely you can understand my – impatience.' He raised Elizabeth's hand. 'I give you Elizabeth Bagenal, the fairest of the fair!'

She heard the approbation and then the jests began anew, with increased innuendo. Bagenal had done it to her purposely, she realized, to humble her. There was no room for pride with him – he claimed it all – and Elizabeth knew she had brought it on herself. As the Queen had said, men were unpredictable.

It became a game, the game of bedding, where the women took Elizabeth to her new chambers and the men went off with Bagenal. She was hardly aware of what was said, although there was multitudinous advice on how to please a man in bed. Elizabeth gritted her teeth and waited until they were done. She stood in the centre of her chamber as the women chattered and readied her for bed, stripping her of her gown and putting her into a night rail of finest, sheerest linen. She stood unmoving, staring at the floor, and when the men came in with Bagenal she did not look.

They were worse than the women. They were coarse and left her no room for dignity, describing in intimate detail what the evening would bring. She looked at none of them, and when at last she and Bagenal were alone she felt like ice and stone.

His hands were on her shoulders. They burned her flesh through the sheerness of the linen. Finally he tipped up her head so she had to meet his eyes, and she saw them watching her as if he judged her. There was no emotion in them.

His voice was quiet and, for him, gentle. 'I will leave you. You were gently raised, unaccustomed to such bawdiness. I will give you time to prepare yourself. It is the least I can do.'

Elizabeth did not believe it of him. Tenderness, understanding, from him? Compassion? She searched his eyes for the truth and saw only what he wished her to see, which gave her no answers at all.

But she was grateful. 'Simon,' she said, 'I thank you.'

'Of course.' He kissed her very softly on the lips, seemed to check himself from something more, then put her aside. 'I cannot give you very long.'

She smiled a little. 'It will be enough.'

And then he was gone, and she felt a marvellous sense of relief.

But it faded soon enough. He would be back, as he said. She was trembling a little, frightened, full of imaginings, but she would have to receive him nonetheless. She was *his* now. Not O'Neill's, whose lightest touch stirred her, but Bagenal's, who took. She recalled clearly the day in the gallery when Bagenal had kissed her so deeply and demandingly and knew he would expect much more.

But can I give it to him? she wondered numbly. *Can I be the woman he expects me to be?*

She shut her eyes a moment, pressing a hand against her mouth. Silently she stood in the chamber, shutting out the room, the light, the bed, the knowledge of what she would do. She summoned what she could of dignity, of assurance, of calmness. Then she turned and went to the huge, canopied bed. She made her hand draw back the coverlet, baring white silken sheets, and finally summoned the courage to climb into the massive bed.

Elizabeth drew the coverlet over herself and lay down on her side, legs drawn up tightly and arms clasped over her breasts. She prayed he would be gentle.

She heard the door open, then click closed. Her back was to him. She lay very still, very quiet, but her breath sounded loud in the silence.

'Och, no,' he said. 'Such a bonnie lass should ne'er hide hersel'.'

Elizabeth shot upright in the bed and twisted around, coverlet falling from her shoulders. She stared at the King in utter shock.

James smiled. 'Ah, lass, ye're so bonnie . . . and I hae waited unco' long.'

'What are you doing here?' The whispered question hissed in the shadows of the room. 'Where is my husband?'

'Elsewhere. I hae sent him on an errand.'

'*Errand!*' Elizabeth gaped at him. He wore only a long velvet robe and his feet were bare. Already his hand plucked at the fastenings of his robe.

'I dinna want him here,' James said calmly. 'I want this private between us. I thought ye might prefer it.'

She could hardly get her breath. She was conscious that the sheer linen hid nothing of her body, moulding itself to her flesh as she sat upright on her knees, but she could not worry about that. Not when she faced the King himself. 'No,' she said. 'You must go.'

One royal brow rose. 'I must go? *I*? No, my Lizzie, I think not. 'Tis to be *our* evening, lass.'

A shudder wracked her from head to foot. 'No!'

His eyes narrowed. 'Ye canna gainsay me. I am yer King.'

Mutely she shook her head.

'Coom, coom, 'twill nae be so bad.' He advanced; she retreated to the farthest corner of the bed. James laughed. 'Coom here, hinnie. Dinna hide like that. I mean ye no harm.' When she made no movement to comply he frowned. 'I am yer King, madam. Ye will do as I say.'

'No.' She said it clearly, distinctly.

'Oh aye, madam. Or I will hae the guards in to hold ye, and ye'll nae be enjoying that. 'Twould be much easier to gie in to me.' He advanced yet again. 'Ye hae no choice, bonnie Lizzie. 'Tis what I've decided on, and there'll be nae gainsaying me. I am yer King.'

Panic settled in a tight band around her chest. She was shaking so hard, she thought she might break apart, and tears were not far away. She knew he had the right. He was the King. He could command her to do anything at all, and if she refused he could have her executed for treason. Elizabeth doubted it would go as far as that, but his threat to have the guards in held the ring of sincerity. James would not hesitate to do it, and then her humiliation would know no bounds.

'What of my husband?' she demanded. 'Would you do this to *him*?'

'Aye,' James said. ''Twas his idea, madam.'

Ice descended upon her. '*His* idea – '

'He knew I wanted ye. And he wishes a title, madam. I think it likely I'll confer one on him . . . for services rendered to the Crown.' His hand dropped down to cup

237

his genitals and his dark eyes gleamed. 'Why else did ye think I gave my permission for the wedding, madam? I knew I'd hae the bedding of ye first.'

'You're lying.' She said it numbly, out of reflex; such an accusation could be construed as treason, and she could, therefore, be killed for it, but somehow she didn't care.

The King's hand was on her wrist. 'Nae, madam, I dinna lie. 'Twas settled between us that very morning. The man wishes to rise in my service, and how else to better show his loyalty? The sacrifice of a bride's virtue is proof indeed, I'm thinking. Now coom, 'twill nae be so bad. I am not a cruel man.'

Elizabeth tried to jerk away. But he was stronger than he looked. He reached out and ripped the night rail from her. She saw his eyes darken and his mouth go slack.

'Holy Christ,' he whispered. ''Tis a sin to hae such breasts . . .' His hand went out and touched them and she flinched, shutting her eyes as his fingers closed on one nipple. 'Aye, madam . . . should be a guid ride for yer lord.'

Elizabeth summoned what calmness she could muster. 'Please,' she said, 'do not do this.'

James's breath was uneven and harsh. 'Hae ye anything better to gie me, then? D'ye hae the means to turn my favour from ye? I think not, madam. I think ye'll hae to obey me.' His voice turned rough. 'Lie doon, woman, and do as I say.'

His hands were on her. She felt them move over her breasts with a sickness rising in her stomach, and yet she acknowledged the futility in any protest. Tears ran down her face as she slumped against the pillows, and then James was in bed next to her.

He slipped out of his robe and she saw he was naked beneath it – a small, thin man with a heavy belly and sparse hair at his loins. His manhood was small and slack and he dragged her hand down to place her fingers around it.

'Love me, hinnie,' he said against her throat. 'Love me, bonnie Lizzie.'

Elizabeth recoiled. 'I cannot! *I cannot!*' And then, as she cried out her denial, she recalled the knowledge she held. The knowledge that could buy her escape.

O'Neill, her conscience whispered. *Kieran O'Neill, Irish rebel, traitor to the Crown.*

The King's hands were on her, caressing her flesh feverishly. He muttered something she could not understand, pressing his slackness against her. And then one hand slipped down between her legs and parted her thighs, encroaching into the softness between her legs. She cried out at the invasion.

'D'ye like it?' he whispered. 'Aye, madam, I thought ye might. And ye've kept it hidden for all these years.'

O'Neill. Ah God, to sacrifice a man's life in the name of my virtue . . . As James's hand slid deeper, her head pressed back against the pillow in mute denial. *Irish rebel, Irish traitor – I have only to tell the King.* But she thought of O'Neill's passion and pride and intensity, and how it affected her. She thought of O'Neill, headless, and the trophy put up on London Bridge, and she knew she couldn't do it.

James came erect against her hand. In shock she tried to withdraw her hand and could not, for he trapped it with his own, working it to work him. He was suckling at her breasts.

O'Neill, she cried, *what have you done to me?*

'Now, madam.' The King's voice was harsh. '*Now,* madam!'

She did not know what he wanted, only that his hand was between her legs and he sought some manner of entry into her body. Her own breath hissed between her teeth as she squirmed against the sheets, trying to twist away. And then, abruptly, he was crying out in a mixture of frustration and anger, and she felt his seed spill out across her thighs.

He lay atop her, quivering, sobbing out his release and the manner of it. 'Damn ye,' he husked against her breasts. '*Damn* ye for what ye hae done.' And then he reared up on his knees, glaring down at her. 'D'ye think to discredit me before the court, madam, ye had best think of yer *own* reputation.'

She shut her eyes, locking out the sight of her dishevelled sovereign. She waited until he was gone. And then, very slowly, she got out of bed and found the chamber pot behind the privacy screen, and lost the contents of her stomach.

21

Deep in her dreams, Elizabeth heard a soft soughing sound. She could not identify it. It intruded into her mind like a warning, and at last she dragged herself into the realm of wakefulness. She lay curled on her stomach and slowly turned her head, and she saw Simon Bagenal divesting himself of his clothing.

Full awareness came back instantly. 'Simon?'

He looked at her. Already his doublet and fine linen shirt were discarded, exposing broad shoulders and a flat, taut abdomen. He was very fair; only a faint line of hair traced its way down his chest to disappear beneath his breeches. His eyes, as he looked at her, were cool and expressionless. 'Did you sleep well?'

Elizabeth pushed herself up in the bed. 'Simon – *the King* – '

'Are you ready for your husband, madam?'

His tone stopped her dead. She stared at him, knowing James had indeed spoken the truth. 'My God,' she said numbly, 'what manner of beast are you? To give your bride over to another man on your wedding night?'

'It served a purpose, madam. I do nothing that does not.'

She stared at him in shock as he stripped out of his breeches and trunk hose. Unlike James, Bagenal required no time, no manipulation to bring him erect; he was ready for her. But she was hardly ready for him. The thought of being bedded so soon after the King's pitiful attempt made her ill. 'Simon,' she said without much hope, 'please – '

241

'Madam, you are my wife. I have no intention of denying myself the pleasure of this night.'

Elizabeth rose up on her knees as he approached the bed. Suddenly she was no longer afraid but angry, intensely angry, and she could not hide the snarl of rage that twisted her lips away from her teeth. 'You will not touch me! I will not allow it!'

He laughed. 'You have no choice.'

'He said it was *agreed* between you. He said you did it for a title.'

'I did, madam.' He stood by the bed, big and hard and powerful, and she smelled the demand on him. 'And I think now I shall get it.'

She lunged, reaching for the single candlestick by the bed. But Bagenal was there before her, snatching it from her grasp and holding it quite beyond her reach. He was smiling, but the smile did not touch his eyes.

'Get out of here!' she cried. 'Do you think I will allow you in my bed after what you and the King conspired to do? By God, *my lord-to-be*, you will know no happy marriage!'

He laughed, dropping the candlestick out of reach. 'Do you think I wanted marriage with you? No. But I knew you were valuable within the confines of the game, and so I was willing to take you however I could. It has paid off handsomely, I think, for James will surely give me the title I deserve. No more of this toadying to a Queen who is coughing out her life into a handkerchief. Now I have only to put out my hand and it will be filled, and all because of you. A virtuous woman at a court so filled with depravity and licentiousness it is a *wonder* God does not turn us all to pillars of salt! I could not bring myself to lie with the King, as he might have preferred, but I have used you in my place.' His breath was unsteady as he looked at her. 'Madam, you have served your purpose with the King . . . now you may serve *mine!*'

Elizabeth threw herself across the bed, trying to escape him, but his hands came down on her shoulders. He pressed her against the bed facedown then turned her over. He knelt across her, one leg on either side of her hips. His straining manhood and the sac beneath it pressed against her stomach.

Bagenal smiled. He shifted his body and pulled her quivering thighs apart with one big hand. 'What, madam, no blood on the sheet? Are you not so virtuous after all?' Then his exploring fingers found what he sought, and she saw amazement in his eyes. But it was quickly replaced by amusement. 'Was Jamie so impatient, then?' He laughed as he saw her expression. 'What a jest, indeed, that he has left you all for me!'

He came down on her before she could draw breath. His hands were on her breasts, squeezing her nipples until she wanted to scream with the pain, and his shaft was at the entrance between her thighs. His flesh was warm and sticky, adhering to her own as he leaned down against her breasts, and she felt the breath pushed out of her lungs entirely at the force of his assault.

She was tight against him, trying to deny him, but he was too hard and too strong. He tore into her, ripping tender flesh as he moved, and she felt the pain stab through her body.

He began a rhythmic pumping that only brought further pain. Tears rolled down her face even as she fought to keep them back. Her breath was being expelled from her lungs in little gasps she could not control. Even as she pushed against his chest, trying to shove him away, he crushed himself against her.

No kisses from him, no caresses, no soft words or tender intentions. She realized, dimly, that O'Neill's intensity was far preferable to the cold dispassion Bagenal used, for this was no mutual union. This was little more than rape, and by the man who was her husband.

He moaned, then shuddered, crying out; lay spent and silent across her. Elizabeth was trappped beneath him, so cold she shook with it, though he was warm; she wondered if her entire life was to be poured out so futilely in Bagenal's bed. She had heard women speak of it as a thing to be endured, lacking pleasure and offering little more than degradation, but she did not think she could endure it. Not again. Not ever.

Bagenal withdrew at last, rolling on to his side. She felt the dampness between her legs, but mostly she felt his eyes upon her. She turned away, curling up on her side as if she sought her mother's womb.

And then the realization stabbed through her that a child might come of such a union. A child conceived by force and cruelty. And that undid her more than anything else.

Elizabeth cried silently, clutching the pillow. She hoped he would not know, but how could he not? Her shoulder shook with repressed sobs and she felt a throbbing settle behind her eyes.

His hand was on her shoulder. She flinched, stiffening. The hand travelled the length of her arm, then traced out her ribs, lingering at her breasts. Then it went down across her hip and moved the length of her thigh. 'Lovely.' It was a dispassionate tone, as if he admired a painting. 'A Greek statue fashioned out of living flesh.'

She wished she were stone instead.

His hand continued its journey, sliding down her calf and stopping at last at her foot. His fingers curved around her instep a moment, even as she curled her toes against him, as if appreciating the shape of her small foot. Then the hand released her. It settled over one breast. He did not stroke or caress her again; she knew it was more a gesture of possession than anything else.

244

'I think, when the King comes again, he will find you a trifle more accommodating.'

Elizabeth felt a prickling sensation in her scalp, lifting the hair on her head. Her flesh rose up on her bones. 'The King will come *again* . . . ?'

'I think so, when he has recovered from the humiliation of his failure. He will have something to prove, to you as well as himself. And perhaps then you may service us both together.' The fingers tightened on her breast. 'I have heard it is a diverting pastime.'

Elizabeth cried out, stumbling as she leapt out of the bed. She retreated across the chamber, hugging herself against the cold waves that coursed the length of her naked body. She cared little enough that he saw her; his words had destroyed any semblance of modesty.

'You will not.' She shook so hard her voice trembled. 'You *will not*. I will let neither of you touch me again!'

He sighed and got out of bed. 'Madam, you will have no choice.' But he did not move towards her. Instead he slowly and casually dressed himself again and then took his leave, without another word.

'You will *not,*' she told the closed door.

She did not call Alice to her. The thought of facing the little maid was too much to bear. So she washed and dressed herself, wincing against the pain in her abused body, and pinned up her hair as best she could. Then she went in search of her father.

Edwin Stafford received his daughter silently, guiding her to a chair she wished was padded. But she sat down and hid her discomfort, hoping she presented him with a calm face. His own was implacable as ever, but there was a new coldness in his eyes.

'I wish the marriage ended,' she said evenly.

'Why?'

Elizabeth felt heat rise into her face. But she could not lie to him or he would never see her side. 'He expects me to be his whore. He expects me to lie with the King, so as to buy himself royal favours.'

Stafford smiled, but there was no humour in it. 'You wed Bagenal to *escape* the King. And yet now you have discovered your husband intends to use you far worse than what you would have known with James. At least as the King's mistress you would have known one man; now you must pleasure two. You have, I think, worsened your position significantly.'

She stared at him. A slow pressure was building in her chest. Its name was dread, and she felt a hollow fear spring up. 'I thought you would help me.'

'Help you end a marriage that will restore my name and holdings? I think not.' His eyes, though brown instead of blue, were hard as Bagenal's. 'You proved stubborn, Elizabeth, and I do not care for stubborn tools. You have placed yourself in this position by going against my wishes, and I have no intention of getting you out of it.' He rose from his desk and moved silently towards her. His thin face suddenly resembled a predator's. 'You called me a whore, madam, and – by God! – *you* are the whore! Learn what it is to be one!'

'You are my father,' she said numbly. 'How can you do this to me?'

'I will do anything,' he told her calmly, 'to restore the pride of the Stafford name. The Old Queen stripped it away like so much useless baggage and made it an epithet in this land. I will not stand for it! I have the power to change it, and I will.'

'Did you know what would happen?' she demanded. 'Did you *know* my wedding night would be spent with the King as well as my husband?'

He did not alter his tone or expression. 'A whore must do what she can to please her man.'

Elizabeth rose stiffly. She shook the folds from her gown and faced him. 'Whatever I am,' she told him clearly, 'you have made me.'

He did not answer as she left.

For two days Bagenal did not come to her, and Elizabeth began to feel a little less tense. She kept herself mostly to the new rooms she was to share with her husband, for her old ones in the wing she had shared with the ladies-in-waiting were no longer hers. Alice was still engaged in transferring Elizabeth's belongings from the small rooms to the larger suites, and so Elizabeth found herself listless and bored. Finally she gathered her courage and went to join the other peacocks and peahens, for she found solitude unhealthy.

She discovered almost at once that the brief respect – albeit hypocritical – she had enjoyed the day of her wedding was gone. Once again the piercing eyes slewed in her direction, and the hands went up to hide whispering mouths that made quite certain she heard every word. At first she ignored the sounds because she had heard them before, but this time the content had changed. This time the mouths linked her with the King, and quite suddenly she discovered everyone in the Presence Chamber was calling her the King's whore.

Elizabeth felt the colour drain out of her face. Nothing had prepared her for this. How could they know already?

She saw her father in a small knot of courtiers. Almost at once she recognized them all – the men had prouder names and larger fortunes than those in the last group Stafford had attached himself to. But they were the sort of names that saw profit in royal favours, and she realized Stafford had wasted no time informing those who cared about such things that the King had made his daughter his mistress and great honour would surely follow.

So quickly was she undone. There was no room for pride and very little for dignity; both were out of place in this court. She could only fasten herself on the little bit of integrity she still possessed, knowing none of it had been her choice.

The King and Bagenal were absent, and so the whispers became louder until the topic was the only one she heard in the chamber. But she dared not leave immediately or such a retreat would only fuel the fire. So Elizabeth turned and walked composedly to a tapestry hanging on the wall and pretended to be immersed in the battle scenes woven into the fabric. It did not matter that she had seen it a thousand times before; suddenly it drew all her attention, as if she had set out solely to look upon the stitchwork.

The voices went on and on, snaring her in a sticky web of jealousy and contempt and hatred. She could not bear it. She gazed at the tapestry and tried to keep the tears at bay, but the last few days had stripped her of herself. She could only recall the King's hands on her and his humiliation; Bagenal's quick, cold, painful possession that held none of the warmth and tenderness she had hoped for. The thought of having either one of them in her bed again was sickening, and she felt a long wave of horror and helplessness break over her head, sucking her down into its depths.

There is nothing I can do . . . a woman is chattel to her husband . . . subject to her King.

Had she tried, she could not have got herself more firmly caught in a trap.

'The victor *faces* the crowd, *madonna*, so he – *or she* – may better accept the accolades of the people.'

It was O'Neill, still edging his words with the Italian

248

accent. But the mocking tone was without pretence or subterfuge, and she felt the slow pain in her heart as it turned over within her breast.

She did not look at him. 'You hear their *accolades,*' she said bitterly. 'Would you accept them?'

'Had I worked so well and hard to gain them, of course.'

She snapped her head on her neck as she stared at him furiously. 'I did nothing to warrant that! Nothing at all!'

His mouth was stretched thin. 'In a single day you wedded one man and bedded another. You could have done no better unless the husband were the King himself. But he already *had* a wife, so he was somewhat out of reach . . . except, of course, in bed.'

She longed to answer him angrily, but she dared not do it so openly. And then her attention was drawn by something else. 'You wear a sword. Why?'

His hand dropped to the hilt. 'I am taking my leave, *madonna.* Returning to Italy can be a dangerous journey, so I always go prepared.'

He means Ireland. And suddenly, incredibly, she knew how badly she would miss him. How much she longed for him.

But then she felt the slow horror move within her soul again, and knew she could never want a man. The King and Bagenal had taken that from her.

Elizabeth put out a hand and touched his arm, caring little what the court might say. 'I must speak with you.'

His brows rose insolently. 'Speak with *me*, madam? What could we possbly have to say to one another?'

'Please,' she said. 'It cannot be here. Will you come to the small chapel?'

His green eyes were dangerously dark. 'Do you seek absolution for your sins, madam?'

'*Will you come?*'

'Once before you waited for me, madam, and it proved somewhat – discomfiting.' She knew he referred to their confrontation in the gallery. 'Why should I risk it again?'

'That time *you* asked,' she answered evenly. 'This time I ask it of you.'

His hand plucked hers from the sleeve of his fine doublet, as if her touch sickened him. 'Madam, if you wish to maintain any semblance of decorum, I suggest you keep such advances for your husband . . . or your King.'

'Will you come?' she repeated.

His nostrils were pinched and white. 'No,' he said. 'I will not.'

She shut her eyes as he turned and stalked away from here, and then he was pausing to exchange pleasantries with several of the courtiers and she knew herself alone again. Slowly Elizabeth gathered her skirts and walked from the Presence Chamber, and when she went to the chapel it was not because she expected O'Neill, but because she truly felt in need of absolution.

The little chapel was empty. Her eyes passed over the fluted columns stretching upward to support the fan-vaulted ceiling; ignored the jewel-paned stained-glass windows and the ornate tiles that intaglioed the walls. She walked slowly down the aisle until she reached the transept, facing the apse, and stood in the very centre of the chapel.

She closed her eyes. She felt the silences and sanctity settle over her like a shroud.

And then it was broken. ''Tis customary to pray on one's knees, madam . . . or has the Protestant faith led you away from that?'

Her eyes snapped open but she did not turn. He had said he would not come, and yet he had. But his voice still held the arrogant irony she hated, particularly when it was directed at her.

'Have you lost your way?' she inquired, staring at the altar and ignoring O'Neill entirely. 'Surely you could not have *meant* to come here.'

'But I did, madam. I spoke too hastily before. There are other things I have to say to you.'

He was just behind her. Slowly she turned and faced him, and found cold anger burning in his brilliant eyes. His hand was on his sword hilt again, clasping it so hard the knuckles were white, but his other hand hung slack at his side.

'What would you say to me?' she asked.

'That I am not entirely without manners, madam.' The Italian accent was gone. Ireland echoed in the chapel, and Elizabeth wanted to caution him against it. 'I would be wishing you happiness in your marriage.'

She nearly flinched beneath the scorn. '*That* is not why you came!'

'No,' he agreed grimly. 'But 'tis customary to wish the bride well. So now 'tis done, and I can say what I mean.' She heard the rasp in his throat. 'I am curious, madam, as to why you wed Simon Bagenal to escape a man who desired you to be his mistress – apparently against *your* desires – and yet you practically bedded the King the moment after the Anglican said the blessing!' His teeth showed briefly. 'Or was that merely a ploy to keep *me* from a bed that seems available to everyone else?'

'No!' she cried. 'Oh, no! It was the King I sought to escape. Do you think I would have done that to refuse another man? My God, O'Neill, I am not so spineless as that! Another man I would have reviled and sent at once from my presence. I *could not* with James. He is the King!'

'Do you say you do not want him?'

251

Elizabeth laughed wildly and heard it spiral through the chapel. 'I wed Simon only because I thought James would not trouble a married woman. It was said about him. But . . . I was wrong.'

'And the taste, madam?' he inquired coldly. 'Have you found you like royal wine better than Irish *uisge-beatha?*'

'It is foul!' she threw at him angrily. 'And could I spew it into his face without fear of losing my head, I would! My God, O'Neill, surely you know what it is to do one thing to escape the consequences of another, only to discover your plight is worsened. You must!'

'And would you undo it?'

'Yes!' she cried. 'Do you think I want this? I have no love for Simon and I want *nothing* to do with the King. But there was no other way.'

'There was,' he said heavily. 'I gave it to you, and you threw it back in my face.'

'You wanted me to be your mistress,' she said in exasperation. 'It was what I sought to escape to begin with – with the King – so why should I climb into *your* bed when I was trying to avoid *his?*' His face was expressionless and suddenly she struck out at him, banging her fist against his chest. 'Curse you, O'Neill, do you think it was easy letting him paw me? Do you think I *liked* it?'

'You wed him.'

'I am not talking of Bagenal!' she cried. 'But perhaps I *should* – what manner of man is it who encourages his King to lie with his bride if only to gain a title?'

O'Neill's face turned a peculiar shade of white. It was pallid as death and his eyes glittered like cold, hard emeralds. For just a moment Elizabeth thought he was ill. Then she realized he was very, very angry. 'Bagenal *willingly* gave you over to the King?'

'I'm sure it was *his* idea,' she said bitterly. 'Perhaps from the very beginning.'

O'Neill was silent. And then he began to swear in a Gaelic so violent she was glad she could not understand.

'O'Neill,' she said, 'it is done.'

'Would that the bastard were here to face me *now!*'

'But he is,' said Bagenal's voice. 'And more than ready to slay another Irish pig.'

Elizabeth, turning, cried out. And then she saw the sword in her husband's hand.

22

O'Neill smiled without heat. 'Well met, *co-ogha*.'

Bagenal's face flushed with colour. 'Use none of your barbaric Gaelic on me, *cousin*. It is my misfortune to be linked to you by blood, but as I now intend to spill most of yours, I think this day will see the end of such a misbegotten relationship.'

'She was your *puithar athar*,' O'Neill said. 'Your aunt. You owe her some respect.'

'I owe her nothing!' Bagenal said sharply. 'She wed Hugh O'Neill against my father's wishes. He was her guardian and had every right to forbid the marriage, particularly to an *Eireannach!*'

'But he was thwarted,' O'Neill said coolly, 'when the woman went freely to the man, and married him according to Irish – Eireannach – custom. In a church, man . . . a Catholic church!'

'She paid for her sins,' Bagenal said grimly. 'She was dead five years later. And now it will be my pleasure to rid this world of her son!'

'Simon!' Elizabeth cried. 'Have you known all this time?'

His eyes did not leave O'Neill's face. 'I was told my wife had left the Presence Chamber in some agitation, after having conversation with the Pope's emissary. And while it is quite true I had no knowledge Andrea Lucca was indeed Kieran O'Neill, the discussion I have overheard leaves me little doubt.' His mouth was a thin, pale line. 'How did you come to know an Irish rebel, madam?'

'This business is between you and I, Bagenal,' O'Neill said curtly. 'Let the woman go from here.'

'No. She shall watch. I shall enjoy seeing her reaction when you lie dead at her feet within the King's own chapel.'

A muscle ticked in O'Neill's bearded face. 'We will go from here, *co-ogha*. I will not profane this place with a sword fight.'

Bagenal laughed. 'I have no wish to go from here, O'Neill. And if you are truly so pious as all that, it should please you to know you will die in a holy place.'

'Where is Bard?' Elizabeth asked urgently. 'I will fetch him here – '

'No.' O'Neill's voice was sharp. ''Tis for the man and I to settle, Eilis, without interruption. Wait you a moment, and I will free you from this travesty of a marriage.'

His hand, ungentle, was on her shoulder. He pushed her aside and she stumbled, going to her knees by one of the pews. And then Bagenal and O'Neill were engaged and she knew she would witness a man's death.

Elizabeth, who had never before seen a sword fight, was astonished by the viciousness of it. The blades clashed in the chapel, echoing, and she saw the flashing of steel so hard and true it nearly blinded her. She hung there on her knees, one hand grasping at the pew, and waited for a man to die.

It was almost like a dance. Bagenal circled, dipped, feinted, then lunged forward again against the steel curtain O'Neill raised. The belling of blades rang loud in the chapel, destroying the sanctity of the place, and suddenly she was sickened by it all. She saw men changed into beasts, living by their reflexes and strength without the slightest sign of intelligence, surviving on instinct alone and the knowledge that a single misstep could result in instant death.

255

O'Neill's thick black hair flew as he moved, and she saw the curling ends become damp spikes. Bagenal's fair, shining cap of hair fell into his face, gleaming in the candlelight as he parried, feinted, lunged. His cold eyes had taken fire, burning with a fierce joy she had never seen in him before, and quite suddenly she understood that this was what he lived for, to walk at the edge of death and accept the risk involved. And that risk was what O'Neill might die for.

They were very well matched. Elizabeth could tell that even in her ignorance. They were of a like height, although O'Neill was heavier, and their reaches were much the same. Neither had an advantage, unless it was that O'Neill fought with a handicap knowing he was in a church, thereby giving it to Bagenal.

She cried out as Bagenal drove O'Neill back, back, until he fetched up against a pew and nearly tumbled over the wooden back. An outflung arm saved his balance, but the sword hilt knocked against the wood, loosening his grip. Bagenal saw the opening, lunged through, and plunged his blade deeply into O'Neill's right shoulder.

Again she cried out. O'Neill bent back, back, until his spine was bowed over the pew. But it freed him of the blade in his shoulder, and he twisted out of Bagenal's reach. But even as he twisted the sword fell free of his hand and clattered against the floor.

'*Cousin*,' Bagenal mocked, 'what curses do you mouth now your death is at hand?'

O'Neill leapt back, dodging the Englishman's sword. Unarmed, he was helpless; wounded, he was fast losing strength. And so Elizabeth caught up the sword from the floor and thrust it hilt-first towards O'Neill as he leapt back in her direction.

'*O'Neill!*'

He caught it at once. She hissed as the edge, whipping

free, cut into her palms. But she had no time for herself. There was O'Neill to think about.

He laughed. Even with his face wet with the sweat of pain and exertion, he laughed at Bagenal. And then, spying an opening he thrust the blade into the Englishman's ribs and drove him to the ground.

'Sassenach!' O'Neill cried. 'What pig is slain *now?*'

He jerked the sword free. Bagenal's cold blue eyes were haunted and utterly astonished, and his chest rose unevenly. Blood spilled out of his mouth. Elizabeth, who had not wanted to see O'Neill die, found she could not watch her husband die either.

She turned away abruptly, still on her knees with her hands doubled up to stop the blood from the cuts across her palms. And then O'Neill's hand was on her shoulder. 'Eilis, I must get free of here.'

She flinched, then turned to look at him. Like Bagenal, his breathing was ragged, and she saw he was in much pain. He was clearly exhausted. The sword hung limply in his right hand, and she saw the first line of blood escape from under the sleeve of his black doublet and crawl across his hand.

'Is he dead?' She was unable to look at the body.

O'Neill's booted feet were planted squarely, but for just a moment he swayed. 'If he is not yet,' he said between his teeth, 'he will be soon enough. 'Twas a death wound, Eilis.'

She was on her feet again, sore hands seeking the clasps of his papal livery. 'O'Neill – you are badly hurt.'

His hand was on her wrist, turning it over so her hand was palm up. He saw the blood there, her own; he saw the bloodied fingerprints he left. He let her go. 'I must get free of this place, Eilis. I will tend the wound another time.'

'Put up your sword.' She spoke calmly, knowing action

was all that would keep her from giving in to the moment. 'You cannot walk through the corridors with it bared, nor dripping blood.'

His brows drew down into a scowl, but she realized it was intense concentration against the pain of his wound. He started to clean the blade against Bagenal's doublet; stopped as she protested. Grimly he slid the blade home in its sheath at his belt.

Elizabeth took a steadying breath. 'The colour of your doublet will hide the blood for now, but I must get linen for it quickly. Come with me, and say nothing.'

'I think the Italian has deserted my tongue,' he said thickly. ''Tis a poor dissembler I am.'

For once, she agreed. He was no more the strong, powerful rebel she knew but a man sorely wounded and swaying on his feet. 'Walk with me,' Elizabeth said quietly. 'Say nothing, but if you can you must look as if nothing untoward has happened.'

'And you?' he growled. ''Tis your husband who lies there, Eilis. D'ye not feel it? D'ye not feel *something?*'

'Close your mouth, Irishman!' she answered angrily. 'What you fought over has nothing to do with me, and what I feel is my own affair.' But she would not tell him she felt sick with the fear he might die also, and leave her with no one at all.

They walked from the chapel like two people who meet unexpectedly, sharing one another's company out of courtesy. Elizabeth chattered on about inconsequential matters when they passed anyone – O'Neill remained uncharacteristically silent – and she thought it unlikely anyone would tumble to the truth.

She took him to her old rooms, hoping Alice had gone. But the little maid had not completed the move from old rooms to new, and as Elizabeth brought O'Neill into the bedchamber Alice cried out. There was no hiding the dark stain, even against his black doublet, or the blood that ran from his hand.

'Bandages,' Elizabeth said crisply, and urged O'Neill towards the bed.

'I cannnot stay here,' he protest. 'They would find me in an instant. Eilis – '

'*Hush!*' she interrupted, thoroughly aware of the startled glance Alice threw O'Neill as the Irish brogue took possession of his tongue. 'Lie down until I can get you bandaged, and then we'll speak of getting you free.' Her sore hands worked feverishly at the clasps of the doublet. When she had them undone she pushed the material aside and bared the wound, hissing as she saw the hole in his flesh. It bled freely, which would wash it free of infection, but she must get the bleeding stopped if he were to live. 'Alice!' Her voice was sharp. '*Bandages* – at once!'

The maid thrust linen into her hands and Elizabeth realized it was one of her old night rails. Quickly she tore the fabric and made a thick pad of it, binding it against the wound in long strips.

'Deft,' O'Neill muttered. 'Almost you'd have me thinking you are a leech.'

'No.' Her words were curt as she finished tying the bandages. 'But I've cared for horses before . . . and methinks you are not so different – ' She glanced over her shoulder at Alice. 'Do you serve *me*, girl, or this place?'

'*You*, mistress!'

'Then will you do as I ask?'

'Of course.' Alice's blue eyes were huge. 'Will he die?'

'No,' Elizabeth said grimly, cursing the girl's question. 'I want you to go to Matteo Pelli's chambers. You know him? . . . Good. Bring him here at once.'

'Now?'

'I need his assistance with Messere Lucca.'

Alice slanted O'Neill a sharp glance. 'He's no Italian,

mistress, not with that accent. I know the sound of Ireland when I hear it.'

'Will you go?' Elizabeth asked. 'Now!'

Alice went, but not before she flung O'Neill another glance over her shoulder.

'She'll bring the guard.' O'Neill tried to rise again. 'I must go, Eilis.'

'When Bard comes,' she agreed. 'Lie still, O'Neill!'

He hissed as she tightened the bandages. His pallor was alarming. 'I have stood worse,' he told her, as if he understood her fear. 'I took my first wound when I was but thirteen, and I did not die then. You'll not be having a corpse in your bed, Eilis . . . not when I have only just now got myself here.'

She smiled against her will; incongruous words in light of his situation. Her fingers lingered a moment on his chest, liking the warmth of his flesh and the silky feel of the black hair that hid skin left pale and smooth, so different from the darkness of his face and hands.

'You are so fair,' she said softly, 'like a child.'

'Have you never heard of the Black Irish?' He was amused. ''Tis said we have the black hair from our faerie fathers and the ivory skin of our mortal mothers.'

'Your mother was an Englishwoman.'

'Oh, aye . . . like you,' His hand was on her face, tracing the line of her cheek. 'Eilis . . . I had to kill him.'

'I did not love him.'

'But 'tis a harsh thing to see a man die when you have lain with him.'

She shut her eyes against the bitterness in his voice. His hand was gone from her face, and when she looked at him again she saw his own were closed. 'O'Neill,' she whispered. 'Do not die.'

The door opened and Bard was suddenly there. Elizabeth saw his face go pale and strained as he saw O'Neill, but his eyes and voice were steady. 'Stand aside, madam. I will see to him.'

'Do not dismiss me so easily,' she said sharply. 'I mean to save him, not give him over to the King's guard.'

'You have done enough already,' Bard said grimly. 'Was it not you who put him here?'

'*I*?' She twisted on the bed to face him. 'What had *I* to do with this thing between O'Neill and Bagenal?'

'You wed the Sassenach,' Bard said flatly. 'We were to leave five days ago, but O'Neill insisted he must speak with you once more when he learned you would wed so soon. And see what it has accomplished?'

'Enough,' said O'Neill. His eyes glittered. 'Must I spill out my life into these sheets while you bicker over me like babies over sweetmeats? Have sense, Bard . . . and *you*, Eilis.'

Elizabeth rose. 'You must get him from here before they find Simon's body.'

Bard's blue eyes flickered. 'He is dead?'

'O'Neill put a sword in him.' She thought it was enough.

'And him into me.' O'Neill thrust himself up against the pillows, strain leeching his face of colour.

Alice, whom they had forgotten, pushed herself among them. 'He is dead?' she gasped. 'My lord Bagenal?'

Bard's arm was around her throat instantly, cutting off her words. His other hand was on her temple, preparing to twist her neck. 'O'Neill?'

Elizabeth interrupted. 'Will you kill so easily, then?' she demanded. 'My God . . . do you know what you do?'

'I know very well,' Bard's voice was grim. 'I serve The O'Neill. Would you rather have him taken, then, and executed? Would it make you happy?'

'Would it?' she threw back. 'I have committed treason by saying nothing of O'Neill's presence here at court. Oh yes, under duress, because you both had threatened me –

but did I give him back his sword when he dropped it because he *threatened* me?' She thrust out her hands and showed the cut palms to Bard. 'I did it because I had to, and I would again. I do *this* because I have to. No longer are you and O'Neill the only ones eligible for execution!'

Bard's face was white. Briefly his teeth showed in a grimace of frustration. 'And the maid? Does *she* do this because she *has to?* I say we are better to silence her now.'

'Alice will say nothing,' Elizabeth answered. 'That I promise.'

'A Sassenach's promise is worth less then nothing.' Bard looked at O'Neill. ''Tis for you to say.'

O'Neill's eyes held Elizabeth's. 'Treason, madam,' he said. 'Aye. But what will you tell the King?'

Elizabeth drew in a deep breath, then blew it out again. 'I will tell him the truth, insofar as I can. I will tell him my husband and Andrea Lucca duelled over me.'

His eyes did not leave hers. 'Your reputation, madam.'

Almost, she laughed. 'I have no reputation. *This* lie will tarnish nothing.'

After a moment O'Neill looked at Bard. 'Let the girl go.'

''Twill be our death!'

'I think not,' O'Neill said, and shut his eyes.

Alice whimpered. Bard released her and she fell to her knees. 'I swear I'll say nothing. *Nothing!*'

Bard said something sharply in Gaelic but O'Neill made no answer, and Elizabeth wondered what had been said. She had seen the perfect willingness in Bard's eyes to snap Alice's neck, and for the first time she fully understood how dedicated they were to Ireland's cause. They had come willingly into the King's presence, risking their lives, and they expected everyone else to do the same. A man or woman in their way was put out of it, and

Elizabeth realized Bard would not hesitate to slay her as well. He had said it once. And because that perfect willingness to kill was tempered by O'Neill, and Bard's love, it had an integrity of its own.

But she could not condone it.

'I will go to my new apartments,' she said, carefully dispassionate. 'They will come soon to tell me of Simon's death, and I must ready myself to play the part of a grieving bride widowed so soon after her wedding.' Her eyes were on O'Neill. 'Stay here as long as you can; no one will come. Gather your strength . . . and use it well. I can do no more.'

''Tis enough.' O'Neill's tone was harsh and she saw the pain in his eyes. She knew there was every chance he might not live to see the morning, and she could do nothing. Nothing at all. She could only wait in her chambers for news of her husband's death, knowing all the while she might yet lose O'Neill.

'Alice,' she said quietly, and took her leave at once.

They came an hour later as she sat embroidering with awkward hands in her new apartments, and told her Bagenal lay gravely wounded.

For a moment Elizabeth could only stare at the men in shock, wondering if she had heard them aright. But her reaction was ideal for her purposed and quite unfeigned; she had believed Bagenal dead.

Alive? My God – he will tell the King about O'Neill!

And so she went mutely with the men as they led her to her husband, and all the while she hoped he would die before she reached him.

263

23

For three days and nights Elizabeth sat at Bagenal's bedside, knowing it was not through love or loyalty that she held the vigil, but fear. Fear he would waken and tell someone of O'Neill's presence within the palace, although Alice had told her that first long night O'Neill was gone. Alice had disposed of the bloodied sheets and returned at once to her mistress, and Elizabeth was greatly relieved the maid intended to tell no one the truth of what had transpired. That worry was gone, but the one about Bagenal remained.

O'Neill had spitted him on the sword. But he rallied; in the third day his fever broke and the royal physicians said he would live. He remained in a stupor, and Elizabeth stayed at his side, watching, waiting. She slept rarely, fearing if she left his side whoever took her place would have the truth from him, and so when Bagenal finally did rouse she found herself gazing at him stupidly, slow of wit and speech.

His eyes on her were clouded, but they knew her. His lips curled back from his teeth in a feral baring. 'You – *here?*'

She stared back a moment, trying to recover her senses. She felt sluggish, too weary for careful speech, but somehow she summoned a light, neutral tone. 'A wife's place is at her husband's side.'

'Bitch!' he said hoarsely. 'Why not go with your Irish pig?'

'I have told you where my place is.'

He was so pale as to be nearly transparent, so fair was

his normal colouring. His hair was lank against the pillows and dark circles lay under his eyes, but there remained the cold, passionless fire she had come to know.

'It is your fault.' His voice lacked its normal vibrancy, but the bite of contempt remained. 'By God, I should see you slain for it! Traitoress!'

'Will you?' Elizabeth felt exceptionally calm, almost exhilarated by the reversal of their positions. 'Will you tell them what I have done? It was *you* who fought him alone, over a personal matter, when you should have called the King's guard and had him taken.' She was amused by the answering anger in his eyes. 'Will the King be so willing to overlook your behaviour?'

'Whore . . .' he said unevenly.

'You should know better than that.' Her tone was cool. No longer was she touched by the insult or the man who said it. 'It was you who had my virginity of me, before I hardly knew what it was to lie with a man.'

'It was you who got him away – '

'Yes,' she said clearly. 'And I would do it again.'

'He is a traitor to the Crown.' It was obviously an effort for Bagenal to speak. His face was the colour of death. 'Elizabeth, you are an *Englishwoman* – '

'So I am,' she interrupted smoothly. 'But I will not have a man such as you telling me about traitors when you desire only titles and improved standing within the realm. You are no better than my father, seeking to use whatever is at hand. O'Neill wanted me in his bed, yes, but never did he *use* me! He wanted me as a man wants a woman, not as you desire a tool. There is a difference, *husband*.' Elizabeth sucked in a deep breath. 'If you tell the King about O'Neill, I will swear you knew it all along, planning to sell the information for greater wealth and position. He will believe it, knowing how willing you were to sacrifice even your bride on her wedding night. Do you

265

think he will listen to your protests when *I* have done with him?' She laughed. 'You made me his whore, Simon . . . now learn what it is for the whore to master the man who thinks to rule her!'

'Get you gone from my sight!'

'*Only* after I have a promise from you.'

'That I will say nothing? No. I promise you nothing.'

Her smile was grim. 'Then I suggest you bid farewell to court, Sir Simon, for I think you will not see it again.'

'Damn you!' He was weak, spent. 'May God see you burn in the fires below!'

'No doubt I shall burn,' she agreed, 'but no less hot than you. Your promise, Simon.'

High colour stood in his pale face. 'You have it!' he choked. 'But what, madam, do you suggest I *do* say?'

She smoothed her skirts with healing hands. 'I have let it be known you and Andrea Lucca fought a duel over me. As the entire court is talking about how I am the King's mistress, everyone will readily believe *this* story. They have seen me with him, have they not? And you all unknowing?'

He spat out a curse. 'Now, madam, I want a promise from you.'

Elizabeth frowned. 'What would you have of *me?*'

'That you will take yourself from my presence.' Breath rasped in his throat. 'That you will go from this court so there is no more need for me to look upon you. Go home to your father's cow byre in Kent. I have no wish to set eyes on you again.'

Trembling, Elizabeth rose from the chair. She had never seen such hatred in a man's face before, and it frightened her. But she dared not show it to him. 'I will go home to Kent. Gladly. But be certain I shall get word to the King of your duplicity if so much as a whisper reaches me about O'Neill.'

'By the time I am up from this bed he will be in Ireland,' Bagenal said weakly. 'The Eireannach fox will go to ground. By God, madam, do you think I intend to chase him to his stinking island? I am well rid of him, and I have no intention of telling the King what has transpired.'

'Of course not,' she agreed scornfully. 'Sir Simon Bagenal, Queen's champion, defeated by an Irishman? What honour would *that* bring you?'

'Go,' he said hoarsely. 'Take yourself from this room and hide yourself in Kent. Your days at court are finished.'

'And I thank God for it.' Elizabeth gathered her heavy skirts and walked stiffly from his presence.

With Alice, she went to Rosewood. There she lost herself in reacquainting her fingers with the satiny touch of the panelled walls and the heavy, dark furniture she loved. She rode again across the downs, hair flying free and skirts kilted up like a hoyden, revelling in the freedom she had not known for too long. And she laughed aloud to know that while Bagenal believed O'Neill on his way to Ireland, he lay instead at the house in the woods that had belonged to his mother, who was Simon Bagenal's aunt.

And then Bard came, silent and solemn and watchful, as ever. 'He is ill,' he said. 'Will you come?'

And so she left Rosewood in secrecy, saying nothing to anyone, and went with Bard to the old house in the trees. There she found Fiona and the dogs, and O'Neill, sick unto death.

He had taken wound fever, common enough in men who travelled before it was safe enough to do so. But she said nothing of it to Bard, who had had no choice, or O'Neill, who could not hear. She sat by his bed, as she had sat by her husband's, and prayed for O'Neill to recover even as she had longed for Bagenal to die.

'He called for you,' Bard said quietly. 'For three nights, until I could bear it no longer.'

'You would not have come to me otherwise?'

'No.'

'Bard . . . I mean him no harm.'

'You do not intend it, perhaps, but you will bring it to him. You have already.'

'I have said I had nothing to do with this battle between O'Neill and Bagenal.'

'Not with that, perhaps,' he agreed. 'But with more than you believe.' And he left, as if he could not bear to see her with the man he loved.

Elizabeth kept O'Neill's burning brow cooled with damp cloths and spoke to him softly, though she knew he could not hear her. He was fitful, tossing in the bed even as she sought to hold him down, for movement worsened the fever in the wound. She rebandaged it regularly and found the edges swollen and stinking of infection. Hot poultices from Fiona she bound against the wound, hoping the herbs would draw the pain and infection until he could sleep cleanly again, untroubled by what hounded his soul. She could say little of what ate at him for when he spoke it was in Gaelic, and in such a broken, wandering tone she doubted even Bard could decipher it.

'Eilis . . .' he whispered. 'Why do you turn your face from me? Is it because I have Ireland in my blood? D'ye love the Sassenachs so much?'

She longed to answer him but he was gone again, muttering in Gaelic mixed with a smattering of French. His face was dry and hot to her touch, burning her flesh, and she wondered how a man could retain his senses while his brain was being parboiled. He quieted a little under her hands, as if he heard her soothing whispers and understood, but then he became fretful again and full of mutters, and she could only wait.

Elizabeth took most of her meals in the bedroom, eating food that was tasteless in her mouth. One night she dropped the mug of broth Fiona put into her shaking hands, and the woman went away after gathering up the pieces. A moment later Bard came in with a glass, knelt down by her chair, and held it to her mouth, helping her drink even as her own hands shook, and she tasted again the fiery water of life.

She choked, pushing it away. 'Do you wish to kill me?'

'No,' he said solemnly. 'You are half dead already, needing none of my help. You must rest.'

She pushed the back of one hand across her brow, dragging loose hair out of her face. 'Not while he is so ill.'

'You have done what you can.' His voice was gentle, evoking the first Bard she had known. 'You have been with him night and day for nearly a week, and you will sicken yourself if you do not rest. I will see to him now.'

Elizabeth looked at Bard, so weary she could hardly speak. 'Will you never share him? Will you never let me know him?'

He, still kneeling by her chair, looked only at the floor. 'He is – all I have ever wanted. To share him is to give up what little of him I have, and it comes hard. Too hard for you to understand.'

'Do you think I cannot?' She pushed more hair from her face and felt the lifelessness of her flesh. 'Oh, Bard . . . I love him too. I cannot pretend to understand all that you feel, but surely I know a portion of it. We both love him. You have had him so much longer than I . . . can you not share him for only a brief while? You will go back to Ireland, while I' – she paused as her voice wavered – 'while I remain behind and wait to hear word of Ireland's army and the battles that will be fought.'

Bard's face twisted. 'If I let you have even a portion of him, Elizabeth, he will be gone from me forever.'

It was the first time he had ever called her by her Christian name. Somehow the simple entreaty in the statement broke through the reserve she had built against him. Bard had always been able to hurt her, from the very beginning, yet it was now – when he did not seek to – that he hurt her worse than she could bear.

She sat on the chair with the whiskey in her hands and looked on his grieving face, and let the tears roll down unchecked. She did not care anymore.

'Oh God . . .' she whispered. 'I could not bear it if he died – '

'He will not die.' Bard pressed himself off the floor and rose. 'Ireland's need is too great.'

'Ireland!' Elizabeth stared at him. 'Is that all you can think of? *Ireland?* How can you be so cold?'

'Because Ireland is here.' Bard tapped his chest. 'Without it, we are nothing. And without The O'Neill, Ireland is nothing.' His face hardened. 'But you are a Sassenach, and you could not possibly understand.'

'I understand he is a man, not a country,' she said helplessly. 'Do you ever think of him as nothing more than that? And what of yourself? Are you so willing to pour out your blood upon the ground for nothing more than a thing called *Ireland?*'

'Oh, aye,' he said. 'I will die for Ireland, and I will be happy doing it. There is no greater thing in this world than for a man to die for his land.'

'Will you think so when *he* is dead?' Her eyes went to O'Neill's pale, haggard face. 'Will you think so when he lies dead of an English sword, or headless by the order of a Scottish King?'

But Bard did not answer, and when Elizabeth looked for him she found he had gone.

* * *

She was sound asleep in the chair when O'Neill called her name. Elizabeth roused and moved to take his hand at once, speaking quietly. It was full dark outside but the candle Fiona had lighted burned brightly, illuminating his face. It was gaunt and waxen, lacking the vitality she had come to love so much, but for once there was sense in his eyes. He stared up at her from the pillows and said her name again, but this time no sound escaped his lips.

He was lucid, she realized with a jolt of surprise. She put her hand against his forehead and felt the clamminess of sweat, knowing the fever had broken at last. Elizabeth closed her eyes a moment, sending her thanks towards heaven, then smiled at him in relief.

'I dreamed of you,' he said hoarsely. His eyes were fixed on her face. 'Are you here?'

'I am real,' she told him. 'You are not dreaming.'

His hand burned against hers. 'Eilis – '

'Hush, hush . . .' she said soothingly. 'You have been ill. You must rest. Sleep now, and I promise that in the morning I will still be here.'

'How did you come?'

She saw he would not rest until she answered his questions. 'I was banished by my husband to my home estate – my *father's* home estate. I have been cast off.' She smiled sardonically. 'Bard came for me there.'

'Bagenal *lives?*'

Elizabeth pressed his chest as he fought to sit upright. He fell back against the pillows as his meagre strength gave out and cursed himself repeatedly.

'Be silent!' she insisted. 'You have only just now come back to your senses and yet you seek to make yourself ill again. I promise I will tell you everything when you are better.'

His eyes burned in his face, so shadowed and haggard in the candlelight. 'Bagenal is *alive?*'

She sighed. 'Yes. But he was badly hurt.'

O'Neill swore, his face twisted. 'Would that he had died!'

'Yes. Now – will you sleep?'

'I weary of sleeping.' His voice lacked the dark timbre she loved, but his frustration was evident all the same. 'I have done nothing else these last days. And do you mean to tell me you have been here all the time?'

'Nearly.'

The fever lent his eyes false brightness, but now there was life in them again. She knew what she saw was O'Neill once more. His mouth, nearly hidden in the beard that needed trimming badly, moved into a faint smile. There was no irony. 'A Sassenach tending an Irishman?'

'As an Irishman tended a Sassenach, so many weeks ago.' Elizabeth smiled at him. 'Almost four months, now.'

'My Christ!' O'Neill swore. 'I must get to Ireland!'

'When you are healthy,' she agreed.

'Christ, woman, would you have me wallowing in bed like a sickly, puling child? I cannot wait, nor can Ireland. I must go – '

'If you go now, it will kill you,' she said evenly. 'You can be of no help to your land if you are dead.'

He tried to shout at her but had not the strength for it. Elizabeth, smiling to herself, held the glass of whiskey to his mouth and watched him drink, and then she saw the quick colour rising in his face as he choked. 'Holy Mary, Eilis – 'tis whiskey!'

'*Uisge-beatha.*' She curled her mouth around the unfamiliar syllables. 'You told me once *whiskey* is a heathenish twisting of its proper name.'

His coughing done with, he drained the rest of the liquor and slumped back against his pillows. Colour was in his face, but it did not hide the dark shadows etching themselves beneath his eyes, nor the hollowness of his face. He had lost strength and flesh during his illness, and suddenly he reminded her less of the powerful warrior she had come to love than a small boy who needed mothering.

But she dared not mother him. Not O'Neill.

'Well.' Her tone was brusque as she rose. 'I will tell Bard and Fiona you are awake again. No doubt you'll want food before long.'

His hand, quicker than she had expected, shot out and caught her wrist. She sat again hastily, off balance, and then he pulled her down against his chest. 'No,' he said roughly, 'let them wait. 'Tis *you* I want by me.'

The glass fell to the floor and broke. Elizabeth thought to rise and pick up the pieces, but O'Neill's arm was crooked around her shoulders. She could tell by his breathing he was asleep again, the sleep of a healing man, and for the first time since Bard had brought her, Elizabeth allowed herself to relax.

The tension seeped out of her body. She felt the warmth of O'Neill next to her, his fingers curving around her arm, and sensed the possessiveness in him she had thought never to see directed at herself. For a moment it confused her, then pleased her, and finally – when she could allow herself to forget what Bard and Fiona might think if they found her with him – it soothed her.

She turned her head against his shoulder and slept.

24

It was a strange interlude for Elizabeth. She watched as O'Neill healed and recovered his strength, seeing the man evolve from the patient, and knew she would lose him. Yet for now she had him, for she was with him most of the time. He seemed content to share her company even without the physical intimacy he had demanded before. But she wondered how much of it had to do with his illness; O'Neill did not strike her as a man who asked nothing of a woman if he truly wanted her.

The beard came off and she saw the face she had first known, though lacking the colour of those earlier days. He had left behind the sun of France and Italy and lost the tan that had made the green eyes so brilliant. Black Irish indeed he was, with the sort of colouring a woman would kill for, and him so masculine that Elizabeth could scarce draw breath when he was near. And yet, as vigour and life crept back into his body and made his movements smooth and lithe again, she felt the flutter of fear she experienced whenever she thought of sharing a man's bed. It had been one thing to sleep in his arms the one night he had seemed to need it, for they had done nothing but sleep. It was another to consider him desiring more than that. It frightened her. Elizabeth could not banish the memory of the King's pitiful futility or Bagenal's cold assault. Not even for O'Neill.

He walked out with the dogs as he had done so long before. The huge wolfhounds gambolled at his side as if they were mere pups. She heard their joyous barks from the house and wondered that O'Neill allowed them noise after telling her they so rarely barked. But perhaps he did not feel threatened. Perhaps he was at ease, trusting her now as he had not before.

That in itself frightened her. Had she convinced him she would not betray him or his cause? Had she *meant* to?

Yes, she told herself. *By convincing him I mean him no harm, he will no longer threaten me*. And yet she thought O'Neill would not hurt her. Not now. *Because I have betrayed my country for the sake of an Irish rebel. He has only to look at me and I am made a traitor. I could no more risk his life than my own.*

Such conviction, such certainty, frightened Elizabeth. When had she changed? When had she willingly become an ally to O'Neill? When had she set aside her perceptions of the Irish race so that understanding could fill the void?

And yet she knew it was not understanding. It was not for Ireland she did what she could for O'Neill, but for the man himself. For another she would not do so much. For another man she would not turn traitor to the Crown. Not even an Englishman.

Tentatively she began to test the bonds of her feelings for O'Neill, asking herself questions for which she had no answers. Already she had betrayed so much for him. She had been willing to watch her husband die. She had even been willing to help O'Neill kill him, for it was *she* who had given the Irishman back his fallen sword.

What am I? she wondered. *Murderess, had Simon died? And would they cut off my head as well?*

She found no answers. No answers at all, for the one that waited was not the one she could acknowledge.

Bard kept very much to himself, but Elizabeth was quite aware of his eyes on her, watching as she moved around the house. She and Fiona had grown closer, sensing a sameness in their loyalty to O'Neill, but Bard withdrew

275

even further. She saw a desolation in his eyes from time to time and a desperate loneliness, as if he knew he had lost O'Neill, but she dared not say a word to him. Bard had his own sort of dignity and she preferred not to disturb it more than she already had.

The November mornings were cold and gloomy, but lacking the bitter bite of deepest winter. O'Neill wore warm clothes and made Elizabeth wrap herself in a heavy woollen mantle when she walked outside with him. No longer did she trouble herself to clothe herself as a lady of the court but wore instead her plainest gown and let her hair hang free in a single loosely plaited braid. The only thing she missed was the freedom to ride across the countryside, but that O'Neill would not have her do. And she understood.

She could tell when he tired, and then she made him go indoors again where the fire warmed the room and Fiona's hot cakes were washed down with tea and whiskey. Elizabeth had grown to like the taste of *uisge-beatha*, though O'Neill raised an eyebrow whenever she drank it, and she found herself longing for time to stop in its tracks. Then he would not have to go to Ireland and fight his foolish battles. But the same pride and spirit that made his intentions so frustrating were what made the man himself, and she found herself hating O'Neill nearly as much as she hated herself. He was taking her heart prisoner and she thought he would ask no ransom.

Bard took his leave early one night and Fiona disappeared to her room near the kitchen. O'Neill sat by the fire, nursing his *uisge-beatha*, with Boru and Cuchullain at his feet. He looked tired; there was a feverish brightness to his eyes Elizabeth did not like.

'You should go to bed,' she told him.

'Oh, aye, I will.'

His voice was vague as he stared into the fire, and she frowned. 'O'Neill – you are not ill again?'

'No. Not ill.'

'Then what is it?'

He sighed and rolled his head back against the chair. 'I cannot say, precisely.'

Elizabeth was up at once, moving to place her hand against his brow. His flesh was quite cool, but she felt the heat of his fingers as he reached up to catch her hand. And then he rose to tower over her, himself again, and she knew what he wanted from her. 'O'Neill – '

'Hush,' he commanded. 'I'll have no more talk from you. We have shared little more these past days, and I cannot wait any longer. My Christ, woman, did you think I was gelded by this illness?'

'O'Neill!'

He swept her up into his arms with no trace of weakness. 'No more talk,' he said, and took her from the room.

He carried her up to his own bedroom, said a word to the dogs to keep them outside in the corridor, and shut the door with his foot. He set her on the bed gently and looked down on her. ''Twill be done right this time,' he said quietly. 'No more words between us, when we both know what it is we've been wanting from each other.'

She watched him strip out of his doublet and linen shirt. Then the boots and the breeches, and suddenly he was nude before her and so beautiful she could hardly stand to look at him. In the dark velvets he had always worn he had cut a fine figure of a man – broad-shouldered, lean-hipped, with powerful arms and legs. But she had not seen him nude before, and she had not known what to expect.

Somehow, though she had seen Bagenal naked before her, Elizabeth had not envisioned the flat abdomen ridged with muscle or the bunching of his thighs; the long, firm calves taut with chiselled muscle; the length of his arms and legs in perfect proportion to the breadth of his shoulders; the broad, powerful hands. The flesh he had lost to illness was mostly replaced. There was nothing about him she would change.

Save the weapon rising between his legs.

Elizabeth saw in one frightened moment that he would hurt her, hurt her as Bagenal had, perhaps worse. He would tear her as Bagenal had torn her; bloody her as Bagenal had bloodied her; bruise her as Bagenal bruised her. For all her senses clamoured for his touch, her inner self recalled only Simon Bagenal, and fused him with Kieran O'Neill.

His hands were on her as she sought to scramble from the bed. Elizabeth cried out, but the sound barely got past the constriction in her throat. She felt the convulsive trembling take hold of her, deepening to shudders, and knew she would vomit if he even touched her again.

'Eilis, Eilis . . .' he said softly. 'Why do you run from me?'

'Not from *you* . . .' she choked. 'From what you will *do* to me.'

Naked, he sat down beside her on the bed. 'D'ye not want it?' he asked. 'Eilis, I think you do.'

'No more,' she whispered. 'No more . . . I will not give myself over to that. You may have put your sword in him, but you did not lie with him. You cannot know what it is to be so frightened, and have him mount you without the slightest hint of care. He *used* me, O'Neill, as if I were a whore who had no need of sweet words and gentle hands. He mounted me like a stud with a mare and was done nearly as quickly. Do you think I want that again?'

He did not touch her. He merely looked at her, frowning slightly, and she knew a sudden yearning for his

278

understanding. But what could he understand? O'Neill, who was a man, not a woman, a man who bedded women as easily as others made water.

'Eilis,' he said softly, 'listen to me, now. Hear me when I say I am not Simon Bagenal.'

'But you are a *man!*' she said vehemently. 'Will you not hurt me, even if you do not mean it?'

'I am not a stud . . . and you are not a mare. We are man and woman, and we are meant for this union, Eilis.' His hands were on her shoulders, pulling her towards his chest. 'D'ye think I could hurt *you?*'

'O'Neill – oh God, O'Neill, I think you could do anything you desired to do – '

'Then let me love you,' he said. 'Let me show you how it is supposed to be, my Eilis . . .' His mouth was against her throat, hushing her gently, speaking so softly she could hardly hear him. She strained against his arms, which held her so tightly, but he did not let her go, and she knew he would not. She sobbed once, then bit her lip so she would not do it again; she wished to show no more weakness to him.

He spoke in Gaelic. She could understand none of it, save her name, but his voice had a soft, soothing sound to it. He could win the trust of a newborn colt with that tone, so warm and tender; was she a filly, then, answering his care?

Elizabeth thought to pull away. But his arms would not let her; his hands stroked her back. 'O'Neill,' she begged. 'Please . . . I cannot – '

'Husshhh,' he said again, this time speaking English. 'My sweet Sassenach, I promise it will not hurt. Not from me.'

His mouth closed on hers and she groaned, tasting his mouth and the whiskey as she had that very first time. She thought fleetingly of Bagenal's kiss in the gallery, when she had thought she wanted him. But this was O'Neill. Who held her; whose mouth set her lips afire and made her long for more even as she sought to deny it.

Suddenly her body came alive beneath his mouth and hands, crying out for him, and Elizabeth found herself lost in a depth of desire she had never believe possible. Her senses clamoured for him, drowning out the vestiges of fear. Deep down she felt the final quiver of that fear, and then she was free to love him back.

Tentatively her hands went up to clasp his neck. She felt the smooth, warm flesh and the taut sinews beneath her palms. Thick hair twined around her fingers. Her breath was ragged in her mouth as she pulled him closer still.

His response was immediate. His kisses grew deeper, more demanding as their tongues met in a courtship of the mouth. His hands were on her aching breasts and she felt the heat of his flesh even through the fabric of her gown.

Suddenly she wanted it off. She want the sensation of flesh on flesh, her own pressed against his, and the cessation of the pain that formed so taughtly in her belly, so taut she could hardly stand it. Her thighs and breasts sang with it.

Elizabeth twisted away from him and turned her back. For a moment she felt him go very still, until she lifted her braid out of the way and told him to untie her laces. And then O'Neill laughed deep in his throat and she knew he was thinking of all the times the laces stopped him before, because she had wanted them to.

His hands were deft but he did not rush. Her eyelids grew heavy; her mouth slackened as the slow heat spread through her body. She felt the fabric fall slowly away from her back, sliding off her shoulders. His hands were against her flesh, slowly pushing the sleeves down her arms until she was free, unfettered by bodice or undershift. In one twisting motion she was free of it all. Naked, she knelt on the bed before him.

He traced the silk of her flesh. His fingers slid over her back so softly she could hardly feel them, aching for his touch, and yet she tingled at even the slightest sensation of contact. Then his mouth closed at the nape of her neck. His tongue raised her flesh upon her bones; one long quiver ran the length of her body. 'O'Neill,' she breathed, because she had no voice with which to speak.

On her knees, she rose. Arched. Head tipped back, back, spilling the braid down her spine. Behind her, O'Neill knelt as well, head bent over hers. She felt the line of his hips in the small of her back; pressed against her buttocks was the jutting of his manhood. Taut. Impatient. Demanding her attention.

But she did not give it. She knelt as O'Neill knelt, not in supplication but in abject pleasure, the sheer delight of tactile sensation. His arms slid under hers, encircling her ribs; she felt the taut soreness of her nipples impress themselves upon the underside of his forearms. And then his hands, as he moved them, settling his palms against the aching roundness of her breasts.

His breath was against her neck as he bent his head over hers. She heard the rasp in his throat, the twin harmonies of their ragged breathing. And then one arm slid down, deserting her left breast, and she felt the hand caress the slight curvature of her abdomen. Lower still, raising her flesh in an instant response, until his fingers were in the tawny curls between her legs.

'O'Neill,' she breathed, knowing no other word to speak. His name had become her world.

With his other hand he caressed her breasts until she could hardly bear it. And then his fingers were within her, and there was no pain, no discomfort, only a yearning that filled her being.

'O'Neill!'

'No,' he whispered against the nape of her neck. 'There will be nothing hasty about this union.'

Her head tipped back, back, until it pressed against his shoulder. She was the string on a harp, taut with the need to loose the music. Vibrating, vibrating, filled up with tension and yearning.

And then his hands were on her shoulders, turning her, and he lowered her down on to the bedclothes. He was gentle and tender as he ministered to her, so at odds with the impatient, impassioned O'Neill she had known before. He hurried nothing, taking his time, caressing her breasts and belly and the length of her legs, from thighs to toes and back again, until she quivered against the bedclothes.

'*O'Neill!*'

But what he said to her was in Gaelic, and she could understand none of it save the tone. Incredibly, he seemed as lost as she within the torture he inflicted.

She took the palm of his hand against her mouth and kissed it, letting her tongue linger. His flesh was salty and callused, but she loved it no less for its toughness. All she knew was she wanted him to feel what she did, so he would understand what he did to her.

From deep within she felt the tension and heat expand; expanding, she thought she might burst. She cried out for him, not really knowing what she wanted, needed, demanded, knowing only she had to have it.

He played her. He played her as he had played his harp. She was taut as a tight-wrapped string, her body ringing to his touch, and yet her newly learned musicianship promised the crescendo had not been reached. The song had just begun.

His mouth was on her breasts even as his hand moved

yet again between her legs. She felt the tight tingling pain as he tongued her nipples and sucked gently, gasping as the pleasure flooded her senses. And then his mouth moved slowly, slowly, tracing the line of her quivering belly; lower, until she felt his lips replace his hand.

'O'Neill!' she cried. '*Oh God* – '

'No,' he said against her, 'only a man, my Eilis.' And his breath mingled with the warm moistness of her essence.

She felt herself arching upward, upward, straining against his mouth, and suddenly there came such a desperate demand within her, she thought she might die from the need. And then O'Neill, shifting, moved her legs apart and entered so smoothly and easily that she thought she had dreamed it all, except she knew she did not.

For one moment she feared the pain Bagenal had given her, but it never came. O'Neill had given her time, more than enough time, so that her body answered the clamouring of her senses. With him she was whole, wanting it as much as he did; there was no pain, only pleasure. And as he began to move deep within her she felt that pleasure spiralling upward until she thought she might burst.

O'Neill. A silent plea.

He moved within her, rocking, rocking, so smoothly, without violence, only an intense, compelling need that asserted itself and carried her along. Faster. Faster. She gave herself over to raw sensation, forgetting who she was, what she was, knowing only *that* she was, and so was he – O'Neill, O'Neill, who took her higher and faster and farther until she wanted to fall, to fall and shatter, because she could bear no more. But she bore it, she bore it, because to stop it was to stop life itself; to stop O'Neill was to stop, period, and she would never give him up.

He moaned. Quivered. Shifted upon her body. Closer yet, closer, so that he was deeper, deeper, so deep she thought he would fill up her soul as well as her body. She felt the tension building in his body even as it did within her own. She was lost, she was lost; he had banished her forever while he also banished himself. And then he cried out as she did and she felt the spurt of his seed deep within her. Her hands clutched at him, pinning him against her even as he held her, and slowly, so slowly, the world came back into being again.

She lay beneath him, secure in the weight of his flesh. He was so warm, so warm, so much a part of her as they lay tangled together in the bed. She felt the pounding of his heart slow until it regained its measured beat; she felt his breath against her throat and wondered if he slept – could a man sleep? Could she? Or had he gone away from her as she had gone away from him in that one blinding instant of absolute unity?

But he moved at last, rolling on to his side and taking her with him, so they lay together in the tangle of the bedclothes, so he could trace the line of her jaw to her breast, where the nipple sprang at once into his palm, and he smiled. 'Oh my Eilis, my Eilis, was that so much to fear?'

'Oh yes,' she breathed, 'oh yes . . . you have taken me from myself. And if it takes me so far out of myself each time, I am afraid I will not come back. And I will die out there, wherever it was I had gone to.'

He propped his head upon one hand, elbow crooked against the pillow. In the shadows she could see only the planes of his face, the fine, pronounced planes of cheekbone, brow, nose, jaw. She had never thought a man could be beautiful, not as a woman was, but she had no other word. And she wanted suddenly to be inside his skin, tight-wrapped around his bones as a string upon a harp, to ring again at his touch. She put out her hand and touched his chest, feeling the silkiness of his hair, the dampness of exertion.

'O'Neill,' she whispered, 'what have you done to me?'

'Bewitched you,' he answered. 'Bound you utterly.'

His hand, stroking, seemed to make love to her flesh, caressing the line of hip and thigh. Almost convulsively she shifted closer, closer, sealing her body against his, so that there was no separation. She could not get enough of his warmth and vitality.

'O'Neill,' she whispered. 'Ah God, how you steal a woman's soul!'

'Have I stolen yours?' He did not smile. He looked at her intently, so intently, from the shadows of the night, with his hand upon her and his voice a whiskey voice, seductive and incredibly tender; from him, incongruous.

From him, it seemed, all she had ever wanted.

'Oh yes,' she answered. 'Oh yes. Now what will you do with it?'

'What would you have me do?'

In the crook of his arm, she sighed. 'Cherish it, O'Neill. And never let it go.'

One broad hand cradled the back of her skull and pressed her cheek against his shoulder. 'Eilis, oh my Eilis, what would the English say? What would the Irish say? To see us like this – to see us so lost, so utterly lost, like fools, like fools, such helpless, hopeless fools . . .' He shut his eyes and she felt the warmth of his breath against the hollow of her neck. '*Eilis, oh my Eilis* . . .' He seemed incapable of anything more.

And she thought, for the moment, she wanted nothing more. What he had given her was enough.

25

O'Neill awoke with the first pearly pink light of the new dawn. He was quite warm and content and felt better than he had in days, as if the last vestiges of his wound fever had indeed gone. He had not known such contentment in too long, and for a moment he could not think why he would now.

Then he became very aware of the body stretched next to his, limbs awry in the abandonment of sleep, and he recalled that he and Eilis had at last achieved the union he had desired so long. After months of wanting her so badly, it had spoiled him for other women, though it had not stopped him from trying to forget her. But he no longer needed to try, for she was here beside him, and as much his as he was hers.

A faint echo of alarm sounded deep within his soul at that, for he had never considered himself a ward of any woman. He was a man who took, giving what he wished in return if they were deserving of it, but never letting them see any part of his soul. God knew women had pleasured him over the years, but he could not recall when – or even *if* – any woman had left him feeling so perfectly at ease with himself. Always before it had been sheer physical release, pleasurable and briefly entertaining, but this time it had been very different.

Slowly he eased over on to his side so he could look at her. She stirred as he moved but did not waken, her face half hidden in tawny hair. O'Neill carefully stroked it aside so he could look at her clearly, trying to see in her face what it was that so bound his soul.

Wryly, he smiled. *She* had spoken of him stealing her soul, asking him to cherish what he had taken from her, and yet he thought she had a portion of his as well, for his was no longer complete. It had gone out of itself to her.

In sleep her face lacked the animation he so enjoyed, but it did not diminish her spirit. Her lashes, gold in the coral dawn, curved against an ivory cheek in an artlessly childish sweep. Her nose was straight except for the slight upward curvature at the end, which lent her face just a trace of impetuousness. It was a saving grace, for she had the aristocratic bones of her father that could be so hard and cold. He had seen that haughty look turned on him enough times to know he did not wish to see it again, not from her. From her he desired only her smile, or her love.

Her skin was quite fair, a true English complexion. The morning light flushed her cheeks and brought a glow of health to her fairness, staining her lips darker as she slept. He remembered the taste of her mouth and wanted more of it, but for the moment he would content himself with looking at her, until he had memorized her.

She stirred again and shifted, twisting her body as if she sought his warmth. One hip jutted towards the roof, emphasizing the narrowness of her waist and the perfect graduation to slender hips and full breasts. O'Neill felt the slow beat of desire intensify and reined it in with effort. Not yet. Not yet.

But how would she fare in Ireland? he asked himself in silence. She was not made for hardships and privation. She had known neither, and now he would give her a surfeit of them both.

And then he could wait no longer but put his hand to her face and traced the delicate lines of her bones. From brow to temple to jaw and below, sweeping at last across her collarbone with a touch soft as a butterfly. She stirred once again and moaned and he saw the nipples tighten.

He smiled with perfect joy to know his slightest touch could so move her. He let his hand linger, caressing her yet again, and her eyes came open and gazed at him in bafflement and wonder.

'I remember,' she said softly. 'It was not a dream after all.'

'Oh, aye . . . no dream. No dream at all, my Eilis.'

Her flesh quivered at his touch as his hand moved down towards her stomach. Without conscious thought, she shifted, moving her hips against his hand, sighing deep in her throat so that it was almost a moan. 'Irishman,' she whispered. 'What madness have you put into my soul?'

'Not madness.' His mouth was against her cheek. 'Magic. I am of the sidhe, and you a mortal woman who will give her soul over to the faeries.'

Her mouth moved into a smile even as her heavy lids fluttered closed. 'But I thought it was the faerie women who did the bewitching, catching a poor mortal man's soul and stealing it away.'

'Well, you have that,' he admitted, 'but now 'tis for *me* to do. I am the Eireannach after all, with faerie blood in my veins, and you only a Sassenach with no proper knowledge of such things.'

'Eireannach,' she said, half laughing, 'where is your barbaric savagery?'

'Here is my weapon,' he whispered, moving against her so she could feel the hardness of his manhood burning against her thighs. 'And would you have me use it?'

Elizabeth did not answer at once. He saw her eyes fixed on him, blackened by desire, and in her face was such a serious intentness as he had never seen before. And then he felt the touch of her hand and knew what she did; that she was trying to overcome the residue of fear she still felt towards that which could so punish her, as Bagenal had punished.

Her fingers were tentative, trembling, moving down through the crisp curling hair that furred his loins to the shaft that rose against her. He heard her indrawn gasp and felt the slight withdrawal, but as he made no move she touched him again, this time with more confidence. But the knowledge of what she did, and why, nearly drove him into a haste that would startle her away. He set his teeth and steeled himself against the passion rising in him.

'How can you want me so?' she asked in wonder.

'As I have wanted you from the beginning.' His breath was ragged in his throat. 'D'ye see now what torture you have put me through?'

'Does it – hurt?'

''Tis sweet punishment, my Sassenach, when a man knows the woman will release him.'

And then suddenly she had turned against him, her hands moving against his back as she wrapped her arms around him. She had taken the initiative at last, showing him how much she cared, and he felt a great welling of pride and triumph swelling within his chest.

He growled deep in his throat as she darted her warm tongue against his ear, her breath soft against his flesh. As he had done with her a moment before, she explored his body, sliding one hand down across the small of his back to the taut buttocks, and lower to his thighs. And then he pulled her beneath him again, taking his weight on to his arms as he sought to enter her.

This time she helped him, guiding him herself, and he heard her tangled moan of need as he began to move within her. Tentative at first, she soon met his every thrust, moving in concert with him, until he could bear it no more and burst within her warmth. He heard himself moan something to her in Gaelic, reflected dimly that she wouldn't understand; then, as he lay sprawled across her, he thought she might know what he meant regardless. He smiled against her throat.

Elizabeth, half crushed by his weight and revelling in it, could not put a name to all the emotions she felt coursing through her. There was great pleasure, of course, and a magnificent lassitude that flushed every pore of her skin, but other things as well. And primary among them was a complete and utter wonder that he could so lose himself in her when he was a man who needed no one but himself.

And then, as he lay in the contentment of her arms, he was not a man but a boy, with tousled hair tickling her breasts as he lay against her shoulder, half asleep as she held him. She put a hand to the thickness of his black hair and luxuriated in it, twining it around her fingers. For one odd moment she felt almost like a mother with a child at her breast, though O'Neill was no helpless babe. And for that moment she felt such a welling of emotion, she could not suppress it, and let the tears fall down her cheeks. One landed on his face and he opened his eyes, shifting to look up at her. A finger touched her cheek.

'Eilis?' His weight was suddenly gone from her. 'Did I hurt you?'

'No,' she said. 'Oh no . . . but you have brought me such joy I can hardly bear it.' Colour rose into her face. 'You see how weak I am, giving in to such foolish fancies.'

'Foolish fancies? Then we are both fanciful fools.' Gently he smoothed the tears away. 'Oh, woman, what you have done to me.'

'What have I done?' She grew braver by the instant, to hear such passion in his voice. 'What is it a Sassenach woman can do to Kieran O'Neill?'

He smiled, but there was a baleful glint in his eyes. 'If I told you, there would be no sense in trying to learn it, and the game all completed.'

She shivered at the reference. Games had been Bagenal's way.

O'Neill kissed her with conviction, leaving her gasping in the bedclothes. Then he rolled over and swung his legs out of bed, perching himself on the edge a moment. She saw the broad expanse of his back and the thick black hair that curled down to brush his neck. Then he was up, pulling on trunk hose and breeches and his crumpled lined shirt, paying no mind to its state.

He ran a hand through his hair, then rubbed briefly at his unshaven cheek. 'I'll have Fiona bring you a tray. And then you must ready yourself.'

'Ready myself?' She sat up, pulling the covers up to clothe her breasts. 'What must I ready myself for?'

His mouth twisted in its old ironic way. 'We leave for Ireland, Eilis . . . and you are coming with us.'

'You cannot mean to take *me!*'

'Only a fool would leave you behind,' he told her flatly. 'You are a traitor to your country, Eilis. If Jamie lays hands on you, you'll find yourself locked up in the Tower, and likely 'twill be *your* head put up on London Bridge instead of mine.'

White-faced, she stared at him.

O'Neill sighed. 'Eilis, Eilis, d'ye think Bard and I have been helpless while we were here? No. Bard has ways of learning things . . . They think we have gone to Ireland, so they do not search England diligently. But they will. And they will go to your father's estate. And when they find you there, they will take you.'

She said nothing as he left. There was nothing she could say.

Elizabeth's world was turned upside down. Instead of glorying in the new relationship with O'Neill, she found herself as much a prisoner as before. She watched Fiona pack her things in a small trunk – she had brought next to nothing from Rosewood – and then Bard carried it down, as he had once before. Elizabeth, dressed in a plain rose-coloured gown that pointed up the high colour in her face, followed them downstairs and saw the coach outside, horses hitched and waiting. Boru and Cuchullain dashed around the coach in wide circles, as if understanding this time that they were to go.

She stood in the doorway, wrapped in a wine-purple mantle, and looked blankly at the coach. O'Neill was atop it, tying down the chests Bard levered up with grunts and Gaelic curses. Suddenly the house was made empty, its usefulness finished; she realized O'Neill gone from England would make her world as empty. She had not acknowledged, before, just how *much* she loved him.

When he came to her at last, doublet hanging open even in the chill of the November morning, she looked at his outstretched hand and shook her head.

For a moment the hand remained outstretched. Then he dropped it to his side. 'You *will* be coming, Eilis.'

'No.'

'You must.'

'Because you say it?' Her chin rose stubbornly. 'England is my home.'

'Your home is with me.'

She felt the anguish rise up in her soul. A single sentence, a jumble of words. Said by O'Neill, they set her afire. What other words could a woman wish for a man to say?

Elizabeth looked into his green eyes and recalled the tenderness in them as he had caressed her so gently and made her know peace and wholeness and happiness in his arms. Then she drew in a ragged breath. 'I cannot go with you. Can you not see? What I have done was for you, not Ireland. For *you*. And for all you and others may call me a traitor, England is my home. I cannot go with you to Ireland and watch as you plan to overthrow the land I call my own. I cannot condone it. I cannot bear to see it done.'

She looked at him in anguish. 'England is my home.'

'Ireland is mine.'

'Then go.' The simple words cost her, but she would not take them back.

His mouth was a grim line. 'Get into the coach, Eilis.'

'I am a Sassenach,' she said clearly, couching it in what words might carry power. 'Ireland is the enemy. Ireland would curse an Englishwoman.'

'Not while you are The O'Neill's woman.'

She could not summon a smile, not even to lighten her words. 'And when it ends?' she asked. 'What will you do with me then?'

'Eilis – '

'I am not blind, O'Neill, or stupid. Ireland will never welcome me. My place is here in England.'

He swore in Gaelic, but she understood the impatience in his tone. 'By Christ, Eilis, be not such a fool! *England* is more dangerous to you than Ireland.'

'No.' She shook her head. 'I have thought about what you have said. But James Stuart is a Scotsman, O'Neill. He was put upon the throne only because he was cousin to Queen Elizabeth, though she would not name him her successor. Did you know that? My father told me. He said the Old Queen would not lie down, even as she died, but stood until she could stand no more. Never once did she say his name. There was no successor to the English throne, Irishman, merely an upstart Scot who was the son of an English lord.' She met his eyes levelly. 'Do you understand what I am saying? James has no stake in what I do. I think he will not trouble himself over me . . . not when O'Neill has gone home to Ireland to raise himself an army.'

O'Neill sighed. 'Then, madam, you may consider yourself my prisoner. A hostage, if you please, against your husband.'

'My husband!'

O'Neill's face was grim. 'D'ye think he will let me keep you without a fight? The very idea of *his* possession in the hands of an Irishman will be repugnant to him, and for that – if nothing else – he will come after me. After *us*, madam.'

'He said he would not chase you to your stinking island.' She recalled Bagenal's words very clearly, and the bitterness as he said them.

O'Neill did not smile. 'When he is recovered he will indeed chase me to Ireland. Even *I* am not so foolish as to be blind to pride and honour. He has been wounded in both by a barbaric Irishman – who also shares his blood – and he will not hesitate to come. He will come to kill me and to fetch you home again, to prove he is a man.'

'O'Neill – '

'You have no choice.' His hands were on her arm, grasping her firmly, and he dragged her out of the doorway into the yard beyond.

'O'Neill – let me go!'

He said nothing. He took her to the coach and thrust her inside, handing Fiona in immediately after. Elizabeth cried out as he slammed the door but by then it was too late. Bard, up on the box, whipped the horses into motion, and O'Neill swung himself up on to the seat next to Bard.

Fiona smiled wryly. ''Tis because he cares for you, Eilis – not because he wishes to be cruel.'

'He has said I am a hostage.' Elizabeth's tone was

bitter. 'Once *more* I am made a tool, a pawn in this foolish game men play!'

Fiona sighed. 'I know himself better than you, having known him since the day he was breeched. I think you will find I have the right of it.'

'Curse him!' she said. 'Curse all Irishmen!'

Fiona's eyes twinkled. ''Tis no need for you to be wasting words on *that*,' she said calmly. 'Those like O'Neill and Bard were born cursed. But 'tis grateful I am for such men.'

26

The second time the coach stopped O'Neill opened the door and climbed inside. He had a strange glint in his eyes. 'Bard says I am looking very tired – from my illness, no doubt. He says I should rest.'

Elizabeth glared at him scornfully. 'You do not look tired or ill to *me*.'

'He does to me,' Fiona said stoutly. 'And I grow weary of being inside. I will ride with Bard.'

Elizabeth sat up straight. 'You can't! *Outside?*'

Fiona smiled. 'I am an Irishwoman, mistress, and very strong. You will see I do well enough.' And she was out of the coach as O'Neill shut the door behind her.

He sat down across from Elizabeth. She scowled at him. 'Have you told her I am no longer Mistress Stafford?'

'She knows.'

'And says nothing.'

'Fiona serves *me*, not propriety.' The coach jolted into motion once again. O'Neill relaxed against the squabs and smiled at her. 'You are better to look at than the rumps of horses.'

Elizabeth said nothing. After a moment of oppressive silence he slid forward to the edge of his seat and took her hands into his, ignoring the stiffening of her fingers. His hands were cold from the ride atop the coach but they took the warmth from her flesh, and she felt one of his thumbs begin to caress her palm. It was a singularly disturbing sensation, for it reawakened her body to the yearning she had thought banished by his rudeness.

'Eilis,' he said gently, ''tis for your safety.'

'You said I was a hostage.'

'Only because you would come with me no other way.' The thumb continued to move and she found it hard to concentrate on what he said. 'D'ye think I wish to be risking you? I want you with me, Eilis, so I can know you are safe.'

'And because I offer you surety against Bagenal and the King.' How cynical she sounded. Court had made her so.

His voice was low and intimate. ''Tis not the only reason.'

'I doubt you will give me another.' She looked into his face and saw a softening in his mouth. The smile was very faint, but it was there. 'O'Neill – '

'You please me, Eilis,' he told her. 'That should be enough for you.'

Rebellion. Bitterness. 'You said once there was a great deal of difference between wanting and loving.'

'Oh, aye . . . there is.'

Scorn. 'And am I to think I satisfy your lust?'

'*Eilis* – '

She jerked her hands away. 'No, O'Neill. I will not play the mare to your stud merely because it *pleases* you.'

'It pleased *you* well enough, last night.' His teeth were tightly shut. '*And* this morning.'

Elizabeth felt heat and colour wash into her face. 'This morning it was because I thought there was more between us than mere satisfaction amd momentary pleasure.'

'I told you once I do not love you,' he said curtly. 'You cannot expect it of me. 'Tis not my way to love a woman, not the way a woman desires love.'

'Then you are a fool.'

His crooked smile was ironic. 'Perhaps. But a wiser one than most.'

It hurt. The pain was a tangible thing; it swelled in her

throat and chest, shutting off her breath. But she would not show it to him. 'I prefer Fiona's company to yours. Stop this coach so you may exchange with her.'

'No,' he said. 'I am weary and wish to rest. You should do the same, Eilis . . .'twill be a hard journey across England into Wales, and the crossing to Ireland is almost always rough.'

He did look tired. There were new lines graven in his face, and she wondered if perhaps the wound fever had not entirely left him. He was a strong man, but he had been very ill in addition to being under exceptional strain during his Italian subterfuge; such things could leave their influence long after a man seemed well again.

But then Elizabeth recalled the night before when she had thought he was ill, while all he wanted was to get her into his bed. And so she sat back against the squabs and crossed her arms, refusing to look at him.

O'Neill, smiling, slid down on to the end of his spine and propped his boots upon her seat. And as he went quickly into sleep she watched him, and found herself incredibly lonely even in his presence.

When they stopped at last at an inn to spend the night, Elizabeth was so tired of riding in the coach, she thought she might scream with it. She was stiff, sore, hardly capable of movement as O'Neill handed her down. Already Boru and Cuchullain had caught up, panting from their exertions. But their tails beat the air as if they could do it all again.

And then she remembered they *would* do it all again, in the morning, and she nearly groaned aloud.

Elizabeth could hardly eat. O'Neill ordered meat pies and a steaming partridge, but even that did not stir her appetite. She stared at the food on her plate, with a knife balanced in one limp hand, and paid attention only when

298

O'Neill took it away from her and cut up the meat himself. Then he pushed the plate back and she summoned a scowling face. 'I will feed myself, thank you.'

'Then do it.' He bit into a slice of new bread and smiled at her, seeming no worse for wear after a day spent in the uncomfortable coach.

Slowly Elizabeth began to eat, though the food was tasteless in her mouth. She was aware of Bard and Fiona at another table, near the one she shared with O'Neill, and suddenly wondered what would be done about sleeping arrangements. Did O'Neill intend her to share his bed? She set down her knife and stared at him. How could he think she would willingly do so *now?*

He put a cup of wine into her hands, then scowled and took it away again. He replaced it with his own cup, which held the familiar amber *uisge-beatha*. 'Drink,' he advised. 'You are too weary to sleep. You need rest.'

She drank, wondering if she were made insensible would he force himself upon her. But by the time she had finished the whiskey she was warm and at ease and very, very sleepy. Her eyes would not stay open. O'Neill said something to Bard and rose, gathering her into his arms before she could summon a protest. She heard him speak quietly to the innkeeper and realized suddenly that he and Bard had used French accents from the moment they had arrived.

He carried her up to the room, with its single narrow bed, and put her down upon it. Elizabeth levered herself up on one arm and stared at him in wonder. 'You do not mean to stay?'

'No,' he said calmly. 'You are a fetching sight with your eyelids all heavy and your mouth gone slack, but that is from the *uisge-beatha*, not desire for my attentions. And I do not want to sleep with whiskey and weariness; they are unpleasant lovers for me. I will share a room with Bard tonight, and Fiona will stay with you.'

She could not properly express her gratitude, for to look at him was too much work. And so she sank down into oblivion knowing only his smile was one of rueful resignation.

They passed at last from England into Wales, exchanging the rolling fields and woodlands of her country for the valleys and rugged blue mountains of Gwynedd, where the mists hung heavy in the mornings and into the afternoons, rolling back to display a panoply of jewelled forests trading late fall regalia for the more muted colours of mid-winter. Sheep roamed the hillsides patch-worked with stone fences and pastel forests. Elizabeth felt a longing such as she had never known, yearning to go home to what she knew and knowing she could not. If O'Neill wished to take the heart from her, he had done so, for he left her with only a memory of England as he took her into Wales.

Through Conwy they went, with its high stone walls and barbican gates and the cold bastion of the turreted castle warding the shores of the Irish Sea. The water was a pale icy blue, capped with white as it washed in against the land. It reminded her of Bagenal's eyes. She shivered and drew the woollen mantle closer about her shoulders.

From Conwy they went to Bangor and crossed to the Isle of Anglesey, nearer, to Ireland with each day and farther yet from London. There had been, so far, no signs of pursuit, but O'Neill was certain it would come.

'They believe us gone to Ireland,' he told her once. 'But they have searched and found nothing, so they will turn again to England while we cross the Irish Sea.'

When at last they reached Holyhead, at the western-most tip of Anglesey, O'Neill sold the coach and horses and bought passage to Ireland on board an Irish ship. Elizabeth heard again the lilting cadences she had come to know so well. And for the first time Bard and O'Neill and Fiona spoke openly again, hiding nothing, for Wales was not England, though the English had beaten the land into submission so many centuries before. In Wales they might know a little freedom.

And in Wales he shared her bed again, saying nothing of prisoners and hostages, and she found a renewed contentment in his arms.

When they boarded ship and cast off for the voyage to Ireland, O'Neill could not get Elizabeth to leave the deck. She clung to the rail and stared longingly at Wales, knowing it was more her country than the one for which they were bound, and that she might never see England again. After a moment O'Neill, seeming to understand, left her to watch alone and went below. And when at last the land was gone and she could see nothing but the Irish Sea, Elizabeth deserted the deck and went below to join him.

He was sitting on a stool with his legs braced against the motion of the ship. His eyes on her were strange, and then he smiled. ''Tis the first day of December,' he said. 'And I have twenty-seven years to my name.'

She felt a pang in her heart. 'You said nothing,' she told him remorsefully, 'and so I have nothing to give you.'

His face was oddly blank, but his eyes were not. And when he spoke his voice held a strange note. 'I have all I need.' He looked at her, and she saw the emotion in his eyes. 'I am going home to Ireland.'

And she realized, in that moment, all the longing and sadness she felt for leaving England behind was matched by what he felt for Ireland. He had been gone from his homeland for eleven long years, not knowing what he would find when he landed again on its shores, and such ignorance in a man like O'Neill could only be a goad.

Elizabeth went to him and bent down, clasping his neck in her arms as she stood behind him. 'O'Neill, I am sorry I was so stubborn. But surely you must understand that I have left England no more willingly then you left Ireland.'

He slid a hand up her arm. 'I know. I know it. And I would not take you from it were there another way. But, by Christ, Eilis – they would harm you if you fell into their hands, for all you have done for Ireland!'

'I have said it before – what I did was done for you. Not for Ireland.'

'I *am* Ireland,' he said intensely. 'And so long as I live and breathe, I will batter back the Sassenachs from my shores.'

'And what of me?' she asked softly. '*I* am English, my proud Eireannach warrior.'

'No.' He pulled her down on one muscled thigh. 'You are my woman, Eilis, and there *is* no more than that.'

'Then show me,' she whispered against his throat. 'Show me, my Irishman.'

He took her to the bed and showed her in the only way he knew how, and she was content with it.

In the morning the ship rolled with the pounding of the waves, and Elizabeth felt deathly ill. O'Neill was gone, for which she was grateful, and she hung over the side of the bunk to spew the contents of her stomach into the chamber pot. Her head throbbed, belly churned; she was flushed with cold, clammy sweat as she clutched the bunk and waited for the wracking spasms to pass.

The door opened. Instantly she thrust out a hand to wave O'Neill away. But it was not O'Neill, it was Fiona, and she shut the door behind her with a thud as she saw Elizabeth's condition.

'Oh, poor mistress, and himself sending me down to

302

see how you fared in all this roughness. He knew you would be sick.'

'He *knew?*' Elizabeth croaked as Fiona dampened a cloth and washed her sweating face and soured mouth.

'The Irish Sea is not a tame beast, mistress, but a serpent that likes to show its fangs. Few men have made the crossing without at least once knowing its violence, and in winter 'tis much worse.'

'How long?' Elizabeth asked weakly. 'How long before we reach land?'

'Depends on the weather, mistress. In calm seas and a good wind 'tis but little more than a whole day's sail. But when the sea goes choppy and the wind blows so hard, may take three or four.'

Elizabeth felt her stomach heave in protest. Fiona smoothed back her hair as she was ill again, and the woman washed her face once more. There was sudden concern in her voice. ''Tis soon for a baby to make itself known, but himself is a lusty man.'

'My God!' Elizabeth's eyes snapped open and she pushed herself up on her elbows. 'You cannot think . . .' And then she recalled that she had missed her monthly courses in the midst of all the excitement, and Fiona would know it well. 'Oh no!'

''Tis not a thing to be ashamed of,' Fiona chided. 'Bearing a child of The O'Neill is something any woman should long to do.'

'Fiona!' Her hand shot out and gripped the older woman's arm. 'You yourself said it was early for O'Neill's child. But it could be Bagenal's!'

Fiona's hands stilled their soothing motions. She frowned. 'I had not thought of that.'

Elizabeth pushed herself upright. 'You must say *nothing* to O'Neill. Nothing – do you hear? It is burden enough for him to drag me all the way across England

and Wales and not to Ireland, but if he knew I carried a child . . .' She put a hand to her throat. 'If he knew it was *Bagenal's* child – '

'Mistress, the man should know. Might be himself's wee babe.'

Elizabeth counted back. There had been but three weeks between the morning Bagenal had taken her and the first night she had lain with O'Neill, and four weeks since then. It *might* be O'Neill's child, yet even Fiona said it was probably too early. But if Bagenal's seed had taken root, it was not too early at all.

'Seasickness,' Elizabeth said firmly. 'That is all.'

Fiona's face was grave. 'But if 'tis not?'

Elizabeth closed her eyes and wrapped her arms around her waist, hugging herself as tightly as she could. The only thing she could be certain of was that the child was not the King's, and for that she was very grateful. But she had no wish to bear Bagenal an heir.

'Fiona,' she whispered, 'what shall I *do?*'

'What nearly every woman has done since God made Eve,' the woman answered. 'Bear a healthy child.'

'And if it is Bagenal's?'

'You cannot wish away a child because you do not love the father,' Fiona told her gently. 'But if 'twill stop your fretting, let me say again the babe could be O'Neill's.'

'You must *promise* me not to tell him.'

'He will have to know before much more time goes by.'

'*I* will tell him when the proper time is come,' Elizabeth said grimly. 'Fiona – promise me.' Her eyes beseeched the woman for understanding. 'He has too much to worry about right now. It would only be one more burden. I will tell him – I *will* tell him! – but not yet. Oh, not yet. Let him see Ireland again without this weight upon his soul.'

The older woman's ageing face was creased with lines of worry. Her mouth twisted as she struggled with the problem. ''Tis true he is worried. 'Tis true he needs to be Irish again before he can be The O'Neill. Perhaps you are right – '

I *am* right,' Elizabeth insisted. 'Fiona, I promise you I will tell him . . . when his war is done.'

Fiona's gnarled hands clasped Elizabeth's. 'But this war will never be done. D'ye not know that? England and Ireland will never know peace between them, not for all the centuries to come, and your own child may spill his blood in the name of the cause.' She smiled faintly. 'English child or Irish, it makes no difference. You will bear sons who will fight for what they believe in as strongly as does himself.' Quickly she crossed herself. 'And a man should know he has sired a child before he goes into war.'

A cold grue slid down Elizabeth's spine. 'But it might not be his,' she whispered. 'It might not be his at all.'

Fiona sighed. 'For that reason, mistress – *madam* – I'll be saying nothing to himself. And now you must get yourself up and come on deck, for 'twill make you feel much better.'

Elizabeth listlessly allowed Fiona to dress her in a fresh gown, though all were crumpled from packing, and felt a little better. She went slowly on deck, wrapped in her wine-dark cloak, and saw O'Neill standing at the rail. The ship pitched alarmingly and sea spray whipped back to cream her face, but even staggering against the rolling she felt better almost at once. Her nausea subsided and for one marvellous moment she thought it might only have been seasickness after all, but then she recalled the absence of her courses and knew it was more than that. But she put a smile on her face and felt his hand close firmly around hers, steadying her against the violence of the sea.

He pointed with the other hand into the writhing wind. 'Ireland, Eilis.'

'I see nothing,' she said. 'Nothing but sea and sky.'

''Tis there, Eilis. I promise you. I feel it in my bones.'

She smiled. 'You feel your birthday in your bones, old man.'

He grinned, one arm sliding around her shoulders. 'Then at least these old bones will lie in Irish soil.'

But Elizabeth could not smile with him, because she feared they would indeed.

27

'There!' O'Neill cried. 'D'ye see it, Eilis?'

Elizabeth followed the line of his pointing finger and saw the dark border of land spreading across the sea. It was first light and quite cold, but O'Neill – perhaps sensing landfall in his bones – had wrapped her in her cloak and then a blanket as he pulled her up on deck. They stood at the rail, staring westward, as Ireland hove into view.

'I see it,' she said softly.

'By Christ,' O'Neill whispered, 'I am come home again!'

She turned slightly in his encircling arms and looked on to his face. She saw a vividness, a vibrancy she had never seen before, even in him; he was so intent he nearly trembled with it. But more than that she saw the tears welling into his eyes, eyes green as the hills of his homeland.

'O'Neill,' she said, and her own throat constricted so much she nearly choked.

'Oh God,' he said, oblivious, '*to see Ireland again!*'

He was not shamed by the depth of his emotion, that much she could see. And she was not shamed or embarrassed to see it in him, for he was a man of deep and violent passions she could hardly begin to fathom. But to see him standing so tall and so proud upon the deck of his Irish ship, with his Irish wolfhounds behind and Ireland before him, filled her own heart with such exquisite pain that she could hardly bear it. It was not she who held his soul, but Ireland. And undoubtedly always would.

Elizabeth glanced behind to the dogs and went very still, for Bard was there as well. Like O'Neill, he stared westward, but his eyes moved from the land to O'Neill himself, and there was such stark pain in his eyes, she could not look again. So she pulled from O'Neill's arms and left him; O'Neill, turning to see where she had gone, looked past her and saw Bard.

Elizabeth saw the sudden flaring union of the mutual joy in their homecoming. O'Neill's grin was so wide it nearly cracked his face, and his arm went out as if to snare Bard and bring him in. As if he needed to.

Slowly Bard crossed the space between himself and O'Neill and Elizabeth watched them embrace like kinsmen who had not seen one another for too long a time. She felt oddly alone and entirely excluded, but sensed a bittersweet happiness. It was a moment no one could share with them, and she was sorry it could not last.

Bard broke away first, as if he could not bear to be so close to O'Neill without giving himself away. There was no doubt in Elizabeth's mind that O'Neill had no knowledge of his place within Bard's heart; she presumed he felt Bard served him out of loyalty and personal ambition, in addition to family tradition. But as they stood together at the rail, eyes fastened on the shoreline of their homeland, she could only turn away and wish she could share in a measure of it.

But she could not, for she was a Sassenach, and no one in Ireland would allow her to forget it.

'Dun Laoghaire,' O'Neill announced as he took her off the ship. The Gaelic sounded like *Dunlarry* to her English ears. 'From here we go to Dublin, but a short way up the coast, and then on to Tyrone.'

'Tyrone,' she said. 'Was that not your father's title?'

'His English title,' O'Neill agreed. 'Before he put it off and took up the clan chieftainship.'

'Then he was considered an English nobleman when he wed your mother.'

'Aye,' he said grimly. 'No one doubted he was Irish, but Queen Elizabeth thought it in her best interests to show folk how tame her Irishman was by offering him a peerage. And so he was a belted earl until he could no longer bear what was being done to his country, and gave the old woman her title back again. He became The O'Neill, and showed Ireland what it was to fight the Sassenachs and win.'

'But, O'Neill – he lost.'

They stood on the quay. O'Neill turned to face her. 'Aye,' he agreed. 'But not until James Stuart sought to have him assassinated, and then he knew he must leave Ireland.'

The cold beat of fear rose up into her chest. 'What will you do now?'

'Nothing in Dublin. 'Tis an English town, now. The heart is gone from it. What Bard and I will do must wait untl we have gone home again, to Dungannon across the Pale.' He smoothed a strand of hair from her face. 'You look so weary, my Eilis, and I must have you travel yet again.'

She summoned a smile, knowing her weariness sprang from worry and the knowledge of what she carried, not from travelling. 'I will do well enough, my lord earl.'

'Call me no earl,' he said roughly. 'I am no English lordling!'

She closed her eyes against the vehemence in his tone, and then he pulled her head against his chest. She felt his kiss in her hair and longed to tell him the truth so he could share her burden, but she would not do it. He bore too much already.

309

'Eilis and I will wait here,' Fiona said, for the new closeness between them had banished the formality of honorifics. 'You and Bard fetch us a coach.'

O'Neill let go of Elizabeth reluctantly, but his eyes went past her to Bard. He grinned. ''Twill be good to speak the Gaelic again, and not be wary of it.'

'And who's to say the English have not been warned we will be coming home?' Bard retorted. 'Because it is Ireland does not mean we are safe.'

O'Neill scowled, swore, turned on his heel, Boru and Cuchullain flanking him. Bard grinned and went after him, and Elizabeth felt Fiona press her down upon one of the chests. 'Rest, now. Himself is right to say you look weary. 'Twill take the heart from you if you let him push you so.'

'I will not stay behind. Not now. In England, yes – but this is not England.'

Fiona's faded eyes looked up towards all the rooftops. 'Thanks be to God and St Patrick, 'tis not,' she said fervently, and crossed herself twice.

O'Neill and Bard came back with a hired coach and loaded everything as quickly as could be done. Elizabeth did not view riding again in such a conveyance with any favour, but resolutely climbed in when O'Neill gave her his hand.

'Sleep, if you can,' he said. 'We dare not stop for long. Bard said he saw a parchment with my name on it; gold is offered for my whereabouts.'

'Already?' she asked, stricken.

''Tis what I expected. James wants his Irish rebel back. I doubt not he is angry I fooled him with my mission for the Pope.' O'Neill smiled grimly. 'I am a wanted man, Eilis.'

'You were wanted before.'

'But then they thought me in Italy. Now they know

precisely where I am and what I intend to do. 'Twill be a fight, Eilis.'

'You have wanted nothing more.'

'Aye,' he said roughly, and slammed the door closed. Elizabeth put her hands against her head and rubbed her aching temples.

She did sleep, but poorly, for the roads were rough and the old coach badly sprung. She lost herself in nightmares of blood and fire and screams, seeing O'Neill's severed head struck upon a pole where it was carried aloft by English soldiers revelling in their brutality. She saw her child born in blood and pain and cruelty, trying to survive in a world gone mad with hatred and old feuds. She saw herself in Bagenal's arms again, forced to do his will and the King's, and she awoke with a cry of fear in her mouth.

Fiona's hands were against her brow. 'Hush now, hush now – 'tis nothing but a dream. 'Tis nothing new in a breeding woman. 'Twill be better, I promise, and then you will forget all about such horrid things.'

Elizabeth pulled herself upright and looked out the window, staring at the alien, misty green landscape. She could see nothing but grey skies and emerald hills, and the promise of too much heartache.

'It is December,' she said. 'Surely O'Neill would not be such a fool as to start a war in winter!'

'The O'Neill is no fool,' Fiona answered sternly. 'What he does, he does for Ireland. You – being English – might not understand, but he'll not be letting cold weather stop him. You don't know the Irish, Eilis.'

'But I know pride,' she retorted, 'and I know he has that in abundance. Will he let it kill him?'

'If he must,' the woman said firmly. 'And he won't be the first Irishman to die for the cause of freedom and independence.'

'But I don't want him to die for *any* cause!' Elizabeth cried. 'None of it is worth it!'

'There speaks a Sassenach,' Fiona said sadly.

Elizabeth sat back on the seat again, letting the ragged leather curtain flop down. 'Yes,' she said steadily, 'I *am* a Sassenach. As much as he is an Eireannach.'

She slept again; this time it was a dreamless rest. She was dimly aware of the jolting of the coach and the occasional barking of the loping dogs, but nothing else penetrated the darkness behind her lids. She knew only that with each mile they drew closer to Tyrone, closer to O'Neill's fate.

Elizabeth wakened when the coach was stopped abruptly. She was barely upright when O'Neill snatched open the door. He drew her out, steadying her against the turf, and she saw in his eyes a bright, intense hunger. 'There is something you must see.' He dragged her to the front of the coach.

The sun was going down, setting the sky afire with pale yellow and ochre-orange. Against the brightness was silhouetted a bulky stone shape, and as she squinted her eyes she made out the keep and surrounding walls.

'Dungannon,' O'Neill said harshly. 'My father's castle, and where I was born to Mabel Bagenal.'

The castle was black against the setting sun. She saw her breath pluming in the air and felt the beat of O'Neill's heart as she stood against his chest. 'Are we going there?'

His laugh lacked all humour. ''Tis held by the English, now – like most of Ireland. You'll find no Irish landowners and tenants . . . only Sassenachs and Scots, who have stolen away our lives.'

'O'Neill – '

'I am not lying to you, Eilis. 'Tis plain, if you have the eyes to see it.'

She sighed. 'Then where *are* we going?'

'Not far. Back into the coach with you, my girl, and soon we'll be done with such travel.'

Elizabeth allowed him to hand her back in again, but not before she clung to his doublet. 'Promise me you will be careful.'

'I am always careful,' he answered, somewhat brusquely. 'How else d'ye think I have survived this long? Now – up with you, Eilis. I have no time for such natter.'

Natter, she thought bitterly. *Can he not see how much I care?*

But the door was closed yet again as once more they headed north.

When the coach was stopped again Elizabeth was too weary to move a single step from it. She thought she had best spend the night in it, no matter how cold it got, for she felt her abused bones might break if she set foot outside. But when O'Neill came in for her she gladly accepted his strength and climbed out on to solid, unmoving ground.

She stopped dead, staring at the small thatched cottage. Two crude windows stared back at her, glowing with candlelight, and the rough grey stones that formed the walls resembled little more than a pile of forgotten fence material. It was no more than a hovel to her eyes, after the cosy dwellings on Rosewood's acreage.

She turned a bewildered face to O'Neill. 'Will we go on again?'

'No. This is where we will live . . . for now.'

'But . . .'

His eyes, so watchful, narrowed. 'Oh, aye, I know – 'tis not what you are accustomed to. Nor am I. But 'tis what all Irish people must call home now, Eilis – even former chiefs – because the English have taken the good houses and castles and farms for their own. Did you think I had a fine house to bring you to? No, Eilis . . . only this.'

She swallowed heavily as the pegged wooden door creaked open on leather hinges. A grey-haired man came out. He was missing his right eye and three fingers on his left hand, clad in rough woollens, but the lantern he held lighted his lined face into a gap-toothed grin of welcome.

'By God and St Patrick, O'Neill, 'tis true! You have come home again!'

'I swore I would, Seamus,' O'Neill answered. 'It has been too long, too long . . . but I am come back.'

'I hardly know you' the man cried, tears shining in his one eye. 'You were a tall lad even then, but *now!* My good Christ, O'Neill . . . 'tis the answer to our prayers!'

'And I'll be needing all of them if I am to succeed,' O'Neill said grimly. 'You know what odds we face.' He gestured with a sideways motion of his head. 'You recall Bard, of course.'

The old man's eye moved to Bard as he stood so quietly in the shadows. For a moment the lined face was very still, and then the tears spilled over. 'You were but a boy when you went – good Christ, O'Neill, did you think I'd be forgetting my own grandson? Come here to me, boyo, come here!'

Bard moved stiffly, as if he were reluctant. But Elizabeth realized it was not reluctance, only great emotion, and as the men embraced she felt a sudden loneliness that drove a blade into the depths of her soul.

They have all come home again . . . and I am so far from mine.

'There is someone else,' O'Neill said quietly. 'Fiona – come out of there.'

Seamus let go of Bard at once, mouth dropping open in astonishment. 'Fiona! 'Tis true?'

The woman moved towards him steadily. 'Did you think The O'Neill lied to you, then, when he swore he would bring us home again? *Pah!* You always were a doubting Thomas, Seamus! Of *course* 'tis true!' And then she was in his arms, crying against his neck while Bard looked on with a faint smile. When he saw Elizabeth's eyes on him in bewilderment, his smile grew, though it was wry.

'Fiona is my grandmother,' was all he said in explanation.

'But – why did you say nothing? Or Fiona herself?'

'You are a Sassenach,' he said evenly, and she felt the familiar pain spring up in her chest.

'Enough,' O'Neill said. 'There is much to be done this night if we are to begin so soon.'

Bard nodded and went back to the coach to unload, and after bestowing a kiss on Elizabeth's cold nose, O'Neill joined him. Fiona turned and reached out to catch her hand, drawing her close. 'This is my husband, Seamus. And this lovely woman is Eilis, *ceile*, The O'Neill's woman.'

Seamus's single brown eye observed her gravely. 'A Sassenach, Bard said.'

'Aye,' Fiona agreed firmly. 'But none of that from you, old man. 'Tis a good woman she is, English or no – d'ye think The O'Neill would be bringing her otherwise? And wasn't his own mother English?'

Seamus sighed. 'I won't be arguing it with you, Fiona, not this night. Come in, come in – 'tis no good to keep you out of your own house. I have a fire.'

Inside, Fiona made Elizabeth sit down before the fire on a crude wooden bench, stripped off her shoes, and began to massage her half-frozen feet. 'Have you *uisge-beatha*, Seamus?'

'I am an Irishman, woman!' he thundered, and gave Elizabeth a cup of the fiery liquor that cut right to the

315

bone, and beyond, warming her as it melted through her weary body.

O'Neill came in with Bard and the dogs, stamping his feet to warm them in their heavy boots, and drank down the whiskey Seamus poured for him. Colour stood high in his face and his green eyes glowed; Elizabeth saw a new life in him, as if Ireland had lent him strength. She thought it probably had; he was not the man she had known. When he looked at her he did not see her, though his smile was warm enough, and when he sat down by the fire she saw his hands were counting off plans she could not know.

Seamus diffidently refilled O'Neill's empty cup and she saw the proud, bright look in his remaining eye. *The O'Neill*, she thought. *They do not see the man, they see the symbol. He is Ireland come home again, and they will care little enough if he sheds his blood for them.*

'How many?' O'Neill demanded of Seamus.

The old man sat down and lighted himself a pipe, nodding as he hunched before the fire. 'At least sixty since we had your last letter.' He bit thoughtfully on the stem as the scent of peat and tobacco drifted through the room. 'But a hundred thousand more when they know you have come home.'

O'Neill's smile was appreciative, but mostly amused. 'Not so many, I think. The English have ruled too long. There will be talk of the gold on my head instead of war, even among the Irish.'

'Not when they know you are here,' Seamus insisted. He glanced sharply at Elizabeth. 'My wife has spoken for her, O'Neill, but I am uneasy with an Englishwoman so close to us here.'

'Eilis won me free in England when I'd got a Sassenach blade put through my shoulder,' O'Neill said quietly. 'She'll not be harming us here. My word on that, Seamus.'

316

The old man nodded. 'But you'll be knowing why I had to speak.'

'Oh, aye . . . and I'd be doing the same. But she is staunch as any man, I think,' His eyes on her were level, grim, but she saw a light in them that she had to answer with a smile of her own.

Bard, hovering in the background, put forth his opinion. 'If we wait until spring, 'twill give us more time to gather an army.'

'And if we wait until spring, 'twill give the English time to locate us,' O'Neill answered. 'We would do better to begin the battle now.'

'How?' Elizabeth demanded, against her better judgement.

O'Neill ignored her, but when he spoke to Seamus he answered her sharp question. 'We have only to put out a call to the Ulstermen, and those of Donegal. They'll be coming. They recall how Rory O'Donnell died within a year of his exile. And those who've been put out of their homes – they have a quarrel with the English. And any man who's lost a son or a brother or a father to the wars – they'll come. I think we'll have our Irish army.'

'The O'Neills are scattered,' Seamus said reluctantly. ''Twill take time to gather them all, to get you elected chief.'

'I need no gathering for that,' O'Neill said. 'I'll be claiming no title they do not give me, but they know who I am. So do the English. Kieran O'Neill, son of Hugh O'Neill and kin to Shane the proud . . . I think 'twill be enough. I can fight for myself without any added title.'

'It would help,' Seamus insisted. 'With The O'Donnell dead all these years, and now your father, and the other old chiefs chased into the hills, we'll be needing what pride we can gather.'

'Our blood is pride enough.' O'Neill stared into the

317

flames. ''Tis Ireland I've come to claim, for the Irish – not a title for myself.'

''Tis yours,' the old man grumbled. 'You are heir to the chieftainship.'

'Heir, perhaps, to the regard my father received.' O'Neill agreed, 'but there is no time to gather the clans for an election, only for an army. And if we did call a formal election, the English might swoop down and take us all, and none of us ready for blood on the naming day.' He shook his head and sat back in the chair. 'No . . . I'll be needing no election. I am myself, and no more.'

''Tis enough,' Bard said solemnly. ''Twas always enough, with you.'

Elizabeth, glancing back at him, saw his blue eyes go dark and detached as he stared at O'Neill, and she wondered what he thought. She wondered if he knew he had lost O'Neill for good. *To this war, if not to me.*

Fiona's hand were on Elizabeth's shoulders. 'Come, Eilis, I'll be putting you to bed. We'll be leaving the men to their talk.'

Elizabeth looked at O'Neill and saw he was lost in thought, staring into the fire so fixedly she believed he had forgotten them all. Without the beard he looked less compellingly sinister, and yet there was a power in his face that transcended that in an ordinary man's.

She felt the familiar yearning for his touch rise, as it always did when she looked at him, but it was tempered with a grave sadness in the knowledge that she, like Bard, would likely lose him soon. What they shared would be usurped by Ireland.

'Good night, O'Neill.' She rose, but he did not hear her. She went into the tiny room with Fiona.

The woman helped her out of her crumpled gown and put her into a fresh night rail. Generally O'Neill took it from her body once they were in bed, but she thought it unlikely this night. She doubted he would go to bed at all, and if he did, it would be elsewhere, alone, to work out his plans. Listlessly she allowed Fiona to guide her into the rude bed and slid down beneath the feather quilt.

'You never told me you had a husband,' Elizabeth said.

Fiona tended the peat fire in the tiny fireplace. ''Tis not so easy to tell another woman how you have left your wedded husband in somebody else's service,' she said quietly. 'But 'twas The O'Neill I served – Hugh O'Neill – and so did Seamus. And when time came for them all to flee Ireland, I was terribly torn. Seamus could not go – The O'Neill would not ask it of him – but O'Neill's wife needed someone to help her with the children, and so Seamus said I should go.' She turned to face Elizabeth. 'No doubt you're thinking that The O'Neill's wife was already dead, thinking of himself's mother. Well, Hugh was a lusty man. Four wives he had in all, but it was the last one who went with him into exile. Catherine Mac-Guinness she was, daughter to The MacGuinness himself. She was the one who bore the other three boys . . . himself is the only child of the English marriage. And the only legitimate son left alive.'

'But you had a child,' Elizabeth said. 'You must have – Bard is your grandson.'

'I had a daughter.' Fiona clasped her gnarled hands. 'But she's been dead for years. Bard has known no parents.'

'His father . . . ?'

'Bard was a bastard child, Eilis.' The woman's faded eyes were bleak. 'Happens often enough when you serve the chief's house.'

'He said he was an O'Neill.'

'He is. But then that is not so much to be claiming.' Fiona's smile was wry. 'Knowing himself, d'ye think the O'Neills would be anything but lusty? In chief's houses, there are legitimate and bastard brothers, uncles, sons. There are more O'Neills in Tyrone than there are Catholics, I think.'

Elizabeth laughed at Fiona's tone and snuggled farther beneath the quilt. 'Good night, Fiona. I am glad you are home again.'

'Good night, Eilis . . . and for that I thank you.'

Elizabeth stared into the flickering shadows as Fiona shut the door and wondered what would become of her. Slowly one hand crept down to splay across her belly, trying to feel the child, but she knew it was too soon.

The drone of voices went on into the hours, and at last Elizabeth drifted on the edges of sleep. She heard the final toast in Gaelic with the now-familiar *slainte* and then there was silence. She waited.

But O'Neill did not come. She pictured him slumped in the chair before the fire with his wolfhounds at his knees, thinking and planning as all the mill wheels turned in his head, trying to know how best to destroy the English.

She slipped out of bed and went across to the door, opening it silently. She stood in the doorway, meaning to call his name, but she said nothing. She saw the harp in his hands, his beautiful Irish harp, and knew what he intended.

The music was very soft, hardly more than a whisper. His big hands picked out a poignant melody that was clearly a lament. She watched him, black head bowed and green eyes fixed on the distances as he played, and thought she had lost him already.

28

Over the next week O'Neill hardly had time for Elizabeth. He spent most of his hours closeted with Bard and Seamus, concocting strategies to gather rebel forces, and Elizabeth learned very quickly it was not a woman's place. Not even an Irishwoman's place; although Fiona was present during discussions, she interjected nothing. She merely fed O'Neill, her husband, and her grandson, and kept herself in silence.

For Elizabeth it was much worse. Because they were bound by the confines of the tiny two-room cottage, she could hardly help overhearing. But it was impressed upon her that she must make herself unnoticed. And so when the men spoke in Gaelic mixed with English, she learned only bits and pieces of what they planned and how they planned it, knowing only that it was destroying the fabric of her existence. In Ireland her life was O'Neill; in Ireland his life seemed not to include an Englishwoman.

Nor any woman? she wondered. *No . . . were I Irish there would be none of this subterfuge. Were I Irish no doubt I would be as committed to this folly.* But she was not Irish, and she knew it more and more with each passing day.

One evening after dinner O'Neill called her to him and she went, seeing the compelling light in his brilliant eyes and thinking, at last, he realized how it was for her. But he only took her by the shoulders, looked down into her face, and said each evening after dinner she must keep herself to their tiny bedroom.

She looked at him in surprise. 'Why? This cottage is

321

small enough with *two* rooms – why must I give up one?'

'Do as I say, Eilis.'

No explanation. She stared up into his serious face and saw no levity, no earnestness, no tenderness. Merely command, and an assumption of her acquiescence.

She pulled out of his hands. 'Must you *imprison* me? Have I tried to escape?'

'No.' His mouth was a grim line. 'Eilis – 'tis for the best. For all of us.'

And then there came a knock at the door and Seamus, in calling out to ask who was there, was answered in Gaelic by a man's voice Elizabeth had never heard before. Seamus answered, seemingly requesting a moment's patience; he turned and looked first at her, then at O'Neill, and he waited.

O'Neill sighed. 'Eilis, you must go.'

'Do you think I would do anything to betray you?' she demanded. '*Now?*'

'Not intentionally.'

'O'Neill – '

A firm hand on her arm led her towards the crooked door. 'You will wait in this room, Eilis, until you are told you may come out.' And he opened the door, pushed her through, and shut it in her face.

Trapped within four short walls and outraged astonishment, Elizabeth stared at the closed door. There was no lock, not even a proper latch – she could snatch it open and confront O'Neill *and* the stranger if she wished. And part of her, angry, did wish. But the other part of her recognized the need for careful voyaging; O'Neill was not now precisely O'Neill, and she did not know how to speak to this man. In England she would, but here she was a stranger, a Sassenach, and she felt the distinction acutely. It was more than simple loneliness and the fear of the unknown that accompanies a stranger on a journey. It was the knowledge that in Ireland she was utterly alone, and at risk.

Unless, of course, she located one of the English landowners O'Neill had spoken about. They would undoubtedly aid her, did she wish to get away.

But only until they learned who she was and what she had done to aid O'Neill, and then she would be little more than a prisoner to James, subject to execution. At least with O'Neill it was an imprisonment not so taxing.

Elizabeth stood at the crooked door. It did not screen out the conversation in the other room. She could hear well enough. But the language was Gaelic. O'Neill may as well have let her remain in the other room; she could learn no secrets if they keep themselves to Gaelic.

She tried to count the voices. Four she knew already: O'Neill's, Seamus's, Bard's, Fiona's. The others ran together, overriding one another as the visitors vied with each other to speak, but she thought there must be seven, eight, perhaps even more. Dangerous in itself; O'Neill had told her the English had forbidden gatherings of more than three men at a time.

They spoke forever. Elizabeth, tiring of indecipherable consonants and vowels, turned away and went to the narrow bed. Fiona and Seamus had given up their bedroom to O'Neill, and therefore to her. They, like Bard, slept on pallets in the other room. The privacy was valuable to her, for it was difficult enough to reconcile herself to the fact that the nighttime intimacy between her and O'Neill was not intimacy at all. How could it be, in a tiny, two-room cottage sheltering five people?

She thought of Rosewood, full of rooms and halls and corridors. Lush acreage encompassing miles of Kentish downs and furrowed, curving fields. No, the Staffords were no longer wealthy or influential, but what they owned was so superior to the poverty of the Irish that even Elizabeth understood why some of the hostility existed.

And if what O'Neill said were true – that the Old Queen and then her Scottish successor had stripped the Irish of their holdings, giving them over to English and Scottish subjects – it was no wonder the Irish were suckled on hostility. Jealousy? Not precisely. A man robbed by a thief is not *jealous* of the thief's newfound wealth, but angry. And, robbed often enough, the man might turn to retribution.

Elizabeth lay down on the bed. In the shadows of the room, warmed by the peat fire, she stared at the thatching and thought about the future. The Irish were doomed. Surely even O'Neill could see it. Against the superior fighting ability of the English – *and* superior numbers – rebellion was nothing more than suicide.

And yet she knew he would continue. She knew nothing would change his mind.

Not even if she asked him.

One night, after they had made love and O'Neill had fallen asleep, Elizabeth lay awake. Her eyes, wide open and tearless, ached as she stared into the darkness. But there were no tears in her to relieve the ache. Only an emptiness filled with desolation, a yawning chasm of futility and grief. The tenderness they had shared before no longer existed; he was not O'Neill but *The O'Neill*, and she found she hated that man.

All the sweet passion had dissipated beneath a new violence. It was not directed at her but at what he planned, and yet she was the one who suffered it. She knew a different sort of love in his arms now, and while it satisfied the craving of her body, it did not begin to touch the requirements of her spirit.

Filled up suddenly with pain and anguish and a mute,

unnamed hostility, Elizabeth slipped out from under the covers and left the bed. She wrapped herself in a blanket and went at once to the glowing peat fire, ignoring the complaints of her bare feet. She knelt down on the hard-packed sod floor and stared into the fire, aware of frustration and anger and pain.

Bitterly she bared her teeth. *Curse you*, she whispered inwardly, with all the venom she could summon. *Curse you, Ireland. What little I had you have stolen.*

Her hands were fists wrapped in the coarseness of the blanket. It scraped against her knuckles. But she did not care. She thought only of England and Ireland, and the warrior born of both.

'Eilis.' O'Neill's voice from the bed. And then the susurration of covers sliding back and a body exiting the bed. But she did not turn.

He came to stand over her. He had banished sleepiness; O'Neill was like a cat – he slept hard when he slept, but he awakened instantly, with all his faculties. He had not stolen a blanket from the bed as she had. He was nude. Even in the chill of a December night.

'Eilis – are you crying?'

'No,' she said flatly. 'You have not yet brought me to that.'

'*I?*' The tone was startled, and it stirred some unacknowledged resentment in her soul.

'Do you think you could *not?*' She rose and faced him, clutching the blanket around her body. 'Are you deaf and dumb and blind to what you can do to a woman? You fool, you fool, what you do affects others . . . you are not in this world alone, O'Neill, nor for merely your own interests! Do you think you bear no responsibility for the feelings of other people?' Elizabeth shook her head. 'How blind you are . . . how *blind* – oh, O'Neill, think of what you do *here*. The implications for the others. Bard, Fiona,

Seamus . . . all of them serve *you*. What you do affects them, it changes their lives. Without you they would be other people; without you *I* would be another person. And yet you look at me all innocent and astonished because you cannot comprehend how it is possible you could make a woman cry.' She drew in a sharp breath. 'No, I am *not* crying. I am angry. Angry and helpless and frustrated, because I am a prisoner of you in more ways than what we share in bed.' One hand stabbed out to indicate the cot. 'Oh, O'Neill, can you see nothing of what *I* see – feel nothing of what *I* feel? How long must this go on?'

'Till it is finished.' That only; it was not precisely an answer. 'You have known it would come to this.'

She stared into his shadowed face. 'I have lost you' was all she said.

He stiffened. 'And have you forgotten already what we did this night?'

'I have lost you,' she repeated. 'There is a new woman for you, now, and I have no place with you here.'

Softly, he swore. In Gaelic. Then: 'Are you breeding, Eilis? What else would account for such idiocy?'

It was a rhetorical question. But Elizabeth felt the chill of shock flood through her bones. It was only with great effort that she kept her hand from going at once to her abdomen. Instead, she shook her head. '*Ireland*, O'Neill. Her name is Ireland.'

He stood very still for a long moment. She thought he would leave her, but he did not. And then he reached out and caught her in his arms and lifted her, taking her back to the bed, and there he soothed her aching body as if he gentled a fractious horse.

She felt the tension and anguish draining away. Her body responded ardently. Elizabeth turned to him, setting her face against his shoulder, and pressed herself against

326

the hard lean length of his body. His arms held her tightly and she slept at last, at peace, but she did not forget that he had not answered her.

At Christmas, O'Neill gave her a gold locket. Elizabeth stared at it in astonishment, for it was good gold and shone in the firelight, but she could not begin to understand where it had come from. He did not go near the town by the castle and he was not the sort of man who would have someone else buy him what he could not. Elizabeth looked at him as he stood before the fire, warming his back, and saw his watchful eyes.

His mouth twisted in a smile. ''Twas my mother's.'

'But – '

'She would want you to have it.' He shrugged. 'You wed her nephew, did you not?'

And the pleasure was suddenly gone from the moment, for she had not been thinking of Bagenal. The chain pooled in her hand as she held it, knowing he had not meant it *quite* like that – knowing also there was that which stood between them. Ireland was her bane, Bagenal was his.

She had knitted him a pair of gloves, knowing his hands better than any and the length of his fingers, and he thanked her for them gravely. He did not put them on; she thought he was embarrassed by the gift, but she said nothing as he tucked them into his belt. For Bard she had knitted a scarf to wrap around his throat, for he had been coughing lately from the cold, and she feared he would grow worse without proper care. Fiona poured hot broths down him until he said she would drown him; after that nothing more was said and Bard seemed happier left alone. He gave Elizabeth nothing but a startled glance when she put the present into his hands, and then he looked away. Colour rose high in his face.

When she found him later in the stable preparing his horse, she told him what gift he could give her. 'Keep him alive. I ask no more than that.'

Bard, buckling the girth, looked at her levelly. 'Do you think I would not?'

'This will be war,' she answered grimly. 'This will be wholesale massacre.'

Bard's brows rose. 'You have no faith in the Irish as fighting men?'

She heard the irony in his tone and lashed back at it. 'But I *do*. I lost my brother to the wars under Essex, here in Ireland. But your numbers are not as great as the English and you do not have the money to support a war. You can only harry the oppressor for a little while, which will surely end in defeat. James will send troops here to subdue his quarrelsome Irish rebels and you will see Ireland put down again. More will die in a useless cause, because there is no hope of you winning. You *know* that. So do I, so does James, and so, I warrant, does O'Neill.' Her hands were knotted up in the woollen cloak. 'I do not ask you to stop fighting – I know better than that – but I ask you to *think*. I have seen what these wars have done to Ireland – do you think I am blind? – and I wish no more hardship and heartache for the Irish people. But that is what all of you will give them if you continue this rebellion.'

For a long moment Bard said nothing at all, engaged solely in looking at her. She could not put a name to the expression on his face.

Finally he finished buckling the girth. 'Was that for me?' he asked. 'Or O'Neill?'

Elizabeth grimaced. 'He would not listen to me.'

'He would not listen to *that*,' Bard agreed, 'any more than I will. But I think you forget something, Elizabeth.' Deftly his hands checked buckles and fastenings. 'We are

328

not new-come to rebellion. We have been suckled on it. None of what you have said has gone unconsidered.'

'Then why do you *do* it?' she cried. 'If you *know* this rebellion will fail, why must you engage in such sacrifice?'

'Because freedom is never won without a measure of sacrifice,' he said quietly. Then he turned and faced her. 'You bid me keep him alive. No doubt it is something any woman would do. But I wonder that you can say it to *me*.' For just a moment there was a flicker of some hidden emotion in his eyes. 'Do you think I could let him die? Do you think I wish to face life without him any more than *you*?'

Elizabeth closed her eyes.

'Christ,' he said raggedly, 'I have no words for you. I cannot even tell *myself* what it is that makes me love him, only that I do. Since we were children.'

Struck by his tone, his sudden willingness to speak plainly to her, Elizabeth opened her eyes and looked into an anguished complexity of emotion that far surpassed her own.

'I have spent my life knowing I could do nothing save serve him as any man would, for if he knew the truth he would surely order me from his presence,' Bard told her flatly. ''Tis bad enough being with him and knowing I cannot have him, but 'tis worse to think of being without him entirely.' He sighed and scrubbed a gloved hand into his dark brown hair. 'And now that I have said this, I have placed a weapon in your hands.'

'No,' she said softly. 'I have known a long time how you felt. But it is not my place to speak of it to others.'

'Not even to O'Neill?' The tone was bitter.

'Not to O'Neill. Not anyone. It is a private thing.'

He looked at her, seeking something in her eyes, some indication of falsehood or contempt. But she gave him none at all.

329

'And will you tell him now?' he demanded.

'Bard,' she said at last, 'we have always been enemies, it seems, since the truth was made plain for me to see. But I have no wish to divulge your secrets. Why must you think I do?'

His mouth hooked down in irony. 'You are a woman . . . and we desire the same man.' He smiled a little. 'A conflict as old as time itself, though admittedly it usually grows up between two *women*.'

'Do you distrust us all so much?'

'With reason. Would you deny most of you are a conniving litter of bitches doing what you must to snare the hound?'

Elizabeth smiled wryly, recalling the temper of the court. 'Often, yes. And was it a conniving bitch who turned a hound to other hounds?'

His look was angry. 'Why must it always be that? No, madam, 'twas not. It has always been men for me.'

'You mean it has always been *O'Neill*.'

Bard groaned and turned to press his forehead against the saddle. ''Twas *only* O'Neill. I loved him without knowing what the feeling was, only that I felt it, that I wanted – *needed* – something from him. And then there was this man – ' His voice broke off a moment, and when he continued Elizabeth heard a new hardness in his tone. 'There was a man who fancied me, and when he was done with me I had learned what I was. What I wanted. It was not a woman who turned me away from others of her kind, but a man who turned me to *his*. And suddenly I knew what O'Neill was for me, and I could never tell him.' He turned slowly, face contorted. 'I have lived with it all my life. 'Tis a blessing, because it brings me pleasure even as a man brings *you* pleasure, and a curse because I dare not have the one I want. Do you see?' His voice rang in the stable. 'Do you see what I have lived with?'

Unevenly she answered, 'I see.'

'And do you understand it?'

She swallowed heavily. 'Bard,' she said, 'Bard . . . I doubt what I feel for him is that much different from what you feel. And so – and so I think we face the same pain and anguish, knowing he risks himself and that we could not bear to lose him, knowing he might be lost.' She looked into his twisted face. 'Then – it is up to both of us, is it not? To keep O'Neill alive?'

Bard, blank-faced again, untied the horse's reins and turned him from the wall. 'I think there is little *you* can do.'

She felt a brief, intense flicker of pain. 'Perhaps not. But did it come to it, I would risk as much as you.'

He mounted, saying nothing.

Elizabeth put out a hand to catch the horse's rein. 'Where do you go?'

'To town,' he answered. 'To see what I can see and hear what I can hear.'

Her breath caught. 'It is dangerous for you, Bard.'

''Tis dangerous for us all, Elizabeth.' His smile was faint. 'But I think it will not stop us.'

She heard him ride out. For a moment she faced the back wall of the tiny stable, hugging the woollen mantle around her body. She sensed the ambience of the child, though she showed nothing of it. She simply *knew* it lived.

'Eilis.'

O'Neill's voice. Elizabeth spun around in surprise, one hand automatically guarding her abdomen. But she forced it away almost at once, wanting nothing to betray the truth.

He also was wrapped against the cold, grey day, half shrouded in a cloak. His black hair was no longer trimmed as neatly as it had been at court; she saw a man before her with hair nearly to his shoulders and falling into his eyes, the blueness of black stubble on his face, faint shadows under his eyes. Almost, she wanted to put out her hands and beckon him to her, longing to comfort him as a mother with a child, but O'Neill was not a man for *comforting*. He would undoubtedly be offended. So she did nothing. She simply faced him in silence, seeing how he slouched against the wall like an indolent, dangerous cat, wanting nothing more than to touch him and make him whole again.

'Eilis,' he said again, 'have you made peace with Bard at last?'

'Peace?' She did not understand him. 'We are not – enemies.'

One black brow lifted. 'You were once. Clearly, though little was said about it. But now, *now* I sense a difference. Oh, aye, Bard still resents you – I think he always will – and doubtless you still think him somewhat of an *immoral* soul' – O'Neill smiled a little – 'but still I think you have made a peace between you. D'ye not agree?'

Elizabeth wondered why they spoke of Bard when they needed to speak of themselves. 'Bard is – bearable.' She did not smile. 'But what we share is not.'

'Is not?' he echoed in mild astonishment. 'Are you telling me you have no liking for what is between us?' He smiled. 'Eilis, I think you are forgetting what you say to me when we are done with making love, and lie tangled in tumbled bedclothes wet with the sweat of our efforts.' He shook his head. 'There is no dislike in you for *that*, Eilis. A man knows. I know.'

She swallowed heavily. 'Is that what it is for you? An evening spent in bed engaged in *efforts?*' Slowly she shook her head. 'Are you blind, O'Neill? Or is it simply that you have put up a wall against such feelings as I know?'

He ceased leaning against the wall and came into the tiny stable. He did not stop walking until he had reached her, and then he put his hands upon her shoulders. 'You say what we share is not bearable. Why is it not, Eilis? Because I am not an English lordling able to give you a title?'

'Curse you!' she cried. 'Do you think that is what I want? You fool – are you forgetting I *had* that? I married Simon Bagenal – *and left him for you*.'

'I took you,' he said clearly. 'I took you for a hostage. You are here against your will.'

Elizabeth stared up into his face. She saw weariness and tension and a burning, nervous energy, recklessness embodied. He was a stranger to her, a man possessed with the intention of starting a war, and there was no room for a woman in his world.

Unless that woman be Irish-born, she thought bitterly. 'O'Neill, O'Neill, you fool . . . do you think I would stay here if I did not wish it?'

Almost, he laughed. She could see it in the glint of his emerald eyes. 'And would you be leaving me,' he began, 'even *if* I allowed it?'

His hands were still on her shoulders. 'Aye,' she threw in his face. 'If I thought it would serve me, I would leave The O'Neill today.'

'You are a hostage, madam.' Softly, so softly, but with steel beneath the silk.

Elizabeth clutched one hand against her left breast. '*Here*, O'Neill. *This* is your hostage. Not me. Not me. You hold me not by dint of iron or rope or locks, but because of this.' Abruptly she caught his hand and dragged it down, so that the rigid palm was over her left breast. 'Do you feel it? That is my heart, O'Neill. *My heart*, which you have somehow managed to win. *That* is your hostage, O'Neill.'

He looked down at her. She saw the mask of his face, so blank, so devoid of emotion or expression. She thought

333

perhaps the admission had shocked him. She thought perhaps he would turn from her in contempt, to know she was as much a prisoner of her own feelings for him as she was of the man himself.

Is O'Neill a man who wants a woman to love him? Or merely the act *of love?*

Then his hands slid up to cup her face and she heard the rasp in his uneven breathing. 'By Christ, Eilis – what you do to me – '

'What?' she demanded. 'Do I please you? Do I bring you pleasure in bed? Do I fill in the few black, empty hours when you must think of something other than Ireland?' She stopped a moment, then went on. 'Or by taking me do you also take *England?*'

His hands closed on her face abruptly, hurting her; she knew the bolt had gone home by the expression in his eyes. 'D'ye throw this in my face, madam?'

'Ireland, Ireland, Ireland!' she cried. 'I sleep with a *country* when I sleep with you! I sleep with *war* when I sleep with you!' She was trembling, but not in fear. Not in anger. In anguish – in the knowledge that he would go from her one day to sleep with another woman, to bind himself to her loins and spill his seed into her womb. And that womb was Ireland, waiting for his blood. 'O'Neill,' she sobbed, 'can you not see what this is doing?'

'I see it,' he husked. 'Christ, woman, I see it more clearly than you. *But it is what I have chosen to do.*'

29

Bard came back at sundown. He came into the cottage, where they shared the warmth of the peat fire and Elizabeth saw how windblown was his dark brown hair, how flushed were his cheeks. As if he had ridden hard.

He looked at O'Neill. He looked at Fiona and Seamus. And then he looked at her. 'Simon Bagenal is here.'

The warmth spilled out of her bones and left in its place ice. '*Here?*' she asked in a hollow, husky whisper.

'At the castle,' Bard said, still looking only at her. 'It is said in town he wants two people in the name of the Crown.'

'O'Neill,' she said, 'and you.'

Slowly Bard shook his head, and she knew the other name.

'He said he would not come here.' Elizabeth heard the echo of her own voice within the fragile prison of her skull. 'He said he would not come to this stinking island.' She spoke evenly, conversationally; in shock, emotions are stripped bare and born again. 'He said he would not come.'

'He has come in the name of the King,' Bard said, 'to crush this rebellion into the ground. In blood and smoke and fire.' He did not smile; he looked not at O'Neill, but at her. 'The castle has been garrisoned by English troops for some time, keeping English peace so the English landowners may know safety in Ireland.'

She ignored the prejudice in his tone. 'Yes.'

'James now has sent an army, a *true* army, to put down our rebellion. Much of that army is quartered in the town.

The rest is garrisoned at the castle. Bagenal is in command.' He paused. 'He will not leave until the thing is done.'

O'Neill swore. 'Is there more?'

Bard's face was perfectly blank. 'There are Irishman who will do anything to feed their families, O'Neill, even to betraying one of their own. It happened to Shane the Proud – it can happen to you as well.'

O'Neill swore again, more violently. 'So, Jamie hopes for assassination.'

'No Irishman would kill you!' Elizabeth cried.

O'Neill's face was a mask as he shook his head. 'This man Bard mentions – Shane the Proud, Prince of Ulster. O'Neill, he was, *The* O'Neill – a kinsman. And he fought the English to a standstill, then died by an assassin's hand. That hand was bought and paid for with Sassenach gold, and the man was welcomed among the Scots, who supposedly welcomed O'Neill. D'ye see what I am saying?'

For a moment she could not speak. And then she merely nodded.

''Tis one reason I have not allowed you into this room when the others were here, Eilis,' O'Neill told her. 'What Bard says is true – there *are* Irishmen who will do unconscionable things for money. 'Tis the cost of starving, of going homeless, of losing what pride the English have stripped from them.' He sighed. 'I could not be certain one or more would not sell the knowledge of your presence to the English.'

'My presence,' Elizabeth echoed. 'What stake have *I* in this?'

'You have heard Bard,' he told her gently. 'Bagenal would pay good gold to get you back, so he could take you to London and to James, where the King could put you on trial for treason, to make an example out of you. An Englishwoman who abetted an Irishman. An *English-*

woman who threw a sword to the Irishman who meant to slay her husband.' He broke off a moment. 'Eilis, the man will be wanting you as well as me. He'll buy you, my Eilis, with bright Sassenach gold.'

Elizabeth looked at O'Neill. She looked at Bard, Seamus, Fiona. She saw Ireland in their faces. Ireland in their souls. She had no place among them.

'A hostage,' she said quietly. 'And valuable. Why not trade me for Ireland?'

'No,' he said – that only, but it sounded definitive.

'Then what do you mean to do?' She drew in an unsteady breath. 'If you fight him, you will lose. And he will catch you and cut off your head so that all of Ireland might see.'

'No.' Bard said, 'he would not. Not in Ireland.'

Even O'Neill smiled, though it lacked a proper humour. 'Not in Ireland,' he echoed. 'He would take me alive to London, Eilis, so that all of England could see me. So that all of England would know of Simon Bagenal, the man who caught O'Neill. No, not here. In London, where they could put my head up on London Bridge.'

'But Bagenal would never get him to London,' Bard said quietly. 'No. Never. Because he would have to cross Ireland first, and no Irishman would let The O'Neill go out of Ireland.'

Almost, Elizabeth laughed at the conviction in his tone. 'You say *that* when you have just told me an Irishman would stoop to assassination? Have you learned nothing from the murder of your kinsman?'

'They cut off his head,' O'Neill said. 'They cut off Shane's head and put it up on Dungannon's gate. The *Prince of Ulster*, Eilis, who was a suitor for Elizabeth's hand. As much a king as Ireland knows in these days of Sassenach domination.' His eyes did not waver from her face. 'D'ye see, Eilis? When the Irish traitors saw Shane's head up on that gate, they knew what they had done. They had put a sword through Ireland's heart. And I think they would never do that again.'

Elizabeth felt the anguish and anger well up in her chest. 'But does it make a difference *where* the head is put? If it is yours, you will be dead *regardless!*'

O'Neill said nothing at all for a very long moment. And then he rose and put out his hand to her. 'Come, Eilis. 'Tis time we were in bed.'

When he had shut the crooked door behind them, Elizabeth turned to face him stiffly. 'Do you think to put me to bed like a child, O'Neill? Like a foolish woman lacking sense? Do you think I *embarrass* you before the others, and so you must put me away where I cannot?'

'No,' he said, and his hands were turning her so that his fingers could undo her laces. 'Christ no, woman – I am taking you to bed because I wish to make love to you.'

Deftly he loosened her laces, pulling aside the gown. His mouth was on her spine, touching here, there, gently, so gently, so warm and soft and gentle. She felt the prickle of his stubble and shivered in response, feeling her body answer at once. She shrugged out of sleeves and bodice as he pulled the fabric away, then stood quietly as he slipped shift and gown over the curves of hips and buttocks. And then she stepped free of skirts and shift and faced him in the shadows, naked and vulnerable before the sheer intensity of the man.

He will swallow me, swallow me whole, he will suck me down into the depths until I drown on a surfeit of my emotions.

'Eilis,' he said softly, so softly, and then as deftly as he had stripped her of gown and undershift, he divested himself of his clothing and moved to stand in front of her, flesh against flesh, the warmth of his risen manhood burning against her abdomen.

338

Where Bagenal's child sleeps.

She felt his fingers sweep up across her brow, hooking gently in her hair, combing it free of its loosened braid to fall unbound about her hips. Hands slid over the ridges of her spine, callused hands, hands that had held a sword and would hold a sword again. Hands that soothed, soothed, smoothing the texture of her skin until it demanded further attention. And then he gave it with lips, with tongue, with teeth, rousing her with the whisper of his breath.

Shoulders, collarbone, breasts. Her head tipped back, back, spilling the weight of hair down her buttocks to her knees; arching back, back, until she pressed her aching, heavy breasts against his hot, moist mouth, knowing only she could not bear for him to continue, could not bear for him to drive her to the point of abandonment, of loss, such loss, such *absence of self*, to that place where she was nothing but a harp string thrumming under his hand, ready to snap if he took that hand away.

Lower, lower, lowest, until she felt the hot, moist mouth in the hot moistness between her thighs, and she cried out softly at the soft, warm, welcome intrusion.

'*O'Neill*,' she said into the silence of the night.

But he said nothing. He merely knelt before her on the hard-packed earthen floor and loved her with his mouth, until she could not speak at all, only drown in the sensations of the flesh.

When she feared she could no longer stand he carried her to the bed. The narrow, hard, lumpy bed they shared in the chill of winter nights. But the chill was gone, banished by his warmth and the heat of his demand. She was warm, so warm, so flushed she thought it summer instead of winter, a summer where they could forget smoke and blood and fire and lose themselves in the pleasure of their bodies. But it was winter, an Irish winter, and even as she reached to pull him down against her breasts Elizabeth knew she shared him still. She shared him with Ireland.

'Jealous,' she whispered, 'so jealous. Can she not spare us a little time?'

And then O'Neill entered and she had no more knowledge of time, no more knowledge of jealousies, no more knowledge of days and nights, only the pleasure that he gave her – the pleasure that he was given.

I love you, she told him silently, when she could form the words again. *Oh my Irishman, how I love you.*

But she did not say it aloud because she could not say it in Gaelic.

She dreamed. She dreamed of blood and smoke and fire. She heard the screams of wounded horses, the cries of dying men, the raucous shrieks of carrion birds settling over the field. Bodies lay in tangled piles, one of top of another, legs and arms overlapping, mouths gaping open and empty eyes staring at the sky. She saw the flash of sunlight on steel; heard the crack of musketry. Tasted the blood and smoke and fire.

'O'Neill!' she cried out into the pallor of the dawn. And realized he was gone.

Elizabeth caught up a blanket and went at once to the other room. Seamus was not there. Fiona was. And the woman waited for her.

'Why?' Elizabeth said.

The older woman sat quietly in a wooden chair before the peat fire. 'Because he had to.'

'*Why?*'

'Because to stay here might get him caught, and spoil the rebellion.' Fiona's faded eyes were full of tears. 'He didn't want to leave you – I could see it in his eyes. I could see it in him when he came out of that room, so soft-footed and silent, so full of Irish melancholy. And he was looking at Bard, who waited, and said only they must go, and Bard was showing him the things he had already packed, and the dogs, and so they all went out into the dawn.'

Elizabeth felt the futility rush up to fill her chest. 'What will he do now?'

'Go to ground. He'll be gathering his forces. This war will be begun.' Fiona's eyes did not waver. ''Tis what he was meant to do.'

'He was not *meant* to die!' Elizabeth cried. 'Bagenal will kill him! Oh I know what Bard said, how O'Neill would be taken to London for execution there, but what if he was wrong? What if my husband would sooner see him dead in Ireland, merely to have it done?' She pressed her hands against her mouth. 'Oh my dear, sweet God, what will happen to him now? What will happen to *me* now?'

Fiona rose. She moved to Elizabeth and set her arms around her shoulders. 'D'ye think he'd go without tending to your fate? D'ye think he'd leave you here? D'ye think he'd be forgetting about you? Oh, Eilis – he'll be coming back for you. That I promise. When this war is done – '

' – and he comes home to Bagenal's wife?' Elizabeth finished. '*If* he comes home at all. What will he do then?'

Fiona's face looked older. 'If himself comes home, your husband will be dead.'

'But not his child,' Elizabeth said. 'Not the Sassenach's child.'

'A child is a child,' Fiona said, but there was worry in her eyes. 'A child becomes what he is made.'

Almost, Elizabeth laughed. 'An English child born in Ireland. What irony in that!' And then she hugged herself in her woollen blanket and felt the bitter tears fill up her eyes.

'He'll come,' Fiona promised. 'He will come.'

O'Neill came. Three weeks later, he came. He did not tell her where he slept or if he would come again. He merely said he would stay an hour or two, and then he would leave again.

With him came Bard to see his grandmother and grandfather, and he and O'Neill spoke of the battles that had begun. How they burned the barns that had once belonged to Irishmen, now in the hands of the Scots and English, and how they would slowly raze the land. Ireland they would tear down if they had to, to rid its shores of the Sassenachs, and from the ruins would come a new Ireland, forged in blood and steel. They would pull down the old order if they had to, to make room for the new, and in their voices rang the sound of revolution. No more were they dreaming of rebellion, but living it. Causing it. And Elizabeth, hearing them, felt her blood run cold.

They stayed an hour. And then they were gone.

Alone, Elizabeth thought of her husband. Of his icy, expressionless eyes; his icy, expressionless face. Of Simon Bagenal, who was a dangerous, frightening man, because what he did was made of ice, not heat, lacking all emotion, as if he had no heart. And yet she had heard him speak to her out of his bed of pain, swearing he would say nothing to the King. And she had known he would; had known somehow he would put her in jeopardy.

She should have known he would follow them.

At night she dreamed of O'Neill juxtaposed with war. There was no separation. She smell the blood and smoke and fire; heard the cries of dying men. Saw the steel flashing in the sunlight; the axe, raised, falling upon the neck to sever the head from the body. And O'Neill, slain. O'Neill, dead of his rebellion, with his head hammered up on Dungannon's gate.

'*O'Neill!*' she cried out at night in the emptiness of her bed, and cradled the child within her belly. The child of her husband, who wished to kill the man she loved.

O'Neill came, and Bard. O'Neill took her out of the cottage to the tumbled wall behind it, and sat her down upon it. He did not look at her. She saw how his eyes fastened themselves on the land that rolled in every direction of the compass; how he caressed Ireland with his eyes – green, velvet Ireland with his green, brilliant gaze. The eyes of a visionary. The eyes of a fanatic.

'The O'Neill,' she said, mostly to herself, but the name – the title – hung in the air, rife with ramifications.

O'Neill looked at her. 'No,' he said. 'A man. An Irishman. A rebel, with no money to pay the men who serve memories of other O'Neills, not wishing for coin but for pride, though pride will not feed their families nor rebuild their homes nor get them back their lands. They ask for nothing of me, nothing save my presence, and I look at them and see them as they die.'

She looked up into his face and saw the anguish in his soul.

He turned suddenly and sat down next to her on the wall. 'Oh, Eilis, I am destroying my own land. We burn and tear down and destroy what others have built – Irishmen! – all in the name of this war. We call the English the enemy even as we do what they have done, and all in the name of Ireland. But can the land forgive me? The people do – those who understand – but can the land forgive me? Does a house understand when I put it to the torch? And what of the poor tenants who had no choice but to work for the English or Scottish landlord? They only know my name, not me. They cannot understand why I burn them out of what dwellings they have left.'

'You have an army,' she said. 'They cannot blame only you.'

'An army,' he echoed. 'Oh, aye, such as it is. Proud men all, and strong, and loyal to Ireland's cause, but it makes it no easier. We are little more than reivers sweeping across the land, intent on razing what is left of an island far gone in desolation.'

Quietly she said, 'You knew it would come to this.'

'Aye.' The voice scraped out of his throat, leaving rawness in its place. 'And I do not regret what must be done, only the manner of it. But 'tis the Sassenachs I must blame for that, for if they would go from Ireland this war would end at once.'

So close to him on the wall, she felt the tension in his soul. 'Once,' she said, 'you asked me what I would have felt when William the Conqueror came. *Then* I could not answer, for I did not understand. Now I think I do.' She looked at the ground, not at him, for fear her words would fail. 'I can think now what it must have been like for the Saxons, who fought with bow and scythe and ploughshare, defending their land against the Norman invader. How the survivors must have cried and screamed and torn their hair to see the land given over to William and his Normans. We lost even our language for many years, for it was Norman French and not Saxon English spoken at William's court. And how did the Saxons feel when the Bastard began his Tower on the Thames, knowing it was meant to mark his fist upon the land?' Her hand crept out to his, folding around his fingers. 'Much like the Irish must have felt when Elizabeth and James began giving their land over to the English and the Scots.'

344

Now she looked into his face. 'Oh, O'Neill, I do not question your reasons for this war, or your dedication – I question only the need for so many lives to be lost when the only outcome is defeat.' Her fingers tightened. 'My proud, fierce Irishman, do you think I wish to see you killed? Even in the name of Ireland?'

He did not lift his head. 'I have no choice, Eilis.'

'I know,' she said, 'and that is why I love you.'

He did not move for a moment, but when he did she saw the bitter regret in his eyes. 'Do not love me, Eilis . . . I am not worthy of it.'

'You are.' She reached up, clasping his neck to pull his head down to hers. 'Oh . . . O'Neill . . . *you are* – '

As his mouth moved on hers she felt the familiar flaring of heat and weakness, the bonelessness of sudden desire as it burst and ran through her limbs. It had been so long, so long, too long, and her body cried out to him even as her voice did. His arms were around her, crushing her, and she revelled in the sweet pain. There was no tenderness in their kiss but a violent possession, each trying to brand the other with their need. She felt the scrape of stubble against her face, the sweep of black hair against her face, glorying in the sensation of his warm flesh against the fabric of her soul.

He rose then, scooping her up, and she knew he meant to take her into the cottage, into the tiny bedroom. He was hers again, and she his, and she wanted only to know the power of his passion as he took her to the heights.

And then she saw Bard, and so did he.

'O'Neill.' There was a hint of colour in his face. 'O'Neill – Seamus has a thing to tell you. I think it is important.'

She felt the conflict in his body. And then he set her down. 'Eilis,' he said, 'I will come back for you.' And he walked away from her and left her facing Bard.

'What is it?' she asked when she could. 'Does it have to do with this rebellion?'

'It does not concern you, madam.' A clipped, harsh tone, full of tight-coiled pain. She had been deaf to it before. Deaf, and very blind.

'It concerns me,' she told him levelly. 'Tell me how it *does not*.'

His mouth went flat. 'Very well, madam – O'Neill's support is failing. Oh, we add men every day, but we lose others as well. To battles, dying. To heartache, seeing the houses and cottages burned. To desolation, not knowing what will become of themselves and Ireland. And because we have not so many as the English, every lost man hurts us. Because in failing, we fail Ireland.'

'And because Bagenal will win.'

'Aye, madam,' Bard said. 'Bagenal will win.'

She looked into his face, into the face of Ireland and futility. 'I do not want him to die.'

'Nor do *I*, Elizabeth.'

'Then will you help me make certain he does not?'

Bard frowned. 'What are you trying to say?'

'That I know a way to keep O'Neill alive, even if this rebellion fails. If he is caught, my husband will have him killed. Oh, I know – ' She put up a silencing hand. 'I know – you have said he would take him to England. But you cannot be certain. What if he knows about Shane's fate also, and seeks to mimic it with O'Neill? And he would be dead, and we would be helpless in our grief.'

'Say what you mean, madam.' But his gaze did not waver from hers.

'I ask a favour,' she said. 'I ask you to escort me to my husband.'

She saw the shock in his eyes; he had expected almost anything else. 'To *him*, Elizabeth? Are you mad? Bagenal will take you to the King!'

She nodded. 'But if I go to him freely, offering a trade, perhaps he will keep O'Neill alive. Perhaps he will try to take O'Neill to London, and the Irish will see to it The O'Neill does not go out of Ireland.'

'A risk,' Bard said. 'You cannot know he would be willing to agree.'

'He will agree,' Elizabeth said. 'You yourself have said he will give me over to the King. He wants me for that purpose. But I give him one more thing, one more item of value that may well surpass whatever value *I* may claim.' She paused. 'I give Bagenal his child.'

'His *child* . . .' Bard's eyes widened and went immediately to her abdomen. 'Is this the truth?'

'Ask Fiona if you prefer. I have known for some time, long enough to be sure.' Her hand dropped down to shield her stomach. 'I will give him his child – perhaps his heir – in exchange for O'Neill's life here. I think he will agree.'

He stared into her face, searching it, and she saw something in his eyes she had never seen before – an odd, grudging respect. And then he smiled, albeit crooked. 'Are you forgetting O'Neill himself? He will never let you go.'

'Then I will go without his knowledge.'

'You would risk that?'

'I will risk anything for him.'

Bard looked at her solemnly. 'You cannot go riding up to the gates of Dungannon without warning, even telling them your name. I doubt they would believe you. They would think you are some Irishwoman trying to win her way into the commander's grace.' He grimaced. 'It has been done before.'

Elizabeth nodded. 'But if I sent a courier with some proof the message is genuine, all would be arranged.'

Bard smiled. And then he laughed. 'I think you have

chosen your courier. But have you the proof Bagenal would require?'

She untied the corner of her cloak and took from it a ring bearing the Bagenal coat of arms. The ring her husband had put on to her finger. She set it into Bard's hand. 'That is proof enough.'

His fingers closed around the ring. When he smiled it was free of restraint and wariness, and she saw the Bard of old. She saw the man she knew O'Neill saw so often, and she understood why O'Neill trusted him so.

Bard nodded. 'Tell O'Neill I have gone to town. We spoke of it earlier; he will believe it. And that I will return to the army when I can.'

'Bard.' Elizabeth's voice was unsteady. 'Perhaps I speak where I should not, but must say it. You are more a man than any I have known.'

He grinned. 'Saving *O'Neill*, of course.'

She felt a bubble of laughter break in her throat. 'Of course. But *he* is the stuff of which myths are made, as Brian Boru and Cuchullain themselves.'

'Not myths,' Bard retorted. 'Irish heroes out of man and woman and faerie folk. And if you name all of those myth, you are not the woman for O'Neill.' He jerked his head in the direction of the cottage. 'Now go back, before he comes looking for you.' And as she hesitated he put out his hand and touched hers. 'Go, Eilis. Or this thing will not be done.'

30

Bard came in the morning. No questions were asked of his presence. He waited until Elizabeth was free, then took her outside and told her the arrangements had been made.

She looked into his face and saw the familiar mask. 'They gave you no trouble?'

'The English? Oh, aye, what I expected. But the ring convinced them I meant what I said, and I saw Bagenal at last.' His face turned grim. 'He had little to say, other than he would await your arrival.'

She felt the pang of fear mixed with sorrow. And pain. 'When do we go?'

'Now,' he said. 'The horses are saddled and waiting. If we tarry, we will not get it done.' He put out a hand to stop her involuntary movement towards the cottage. 'You must come now. If you say good-bye to Fiona, she will seek to stop you. Seamus also; they serve The O'Neill.'

'So do you.'

He grimaced. 'Aye, though he will not thank me for this. I will be lucky to survive his wrath.'

'He would not *punish* you for this – '

Bard laughed. 'I doubt not he'll be having a few choice words for me, and will likely knock me down a time or two with his fists, but I'll take no harm. 'Twill be no different than what I've got from him before, even as children. I have developed calluses on my jaw.'

Elizabeth's hand stole to the locket she had hung around her throat at Christmas. It was all she wanted; she would miss nothing else she left behind.

Except O'Neill, she thought

'I will tell Fiona when I am back,' Bard said. 'She will understand.' Then he took her arm and led her towards the tiny stable.

The ride was cold, whipping back her cloak no matter how hard she tried to keep it closed. Her gloved hands slid on the reins and she could hardly feel her feet. Her eyes teared and her ears burned and her lips were numb, but she said nothing. She said nothing at all, only lost herself in silence and the knowledge of what she did, and for whom she did it.

When at last Dungannon jutted out of the land and beckoned her within the high stone walls, Elizabeth felt the welling of pain and grief and fear. The sacrifice she made paled in comparison to the bereavement she would know. O'Neill would become a portion of her past, a myth as much as Brian Boru and Cuchullain, and as real. He would be the dream in her heart as they locked her in the Tower and he – and she – would never leave it, unless they took her to the block. And O'Neill – O'Neill the *man* might die – but O'Neill the dream would not. Ever.

For a moment she nearly turned back. She stopped the horse and saw Bard turn to look, and the understanding in his eyes. And then she recalled that he and O'Neill had their own sort of honour and she must respect it; Bard had given his pledge he would bring her to her husband. She had no choice.

She tapped the horse with her frozen heels and went on, steadfastly refusing to look at the castle.

But the time came when she had to, when they stood before the gates and Bard called to the guards that he had the woman Bagenal awaited. She watched the portcullis rise up, the thick leaves swing apart. And then Bagenal himself rode out of the castle bailey.

She saw the fair, shining hair and the cold implacability

of his eyes. He looked at her briefly, saying nothing, but she sensed the anger burning in him. No doubt he intended to make her see what she had cost him when he had her inside the walls.

'Madam,' he said briefly.

'Husband.' She met his eyes unflinchingly.

'How have you fared among the savage Irish rebels?'

'Well enough,' she answered calmly. 'They have done me no harm.'

'But they have done *me* harm, madam.' His voice was suddenly full of malice. 'They have harmed my person and stolen my wife, and they must pay the cost.'

'And I?'

Bagenal did not smile. 'You will pay it also. Of that I am assured.'

She did not feel brave. She felt cold and frightened, so very, very frightened. 'Simon,' she said, 'you may have me. But only if you allow O'Neill to live.'

'So the catamite has said.' His tone indicated contempt for the Irishman at her side. 'You wish to bargain with me, madam, when you bear the taint of treason?'

'I *will* bargain with you,' she returned. 'As Bard has said, I will give myself over to you – *and our child* – in exchange for clemency towards O'Neill once you have him.' She lifted her head. 'Yes, I know you will win. The English always do. And I know O'Neill will be captured, because no doubt you have set all of your men at the task of taking him. And I know you will wish to execute him yourself, here at Dungannon, so all the Irish may know what happens to men who rouse the Irish into rebellion against the Crown.' She challenged him with a look. 'Would you not?'

'I will hang his head upon these gates,' Bagenal agreed. 'He will be the second O'Neill to view Ireland without his body attached.'

351

Elizabeth drew in a careful breath, knowing she risked the loss of the game she played. 'No,' she said calmly, 'you would be a fool to do it here. It would only inspire the Irish to further bitterness and rebellion, not grind them into submission. You would do better to make an example out of him in London, where England can witness what happens to Irish rebels.'

Simon Bagenal smiled. 'Madam, you almost convince me you *desire* his execution.'

'No,' she said, hearing the hollowness of her voice. 'O'Neill is a dead man. But I wish not to have him killed before the people who worship him.'

'What makes you think I would not prefer such a death for him?'

'Because, in the end, the King will favour a London execution,' she pointed out. 'How better to prove to his subjects how far-reaching is his power, how masterful he is – and how well he is served by you?'

'And if I do not accept this bargain?'

Elizabeth shrugged a little. 'If you take O'Neill and kill him in Ireland, I will put a knife to my throat and cut it, and you will not have the pleasure of delivering your traitor-wife into the King's justice.' She held his eyes with her own. 'And you will never see your child.'

He bared his teeth as colour came into his face. 'Agreed,' he said tightly. 'I give O'Neill his life . . . until he reaches London. And now, madam, you will come to me.'

'When I have your promise that Bard will go free from here,' she countered. 'He accompanied me in good faith, and I will not have his freedom taken from him merely because he did as I requested.'

'Agreed.' The tone was flat. 'I assure you, madam, it matters little to me if we take him now or later. He will still be quite dead. Now, come.'

Elizabeth turned to Bard. 'You know what I have done, and why. I trust one day you will tell *him*.'

Bard's mouth moved into a faint smile. 'I admire your spirit and loyalty, if not the manner of your tactics. Very well, Eilis, one day I will tell O'Neill how you bought his life at the cost of your own. But I think he will not be pleased by the sacrifice.'

'Elizabeth.' Bagenal's clipped, English voice.

Briefly she leaned across to touch Bard's hand. 'I thank you, Irishman.'

He grinned. 'And I you, Sassenach.' He spun his horse and left her; Elizabeth turned resolutely to face her husband.

And saw him give the order to the bowman atop the wall.

'*No!*' She jerked her horse around, crying a warning to Bard. But the arrow had already been sped. He lurched in the saddle, jerked forward, then tumbled limply from the galloping horse in a tangle of arms and legs.

When Elizabeth reached him she saw the shaft had broken off. She tugged him over on to his back and looked into his face. His eyes were closed, his mouth open, and a trickle of blood spilled between his lips. As she held his hand she felt the warmth pass from his flesh.

Bagenal jerked her away from the body. She saw a dozen soldiers surrounding Bard. One carried an axe.

'Cut off his head,' said her husband, 'and put it on the spike above the gate. Let him look his last upon Ireland as the crows pluck his eyes from his head.'

Bagenal dragged her up the stairs, ignoring her struggles and curses, until he reached a closed door. He flung it open and tugged her into the room beyond, then threw her towards the bed as she fought him. Elizabeth sprawled across it awkwardly, then scrambled up to face him.

'You *bastard!*' she cried. 'You agreed to let him go free!'

'You are a fool to ever think I would have done so,' he retorted. 'And far more foolish to believe I would let O'Neill live more than a single day once I have him in my hands.'

'Bastard!' she repeated.

Bagenal laughed. 'Oh no,' he said. 'No. *I* am not the bastard. *That* title belongs to the child in your belly.'

She wanted to spit in his face. 'Unless you somehow contrive to get a divorce, the child will be born legitimate.'

Bagenal did not smile. His tone was casual, almost negligent, and yet his words were exceptionally distinct. 'Of all the women I have bedded since I was able, not one – *not one, Elizabeth* – has ever conceived by me.' He paused, studying her coolly. 'Do you understand? An unusual situation for you, is it not? And quite telling. Because unless a miracle has suddenly occurred, there is no possibility you conceived that child by me.' Again, he paused. 'You *do* understand, I trust. That child is not mine, Elizabeth, but a bastard by O'Neill.'

She felt her heart skip a beat, then resume laggardly, as if it could not continue to push blood throughout her body. Her hands and feet were cold. '*O'Neill's* child – '

'I will take him,' Bagenal said. 'I will take him, and I will kill him, and I will put up his head beside the catamite's so all of Ireland can see them.' He smiled. 'I thank you, madam, for putting the means into my hands. For making it so simple. Do you see?' His icy eyes were bright. 'Do you see, Elizabeth? O'Neill will come for you, and he will come for his bastard child, and I shall sever this rebellion even as the steel shall sever his head!'

She said nothing, nothing at all. She was incapable of speech.

Bagenal put out a hand to the door, preparing to shut

it in her face. 'You shall join me at dinner, madam. So we may discuss *your* fate.'

At dinner she was seated at one end of a long rectangular table of Irish oak, flanked by silent soldiers. Bagenal sat at the other end; they faced one another across an expanse of wood and acres of contention. She did not avoid his challenging eyes in any way but met him stare for stare.

'Unrepentant,' he remarked. 'I see it in your eyes.'

'What should I repent? My aid to him? No. I only wish he had killed you in the chapel.'

'Nearly,' Bagenal said. 'Nearly, Elizabeth. And yes, you should repent. Repent of your broken marriage vows, the sin of adultery, the foulness of abetting murder. You are damned, madam, and will surely burn in hell.' He smiled coolly and poured more wine into his glass. 'Now, would you care to discuss the manner of your death?'

She did not drink. She did not eat. She wanted nothing from Bagenal except to be free of his presence. 'I assume I am to be executed. For treason, am I not?'

'Perhaps,' Bagenal agreed. 'There is that charge, and it is a weighty one. It cost Essex his head, did it not? And others. And others.' He smiled. 'But there is also adultery.'

'Adultery is not enough to get me executed,' she retorted. 'Only when a woman is married to the King, which I am not. *My* husband is only a knight.'

For the flicker of an instant his mouth tightened. Then he smiled. 'I think treason will be charge enough to get you death. But it *is* possible you may suffer only imprisonment.' He sipped at his wine. 'Years upon years shut up in the Tower of London, perhaps in the Bloody Tower, where so many have waited for death. Years upon years, while you grow old and feeble and witless, with all your beauty gone. So sad a fate for a woman; so harsh to see it happen.' His eyes were steady on her face. 'And I will watch it happen, should the King grant you – clemency. I will come to see it, to see you fade away.' He waited. 'Which do you want, Elizabeth? A quick or lingering death?'

'If death gets me free of you, I will welcome it however it comes.' She said it coolly, distinctly, matching his habitual tone. And saw the recognition in his eyes.

For a long moment he only stared at her. And then he laughed out loud. 'By God, O'Neill has honed your tongue! Had you one like that at court, I do not doubt you would have sent all the men fleeing the wrath of Elizabeth Stafford.' But his laughter quickly faded. 'You do not eat or drink. Therefore I must assume this is a form of insult to me. Well, it does not matter – I do not care. Starve yourself if you will . . . it will kill you all the quicker.' He waved a hand. 'I am done with you.'

The soldiers stepped forward to escort her to her room. But as she pushed out of her chair she turned again to her husband. 'If I am imprisoned in the Tower, what becomes of the child?'

Bagenal shrugged. 'Presumably you will bear it there. Women have done it before.'

One hand splayed across her abdomen. 'And will they let me keep it? Will they let me keep it with me?'

His eyes were almost colourless in the candlelight. 'Madam, why would you wish the child to *share* your imprisonment?'

She drew in a breath and tried to steady her voice. 'Because it is O'Neill's, and all I will have of him.'

His face tightened. 'No, madam, I think they will take the child from you. I will certainly ask them to.'

She closed her eyes. And then slowly she lifted the chain from around her neck and dangled the locket in the light. 'Then I would wish this given to the child, so it will have something from its mother.'

Bagenal frowned. 'What is it?'

'Something from O'Neill,' she said quietly. 'It was his mother's locket.'

'His *mother's* – ' Bagenal rose at once. 'Bring it to me. That locket was my aunt's. By rights it belongs to me, not a bastard by O'Neill.'

She clutched it in her hand as if to keep it from him. And then, knowing he could so easily force her, she walked slowly the length of the table and paused in front of him.

He put out his hand. 'Give it over, madam.'

And as she poured the chain and locket into his outstretched hand, Elizabeth snatched up his trencher knife and thrust it towards his throat.

The locket fell. She heard it rattle against the hardwood flor. And then Bagenal had her wrist, crushing the strength from her grip, and the knife fell free of her hand.

His hands were at her neck, fingers threatening the fragility of her throat. She set her teeth and shut her eyes, and felt his breath against her face. 'Did you plan this?' he demanded. 'Did you plan this all along? To give yourself over to me and then try to murder me?'

Her eyes snapped open. 'Curse you!' she cried. 'You broke your word and had him killed . . . you even cut off his head! And you will do the same to O'Neill when you have caught *him!* Did you think I would not know? Did you think I would let you do it? *Yes*, I came here to kill you – *yes*, I planned to do it. And I would do it again if I could!'

'Yes,' he agreed. 'Oh yes, I know you would. But if you think *this* has bought you your death, you are wrong, so very wrong. I will not have you killed because it is precisely what you want.'

She went very still in his hands, staring into his face.

Bagenal laughed. 'Aye, madam, I know you better than you yourself. You came here to kill me in order to save O'Neill. Failing that, you believe I will kill you myself. And you want it. *You want it.* Because you would rather be dead if O'Neill is dead . . . I can see it in your eyes.' He smiled, and then he laughed. 'And so I deny it to you.'

He thrust her into the waiting hands of his English soldiers. 'Shut her away and lock the door. Let her taste imprisonment.'

31

When Elizabeth saw her husband again it was two days later, and he was dressed for battle. For a single moment she felt a flicker of vindictive joy in her soul, glad beyond measure that he would risk his life against O'Neill and perhaps give up that life, but the anticipation was flattened almost immediately by apprehension for O'Neill.

'He *will* die, madam,' Bagenal said. 'Today will see the Irish army broken, O'Neill taken, and his execution. His head will be hammered up beside what remains of the catamite's, and I will let you look long upon them both.'

'He will not die.' She stood quietly before a narrow embrasure. 'He is Ireland, and Ireland will never die.'

Bagenal's laugh was a short bark of derisive sound. 'I assure you O'Neill is not Ireland, madam. Only a foolish, impetuous rebel with a dwindling force behind him.' A scabbarded sword hung at his side. 'He faces the might of England. How in the name of heaven could he survive?'

'He will,' she said. 'He will. He fights for more than injured pride or English tradition or position in James Stuart's ugly court. He fights for himself, for his people, for Ireland herself – what was and what will be.' Still she stood before the embrasure, hands folded against her gown. 'While it is quite true he lacks the might of England, he *has* the strength of a land behind him. *He is Ireland*, my Sassenach husband . . . and England shall never defeat this land.'

'Treasonous heresy.'

'Perhaps,' she agreed. 'I imagine my head will roll from the block at Tower Green. But then, you see, it will not matter. Because if I cannot have O'Neill in life, I will certainly have him in death.'

Bagenal turned from her. He went away from her, locking the door, and she was left alone. And only then did she turn her back to the door. Only then did she look out the embrasure into the castle bailey towards the massive gate where the crows still hedged the walkways, and let the daylight fall full on her face.

'O'Neill,' she said into the silence of her prison, 'O'Neill, you have sired a child . . . and so Ireland cannot die.'

While the tears ran down her face.

The waiting was worst of all. She heard the clatter of hooves as Bagenal led his army out to meet O'Neill's, knowing the Irish were badly outnumbered, for though Bagenal left a contingent of men at Dungannon to protect his holding, the main force of English troops he took with him. Elizabeth stood at the embrasure and stared out, watching the slow procession of soldiers winding through the gate.

No one brought food, even when the morning stretched into afternoon, and beyond. No one came at all. She thought perhaps Bagenal had left orders she was to be kept hungry, in a properly repentant state of mind when he returned victorious from battle. She cared little enough for herself, but the child was undoubtedly hungry. She wondered if it could sense her worry and the tension.

When the sun set and the moon came up, shining silver across the land, Elizabeth went back to the embrasure yet again. In the darkness she could not see the crows. She could see little beyond the torches set about the bailey. But she could hear the footsteps of the watch and brief exchanges of conversation.

English voices, all of them, lacking the lilt of Ireland.

She sat down upon the bed and stared blankly at the far wall, shadowed in the moonlight slanting through the embrasure. She envisioned what so often filled her dreams, the atrocities of war; the slashing of swords and battering axes, the crack of musketry and cannon. Severed limbs and severed heads, bleeding stumps and screaming mouths. And O'Neill, attacked by too many, thrown down against the ground, with Bagenal standing over him ordering the head cut off for the adornment of Dungannon's gate.

And she saw Bagenal returning with his horrid trophy and the head put up on the spike to gaze blindly across the land, even as Bard gazed, never again to know the sound of an Irish harp or the lilt of an Irish tongue. Never to know the trust and adoration of his hounds, the love of any woman, Irish, French, or English.

As last she slept, exhausted by the tension, and lost herself in dreams full of the cries of dying men and the clashing of steel swords; saw the blood spilled across the bailey cobbles and the winding stairs of the keep, until she could bear it no more and shut her mind to dreams.

Elizabeth jerked upright with a cry as the door slammed open. In the rich light of a newborn dawn she scrambled up and set her back against the wall, bracing herself for the sight of her husband with his dripping, grisly trophy, and when he stepped into the room she did not at first believe the head was still attached to the body.

And then she knew it was O'Neill she saw, not Bagenal, and whole, so whole, with only a cut across his face in place of the gaping throat, bloodied from head to toe, but with his head still firmly in place atop his shoulders.

'Eilis,' he said – nothing more.

She saw the sword in his hand, bared and dripping blood. It pooled on the floor like rubies, glowing in the sunlight that slanted through the window. She shivered once, staring at the man, and then she began the endless journey across the room.

He remained on the threshold, one hand clasping the dripping sword and the other braced against the jamb, as if he could not stand. His eyes were bright green in the morning sunlight, fixed on her as she moved, and his black hair hung damp and tangled against his neck and shoulders. The cut on his face stretched from cheek to jaw; Elizabeth thought it would scar, ruining the perfection of his face. But somehow she did not care.

When she reached him she put out her trembling hands and felt the blood and sweat-sodden clothing, the movement of his chest beneath the fabric as he breathed. *He breathed*.

And then she reached up to touch his face with mute, frightened hands. 'O'Neill.' It was the only word she could manage before she broke completely.

'Did you think I would not come?' His voice was hoarse, scraped raw in a throat abused by shouted orders. But there was irony in the tone, the merest shadow of it, and she recalled when he had asked the question before in the King's Presence Chamber.

Elizabeth laughed, and the sound filled up the room.

'My Christ, woman, did you think I would not come?' And he threw down the sword and engulfed her in a hug so hard she thought her breath would stop.

He spoke to her. Between sobs, between the broken hoarseness of his voice, he spoke to her. In Gaelic, as if he could not say what he wanted to say in any other language: '*Tha gaol agam ort, tha gaol agam ort,*' again and again, and other phrases, filled with all the power of his emotion. She understood none of the Gaelic, only the nuances of his tone; it told her what he said. What he could never say before. And she knew she was safe in his arms at last and he safe in hers, alive, alive, with no death wound to spill his blood into the thirsty soil of Ireland, who drank up so many men.

'Eilis,' he said, 'oh, my Eilis . ... *I thought I had lost you forever.*'

Her fingers curled into the fabric of his doublet. She did not care that there was blood on his clothes, only that they clothed a living man, and that man's mouth against her face. She felt her head of its own accord tip back, tip back, and then he was kissing her, drawing the breath from her until she sobbed aloud and the tears ran down her face.

His fingers touched the bruises on her neck. 'Bagenal . . . ?'

'His answer – when I tried to put a knife into his throat.' Her hand went up to linger on his face. 'But *you* – '

''Twill give me a great romantic scar,' he said. 'But will you turn away from me, remembering how I got it?'

'How did you get it, O'Neill?'

'Killing your husband, madam. I have made you a widow at last.'

She looked into his face, into the emerald eyes. She saw weariness and pain, and a grief so sharp she could not bear to tap her measure of it. 'You know about Bard.' It was not a question. She knew by looking at him.

O'Neill flinched visibly, as if reminded of the thing. 'Aye' was all he said; she thought it was all he *could* say.

'O'Neill,' she said. 'Oh, O'Neill . . . *I am sorry for what I have cost you.*'

He pulled her once more against his chest. 'No, no, you have taken nothing, nothing at all from me.'

All the guilt and grief welled up. 'But I have. Oh, I *have!* I asked him to escort me.'

His hand cradled the back of her skull and pressed her cheek against his shoulder. 'Eilis, Eilis – Bard did nothing without knowing the risks involved.' The pain in his eyes belied the steadiness of his tone. 'Eilis, oh my Eilis, what he did, he did for me. And it was for *me* he died, not because of you.'

For a moment she clung to him, taking comfort in his nearness, and then it was stolen from her. He set her aside abruptly and moved away from her, stepping past her into the room. He went directly to the embrasure, as if he could not face her. And she thought, for one awful moment, he repudiated her in spite of what he said.

O'Neill turned; she saw the awesome tension in his body. And she realized he was frightened by the emotions in his soul, as if he tread a treacherous path and knew he might fall off. 'I have seen to it his head was removed from the gate,' he said in his broken voice. 'He will be buried as befits a man, deep in Irish soil.' Then he shut his eyes, and the fists came to rend the air. 'Oh Christ, he loved me, *he loved me* – and I could not give him what he wanted.'

She put a shaking hand to her lips. 'Then . . . you knew . . .'

'Oh, *aye*.' O'Neill, bereft, pushed a grimy hand through his hair. 'He tried to hide it from me, but I knew him so well. So well.'

Elizabeth could not move, could not speak. She could only stare at the man, who was so very close to the point of breaking down.

Slowly, almost awkwardly, O'Neill moved to the bed and sat down upon the edge. 'I hurt him very badly. I called it a sin and a perversion once, when I was in my cups, when his love for me was as clean as that you bear for me.' He raised his head and looked at her. 'Aye . . . I knew, and I wish there had been a way I could have told him that I knew, and that it did not sicken me. I would

364

never have sent him from me. He served me so well. So well.'

At last she could move. And she did. She went to the bed, as he had, longing to vanquish his pain and grief and knowing he must bear them. She sat down next to him, hard by his side, and threaded her fingers into the fingers of his hand.

He turned his head to look at her, and she saw the tears welling up in her eyes. 'We were children together, Eilis, and boys, and finally even men. And now he is dead . . . and I am left to remember him.' Grief twisted his face. 'He was my brother, Eilis. He was my father's bastard.'

Silently she took him into her arms and held him against her breasts, knowing such comfort was all she could possibly offer.

O'Neill, she mourned, *oh, O'Neill, would that I could lift this burden from you*.

'What I have done,' he said in his hoarse, broken voice, 'what I have done to my Ireland – '

'O'Neill, you did what you had to do.'

'But she is broken, broken, beaten down beneath the steel. Oh, Eilis, what I have done to my land – '

' – and would do it all again.' Elizabeth smiled a little. 'Would you not? Is that not the price of dedication?'

He looked at her. He put out his hands and cupped her face in the bloodied, grimy palms. 'I have lost her, my Ireland. She has slipped through my fingers again. Oh, aye, we took Dungannon back from the English . . . but we will lose it again. James will send more troops, more guns, more cannon, and Tyrone will become little more than a quagmire of blood and decaying flesh, feeding the carrion birds.' His fingers stroked her face. 'I cannot give over my Ireland to such a fate again.'

'Ireland without The O'Neill is no longer Ireland.'

Slowly he shook his head. 'I am not The O'Neill. I am

only an Irish rebel who has brought sorrow to his land.'

'And pride!' she said. '*And pride.*'

He put one hand on her abdomen. 'Bagenal told me of the child. He threw it in my face. He meant to hurt me, but all I knew was joy. And great determination not to die before its birth.'

She swallowed back the tightness in her throat. 'What will you do, O'Neill?'

'What my father did.' He took his other hand away from her face. 'I will sail from Ireland and seek my life in foreign courts, recalling my days of rebellion under the Irish skies. Until I die, as my father died, in self-exile from my home.'

'But not alone.'

He shook his head. 'Fiona and Seamus will come with me, and the dogs.'

'And I,' she said. 'You cannot rid yourself of me.'

He looked at her in despair. 'My Christ, Eilis, I want you so badly I ache with it. But what kind of life can I offer you? I can give you only exile. In France or Italy. An existence paid for by foreign kings and queens and popes who find it amusing to keep a tame Irishman at their sides, to be rattling at James Stuart when he grows complacent on his throne.' Slowly he shook his head. 'I have nothing for you, Eilis, save smoke and blood and fire.'

'I care little enough what *manner* of life it is,' she told him clearly, 'so long as you are *in* it. Do you think I could live without you?'

'How could I expect you to come with me?' he demanded. 'I made you betray your King. I made you betray your husband. I made you betray your homeland.'

'And I would do it all again.' Elizabeth cradled his beard-roughened jaw in her hands. 'I would go anywhere